In the
Midst
of
Innocence

In the
Midst
of
Innocence

a novel

DEBORAH HINING

 Light Messages

In the Midst of Innocence
Deborah G. Hining
lightmessages.com/deborah-hining
dhining@gmail.com

Published 2018, by Light Messages
www.lightmessages.com
Durham, NC 27713 USA
SAN: 920-9298

Paperback ISBN: 978-1-61153-244-9
E-book ISBN: 978-1-61153-245-6
Library of Congress Control Number: 2017963046

"The Little Tennessee"

North Sea, Red Sea, Sea of Galilee
None of them are the place for me
If I had my choice, you soon would see
I would pick the river called the Little Tennessee
It is wide and swift, not right for wading,
But you will not see my choice fading.
There are places all over the world that I would like to see
But my heart always comes back to the Little Tennessee.

–Debbie Griffitts, age 6 yrs
Maryville, Tennessee

To my mother, whose heart was broken when the last free-running portion of the Little Tennessee was dammed, and to my father, who carried that poem in his wallet until the day he died.

August

Warm, waning days.
The stars brighten now,
Earth hastens her journey toward darkness,
Even as the great orb pulls me into her silvery embrace.
She wills me to dance, and I am helpless to deny her.
The Spirit broods; light and dark play upon the land.
My children cannot yet see what roves in the unseen places,
But change is coming.

August 28, 1931
Dearest Mother and Father,

I have settled in nicely with the Reverend and Mrs. Miller. The house is quite large, roomy enough to absorb me, all my clothing, and my books, and I can assure you that it is quite safe. No doubt, Thomas and Jonas will attest to that as soon as they arrive home, if they have not already done so. I imagine they will reach you before my letter does as they left early this morning right after breakfast.

It worked out well to go through Memphis to visit Aunt Mildred, even though it was quite a bit out of our way. We had a very nice visit, but I do not think she is as happy in her new marriage as we all had hoped. I did not see much of Mr. Jenkins because he was clearly not desirous of our company. Nevertheless, it was wonderful to see Aunt Mildred again after all this time.

You will be proud to know that I drove the entire way from Chicago to Memphis, without feeling the least fatigue! I am certain I will be able to drive home by myself for the Christmas holiday.

Now begins the next phase, and how I look forward to becoming acquainted with the area and with the people I will be serving! Since there is no church building in this "holler," as the natives call it, Reverend Miller holds services at the schoolhouse where I will be teaching, which is only about half a mile away from here. I expect I will meet several of my students and their families tomorrow, as Reverend Miller assures me that more than a few attend his services regularly.

As you can imagine, I am most anxious to know how the Lord will lead me, and no doubt tomorrow will be the beginnings of my testing. My fervent prayer is that I will measure up to what He expects and desires of me. There is much work to be done, I know, and I pray I do not come up short in His eyes.

Please give my love to Thomas and Jonas, and thank them for attending to my removal here to East Tennessee and for their care and concern for my wellbeing. Also, give my warmest love to Cecilia. Tell her I will write her as soon as I can.

I remain you loving daughter, excited and grateful that you have allowed me to come here to serve the Lord,

Emily

August 31, 1931
My Dearest Sister,

I am here! You cannot imagine how beautiful it is, and how excited I am to be here. I feel as if I have landed in an entirely new, magical world, bucolic and green. It reminds me of Ireland— do you remember how green the hills were when we spent the summer with the O'Seanaseays? It is just as green here, but there are so many different shades of it because there are so many trees!

I found myself longing to climb the huge oak in the front lawn here at the Miller's home—it is much like the one in our own sweet back garden, the one we used to live in all summer when we were children. But whereas we have only a few trees, the Millers have a forest surrounding them. You cannot imagine how leafy it all is!

I attended church service today and met some of the children I will be teaching when school begins in just a little over a week. I believe that Father has been unduly harsh in his assessment of what the people here are like. They are poor, certainly, but I did not see any "slovenly, slack-jawed, mentally deficient characters" that he insisted I would be encountering. Yes, many of the children did not wear shoes, and although their clothing was poor and well-patched, most were clean. I do not expect that I will be catching lice from any of them. At least I hope that is not one of the trials I will be facing over the school year!

Sadly, the service was attended mostly by only women and children. The men, as well as a goodly number of the boys, are laboring in the fields in order to get the crops in. Because almost none of the men are gainfully employed at this difficult time, they rely exclusively on what they can produce in their own farms and gardens to feed their families. It is sad, of course, but not as sad as the long lines of men we have seen in Chicago, waiting for the slim chance of employment, or even a hot meal. It does not seem that this part of the country is suffering any more than the rest of it.

On the way down, we went through Memphis and met Aunt Mildred's new husband, and Cecilia, I must tell you, I am not at all fond of him! He is coarse and rough, and when he bothered to speak to us, he made a slur about us being Yankees. That set us out on the wrong foot, but I believe he is far worse than we initially suspected. The second night we were there, Jonas, Thomas, and I were sitting up late talking after Aunt Mildred had gone to bed. Just after midnight, Mr. Jenkins came sneaking in through the back door, trying to tiptoe past us, but Jonas spoke up, compelling him to come into the parlor and say goodnight. He was stinking of kerosene and soot, and he looked about as furtive as I have ever seen anyone look.

The next day, we discovered that a Negro church not a mile distant had been burned to the ground, and as soon as I heard it, I knew in my bones that Mr. Jenkins had something to do with it! Cecilia, I must tell you, that absolutely terrified me! Down here, many people consider Negroes dangerous and believe they must be kept in line with stern measures at times. However, I never dreamed that someone would burn down a *church*! I cannot imagine why anyone would want to molest *Christian* people of color.

Please do not breathe a word to Father and Mother about it. They are already fearful that I will be in danger here in the land of the Rebels, but if they know that people are burning down churches, they will surely make me come home. Thomas and Jonas have already given me their word they will not tell. Thomas even remarked that Father should have more cause to be worried about me in Chicago, what with all the bootleggers running loose, shooting up the city in their gang wars!

Aside from this one incident all the way over in the far western part of the state, I feel quite safe and happy here. Reverend Miller assures me that there are few Negroes in these parts because virtually none of the mountain community of East Tennesseans ever engaged in the shameful practice of slavery. In Alcoa, about 25 miles from here, a small population of coloreds have been brought in to work at the Aluminum Company ore smelting plant, but they keep to themselves and are considered good, quiet neighbors to the white community in Maryville. I do not think there is any chance that there could be any problem with them, especially since none of them ever venture up into the hills here.

Even so, I am not worried at all. I know the Lord will protect me. I hope, with His guidance, I will make a real difference in the lives of these dear people, bringing light, education, and the love of our Savior!

My love flies to you,
Emily

September

September 1, 1931

Dearest Mother and Father,

Already I know this is the place the Lord intends for me to be. Reverend and Mrs. Miller are the kindest of souls, and it is clear they are devoted to these people here in the hill country. I met many of them at church service yesterday, and although they are poor, and some of them are ignorant, not all of them are without a good grounding in Scripture. Moreover, I find that even the poorest and most uneducated of them have a kind of dignity that you would find pleasing. They also have an interesting combination of humility and pride. They are very deferential toward me, as well as to Reverend and Mrs. Miller, but they hold to their own counsel and refuse to let anyone perform a service for them without repaying it in some way. Yesterday, Mrs. Miller and I visited some of the families in the area, and we took some little cakes that we had made. Each family we visited graciously accepted the cakes, but they hastily assembled some goods they had on hand to give us in return. We came home with canned jellies, bits of hand-tatted lace, an embroidered apron, and several other items of beauty and value. It was more than we brought!

I assure you, they are kind and harmless. Please stop worrying about my safety or the safety of my soul. They are not heathen at all, but quite Christian. Their worship is sober; they do not engage in riotous display of emotion, handling of serpents, or in the more bizarre interpretations of Scripture. I expect I will learn as much from these good hill folk as I hope to impart to them.

Your loving daughter,
Emily

September 6, 1931
Darling Cecilia,

I have been here over a week already, and I am feeling as free and as blissful as a bird who is learning to fly. It is so very beautiful, and all the people I have met are kindhearted.

Today at church, I met a remarkable family, the Wallaces. The mother and children attend services regularly. The father, who is less regular, joined them today, perhaps because three of the children came up in front of the congregation to sing. It was touching and amusing how they performed: with great fervor and a modicum of talent, if not of training! They were much better than you might expect!

After the service, Mrs. Miller introduced us at my request. There are two older boys, two younger girls, and a toddler of about three or four. The mother looks worn out, from breeding, no doubt, as do most of the women in these parts, for they marry young and have large families. I would say at least half of them are in the family way. Sadly, even the young women have that pinched, worried look that comes from a lifetime of cares. Mrs. Wallace has particular cares, I have learned, brought on by the fact that her husband is excessively fond of the drink. I was very surprised to learn this, for he is the picture of perfect health and vitality.

Frankly, I have never seen such striking men as Mr. Wallace and his sons! They are perfectly proportioned, of the hardiest of stock, large, and robust, with fine features, and all of them, including the girls, have the most extraordinary eyes! The oldest girl, Pearl, has golden eyes, exactly like her mother's, and by golden, I mean they are bright yellow and they shine like sunlight.

The older boy has eyes like his father's; one cannot tell if they are blue or green—they are both, all at once, and are as clear and bright as the sky or the sea or the green hills, depending upon the angle at which you see them. The younger of the boys has eyes that are of the palest green, so pale that they look nearly white, and in strong light, they look silver. The two younger girls have eyes of pure Ceylon. I wish you could see them. It almost seems as if they belong to a different race of people that I have never had the privilege to meet before.

Of course, they are not the only family to have handsome features or beautiful eyes. Many of them are quite fine-looking and as hardy as would be expected to survive in this unforgiving environment. The most common eye color is pure blue or the calmest of gray. I do not know why I have not noticed all these extraordinary faces and eyes before. It seems as if I have been looking through a glass, darkly, and now I am just beginning to see these people face to face.

After church, we all, Reverend and Mrs. Miller and I, went for a drive in the country. We followed the Little Tennessee River, a shimmering blue and white ribbon that took my breath away at every bend, and then we traveled high up into the hills. I cannot tell you how beautiful this place is, Cecilia. The sunlight is so clear and golden that I imagine it is what the light in heaven must be like. We drove to the very summit of a mountain, where the air is thin, sweet, and full of the music of birds and woodland creatures. The sky was perfectly azure, but with a golden and silver glow alighting upon every tree, rock, and flower. How beautiful is this part of Creation!

I know I am gushing. I am simply filled with the joy of this day, and perhaps, of this place. I know in my soul that I have not made a mistake coming here.

School begins in 2 days! I am filled with anticipation and trepidation!

Your surprisingly emancipated and excited sister,
Emily

Warm, waning days.
I savor a difference, in the slant of sunlight,
In a creeping vapor,
In my children.
Something unnamed will change how they see themselves.
I cannot taste it yet,
But I catch a scent, not tart, not sweet.
I have smelled something like it before;
It was so long ago, the memory has been washed away.
There is only a trace deep in my bedrock that reminds me.
I breathe more freely now;
The orb's lust fades, as does mine.
My thoughts turn to the rocks beneath me,
To my arms reaching out into the wildness.

September 9, 1931
My School Journal, grade 7, Miss Weston's class
By Pearl Wallace

This has been the best first day of school in which I have ever been. My teacher, Miss Weston, is very nice and pretty, and she wears beautiful dresses that probably came from Marshall Field's department store in Chicago, from whence she came. She teaches at Cheola School, which I attend with my brother Sardius and my sister Beryl. I was supposed to enter the sixth grade this year, but I am in the seventh. I started first grade when I was five years old because I could read by then, and yesterday Miss Weston gave us a test and I got to skip the sixth grade, even though I am only ten years old. Sardius is my next to the eldest brother. He is two years older than I am, and he is in the eighth grade because he also skipped a grade. My sister Beryl is eight years old and is in the third grade. My oldest brother Jasper is too old to go to school, and my baby sister Ruby is only four years old.

Mama says I got promoted to the seventh grade because I read so much during the summer, and I helped her cipher when we were selling berries. I did not tell her I learned to cipher on my own last year when I found where Daddy hides his whiskey and started selling it to Jake Hatton and to my Pap-pa. I get 25c a half pint for it, and I manage to skim that much off a gallon without Daddy noticing. It took me six months to get enough to buy me a new pair of shoes from Sears & Roebuck in time for Easter last spring, and I had to cheat a couple of times and draw down a little more than a half pint when Daddy went on a spree and got too drunk to notice how much I took.

They are beautiful, black patent leather shoes, with straps across the instep that you buckle at the sides. Mama calls them "Mary Janes," which I think is a beautiful name. Just as soon as I saw them in the catalogue, I figured out how much whiskey I would have to sell to get them, and it sure took some ciphering because I do not hardly ever get exactly 25c every time. I had to work out averages and estimate how much whiskey I could steal and how much money I would have left over after I had tithed ten percent to the Lord.

When I sell whiskey to Pap-pa he usually gives me what he calls a "tip," which might range anywhere from a couple of cents to a nickel. Jake Hatton is so stingy he tries to cheat me every chance he gets, and for a while there he told me to put it on his account and he would pay me later, but he never did. I caught on to that pretty quick, but not before he had stolen a good bit of my whiskey. I had to threaten never to sell him any more just to get my jars back, and when he finally did give them back, the lids were rusty. He is trash, just like my mama says, and I ought not to do business with him, but he is my only customer outside Pap-pa, and Pap-pa does not drink half as much as Jake Hatton does. Also, I am ascared if I try to cut Jake Hatton off, he will tattle on me, and that will be the end of that. It is better to put up with a trashy skinflint than to lose my business.

I am keeping this journal for Miss Weston. She has given all of us 2 bound books full of empty pages, one to write in as often as we can, which we keep to ourselves. The other one is to write in once a week to turn in to her. I have started the first book, but I am not sure what we should put in the book that we hand in. I will ask her about that tomorrow.

This is all I have time to write for now. My baby sister Ruby is crying and I have to go tend to her because Mama is busy putting up tomatoes.

September 9, 1931
Dear Mother and Father,

We began classes in earnest today. Miss Halfacre and I spent yesterday administering exams in order to place each child in his or her appropriate grade level. Ruth Halfacre has been here for four years and helps coordinate the lessons. (She is my supervisor, and until now was the only teacher here.) She is native to these parts, hailing from Maryville, and I must say, she has done an admirable job, considering the fact that most of the children attend school only intermittently, and some of them quite infrequently. Most of the children need some remedial training, and some require extensive work to bring them to grade level, but there is at least one very interesting family with disarmingly well-educated children. I met them Sunday at church: the Wallace family. Miss Halfacre informs me that the mother is enthusiastic about her children's education, makes sure they attend school as often as they can, and tutors them extensively at home. It just goes to show you can find intelligence and a love of learning in the most surprising places.

Not all of the children were able to attend today. It is harvest time here, and they are needed to help in the fields. It is a tragedy that even the youngest children are required to help scratch a living from the soil, but at least they have some means to keep from starvation. There are no soup kitchens here to succor those in need, and none is expected. I find myself impressed by the self-reliance of these people, even if it means the children are missing their education.

Yet, despite these disappointments, I am determined to remain cheerful and always mindful that I am here at the Lord's pleasure.

Your faithful daughter,

Emily

Warm, waning days
The great orb has unclasped me for now;
I sink between my green banks,
Basking in the heat of her brother.
The youngest of my upright children still frolic beside me,
But the taste of change grows stronger.
My silver children and the scurrying ones feel it, too.

September 10, 1931. It is hard to think of something to write about that I can turn in on Monday. I asked Miss Weston what I should say, and she said the first book is to write our private thoughts in. We can say whatever comes to mind without thinking about it. Once a week, we should look over what we have written, then rewrite the parts that we like the best in the second one. She says we should always keep the first book so we can remember what life was like here and now, and that we probably would enjoy it a great deal when we are older. Maybe, someday one of us might become famous. If we do, people will want to know what we did back when we were just children.

That is true. I would like to read the journals of many people, like Amelia Earhart who is an actual lady pilot and Albert Einstein who is the smartest person who ever lived outside of Jesus. I do not know if people would want to read about my life, though, since parts of it are not very nice. I hinted as much to Miss Weston, but she did not seem to believe me so I told her I would have to publish it posthumously. She got a funny look on her face, and then she sort of smiled, held my hand, very careful, as if she did not want to hurt my feelings, and told me that it is supposed to be pronounced POST-u-mus-ly, not post-HUM-us-ly, and that it meant after your death. She also said that she thought I meant to use the word anonymously, which means without anybody knowing who wrote it.

I did not say anything, but I surely did mean posthumously because if the law found out about my whiskey trading, they might track me down even if it was anonymous, and I might get sent up the river. I am glad she straightened me out about that pronunciation, though. It would be scundering to go see a book publisher and say the word wrong. They would not even give me the time of day!

September 11, 1931

Dear Jonathan,

I have received your letter, which I must admit surprised me very much. The last time we spoke seriously about our futures, your plans were to travel, and you gave me no reason to believe those plans might include me. I certainly got the impression that marriage was the last thing on your mind.

Frankly, Jonathan, I think your timing is not the best. If you had asked me two months ago, before I made definite plans to come here, I might have seriously considered your offer, but now, while I greatly appreciate your attentions and your earnest declarations, I must tell you that at present, I am dedicated to serving the Lord, at least for the school year. Consequently, I cannot entertain any thought of becoming a wife until I have made certain what my calling is to be. Until I know what the Lord requires of me, I must remain here, in the place it seems He has ordained for me.

I sincerely hope this does not cause you undue disappointment, and I hope that we can continue to be friends. Your friendship has been and will continue to be very dear to me, and I will grieve if I know I have ruined it or that you think less of me for what my father calls "my stubborn refusal to see what is best" for me. I only want to serve the Lord in the best way I can, and I need time to learn what that may be.

I remain your sincerest friend, and hope that you will remain mine.

Fondly,
Emily

September 11, 1931
Dearest Cecilia,

Hold onto your hat with the news I am about to tell you!

At last, Jonathan has proposed! *Now!* After I have already left Chicago and am ensconced into my new life here. I hate to say it, and I know you will not believe it, but I have refused him. I can hardly believe it myself. If only he had resolved to do this two months ago, before I was set on this course. Even if he had done so a month ago, I could have changed my plans, but now it is too late for the board to find another teacher, and I would feel I have disappointed not only the board and the children, but also myself, and, I like to think, the Lord, who has guided me here.

I feel strangely free and calm, having refused Jonathan. If he had been as considerate as he ought to have been, he would not have waited until I was already here and beginning my year of teaching. I feel angry that he should be so thoughtless of my feelings and consider me willing to drop all my responsibilities to come running to him when he has kept me on tenterhooks for so long. And to think how much I once pined for him!

I should not write any more—I shall just vent my anger and my frustration. Give my love to Mother and Father. I am quite safe and happy, although in a dither over Jonathan's sudden expression of his desire for me. Of course, do not even think of telling any of our family. If Mother knew, she would insist I come home and marry him immediately, and I should lose the opportunity to serve my Lord, which I have promised to do.

Good night, my darling sister! Thank you for letting me unburden my heart.

Emily

September 11, 1931. Daddy used to make good money working for the railroad, but now the Depression is on and they have laid everybody off. He has not worked a lick since last February. To tell the truth, half the time he is not worth a hill of beans around here, but I am not complaining about him taking time away to run his still. The more whiskey he makes, the more I can sell. It is hard on Mama, though, when he is not here to help with the heavy work. It is a good thing my brothers are strong, and my Uncle Woodrow, also. They shoulder a good deal of Daddy's burden so that we do not suffer for his transgressions.

I like school very much, and so do Sardius and Beryl. Jasper does not go to school. He is fifteen years old and he would be in the tenth grade, except that our school only goes to the eighth grade, and we cannot afford for him to live all the way over in Maryville for high school. When Daddy was working, Jasper stayed in the boarding house with him during the week and went to Maryville high school, but when Daddy got laid off, Jasper had to drop out because he had no place to stay. Now he helps out my Pap-pa who lives over by Greenback and my Uncle Woodrow who lives on the farm next to ours.

Jasper is still getting his lessons, though. Mama has many books, and she makes sure he keeps up with his studies so that he can get a full education here at home. Her own mother, my Mamma, who has already gone to heaven to be with Jesus and the Lord God Almighty, taught Mama at home, and she knows about everything there is to know, so Jasper is not left out in the cold. It is hard on him, keeping up with his studies in the evenings after working all day on both Pap-pa's and Uncle Woodrow's farm, and taking care of his calf and all the chores around here while the rest of us get to go and loll around at school all day, doing nothing but learning.

My baby sister Ruby is four years old and too little to go to school, but she already knows her letters and Mama is teaching her to read. She can already almost read *The Little Helper*, if Mama helps her sound out the words. I love her the best because I get to take care of her.

September 12, 1931
Dearest Mother and Father,

There has been a tragedy here. Reverend Miller had a failure of the heart during the night, and his condition is very grave indeed. We took him to the hospital in Maryville, and Mrs. Miller is with him now. I went to visit him, but I was not allowed to see him. I am glad I am here for Mrs. Miller's sake. She needs someone to comfort her in this terrible time.

My classes are going well. I have some very bright students, and I am finding that it is not at all difficult to teach several grades at once. The older ones help the younger ones, so it works out well.

Much love to you all, and especially to Jonas and Thomas. I have not had the opportunity to write to them much.

With love,
Emily

September 13, 1931 The most exciting thing happened today! The preacher has been taken sick, and so Miss Weston preached in his place! It is a good thing Daddy was not there because he would grumble about it, being as how Miss Weston is a lady, and he says that ladies have no place in the pulpit. If he had been there, she would have put him to shame for saying that, because she did a fine job. The sermon was about the baptism of the Holy Spirit (that is in Acts). I am very proud of Miss Weston. Not only is she smart, she is also a graduate of Moody Bible Institute, so she knows her Bible very well. Mama and Sardius said she really teaches the Bible, not like those ignorant, wind-sucking preachers down at Big Gully who cannot hardly even read, and all they do is holler and work up a sweat about how everybody is going to hell if they do not straighten up and fly right. I think she is even better than Preacher Miller.

After the sermon, we all went to Pap-pa's house for dinner, like we always do. Pap-pa's wife, Miss Janey Jo, is a very good cook. We had a real feast of vegetables, although we did not have any meat. Pap-pa has been too busy to go ahunting, and no one was in the mood to kill a chicken. I think Pap-pa is worn out from harvesting.

Daddy and Uncle Woodrow did not join us for dinner today because Mama has started a rule that anybody who does not go to church does not get to go to dinner at Pap-pa's afterward. She is hoping that will make everyone get up and out the door of a Sunday morning, but it did not work this morning. I reckon Uncle Woodrow and Daddy just could not manage it because they were too tired from working so hard all week.

I feel sorry for them missing it, and especially Uncle Woodrow because he could use a little more meat on his bones. He is a nice, sober man, but his nerves are bad because he got shell shock in the Great War when he was only 18 years old. He served on the Western Front. When he came home, he was a pure mess, and has been all these years since. Now he is 31 years old and has nothing to his name except the 20 acres next to us, which he has a hard time farming because he gets the shakes if he spends too much time out in the open. It is hard to plow when your hands are shaking so bad you cannot hold the reins. He lives in a pitiful shack all alone. It is a good thing Jasper helps him because he was about to starve when he had to do it all by himself. He is steadier with Jasper keeping him company because Jasper is calm, and he keeps him at his work.

Even though we are not supposed to work on Sundays, we sneaked in a few hours this evening while we still had some daylight. It was nice to get a good start on the week. Five rows of potatoes done tonight means five rows we will not have to do when we are tired to death.

It is past my bedtime, and I still have not written anything fit to turn in to Miss Weston tomorrow. Can you imagine how awful it would be if Miss Weston found out about my whiskey trading or that Daddy is a drunk and too poor to buy me new shoes for Easter? She would hightail it back to Chicago and then we would all be without a teacher!

September 13, 1931
Dear Cecilia,

I bring you more surprises. The Reverend Miller has been taken ill, too ill to preach, and rather than let the congregation be disappointed at the lack of teaching, I stepped into the pulpit in his place today. I cannot believe it myself, that I was so bold as to get up in front of everyone and teach from the Bible as if I were the preacher. I did not have to prepare much—I adapted one of my papers on the Baptism of the Holy Spirit that I had written for a class, and I do not wish to boast, but it was very well received. At first, they seemed a little taken aback, especially the men, but because I used an expository style of teaching from the text rather than exhortation, I think they took it in stride.

DO NOT TELL MOTHER AND FATHER! Father would have a fit, I am sure. It is bad enough that I was so stubborn to go all the way through college without his blessing, but this would certainly send him over the edge.

I am flying high, as you may well imagine!
Much love,
Emily

September 14, 1931
My School Journal, grade 7, Miss Weston's class
By Pearl Wallace

My name is Pearl Wallace. I live in Blount County, Tennessee, and I go to school at Cheola School. I am descended from the great William Wallace of Scotland who bravely fought against the evil Edward the First of England. My great-great grandfather was Wayne Wallace. He used to own all the land between Lookback Mountain and the Little Tennessee River. My grandfather was James Wallace, named after the great King James the Fourth of Scotland who became the famous King James the First of England who gave us the Bible.

My grandmother, Mama Wallace, also was Scottish, although I am not sure what clan she claimed. It is too bad, but most of the Wallaces have died or moved away, leaving only my Uncle Woodrow and my father here on the old homestead.

All of us are pure Scottish on my mama's side, also. Pap-pa is from the Aiken clan, and Mam-ma was from the Blair clan. Mam-ma was Ulster-Irish, which means that they were Scots who moved to Ireland to help the ignorant Irish see the truth of the Gospel and not be bound to the abominations that the pope and the Catholic Church taught them. Even though they were there a long time, they stayed true to their Scottish blood, so all of us young'uns can claim several clans, although we go ahead and claim the Wallace clan because it is the most important one.

September 14, 1931. I am not able to write much tonight because we had to dig potatoes after school up until dark. Mama does not like us to miss school to help with the crops, so Jasper, Uncle Woodrow and Daddy have been doing what they can during the day, and when we came home, we hit the fields for as long as we could. The dark of the moon is already past, though, and we are behind. We still have a lot of potatoes in the ground, and next we have to start in on the beans and okra, so we will have to lay out of school the rest of the week to get it done.

We like digging potatoes when we do not have to stay at it too long. If you do it too long at a time it hurts your back, but if you do it only for a couple or three hours at a time, it almost seems like we are digging for buried treasure. Then we always get a good supper because Mama fries up fresh potatoes with a side of fatback, and sometimes she has fish, too, if Daddy has gone down to the river. I think his still is down there, and he slips in a little fishing in between batches.

I also like potato season because we get to take a bath almost every night when we have been digging. I love sinking down in a big tub of hot water after grubbing in the dirt all afternoon. It is a lot of trouble to haul in enough water for our baths and get it heated up, but it is worth it to get in so dirty and come out so clean. It is like being baptized every night.

Warm, waning days.
My upright children are weary, and they fear want.
I offer them sacrifices of my silver ones,
But they are not satisfied.
They want to hoard the bounty of sister Earth
To slake their hunger for the long cold ahead.
The scent of soil and toil cling to them.

September 15, 1931. Our neighbor, Billy Ray Carlton who has been gone for three years, has come back and moved into his old home place across the creek from us. Billy Ray moved to Louisiana three years ago to work the shrimp boats, right after his Mama died, but now, with the Depression on, he got laid off, along with most everybody else in the country. Now he is back, saying he is going to be a farmer after all. I do not remember much of Billy Ray. He was mean to me when I was little so I stayed out of his way whenever he was over at our place, but now he is back. And guess what? He brought back a wife and a child!

Although they moved in last week, we have not been over to meet them on account of the potato harvest, and Mama says she does not have the time to be hospitable just yet. She sent Daddy over there yesterday with a chess pie, and he came back grumbling to Mama that the woman is a coonass cajun and he said the child is white but looks like a negro. Except he did not say Negro. He said another word that Mama says she will whip us for if she ever hears us say it. A lot of people around here do say it, just like they say G.D. and other words that Mama hates. But if you say it, it means you are nothing but white trash. If you are an upright citizen, you say negro or colored person.

Mama did not like what Daddy said one little bit. She sat up very straight and said in a stern voice, "Richard, you will not use such language in front of my children!"

I was very surprised to see her stand up to him like that. Every time he gets drunk, he cusses us all out and Mama never says a word, but she got her dander up when Daddy said that. I know coonass is not a nice word, either, but is cajun a bad thing? I wish I could ask Mama, but I do not want to make her mad at me, and of course I cannot ask Miss Weston. I do not want her to know that I know bad words.

At first, Daddy looked cowed after Mama blessed him out, and then he got a little pouty. After a while he slipped out, and I knew he was going out to the woodshed. It is a good thing the jug is getting close to empty, or he would for sure be sliding off the wagon over this. I have been hitting it hard of late. Last night I took out about a quarter cup to give to Jake Hatton just to keep him from tattling on me to Daddy. I charged him a dime for it, which I made him pay up front. I hope Daddy does not remember how much he had left the last time he was in the woodshed.

Although I am not happy at the thought of running into Billy Ray, I cannot wait to meet Mrs. Carlton and her child. I cannot imagine how someone can be a black person and at the same time be white, and I am curious about what a coonass cajun looks like.

Warm, waning days, cooling nights.
There is rancor in the hearts of some of my children,
Elusive distress that has not yet been formed into thought.
Rancor and sorrow, hate forming.
None of my children understand, although they feel it.
The upright father succumbs to bitterness and oblivion.
I weep for them as The Spirit grieves.

September 16, 1931. I wish we could go over to Billy Ray Carlton's house and meet his new wife and daughter. Mama says maybe we can tomorrow, if it rains and it is too wet to get in the field.

Daddy left before daylight to go get jar lids. We are about out because he used them up for his whiskey jars, and I hate to admit, I might have taken a few myself. He did not get home until nearly suppertime. He was not drunk, which we count as a blessing, but he was stinking of whiskey, which made us all mad. Here we were, working hard trying to get in enough food to last us the winter, and he trots off to town on the excuse of picking up a few jar lids, leaving us to do all the work by ourselves. We need him in the field this week, and it should not take him the whole livelong day to go buy lids.

When Daddy is sober and in a good mood, he can be a good worker, but it is hard to keep him home. Unless Mama can talk him into promising to stay, he will leave of the morning and not come home until suppertime. Sometimes he goes over to Harvey Madison's garage to tinker on his old automobile, which he gets to running on occasion. Sometimes he takes Jasper with him because Jasper can put right just about anything he sets to. He will sit back on his heels and study it for a long time, then he will just reach in to fiddle with it for a few minutes, and the next thing you know, it is working again. When Jasper goes to Harvey Madison's garage with Daddy, they usually get the automobile started, then they bring it home and take us for a ride in it. Most of the time it breaks down again before we get too far, and we have to hitch up Charley, our mule, to drag it home. Now it generally just sits, getting rusty at Harvey Madison's garage.

Daddy also spends a great deal of time fox hunting or just running his hounds. He sometimes brings in some fish or a squirrel or two for supper, but we do not count on it. I wish he would bring home a deer. They are good eating, and one would feed all of us for a good, long time, but he says it is too much trouble to field dress and drag home a deer. That just goes to show you what a trifling sort he is.

I have just spent this whole evening writing about what a sorry daddy I have, so I will not be able to turn any of this in for my assignment. Miss Weston will think we are trash. I reckon I will just make up another special entry that looks good. That is easier because I am in the right frame of mind after hearing Miss Weston preach.

September 17, 1931. It did not rain today, but I got to meet Billy Ray Carlton's new wife and daughter anyway. Mama had gone over there last evening and invited them to come for coffee this morning, and they got here just as we were clearing away the breakfast things.

They are very different from us and they talk funny, but I like them. Mrs. Carlton is beautiful in a way I have never seen before. She has skin the color of honey, beautiful red lips and lots of white teeth. She has big bosoms, too, and the most beautiful, shining, dark brown curly hair that comes all the way down to her waist. She was wearing a red dress that looked beautiful on her even though it was pretty clear that it was a hand-me-down. It was faded and a little ragged, with a big patch on the skirt. You could tell she had let the hem out all the way, because there was a crease down there where the hem used to be. Even then, it did not quite cover her knees, because her legs are very long. I noticed this because my legs are long, also, and I could not help but feel bad for her. I am always self-conscious when I grow so fast my dress gets too short and my knees stick out. My legs are skinny and not half as pretty as Mrs. Carlton's, so maybe she is not as scundered about it as I am.

Daddy was not here, but Uncle Woodrow was, and he and my brothers stared at Mrs. Carlton when she came in. Mama sent the boys on out to the field, but Uncle Woodrow stayed and just sat there the whole time Mrs. Carlton was here, kind of sunk back in the corner, pretending to read the newspaper, but he kept glancing up and looking at her out the side.

Darlene is a puzzle. Daddy had said she was a white negro, and I was curious to know what that meant. I have never seen one before. Also, do you use a capital N for Negro? I have not figured out yet what any of this means.

I just looked it up. You do spell Negro with a capital letter. It is a proper noun.

I do not know why Daddy said that about Darlene. Everybody knows that Negroes are black, and they are very mean. Walt Bittertree used to have dealings with them before he moved here, and he says they are bad to sneak around at night and rob innocent people who might be out just minding their own business. I reckoned Darlene would be very big and fierce and maybe dark skinned. However, Darlene is not at all mean or scary. She is very, very sweet, with a smile that is kind of shy in a way, but at the same time you get the feeling she might be up for some fun kind of mischief.

She also is very white, even whiter than me. Her hair is as white as mine, but it is wild and curly, like cotton has exploded all over her head. One time at the fair, we saw a magician who had us touch a metal ball and it made our hair stand on end. That is what Darlene's hair is like, except where ours went straight out, hers is kinky. She also has blue eyes that are very pretty, but she wears dark glasses when she is outside so that you cannot see how nice they are. Her nose and lips are kind of fat. At first, I thought she was a little on the ugly side, but the more I looked at her, the more I liked the way she looks, especially the blue eyes. I wish she did not wear those dark spectacles, though. She looks a little spooky with them on.

They did not stay very long because Mrs. Carlton was nervous about Billy Ray coming home and catching them gone, but I am looking forward to seeing them again. I really like Darlene.

September 18, 1931
Dearest Cecilia,

This has been a heartbreaking week. Most of the children have not come to school at all, because they are required at home to help bring in the crops. A few have come for only a day or two, leaving me to feel helpless and worthless for most of the week. I went to see several of them in the hopes of giving them some assignments, but I quickly discovered that was a mistake. It is obvious they do not want me to see them in their native environment, working to exhaustion. I have never seen children so tired, so ragged, and so dirty, and they clearly are embarrassed to be seen in such difficult circumstances. The mothers hurry the children to the well to wash their faces and hands when they see me coming, and then they feel obliged to offer me a meal, which, of course, is a hardship to them. I brought one family a picnic hamper filled with sandwiches, and the mother politely, but firmly, told me that they had already eaten, which I know was not true, because the younger child gasped and looked at her with consternation. His elder brother quickly reached over and pinched him to shush him, while all the others looked hungrily at my hamper. I knew they had not eaten much at all that day. I tried to think of a way to leave it with them, but the mother was firm, dismissing me as soon as she could without being rude. It distresses me that there is nothing I can do to ease their suffering. I believe they would rather die than accept aid from me. Your heart would break to see them.

Please pray for these people in their desperation, and especially for the children.

Love,
Emily

September 19, 1931. It has started to rain, so we get to take the evening off from working in the fields, praise the Lord! I wish it had started raining earlier, because then we could have gone over to see Darlene and her mother, but it is too late now.

Daddy was sober all day today, and he worked hard, but he was not in a good mood. He kept criticizing us, and when we got to acting silly, he said we act like unenlightened peasants who do not know how to behave in a good family.

It burns me up when Daddy puts on airs. He gets especially highfalutin when he gets to talking about his ancestors. He says we are from a heroic line, as great as Lancelot, Arthur, and other knights of old. Every year when we go to the Highland Games over in Maryville, Daddy wears his kilt to let everyone know he is a Wallace. Although none of the rest of us has a kilt, we all wear a scrap of the Wallace tartan so everyone will know who we are. It is nice to be a part of such an important clan, but I wish Daddy would not make over it so much in front of ordinary people.

After supper when we were washing up, I got Mama to myself and I asked her why Daddy called Darlene a white Negro, and she said it is because Darlene might have had a Negro father but she is an albino, which means that all the color has been leached right out of her skin. I said that Negroes are black and whites are white, so why call her a Negro at all? She got a little flustered at that and said it was hard to explain, then went to her bedroom without saying any more. I had to finish up the dishes by myself.

Warm, waning days.
The vast blue has turned to grey;
My body swells with freshness.
The torrents bring again a taste of earth that should not be.
The greenleaves are being slain.
My children will mourn—
The silver, the creeping, and the upright ones—
But for now, they still sing with laughter,

Unaware of what descends from above and ascends from below.

September 20, 1931
Dear Jonathan,

Thank you for your kind words. It makes my heart sing to know that you understand that I feel that I must be where the Lord has placed me, at least for now. I cannot tell you how excited I am that classes have begun, and how I look forward to the blessing of teaching these precious children who have been entrusted to my hands. Surely, God has placed us all here together to give me the opportunity to enlighten these vulnerable, young souls. I know I will bring new understanding to them, and I hope, in the process, I will find ways to ease their burdens and to bring them closer to God's own heart.

Blessings to you, my dear friend! I pray for you unceasingly and beg that you do the same for me. I do so desire to bring Light to these special people!

Your sister in Christ,
Emily

September 20, 1931. Today is Sunday, which is very nice because we get a day of rest. It is still raining, so everything is slushy and muddy, and my hands are raw from picking and shelling beans. We were all a sight by the time we got to church this morning.

Miss Weston preached again because Preacher Miller is still sick from a heart attack. Daddy and Uncle Woodrow joined us for church and for dinner at Pap-pa's afterward, and guess who also came? Miss Weston! We had a wonderful time. Miss Janey Jo really outdid herself with dinner. She had a roasted goose, buttermilk biscuits, green beans, beets, squash, and butterbeans. I ate so much I about popped!

I am happy Miss Weston came. She is very sweet, smart, and beautiful! Every Sunday, she wears even more beautiful dresses than she wears during the week, and she wears hats, too. Mama has one hat that she wears to church, but Miss Weston has so many I cannot count them. She has long hair that she wears in braids that she wraps around her head like a crown. The hats sit on top, nestled in the crown, like a crown of glory.

Daddy did not like going to church with Miss Weston preaching because he says that women are not allowed to preach according to St. Paul, but Mama says it is all right because Miss Weston is not a preacher. She is a missionary, and missionaries are allowed to preach as long as it is not in a real church. St. Paul plainly says that women are supposed to keep silent in *churches*, and Miss Weston preaches at the schoolhouse, so Mama won that argument.

I do not know why she has come here to be a missionary, when everyone knows that missionaries go to heathen places like Africa or India, where people are starving and ignorant and really need to hear the Gospel. We all are civilized around here, and we know the Gospel. We have all been saved ever since we were little. I was only three years old when I asked Jesus to come into my heart. When I told Mama, she cried and hugged me and told me I was the smartest child she had, and the best. When I think about that, I feel bad about selling Jake Hatton that whiskey, but Daddy would never in a million years buy me new shoes for Easter, so I had to do something.

Sometimes I think I want to be a missionary, and now that I know you can be one anywhere, even in the U.S.A., I like the idea even more. When I was little, I used to ask God to send me a sign if He wanted me to go to Africa to spread the Gospel, and every time I prayed for that, I always had a nightmare about being cooked in a big pot, with cannibals stirring me up with canoe paddles. It always ascared me half to death, and it left me fuddled because I could not figure out if God was telling me I had to go and sacrifice myself or if He was warning me not to go because

I would never survive those cannibals. I still have not figured it out, but am waiting for another sign from Him. I reckon there is time, because I have at least another five years or so before Mama would let me go to Africa or maybe Mississippi where people really are poor and ignorant, but while I am waiting, I need to do something to keep the wolf from the door.

September 20, 1931
Dearest Cecilia,

I have had the most wonderful day! Do you remember the family I told you about—the one with the beautiful eyes? This is the Wallace family. They invited me to dinner after church today (by the way, I got to preach again! More on that later), and I met some of the nicest people. First, there is Mrs. Wallace's father, Donald Aiken, and her stepmother, who hosted the dinner. Mrs. Aiken is surprisingly young—I would say in her mid-30s, and I believe she and I are going to be the best of friends. She is quite civilized, as is the whole family. I was astonished when they began discussing the works of Edna St. Vincent Millay! Mr. Wallace quoted all of "Love is Not All." Do you know the poem? It begins, "Love is not all. It is not meat nor drink, nor slumber nor a roof against the rain," and continues with a meditation on if love is more important than peace or a comfortable life or even survival.

He recited the entire poem, quite beautifully in his deep, melodious voice, and then there followed a lively debate about it. Even the children chimed in, expressing their opinions of what might be more important than love. I must say, I was entranced by the whole family, how they seem to revere poetry and philosophy. I believe there is something romantic in the hearts and minds of these people. Perhaps it is because they are surrounded by so much beauty in these hills.

Mr. Wallace's younger brother, Woodrow, also sat at the table. A more intriguing soul I do not think I have ever met. He is very like his brother, tall and beautifully formed, with those astonishing eyes of both vivid blue and green, and there plays about them an air of both tragedy and mirth. Between him and the elder Mr. Wallace, the conversation was alternately so deep, then so lively and fun that I found myself breathless with laughter, and then quite somber with contemplating deep questions. I do not know when I have spent such an enjoyable afternoon.

I wish you could have been here to enjoy it with me. Perhaps you can plan a visit so you can meet some of these wonderful people.

All my love,

Emily

P.S. The Reverend Miller is still quite ill, and although he is past the most treacherous part, it may be that he does not return to the pulpit any time soon. It is quite exhilarating to be up there in front of the congregation, teaching the Word of God to adults, much different than teaching grammar and arithmetic to boys and girls. Fortunately, most of the congregation presently consists mainly of women and children since the men are still busy in the fields. The men who were there were taken aback at first to see me preaching a real sermon, but they were well outnumbered, and now I think they have begun to accept me at the behest of their wives. I am an oddity, but I am THEIR oddity, and I get the feeling that they are secretly proud of me!

September 21, 1931
My School Journal, grade 7, Miss Weston's class
By Pearl Wallace

Miss Weston is the nicest teacher anybody could have. She also is a missionary. That is something we have in common. I want to be a missionary when I grow up, also. I plan to go to Moody Bible Institute and learn everything there is to know about the Bible, and then I will go to India or to Africa where the people do not know the Lord Jesus, and I will tell them all about Him so they will be saved and go to heaven when they die.

It will be hard to go away because I love my home very much. I live in the mountains of East Tennessee, right on the bank of the Little Tennessee River with my family of two brothers, two sisters, my mother, and father in a cozy little house. My father was with the Railroad until the Depression hit and he was laid off along with everyone else. However, we are much better off than most folks around here because we own land, which we put to good use. We keep a garden, catch fish from the river, and we pick berries all summer and fall. It is like heaven, except I expect that we will not ever be cold or hungry in heaven.

September 21, 1931. Tonight we just had cornbread and buttermilk for supper because we were working so hard canning and pickling all day, but we are not hungry because right after supper, Mrs. Bittertree brought over a chocolate cake, made from her special recipe that calls for buttermilk, which makes the cake extra moist and soft, and of course, delicious! We canned well on into dark, and put up 32 jars of tomatoes, so the house smells delicious!

The Bittertrees live on the other side of Uncle Woodrow, on the prettiest piece of land that used to belong to my Daddy Wallace. That land should have come to us, but Daddy's brother inherited it all, and he sold it to the Bittertrees, before he up and moved to Texas. Sometimes I wish Mr. and Mrs. Bittertree were not so nice. It would be easier to be mad at them for getting the best part of Daddy Wallace's land.

They have a son who is spoiled to death. His name is Ralph Lee, but Mrs. Bittertree calls him "Little Ralph Lee," even though he is 14 years old and is mean as a snake. He quit school two years ago because they caught him stealing people's dinners, and he would not admit to it even though blackberry jelly from Danny Ogle's jelly biscuit was smeared all over his face. Miss Halfacre whipped him for it, and then Mrs. Bittertree told him he did not have to go back to school after that. She says she taught him at home, but we all know good and well all he did all day was run wild all over the place, and he still does. He steals from the Greenbrier store sometimes, too, but nobody can ever catch him at it.

One time I caught him pinching Beryl hard enough to make her cry. I hauled off and lamped him good in the eye. He did not tell anyone it was I who did it because he knew that if he told, everyone would laugh at him for being bested by a little girl. Mrs. Bittertree went around weeping about it, saying, "Poor Little Ralph Lee ran into a tree branch and about took out his eye." My brothers and I laughed about that for a long time.

I am going to bed now. I am so tired I am barely able to go wash my feet. I would leave that off, but Mama would kill me if I crawled in between her clean sheets with dirty feet.

September 22, 1931. I love to pick muscadines. The best ones are the highest up, so Jasper, Sardius, Darlene and I skinnied up the tree to the very top and threw them down on a sheet. Mama and Beryl gathered them up and put them in buckets. Even Ruby helped a little, although she ate more than she put in the bucket. From where we were up in the tree, we could see clear across the river and over the first line of hills, all the way to Chilhowee Mountain. The river is bright silver during the daytime, and toward evening, it turns gold. There is no place better to be than up in a tree, smelling that sweet muscadine smell and eating them until my mouth gets itchy. Muscadines bring good cash, too.

We had a picnic, and it seemed like one of those beautiful days of summer when we were not really working, but just having a good time. To top it all off, we managed to get over six gallons! Getting to take all those muscadines home was just something extra good that added to the happiness.

Daddy was home when we got there, with ten pounds of sugar and 6 dozen new jars and lids, so we just ate leftover cornbread and molasses for dinner, then set in to making jelly. Now the kitchen smells so good with the sweet, muscadine smell.

I love making jelly. We all crowd in the kitchen and work like one of those manufacturing machines that pumps things out in a big hurry. Mama starts in singing, and we get to going, and the next thing you know, jars of jelly are all lined up on the table, the counter, the windowsill, and all along the walls. We are going to have some fine eating this winter!

Warm, waning days.
My children gambol amid rocks and sweet grass.
The upright ones sang to me from the tops of the greenleaves
And ate of their bounty,
Dripping sweetness and song through the nothing of air.
The Spirit smiles at their joy,
Even as something dark peers from the edges.
The silver Orb's lust grows strong,
Inciting in me the need to rise.
I leave my silver children tucked in my womb
As I reach for her.

September 23, 1931. Tonight we made apple pies, and the kitchen smells like cinnamon. Mama is not making butter this week, even though she says she will miss the cash from it, because cream makes the pies taste so much better. It puts Daddy in a good mood, too, all that pie with cream for supper. He also is looking forward to fried pies this winter, as we all are. There is nothing better than reaching into your dinner pail and pulling out a fried pie on a cold day.

I wanted Darlene to stay to supper, but when I started to ask, Mama shook her head at me and glanced over at Daddy. It makes me mad that he has such a mean spirit about Darlene. She is just as good as anybody. She is helpful, and sweet, and smart. Mama thinks so, too.

September 24, 1931. Mama sent Jasper, Sardius, Daddy, and me over to Pap-pa's today to help him bring in his beans while she finished with the apples. When we got home, we helped her bring in all the ones she had drying outside. They were everywhere! They were on the roofs of the house, the woodshed, the springhouse, and even up on the barn! At first we were worried because we thought Mama had climbed up on the roof. It is steep and she is very fat, so it would be easy for her to roll right off. Daddy started to fuss at her for climbing up on the roofs, but then Uncle Woodrow popped up to tell us he had actually done the climbing. That also was surprising because his nerves are so bad he usually gets the shakes when he is in a scary place. I do not have time to write more because I must go and help put up those apples. I cannot wait to make apple butter. That is my favorite!

September 25, 1931. We have only one more day before the full moon, but we have made good progress. We have mostly finished with the apples, which is a good thing. Everyone is getting tired of them. Even though they smell good, the smell gets up in your nose and stays there so you cannot hardly smell anything but them. Ruby got a bellyache last night from eating so many.

We spent the morning picking squash, tomatoes, and okra, and after dinner, Daddy said he was going down to the river to fish, but we all know what he was really up to. That means he will be gone until supper, so Mama said Beryl and I could go get Darlene and Mrs. Carlton to come have some apple pie and coffee. We ran over there as fast as we could, and then we had the best afternoon with Darlene, making apple butter and eating it on hoecakes that Mrs. Carlton cooked while Mama canned. Darlene and I went down to the river for a little while, but the sun was so glary that Darlene said it hurt her eyes, so we left and came on back to the house. Darlene told us all about Louisiana and how folks speak French down there. She also told me that a cajun is a person who lives in Louisiana and that it is not a bad word at all, but coonass is not very nice. I did not tell her what Daddy had called her because I know that would hurt her feelings and make her think we were white trash. I wonder if it would hurt her feelings to call her a Negro? I wish I could ask somebody about what is proper.

I told her about school and wondered which grade she would be in, and she said that she would not be going to my school, that her mama teaches her at home. I tried to talk her into going with me, but she just shook her head and said she could not go to my school and she would not tell me why. I had a very good time with Darlene. She already is my best friend outside of my brothers and sisters.

Both Mrs. Carlton and Darlene are big cut-ups. Mrs. Carlton has a big, purple bruise on the side of her face that she got trying to milk their ornery old cow. She told about how she was sitting there, calm as could be, with her head in the clouds while she milked, and all of a sudden, she thought she had been hit by a lightning bolt. She made it sound so funny, mocking that cow thrashing around, kicking her until she saw stars. I laughed until I cried. Mama and Uncle Woodrow did not laugh as much as I did. They are bashful around her and want her to think they do things proper, but I do not mind that she knows I think she is funny. I think that lets her know I like her a lot.

Mrs. Carlton and Darlene left before Daddy got home. Nobody has said anything, but I think Mrs. Carlton knows that Daddy would not like to see Darlene at our house playing with Beryl and me. Uncle Woodrow is much nicer than Daddy. He was very kind to them and even walked them home, even though it is not far or dangerous. It is only a half-mile, just across the creek, and there is a sturdy tree trunk on which to walk across. He wanted them to feel important enough to be escorted by a gentleman. Not everyone is as ignorant as my daddy is.

September 25, 1931
Dear Cecilia,

Did you tell Father that some of the men here are afflicted with a thirst for liquor? And did you tell him and Mother that Jonathan has asked me to marry him? If so, I must say, I am disappointed that you would betray my confidence in that way. Now Father is insisting I come home, and Mother has practically published the banns, but I am more determined than ever not to tuck my tail between my legs and come running back. I have my duty to fulfill here. I will not go back on my word. It is my mission to enlighten the children of this district. I will thank you not to further blab about what is going on here.

Your disappointed sister,

Emily

Warm, waning days.
The great orb holds me high above the greenness.
I arc into her light.
Bellies are full with new life.
We rejoice in the quickening.

September 26, 1931. Daddy went foxhunting last night, as he always does at the full moon, and he has not come home yet, which is a blessing, because a night out foxhunting means he is going to get blootered. I hope he stays out all night again tonight and sleeps it off. We cannot stand him when he comes home roaring drunk, cussing and pitching a fit, and getting us all torn up.

I don't know how Pap-pa does it, but he somehow knows when Daddy has fallen off the wagon, and he always comes over early the next morning to help out and make sure we all are all right. He says he is coming over because Miss Janey Jo won't cook him a decent breakfast, but we know better.

I know that Pap-pa does not like Daddy, even though he does not breathe a word against him. As far as I know Mama does not complain to Pap-pa about the way Daddy treats her when he has a snootfull, but you can tell that he knows by the way he gets very quiet around Daddy when there has been a row. I wonder why he let Mama marry him when she could have had any fine fellow in the county.

I think Mama must really have liked Daddy back when they were young. The way she talks about him sometimes, I think she still likes him. To hear her tell it, he was a handsome boy, and he did not drink when she married him. Also, he was a good daddy to their firstborn, Little Harrison.

Little Harrison died right after his second birthday of the whooping cough. Right after that, Daddy started in on the whiskey, and every time he came in from work on Saturdays, he curled up with a bottle. It did not matter to him that he had other young'uns coming along after that. That is the honest truth. We have had a sorry drunk for a daddy from the minute we first saw the light of day. It makes me mad that I missed out on the good part of what Daddy used to be. I think about him being a good father, and I wonder if Little Harrison had not died, maybe he would still be. I wonder if my big brother knew how much was at stake, he might have fought against that old whooping cough a little harder.

Some people say that Daddy cannot help himself being a drunk because he is still grieving over his baby. I do not believe that. He surely could help himself when the railroad bosses had their eye on him, back before the Depression was on. They would fire anyone who showed up for work even smelling of drink. It seems to me that anybody who can keep himself sober all during the week can keep himself sober any time he wants to. I think he just uses Little Harrison's death as an excuse when he decides he wants to get scuppered and lay out of doing anything around here.

September 27, 1931. Daddy still is not home. We heard the hounds baying all night long, so he must be out there somewhere, staggering around in the woods with his trashy old cronies. I just hate him when he does that. Thank goodness for Pap-pa and Uncle Woodrow who pitch in when Daddy is on a bender. They are both good, steady men who know how to act like men. They think Daddy is foolish to waste his time hunting foxes. You can't eat them, so why go chasing them all over tarnation, making enough racket to wake the countryside and coming home to cuss out your family and then fall into bed to sleep all day?

Pap-pa will not go fox hunting, but he hunts for food, while Uncle Woodrow will not shoot anything on account of he is ascared of loud guns. He will fish, but he will not hunt, not even if he is starving and there is a squirrel sitting not five feet away, digging in his tomatoes. He will not even be in the same room as a gun. Whenever Daddy knows he is coming over, he takes his rifle from off the wall over the fireplace and puts it back in the bedroom. If Woodrow comes over and the rifle has not been moved, he will stand outside even if it is raining ice water and wait for somebody to put it away. One time Jasper laid a bunch of cedar logs on the fire and they got to popping, and Uncle Woodrow liked to have run Mama over getting out of that room. He ran out the back door, then threw himself off the porch, and kept on running. We did not see him for weeks after that. It is no doubt that the poor man has the worst nerves of anybody I ever saw.

After church today, we went to Pap-pa's for dinner, and Miss Weston and Uncle Woodrow were there, but not Daddy, of course, since he is still laying out drunk. Between Pap-pa and Jake Hatton, I am getting rich with my whiskey trading. Today I made 35c! Of course, I will have to tithe 3 1/2 c, which I will round up to 4c. I will not mind that one bit because I know that how I got this money is not pleasing to the Lord. If I give Him the extra half cent, He might not be too mad at me.

Warm, waning days.
I taste the pain of my children.
It wafts through the darkness with the cry of the hound,
With the miasma of rancor.
Even singing loudly, I cannot drown the innocents' sobs.
The great Orb loosens her desire.
I exhale with my release.

September 27, 1931
Dear Cecilia,

I think I owe you an apology. Upon further reflection, I realize that it probably was Jonathan who shared my confidences with Mother and Father. If I had been thinking, I would have known you are not the kind of sister who would betray me. I was in such a tizzy about them having found out about Jonathan's proposal and about the illegal activities of some of the men of this community that I immediately took it out on you. I certainly hope—actually, I am quite certain—that I am right in this. I beg you to forgive me.

I have had another successful Sunday. I preached on Gideon and the fleece, which was very well received, and then I went to Mr. and Mrs. Aiken's house for dinner. Mrs. Aiken, who has asked me to call her Janey Jo, insists that I should come to dinner every Sunday. I am glad to do that because the Reverend Miller is still bedridden and Mrs. Miller does not like to be apart from him for Sunday dinner. If I am away during the mealtime, it allows her to sit with him and eat in his bedroom. I fear I have become a burden to them, and I am grateful for an excuse to get away as often as I can.

Mr. Wallace did not join us today, but his younger brother Woodrow did, and we all had a pleasant time, although the younger Mr. Wallace (I shall call him Woodrow to keep you from being confused) was very quiet so that it was difficult to include him in conversation. I get the feeling something terrible has happened to him. There is an air of tragedy about him, despite his hearty attempts to be engaging. Sometimes I catch him staring into space with such a desperate look in his eyes, I long to ask him the secret of his melancholy. Perhaps I could draw him out more and even help him to overcome it. Please add him to your prayers, that God will deliver him from whatever makes him suffer so much.

Your loving sister,
Emily

September 27, 1931
Dearest Mother and Father,

Thank you for your recent letter and for the advice you have shared with me. I appreciate your concerns, but I see the circumstances differently than you do. The Millers need me here more than ever, now that the Reverend is so ill, for I am needed to keep Mrs. Miller company and help her tend to the needs of the congregation. She spends so much of her time nursing her husband that it is left to me to call on the ill and infirm. It is not a hardship to me at all, but invigorating because I feel as if I am doing God's calling.

Unfortunately, the Reverend will most likely not be well enough to return to his duties for some time, but you will be pleased to know that someone who lives in the community with good training in Scripture has stepped up to take his place in the pulpit for now. Mrs. Miller and I are quite able to handle the responsibilities left to us. Members of the congregation are also taking very good care of me! Today I went to dinner at the home of the Aikens, pillars of the community. They attend the Methodist church in Greenback, but their daughter and her family attend our little church here in the "holler," as they call it. You would be surprised at the tenor of our conversations. Today at the dinner table, we discussed the merits of Billy Sunday's sermons, so you see, they are not all "ignorant, vacant-eyed morons" after all!

Regarding your concerns about the sin of drunkenness, I assure you that the people here are quite sober, for they cannot afford the luxury of missing work in the fields. If they do not gather in enough food to last the winter, they face starvation. There may be one or two stray instances in which someone takes a sip now and then (usually for medicinal purposes), but it is quite rare. I have not seen a single person in his cups here. Besides, may I remind you that Chicago is full of bootleggers, speakeasies, and gin joints, not to mention drunken men sleeping on the streets? If you are going to judge the safety and moral integrity of a place based upon the amount of liquor consumed per capita, then Cheola Community is far superior to Chicago!

I assure you that Jonathan and I remain the best of friends. There is plenty of time for us to plan a future together (if that is what God wills for us) when I return home at the end of the term.

I remain your grateful and loving daughter,

Emily

September 27, 1931
Dear Jonathan,

I am very disappointed in both you and myself. Because of you, I have wrongly accused my blameless sister of an indiscretion. I did not dream that you would be so bold as to tell my parents the contents of the letter that I wrote to you regarding the weaknesses of certain inhabitants of this region, and I certainly did not expect you to reveal to them the personal conversations that you and I have had regarding marriage. I am not my mother, and even if she is in love with you, I am not. I am fond of you, certainly, but I have never declared any affection for you other than that of a friend. Now you, by your excessive boldness, have instigated a campaign by my parents to force me to return to Chicago. I have no intentions of doing so. The school year is already well underway, and I have every expectation of completing it. Whether or not I return to Chicago at the end of the term is entirely between God Almighty and me.

Now, please refrain from appealing to my mother to induce me to come running to you. I am not a child, and I am not under my mother's thumb, nor my father's.

Sincerely,

Emily Weston

September 28, 1931
My School Journal, grade 7, Miss Weston's class
By Pearl Wallace

My name is Pearl because my mama has named all her children after the precious stones to be found in the Throne of God. We are Jasper, Sardius, Pearl, Beryl, and Ruby. By all rights, Ruby was supposed to be named "Carbuncle," because they did not call it a ruby in the Bible, at least not when they were talking about the Throne of God. I am glad she fudged a little. Ruby would have a hard time living down "Carbuncle." The young'uns at school can be mean sometimes. The grownups around here can be mean, also. A lot of them call Sardius "Sardine," and it makes him mad. He does not show it, though, because he is bashful and he does not want anybody to know it hurts his feelings.

I had an older brother named Harrison, who was the firstborn, but he died when he was two years old of the whooping cough. It was after that Mama started in naming us after the jewels in the Throne of God, because she said if the Lord regarded her babies as precious as His Own Throne, then maybe He would look after them a little more diligently.

September 28, 1931. Daddy came home last night. I did not hear him, which means he had already sobered up some by the time he got here. When I got up, he was sitting at the kitchen table, looking like something that had crawled out from under a rock, but he was nice enough. Mama did not speak to him while she was cooking breakfast, but when he mentioned that he had the automobile working and that we should all go across the river and pick muscadines over at Big Sonny Dailey's place, she sweetened up a little. After breakfast, we all piled in, and off we went! It ended up being a good day, but I wish Darlene could have come with us. We have so much more fun when she is along.

Tomorrow we have to get in the rest of the potatoes, cantaloupes, and the squash. There is a lot of work yet to be done. Good night! I will sleep well tonight! Beryl and Ruby are already asleep.

September 29, 1931. We spent the day picking in the fields, even though we are in the waning moon. We just did not get everything in while the signs were right, but Mama says that should not matter because we are canning everything we pick, so we don't have to worry about things keeping. It is a good thing we have plenty of jars and lids now, as we are canning like crazy.

I wish we could go back to school. I am hoping that when we get back, Miss Weston might have a shipment of new books from her friends up in Chicago. She has started a library, so we can borrow books any time we want. Reading is as much fun as fishing, playing in the creek, or climbing trees. In the summertime, sometimes I climb up in the big sycamore down by the creek and curl up in the crook with a book for the whole afternoon.

I learned to read when I was four years old. My mama started me out early on with the *Appleton School Reader*, and I took to it like a duck takes to water. By the time I was in the third grade I was reading from the Bible, and for fun I read *The Story of Mankind*, the *Voyages of Dr. Doolittle*, and just about anything I can get my hands on. This summer Mama said I was getting good enough at reading to try my hand at Shakespeare because I already could read from the Psalms and Song of Solomon, which Shakespeare helped to translate from back when King James was the King of England. King James was a good king because he was actually Scottish, which means he came from a better class of people than the English. He was the son of Mary, Queen of Scots.

I wanted to read *Titus Andronicus* because I heard it was very gory, with a bad man who grinds up the bones of his rival's children and bakes them up into bread, but Mama said that was not appropriate for a young lady, and so I read *As You Like It* instead. She and I sat down every day and read one scene together. I read a little of it out loud and she would tell me what it meant, then I would go back and read it again, and it would make sense to me. I liked it, except for the part that says that only the oldest son can inherit from his daddy, and that everyone else gets left out in the cold.

My own daddy and his younger brother Woodrow got left out in the cold because their daddy believed that very thing and left most of his land and his money to his oldest son, my uncle James, who sold it all off and then packed up and moved to Texas.

Sometimes it just burns me up that people think that the oldest boy is the best and the rest of us are just worthless. When I grow up, I am going to treat all my children the same. I may even treat my girls better because boys can do more and they can get better jobs while girls usually end up just being somebody's wife. If her husband turns out to be a sorry drunk, she is left to try to feed her young'uns on berries and trout.

Cooling, waning days, darkening nights,
I taste the weariness of my upright children.
The young ones feel age in their veins.
The babe lies heavy and weak in the womb.
I wait for the light to drain into darkness,
For the ebbing.

October

October 1, 1931. Daddy is not always bad. He can be kind and fun, but sometimes, he is very sad because he does not know how to be happy with what life has handed him. I think it was Big Daddy Wallace's fault. He made Daddy think that money is everything, so now he does not know how to get along without it.

Big Daddy had been a wealthy man until the Panic of 1907, and to be honest, his boys grew up spoiled. When times got hard, Big Daddy Wallace fooled around trying to keep up appearances, sending his boys off to a fancy boarding school, and then to college, until he went broke. Daddy went to Maryville College for one semester, but then, things got so bad that Big Daddy had to lay off all the workers, and then he had an apoplexy, so he had to call the boys home to do the heavy work. That did not work out by a long shot. Daddy says that the Wallace boys were meant to be poets, not workhands, and of course, once they took over the farm, things went from bad to worse because they did not know any more about farming than Jack. Then, Big Daddy up and died and left about all he had to Uncle James, and the next thing you know, Uncle James has sold out and gone to Texas, Uncle Woodrow has gotten himself messed up in the war, and Daddy does not know what hit him. It was lucky that one of Big Daddy's friends who was a big shot with the Railroad stepped in and got him a job. That worked out until the Depression hit and everybody went bust. Poor Daddy just feels like life has treated him bad, and he does not know how to buckle down and work to make things better.

October 3, 1931. The last two days have been hard. I am so tired I can hardly hold my eyes open, but things are looking up. Daddy swears he will not drink a drop until all the crops are in. The nice thing about Daddy is that once he promises to stay sober, he generally does, at least for a time, so we can count on him to put his hand in for the next little while. Mama says she, Daddy, and Jasper can handle it after this week, so the rest of us can go back to school. I am not sure about that. She is not looking like she is up for much more work. She gets out of breath just walking from the woodshed with a load of wood in her arms.

Beryl has finished her bath, so I am going to take mine now. It will feel good to sit in some hot water and soak out some of the tiredness out of my back.

October 4, 1931. Today is Sunday, my favorite day during harvest season because it is a day of rest. We get the whole day not doing any work at all.

At church today, we sang *Just As I Am* for the invitational, which is my favorite song when you do not sing it too slow. When you sing it fast, it makes you feel sweepy and swoopy, as if you are floating down the river, hitting little eddies, pausing for a minute, then sweeping fast again. That is how it sounds when Mama plays it, but Claire Fellows plays it too slow, which makes it feel like somebody died.

I think Miss Weston feels bad because nobody comes down to get saved, but we all were already saved and baptized before she came. Preacher Miller never has an invitational unless there is somebody new there that he thinks needs to come to Jesus. I like singing *Just As I Am*, but it would be worth it to give it up not to see Miss Weston's hopes dashed every Sunday when no one walks down the aisle. She starts out looking hopeful, with her eyes searching over everyone's faces, and with each verse, you can see the hope become more and more dim. By the time the song is over, she looks so beat and sad I want to cry for her. Sometimes I want to go running down the aisle and make up a story about how I never knew how much Jesus loved me until now just to give her a little encouragement, but that would be a lie, and she would see right through it.

After church, we went to my pap-pa's house for Sunday dinner, but Miss Weston did not come because she has some letters to write. I missed her, but it was nice not to have to put on company manners while we were all so tired. After dinner, we sat around in the front room while Pap-pa whittled and told stories. Mama was so wore out she just sat in Mam-ma's rocking chair the whole afternoon and laid her head back with her eyes closed. Miss Janey Jo took us all outside to look at the calves that Pap-pa will be taking to market in a few weeks.

Being out in the barn with the cows and their calves made me miss Mam-ma. She used to sing while she milked. She had a soft, wavery voice, kind of husky and breathy, and she could carry a tune perfectly. She always sang hymns, but sometimes she sang ballads from the old country where her mama was from. That would be Ulster, in Ireland. The ballads from Ireland are always both sad and lively. They were usually about somebody's lover dying or running off to war, but the music was bouncy and happy. I never knew if I was supposed to feel happy or sad when I heard her sing, so I just let myself feel both. It is the same way I feel now whenever I think about her.

Miss Janey Jo is different. She is always happy and she sings happy songs about bluebirds and fancy ladies. Sometimes, she goes camping with us and fishing in the river.

Mama does not say so, but I know she does not much care for Miss Janey Jo. I can tell because she changes the subject every time one of us talks about how much we like her. I think she is mad because Pap-pa up and married her not seven months after he put Mam-ma in the ground, which Mama thinks was not decent. Miss Janey Jo also is young enough to be Pap-pa's daughter. She is not but two years older than Mama. Mama does not think that is decent, either. She is nice about it though, so I do not know if Miss Janey Jo knows Mama is not fond of her.

For Mama's sake, we tried not to like Miss Janey Jo at first. Beryl managed it for a while, but I just could not from the very beginning. She is the nicest lady you ever met, and sweet and kind to me just like Mam-ma was, but she is pretty and very much fun, which Mam-ma was not. Mam-ma was sickly for a long time before she died, and by the time she gave up the ghost, there was nothing to her but skin and bones. She did not even have much hair left, except for a few little wisps that she tied up in a little bitty knot on top of her head that was not hardly any bigger than a persimmon, but still I thought she was beautiful. She was partial to me and spoiled me, so it is natural that I would take to her.

Now I need to write something to turn in to Miss Weston tomorrow. I sure cannot turn in anything from most of what I have.

October 4, 1931,
Dearest Mother and Father,

This is one of those difficult weeks where nearly all the children have missed school because they are required in the fields to help bring in the harvest. I am constantly amazed at how hardworking and diligent they are. They do backbreaking work, and yet, they apply themselves assiduously to their schoolwork. Unlike some of the children I have seen at home, they understand how important an education is. If you could see them being so brave in the face of poverty, how unselfishly they contribute to their families, how respectful they are to me and to one another, you would be as proud of them as I am.

Yet, even though they work hard to make something of themselves, most of them face hardships that they will never be able to overcome. Their poverty means they will never get the kind of education they need to make a comfortable living, perhaps even a subsistence one. Most of them will be chained to this hardscrabble soil for the rest of their lives. If they are like their parents, they will continue to thirst for poetry and philosophy, holding to well-worn copies of the classics, reading everything they can get their hands on, taking the time to discuss deep topics among themselves. I am astonished at how literate some of them are, and how they yearn for intellectual society!

I long to do something to help them. If I cannot help the adults, I can help the children. The ones who are exceptionally bright and motivated deserve a chance to a good education. There is no high school in this community, so far away from any towns large enough to support one. That means once they complete the eighth grade, they are doomed to a life of labor, without the light of learning, without the opportunity to further study Scripture, philosophy, or any other subject.

Since I have a good bit of the legacy Grandfather left to me, and since I anticipate that I will be receiving additional income from Papa William's estate when the time comes for him to depart this earth, I am thinking that I would like to establish a scholarship fund for the brightest and most motivated of these children to attend private boarding schools for high school. Would you be willing to help me? Would you consider helping me to fund such a scholarship? Would you be willing to lend your name to a request to your colleagues and friends for such?

Oh, Mother and Father! If only you could see these children! How beautiful, bright, and eager they are! How kind and deserving. Your heart would break to see their circumstances, to feel their poverty and understand their limited prospects. Please consider helping! If you were to give just a little, it could make such an enormous difference. If your friends and associates would give a little, it would mean the world to all of us.

Thank you, dear Parents, for listening to my plea, and thank you for considering helping me to help spread the light of education to these dear people.

Much love to you all,
Emily

Cooling, waning days.

A day of singing, the Spirit is pleased.
He presses His hand upon my banks as I grow restless.
The great Orb turns her face toward darkness,
Away from me; she loosens her grasp.
I hum under the palm of the Spirit,
Feeling my silver children shimmer beneath the willows.

October 5, 1931
My School Journal, grade 7, Miss Weston's class
By Pearl Wallace

I love to read. I have been reading ever since I can remember. This summer I read a play by William Shakespeare, called *As You Like It*. My mother said I was ready for Shakespeare because I was so good at reading the *Psalms*. Shakespeare helped to translate part of the *Psalms* and *Song of Solomon* for the King James Version of the Bible. It is the only version that is actually God-inspired, so it is the one we read. All the others bear false witness.

It was a very good play, which I enjoyed, although it was confusing, with many characters who pretend to be other characters. My mother helped me to sort it all out, though. I was happy to see that it ended well, with everyone getting married.

I liked one of the main characters, Rosalind, because she was smart and figured out what to do to make it turn out well. Shakespeare was wise enough to know that girls sometimes make the best heroes.

October 5, 1931. Hurrah! It rained today so we got to go to school and Mama got a day of rest. She is looking very worn out these days.

It also is nice to come home from school and not have to get right to work. We just played with Ruby, and then I ran over to see Darlene. We played jacks for a while, but then Billy Ray came in, and it felt funny to be there with him staring at me the way he does, so I came on home. I do not like Billy Ray one single bit. He is half-drunk most of the time, and he is mean all of the time. At least Daddy does not drink but every once in a while, and when he gets over it, he is nice again. Billy Ray is never nice.

It quit raining during supper. We all went out to sit on the porch to listen to Daddy play his banjo. Sometimes, when we sit out on the porch of an evening, Daddy does not enjoy himself, but he looks at the stars and gets a little bit blue, so we were all glad that Daddy seemed happy the whole evening long.

Daddy is a daydreamer. He thinks about things that no one else thinks about. One time, we were all sitting out on the porch after supper, and he just got up and stretched out in the yard, looking up at the sky. Presently, he called all of us to come out and lie down with him. It was a very clear night, and the stars were as bright as little candles in the sky, all lit up. Daddy pointed out some of the constellations, and he told us that some of those stars are so far away, we could not travel to them in a hundred years, even if we went a thousand miles an hour. It was the most amazing thing to think about. Imagine travelling hundreds of years in cold, cold space, heading toward a star! He looked up at those stars, and he recited a poem that goes like this.

> *O stars, and dreams, and gentle night;*
> *O night and stars, return!*
> *And hide me from the hostile light*
> *That does not warm, but burn;*
>
> *That drains the blood of suffering men;*
> *Drinks tears, instead of dew;*
> *Let me sleep through his blinding reign,*
> *And only wake with you!*

That is from an Emily Brontë poem that is in one of the books that Mama has on her shelf of good books. I thought it was so nice, although sad, that I went and got it so I could read the whole thing. I just cannot help myself. Sometimes I just have to feel sorry for Daddy when he starts speaking sad poetry like that.

Cooling, waning days.

The earth still yields her bounty as my children toil.
They do not stop to see the land turning golden.
Gray clouds gift more fullness, lifting me above my banks.
I flow silver into the sinking sun.

Joy rises, but the weight of sorrow tethers her flight.

October 7, 1931. It rained off and on all day today. It was too muddy to get out in the garden, so we did not have to work after school. A new moon will be coming on in a couple of days, so we had planned on starting in on the potatoes again, but the rain meant we just did not get everything done. This probably means Sardius and I will have to stay out of school tomorrow and Friday. Beryl gets to go to school without us because she cannot work hard on account of her bad headaches. I do not begrudge her that, though. I cannot imagine how hard it must be to have a headache all the time.

Jake Hatton came by today, looking for a pint of whiskey. I told him never to come to the house, but to hide out in the woods down by the creek and wait until he sees me out in the yard. He can whistle a hooty-owl call to me, and I will meet him down by the big sycamore. As soon as I got home, I heard him calling, even though it was raining cats and dogs by then. I got soaked going out to meet him, but I had a pint ready for him, so I made another 50c today. I have $2.63 saved up in my business account, which I keep in the special cherrywood box my Pap-pa made me. I would like to give some of it to Mama, but then I would have to make up a lie to explain from whence it came. I reckon I can say I sold some muscadines on my own.

Jake Hatton is a funny sort. He twitches, as if he has ants in his pants and in his shirt. Sometimes he hops around a little, and he makes funny noises, like barks and squeaks. He cusses up a storm, also, which is why Mama calls him trash. Even when he is trying to be gentleman-like, sometimes he bursts out with the worst language I have ever heard, and then he hangs his head and says, "I am G.D. sorry, G.D. it. I just can't G.D. help it. It just G.D. falls out of my G.D. mouth," and then he walks away, his head low, twitching off into the woods and swigging my whiskey. I feel sorry for him. I think there is something bad wrong with his head. Of course, he does not really say just "G.D.," but the real cuss words. I just write that because it hurts my feelings to see the real words written down.

I hate it, but I must cater to Jake Hatton because I like the way the money is piling up in my cash box. Sometimes I lie awake at night and think about what-all I am going to buy with it. I would like to get everybody new clothes, and I would like to get Daddy's jalopy fixed so we could all go for rides in it. It has been banjaxed off and on for five months now, and I miss riding over to Maryville or up to Indian Gap, which is about the prettiest place I have ever seen. The loggers have not messed up that area like they have over on Little River Road.

October 10, 1931. It has cleared up and dried out some so we have spent the last three days getting in the rest of the crops. Mama has had a hard time of it, especially when she was digging potatoes. She kept putting her hand on her back and making a face. It would help if she were not so fat. A big belly like that is hard on the back, but Daddy says that it is good for her to put on some fat so she can make it through the winter better.

I hope it does not rain, even though we will get to go to school if it does. It is going to be hard to get everything in before the moon turns. Now I am going to bed. I am so tired I feel sick.

October 11, 1931
My Darling Cecilia,

It has been another one of those dreary weeks that I did not get to fulfill my role as a missionary or a teacher. So many of the children are missing school to work in the fields that I wonder why I even bother to hold classes on these days. The church service was next to empty today, as well. In the beginning of the harvest season, people made an effort to take Sundays off, but toward the end, they are so pressed to get it all done, and they are no doubt so exhausted that they no longer can drag themselves in. Their plight is pitiful, and I am in agony for them.

The Wallace family did make it to church today, however, and we all assembled at the Aiken home afterward, as usual. Woodrow seems a mite happier, which cheered me immensely. He wears his heart on his sleeve—I can tell if he is having a good or a bad week the moment I see him. His eyes are so expressive they can hide nothing.

I asked Reverend Miller what might be causing him to be so melancholy at times. He revealed that the poor man's spirit was badly scarred when he served in the Great War. It pains me to think that this extraordinary man was dealt such a debilitating blow whilst serving his country and fighting for our freedoms! If only there were something I could do to help him recover. It would break your heart to see how he suffers sometimes.

Reverend Miller has recovered some, at least enough to spend a good bit of the day sitting in the parlor and to eat dinner at the table each evening. The doctors are worried about his lungs, however. They fear that he does not have enough strength to keep them clear during the winter season.

I am sorry my letter is so dreary. Believe me, this is temporary! As soon as the children return to school and I can also preach to a full house, my spirits will revive.

Thank you for your cheerful letters. They keep me going in times like this!

My dearest love,
Emily

Cooling, waning days.

My breath is slow and deep; I am fat and sated.
The taste of something like a lusty spring sways:
The coming of new life, of unbidden yearning.
Pain will descend upon them, but I cannot warn them,
Even if it were my desire.
The Spirit broods and waits, watching as the pall approaches.

October 12, 1931
My School Journal, grade 7, Miss Weston's class
By Pearl Wallace

My mother is very educated. She did not go to a regular school because they did not have them here when she was growing up, so she studied at home, with her own mother as her teacher. She had already finished the examination to complete high school by the time she ran away and married my daddy when she was 17 years old. She knows a lot about science, and she can even speak French and German. She had planned to go up to the part of Canada where they speak French to visit her great-aunt Sarah Wisnet when she turned 18, but then she met Daddy and she changed her mind and married him instead. I, personally, would prefer a trip to another country to getting married. I may not even get married at all, ever, because I intend to go to college to learn to be a missionary and be a Bible scholar like Miss Weston. Men do not like it if their wives are smarter than they are.

October 13, 1931. Hallelujah! We have finished with the harvest enough that we can go back to school on Monday and not miss any more for the whole winter. I cannot wait! We will be canning all day tomorrow, but after that, it is clear sailing.

It is nice to see rows and rows of jars of food we have put away down in the cellar. We have tomatoes, corn, pickles, molasses, jellies, and beets in jars, and piles of potatoes, sweet potatoes, turnips, and apples laid out on newspapers. Now I am going to bed, and will I ever sleep!

October 14, 1931. We got to go to school today! That is, Beryl and I went to school. Sardius laid out one more day to help, but Mama said she did not need us girls. It was wonderful being back! Miss Weston had on a beautiful dress. It was blue, with a brown belt. She looked just lovely in it. I worked up the gumption to talk to her about how Darlene looks and asked her why she thought Daddy says she is a Negro even though she is white and why he does not like her, even though she is not mean at all. She chewed her lip and told me that Jesus loves all children, no matter what their color is, and then she had us sing *Jesus Loves the Little Children, All the Children of the World*. I got confused, because she never did really answer my question about why Daddy would call Darlene a Negro even though she is white. Black and white are the opposite, are they not?

October 14, 1931
Darling Cecilia,

I have an interesting situation here. Pearl, the little Wallace girl that I like so much, has informed me that an odd family has moved in next door to her. The neighbor, a native of these parts, has married a woman who has a Negro child, and Pearl's father disapproves of her associating with his children. Pearl, in her innocence, cannot understand why Negroes, especially light-skinned ones, should be treated differently than Caucasians.

I do not see it as my place to contradict Pearl's father in this matter, for I see my duty is to eventually convince him of the error of his drinking. If I come between him and Pearl in this point, I may poison any positive influence I may have over him. I just explained to Pearl that in God's eyes, all people are the same, without validating or denying her father's concerns. Sadly, I think

I just confused her more, and I am not sure I am approaching this in the right way. What would you do in this situation? It is clear Pearl loves the little Negro girl and that her heart is crushed that her father is so negative toward her.

I find myself more than a little confused about the situation, and I wonder if I do not also harbor a less than generous spirit toward people of color. I fear that Father's disapproval of the darker races may be influencing me to regard Negroes with some disapprobation. But if the Lord God Almighty loves all people equally, male and female, slave and free, then should not we all love all equally as well? I do wish you were here so that we could talk this over! I never realized how much our sheltered upbringing would hinder me in the fulfilment of my role as mentor, guide, and teacher.

On a lighter note, I was amused at your hinting that I might be losing my heart to Mr. Woodrow Wallace! Rest assured that I merely am concerned about the poor man's fears and weaknesses. I hate to see any potential such as his be undermined. Of course, I would never consider someone like him to be a suitor to me! Our worlds are too far apart.

I miss you, Cecilia, and our long chats. I wish you were here to help me sort out my thoughts. I cannot tell you how important your letters are to me, and how I glean such pleasure from them!

Your loving sister,
Emily

October 15, 1931. We had a good thunderstorm today. Poor Beryl was ascared to death by the time we got home, drenched to the bone. She screamed every time the lightening flashed and the thunder crashed. Beryl is ascared of a lot of things. Thunder and lightning, and big dogs, although she is not ascared of Daddy's fox hounds because she knows them well. She is ascared of snakes and spiders and even hooty-owls at night because she thinks that maybe there are still some wild Indians around who can mimic hooty-owls perfectly. She heard a story once about a woman who was carried off by wild Indians, and before they snatched her, they called to each other outside all around her cabin with hooty-owl calls.

It is a mystery to me why Beryl is ascared of Indians. In the first place, the Indians that lived around here were Cherokee, and they were peaceful, nobody to be ascared of. In the second place, there are not any left around here, not any more. I know there used to be a lot of them because I find arrowheads down by the river and up in the bluffs above it. One time Sardius found the head of a tomahawk, as perfect as if it were just made.

They are gone now, every single one of them, marched off to Oklahoma by Mr. Jackson back in 1838, which I think is a disgrace. The land around these parts was theirs first, and no one had any right to take it away from them and make them walk all across the country to Reservations out West where it is hot and dry. I bet it was hard to get used to after living in these cool, wet mountains. Some of them hid out and did not go, but they mostly live over in North Carolina now. There is a Reservation there, too, but at least it is in the mountains.

I told my Uncle Woodrow about how I did not think Mr. Jackson should have just run the poor Cherokee off like that, and he looked sad, and then said if he had not, I probably would not be alive today because none of my great-grandpappies would have been able to buy land here and my mama and daddy would never have known each other if the Indians still owned it all. That is hard to think about. I am glad I am here, but sad it means somebody else suffered. I do not know what is right.

Except for cannibals, I am not ascared of anything. Not snakes, not even copperheads, not spiders, and certainly not lightning and thunder. There is nothing I love more than a good thunderstorm with lightening slashing all around like Taranis himself is throwing bolts down on our little house. I like to sit up under the eaves in the loft and watch out the window, and I love to be out in it and watch the air turn green and see the trees seem to jump all over the place when the lightening comes fast and furious. I always love it when a storm comes when I am over at Pap-pa's house by myself. That way I know the others are there to be with Mama, and she will not worry about me, knowing I am safe at her daddy's house, and I can go and sit out on the big sleeping porch and watch her rip.

Cool, waning days, cold nights.

A shadow of my first upright children rises from my bedrock.
They gave me the first name that was spoken aloud: Tanasi
As Tanasi, I was revered, I sang with abandon,
Mother Earth lost none of her soil to me;
Her greenleaves numbered many and were not slaughtered.
My memory sees skies blackened by wings of birds,
Banks solid with otter and deer.
The greenness rolled far across the land.

Where have my first children gone?
I know the taste of metal, of hate and fear.
They vanished into the maw of suffering.

October 16, 1931. Mama was sick today and when we got home, she was in bed, Daddy was trying to make up a batch of cornbread and making a right mess of it, and Ruby was sitting in the middle of the floor squalling. Beryl and I took over cooking supper and tending to Ruby, and then Daddy took off right after supper, saying he felt like the house was closing in on him. Jasper and Sardius both went out, too, to patch a leak that had sprung up in the porch during the storm yesterday, and Uncle Woodrow was nowhere to be seen. I had to do the dishes by myself so Beryl could get to bed on time. She had a bad headache. She gets them if she does not get enough sleep, and she has not gotten full rested up from all the hard days of harvesting.

Today was not all bad. Miss Weston asked Beryl and me to sing *Shall We Gather at the River* in church on Sunday. I look forward to that! I like that song very much because I like the thought of the beautiful, beautiful river that flows by the Throne of God, covered in precious gems that look like me and Beryl, Jasper, Sardius, and Ruby. I can imagine our faces stuck all over the Throne, peering over God's shoulder as He makes His judgements. I bet He got mad at Mr. Jackson for making all those Cherokee march off to Oklahoma. I would like to see the look on his face when he found out how much trouble he was in.

Daddy is still not back. I bet he has slipped out to the woodshed, getting blootered.

October 16, 1931
Dear Jonathan,

Thank you for your kind letter, and thank you for your offer to help me help the good people of this community. To be honest, they need everything! Their clothing, household goods, farm implements, books, everything--! is inadequate, and how I wish we could give them so many of the things they so desperately need. Whatever you can do, whatever items you can gather or money you can raise would make a difference in the lives of these people I have come to love so much.

Thank you a thousand times for your kindest of offers! I am so happy that we are friends again.
Fondly,
Emily

Cool, waning days, cold nights.

The greenleaves have changed their mantle to gold and red,
First, slowly, then swiftly, they have begun to undress.
Days are as silver as my children. Nights are gossamer.

For now, I am free of the great Orb, but she begins to turn.
Her face in profile, she listens to the humming of the Spirit.

October 17, 1931. I am sorry to say that we all have brought shame on our family. This morning I put on britches because I was going fishing with Darlene, and we have to wade through a briar patch to get to the best spot, but before I got out the door, Miss Weston came calling. She took one look at me and said, "Pearl, dear, why are you wearing trousers? Young ladies should not dress like boys."

I was scundered to death. I tried to tell her I was going to be wading through a briar patch, but then Daddy came in from a night out in the woodshed, and I could tell right off he was drunk as a skunk. He was hollering at us before he even got into the front yard, cussing and carrying on because Miss Weston had left the gate open and one of his pups had gotten out. It had not gone any further than the springhouse, but he acted like it had been run over or drowned in the creek. Mama came running out of the bedroom, trying to put up her hair as she was coming out, but most of it was still hanging down her back, and she looked just awful. Her face and her legs were swole up bad, so that she looked fatter than ever. Then to make matters worse, Ruby came running out after her, dressed only in her step-ins, and they were so ragged, they barely covered her bottom.

Miss Weston's eyes bugged out, and then she stammered out, "I am terribly sorry I have come unannounced. I will call again another time." Then she ran out the door. Daddy bumped into her on the porch and called her a very bad name, telling her to get off his property before he took the shotgun to her. All I could do was wish I were dead.

October 17, 1931
My Dearest Cecilia,

I have done something terrible, and I think I have ruined any chances of encouraging Mr. Wallace to give up his sin of drink! This morning, I went to visit the family and to take a few baby items to Mrs. Wallace. She looks to be coming close to her term, and I wanted to welcome the new little one to the family. I also was hoping to learn more about the little mixed child who lives next door and perhaps find a way to meet her. It is important that I serve all the members of the community, no matter what their race, and I had hoped to discover if it would be too presumptuous of me to invite her to attend school with the other children.

I should have known better than to go unannounced. When I arrived, the family was not dressed to receive me properly, and Mr. Wallace was not only very intoxicated, but also violently angry that I had come! I had inadvertently left the gate open and one of his purebred foxhound puppies had escaped from the yard as a result. His language to show his displeasure would have made a sailor blush.

Now, I have embarrassed Mrs. Wallace and her children so badly that I do not think they will recover from the incident for a long time. I know I will not! I am so ashamed that I do not think I have the nerve to face them, but I know I must find a way to apologize and let them know all the error was on my part. I wonder if Mr. Woodrow might be able to help me smooth things over? What do you think I should do?

Love,
Emily

Cool, waning days, cold nights.
I taste shame and sorrow among my upright children.
The father weeps upon my banks.
He cannot tame the restlessness of his spirit.
The young ones are wounded in their souls.
The stranger wants more than she can understand.
The mother fears for all.

I turn my face from them,
To the silver Orb who begins to beckon.
The urge to dance rises in me.

October 18, 1931. We did not go to church today. I do not need to say why. None of us can face Miss Weston after what went on yesterday. Mama did not even get out of bed all day. Daddy is creeping around lower than a snake's belly. I hate it that Beryl and I missed getting to sing "Shall We Gather at the River."

October 18, 1931
Dear Jonathan,

I have been thinking of your kind offer to help me find a way to help my students. I have decided to establish a scholarship fund to enable the brightest and most motivated of the children here to attend high school, and college as well, when that is warranted. I have a little money from an inheritance, and although it is too small to go very far, I think it could be the beginnings of something substantial, if I had help.

Sadly, my Father is not forthcoming with assistance. He is holding a grudge, I believe, because I came here against his will, and he wants to teach me a lesson about familial duties and the consequences of disobeying one's parents. Although I understand his position, I am more determined than ever to find a way to pull the children from these beautiful mountains out of the poverty they face.

Ever since you let the cat out of the bag, Father and Mother think I should waste no time in coming home to marry you, and while I appreciate and understand their desires for me, I cannot think of my own happiness when so many of these children are suffering. If only I could find a way to help them further their education beyond the elementary years, I might be more inclined to think of my own future. There is no schooling available for them once they have completed the eighth grade! Can you imagine what it must be like to not be able to attend high school? Dear Jonathan I would be ever so grateful if you could help me find a way for these deserving students. Please think hard about what we can do together!

Fondly,

Emily

October 19, 1931
My School Journal, grade 7, Miss Weston's class
By Pearl Wallace

When I grow up and become a missionary, I will do everything I can to serve God to show Him how much I love Him. I will be a faithful servant all my days, even if I have to go to darkest Africa or India, where the people do not even know how to dress properly. I will bring them all nice clothes from my own store of dresses, skirts, and blouses.

Sometimes, girls and women have to wear trousers if they are going to be riding a horse or if they are going fishing or hunting and have to traipse through blackberry patches that will scratch their legs to pieces if they have on a dress. Otherwise, they should always wear dresses in order to be pleasing in the sight of the Lord.

October 20, 1931. I have not been to school for the last two days, I was so miserable, thinking about what Miss Weston is thinking about us, and Mama did not make me. She has not been out of her bedroom much these past two days, either. I know she is past mortified. Daddy acts as if the world has come to an end.

Sardius and Beryl went to school, though, and they brought me back my lessons so I could keep up. Miss Weston sent a nice note saying she was sorry she intruded upon my family during a difficult time.

Darlene has been a big help. I went to the creek just to get out of the house. I was just moping around when she came skipping through the woods like a little fairy, with the sun glinting off her hair so pretty. We ran off to the woods and had the best time playing, climbing trees, and pretending to be pirates and brigands. I told her about William Wallace, and then she pretended to be Edward the First, and we had a sword fight. We had so much fun I almost completely forgot about Miss Weston and how mortified I am.

Daddy has been sober since Saturday, and this morning he said he was sorry about showing himself in front of Miss Weston. After that, he went to town, saying he was going to look for a job again, which made us all feel better, even though we know he is not likely to find one. It is just nice to get him out of the house when he starts acting pitiful and sorry. It is more like he is sorry for himself than he is for what he did.

October 21, 1931. It was a very exciting day! Daddy woke us up early this morning and told Jasper to run over to Pap-pa's house and bring back Miss Janey Jo, and the rest of us needed to go get firewood for the stove and cook us all up some breakfast because Mama was too tired and he was too busy tending to her. She had been out in the cabbage patch all night picking out a baby, and she was so worn out that she could not get out of bed.

I wish Mama would not do that. If she wanted more babies, she should send me or Jasper out to find them for her. To tell the truth, she does not always pick the best ones. They always are skinny, pitiful little things, and the last baby she brought back died before his first day was out. Mama and Daddy both cried for days, and Daddy got drunk for a whole week. We were all very sad, thinking about that poor little baby boy, not any bigger than a minute, who did not stand a chance from the beginning. I am sure it did not help that he probably had been out in the snow all night before Mama got to him. I would wait until summertime, when the nights are warm, and I would pick out big, healthy ones with pink cheeks and wads of fat up and down their little legs.

I fussed at Daddy and told him that Mama would be a lot better off if she would send me out to pick out babies for her, and he kind of laughed a little, then tears came into his eyes and he said that the baby Mama picks out may not look the best to us, but we do not know what special feeling Mamas have for their little ones, and he reminded me that no one thought Ruby would make it, she was so little, but she turned out to be a good one. I had to admit he was right. I cannot imagine anybody other than Ruby being with us.

The new baby, which Mama named Sapphire, is very tiny. She feels no bigger than a little sugar pumpkin in my hands. She never cries but only squeaks a little now and then. Mama looks very tired and sick. She worked too hard, trudging all over these hills from cabbage patch to cabbage patch to find the one baby that gave her that special feeling. It was especially hard on her since she was so wore out from harvest season. Why she picked this time to go, I cannot fathom. You would think she would at least wait until she had rested up a little bit. I reckon I do not know what all is involved in baby-picking, so I will just keep my mouth shut.

Miss Janey Jo came over and started tending to Mama and Sapphire, and you would never know there was any harsh feelings between them. Janey Jo acts as if Mama is her best friend and she chatters to her while she plumps up her pillows and brings her soup. Mama does not say anything much at all. She just holds the baby and looks ascared.

After we all had a chance to see Sapphire and hold her for a minute, Daddy loaded us all up in his automobile and took us over to Pap-pa's house to keep him company while Miss Janey Jo is over at our house looking after Mama. I told him we could take care of Mama just fine between us all, particularly since Mama was not overly fond of Janey Jo, but he said that they had patched up their old bitterness and would be good friends from now on and it would be good for them to spend some time together to get to know one another better.

October 22, 1931. Today was much better. We all laid out of school again. Pap-pa took us to the fair because Jasper and Sardius entered their calf, Dandyman, for the calf judging. Guess what? He won a red ribbon! Right off, they got an offer of $75 for him, which they will take, of course, and as soon as the fair is over, they will have their pockets loaded with money. They say they will buy us all something warm for winter. They will save a little to buy feed for next year's calf, and then give the rest of the money to Mama. Daddy would love to get his hands on some of it, but Mama hides it from him. She needs every penny she can get just to keep us going. Daddy would just buy up a lot of corn and sugar so he could make whiskey, and if he had more, he would get another dog. If he could get enough, he would even buy himself a horse. Not a good, strong one that we could hitch to a plow, either, but one for chasing after hounds. A horse like that probably would not eat anything but good oats and would drive us straight to the poorhouse.

Pap-pa said we did not have time to go by the house after we left the fair to see Mama and Sapphire, and besides, they needed their rest. We just came on back here to stay the night.

Cool, waning days, brightening nights
The great orb's belly grows large.
She calls to me in sweet song.
I yearn for her, reaching up, as she pours down.

New life whimpers in the warmth indoors
As Death lurks hungrily.
He lusts, but he will be denied.
I taste victory for Life.

October 23, 1931. I went back to school today. It was good to be back. Miss Weston did not say a word to me about missing nearly a whole week of school, and she was as nice as could be. She also did not say anything about Daddy's drunkenness or Mama and Ruby not being properly dressed when she called. Or me not being properly dressed, either.

Although I hid out from Miss Weston as best I could for most of the morning, she smiled extra special to me at dinnertime, and she came over to have a nice talk. She told me she was very happy that I have a new sister and that she hoped she would grow up to be a Godly young lady like me, and that she would be a blessing to all our household. She did not say a word about Mama looking so slovenly or Daddy cussing at her. I am feeling better. Miss Weston is very kind and good.

We went to our house after school to check on Mama and Sapphire and to take care of the chores. Sapphire is the tiniest little thing. She sleeps on a pillow in a dresser drawer, and she looks just like a little baby doll, so perfect and so tiny. I cannot believe she is real! I just love her, and even though she is not the kind of fat baby I would have picked out, I think she is just right the way she is. I have to say that Mama ended up picking out the best one after all.

Daddy has not had a drink since he showed himself so bad when Miss Weston came to visit, and he is being the very picture of a perfect husband and father. He waits on Mama hand and foot, he sings to us, and today he got his banjo out and picked until his fingers got sore. I would rather stay at home with Mama and Daddy when we have good times like this. We did not want to go back to Pap-pa's house because it was so much fun there at home, but Daddy said they do not need us underfoot, keeping Sapphire and Mama from getting their rest, so we brought Ruby and came back to Pap-pa's house for the night.

Jasper stayed at home because he is bringing in the rest of the harvest with Uncle Woodrow. I wish he could have come with us. It more fun being at Pap-pa's when all of us young'uns get to be there together. Pap-pa's house is so big we have plenty of room to spread out, and Miss Janey Jo really knows how to put a good spread on the table.

It is farther to walk to school, and we had to leave before daylight this morning, but the weather is very nice, so the walking was not troublesome. The sun came up just about the time we hit Johnson's ridge, and it is the most beautiful thing you ever saw. The maple trees along there are red and gold, and the sky turns from deep blue to pink and orange, and then, all of sudden, the mist vanishes and the day becomes light blue and gold right before our eyes. I just want to stay out as long as I can, even if it means missing school, but I am glad to get to go to school, too. It is hard to make the choice to go inside sometimes.

October 24, 1931. We are back home now. I am glad to be here, although I also miss Pap-pa and Miss Janey Jo. We did not get to go to church today, because Mama is still very tired from being out all night looking for Sapphire, and Daddy has to stay here to look after her.

Daddy is not good at cooking, so Beryl and I are in charge of supper. Thank goodness for Miss Janey Jo, who brought over some cold ham, sausages, a couple of pies, and a pot of beans. All we have to do is heat it up and make up some hoecake or cornbread. The boys help us wash up. Mama sits in the rocking chair with Sapphire while we fix supper, and it is a good, friendly time together. Daddy milks Buttercup every morning and evening so we do not have to.

I have ordered myself some new shoes from the catalog. These are getting tight. It is too bad that with winter coming on I will need stout ones rather than pretty ones, so I had to get some clunky old brogans. It breaks my heart, but at least my pretty ones are still in such good shape, they will be good for Beryl in time for Easter, so I can enjoy seeing her wear them. I also ordered some diapers for Sapphire. The ones we have are so old and worn out they do not hardly do much good. Mama has taken to tearing up old flour sacks to wrap her in.

October 26, 1931
My School Journal, grade 7, Miss Weston's class
By Pearl Wallace

I have a new baby sister! Her name is Sapphire, which is one of the precious stones found in the Throne of God. Sapphires are blue, which is perfect because Sapphire has blue eyes. Mama says they might change, but for now, they are the color of sapphires, which are very pretty.

Sapphire is tiny, but she is perfect. She is the most darling baby I have ever seen! I love her very much and pray that she will grow in wisdom, and in stature, and in favor with God and men. (Luke 2:52). I will do what I can to help her to become a Godly woman.

October 26, 1931. We have a full moon tonight. It is the full hunter's moon, and ordinarily Daddy would not miss the chance to go run with his hounds on this biggest hunting night of the year, but lo and behold! He did not go! He stayed home to tend to Mama and to help with the chores, then after supper he went over to Pap-pa's place to collect some flour sacks so Mama could make Sapphire some diapers. Mrs. Carlton and Darlene came over for a little while to meet Sapphire and to bring over a cake. You should have seen how they made on over Sapphire! Darlene wanted to see her little bitty tiny toes, and Mrs. Carlton danced around the room with her, and just laughed up a storm when she sneezed a tiny little sneeze.

Mrs. Carlton was wearing a yellow dress with a full skirt. When she twirled around, dancing with Sapphire, it fanned out around her knees, and I could see how ragged it was at the hem, with a big tear right in the back, and how it was too short, even though she had let it out all the way, and her long legs were showing up past the knees. That tear in the back sometimes flapped open, and you could see way up the back of her thigh. Uncle Woodrow and the boys all stared at it, and I wanted to tell them to stop because it is not nice to let people know you can see how ragged they look, but I did not have the chance. It was like they had never seen people with ragged clothes before. I was scundered for her. They kept right on staring until Mrs. Carlton sat down and handed Sapphire back to Mama. Thank goodness both Darlene and her mother were both too taken with Sapphire to notice.

It turned out to be a very nice evening. We lit the fireplace in the front room for the first time this season and made popcorn. Mama went to bed, and so it was just Uncle Woodrow, Mrs. Carlton, and all of us young'un's out there, having a good time, passing little Sapphire around so we could make on over her. She slept in my arms for a good bit. I just cannot get enough looking at her! Uncle Woodrow is very happy about Sapphire, also. You should have seen how much he laughed and talked.

They stayed for a good while, then Mrs. Carlton said they had taken up enough of our time and stood up to leave. I sure hated to end the evening, but I know she was nervous about Daddy coming home and catching them there, so I did not beg them to stay, as I wanted to. Bless Uncle Woodrow's heart. He jumped right up and offered to walk them home. He is such a good man. Just when Mrs. Carlton is feeling bad about Daddy having a mean spirit toward Darlene, he bends over backward to make her and Darlene feel important. I just love him.

Cool, waning days, cold nights.

The earth grows drowsy,
Life stirs in my upright children
Just as it snugs down deep in my silver ones.
Softness settles like a mantle.

My desire rises in a sweet frenzy
To dance in the silver light with the great Orb.
Other desires rise in my upright ones,
Desire that cannot be spoken or known

October 27, 1931. Today when we got home from school, Miss Janey Jo was there. She had come over to do the washing, for which we were all grateful. Everything was washed and dried when we got home. I helped her bring it in and we made up all the beds. Mama was so grateful she about cried when we put clean sheets on her bed. After that, Miss Janey Jo stayed long enough to fix supper. I helped her, and we made up a double batch of cornbread and some fried ham that will keep for a few days. It was already getting dark by the time we were done, so Daddy drove her home in the wagon while the rest of us ate and cleaned up.

Jake Hatton came by while I was getting the washing in. Miss Janey Jo had gone on inside to start supper, and I was out in the back all by myself. I was yanking the sheets down right quick, to get them in before the dew fell, when he came up from the creek, hippy-hopping and twitching along, and he did not say a word. He just waited for me to take them down and fold them, the whole time muttering about how he needed him some G.D. whiskey. I made him go back down to the creek to wait for me to get it because I do not want him seeing me going into the woodshed where Daddy keeps his jars.

You should have seen how happy he was to see me coming with my pint jar! He about fell into the creek, doing his hoppy little dance, grinning so big I thought his face would split open. I reckon he was not glad enough to give me a tip or to pay me what he still owes me, though. He is a skinflint, but I reckon I should not begrudge him too much. It was nice to get the 50c.

October 28, 1931. As soon as we got home from school today, I ran over to Darlene's house. We went out to the barn to look for eggs, but Billy Ray came out while were there and stared at us until we got to feeling funny, so we left and came on over to our house.

Whenever I look at Billy Ray Carlton, I cannot help but think we are a whole lot better off with Daddy than with him. When I complain about Daddy getting drunk, Darlene rolls her eyes and says, "Pearl, you don't know anything. Billy Ray is a whole lot worse." I do not tell her how bad it can get, with Daddy cussing and yelling and throwing things, and then passing out on the floor sometimes, because I imagine Darlene and her mother might have to put up with a lot, too. We are a lot alike, even though she is a Negro and I am Caucasian.

I wished Mrs. Carlton would come over with us, but Darlene says she does not go anywhere when Billy Ray is at the house. Darlene generally can go, but Mrs. Carlton says she should stay at home to be with her husband. It is a good thing Billy Ray is not at home very often. He goes over to Johnny Joe Sunders place a lot because Johnny Joe has a still and he lets him drink whiskey. I bet he gets extra mean when he is drunk, but I did not say anything to Darlene about that.

I just found out that they finally got old Al Capone. That worries me a little bit. Al Capone is a lot smarter than I am, and he has been running liquor for a long time, so he knows what he is doing. I do not know how to duck and dodge the way he does, and if I get caught, they might send me up the river for life because I do not have a fancy, slick-talking lawyer who knows how to finagle the justice system. I am praying the Lord will let me get by with this for just a little while longer so I can buy everyone nice presents for Christmas. I have already spent a lot for diapers for Sapphire and new brogans for myself. I hope I can get pretty patent leather Mary Janes for Easter.

October 29, 1931. This evening, before it got dark, we picked pumpkins and made jack-o'-lanterns for the mumming on Saturday night. Jasper is an artist. He can carve a pumpkin to look just like a ghoul, so his pumpkin will be the best of all. Daddy helped us. He has not had a drop to drink, which is very good news. He will not be getting drunk and ruining our mumming on Saturday. We will finish up our jack-o'-lanterns tomorrow.

Mama is tired and sickly. She still has not gotten over all it took out of her, traipsing through the countryside all night long when she went out looking for Sapphire. She had been nice and fat before that, but she has fallen off something awful. She is nothing but skin and bones, and she looks sickly all the time. Daddy tells us that she will recover soon enough, once she can get fully rested up again, but she is not able to sleep much as little Sapphire is always whimpering to be fed. Sapphire seems to be falling off, too, even though she is nearly always latched onto Mama's titty. It is too bad cow's milk does not agree with her, even if we water it down and mix molasses in it.

October 30, 1931. Hallowe'en is tomorrow, and I was happy about it until dinnertime at school today. We always celebrate Hallowe'en at Pap-pa's house by having a mumming, which is always very much fun. I already have my costume made up. I soaked an old black hat and hung it on a broomstick to dry so that it has a pointy crown, and I am going to carry the broom and dress up like a witch in one of Mam-ma's old black dresses. I will have the best costume of everyone.

At school, everyone was talking about the mummings they would be going to on Saturday. Most everybody is going to be a ghost or a witch. Sam Hutchinson said he and all his brothers are going to dress as clansmen and ride over to Alcoa to scare the coloreds over there. I am pretty sure Sam is not Scottish, and I have never heard him talk about his clan before, so I asked him what their tartan looked like. He looked at me funny, then laughed, just as Miss Weston came over and asked us what we were talking about. After we explained that we always hold mummings on Hallowe'en and how we dress up as goblins and witches, she got mad at us and blessed us out! She said we should not take part in such devilment and heathen practices, that it was against God's holy orders to have dealings with witches, divination, or evil spirits.

That made me feel just terrible. We explained to her that it was all in fun, but she told us that celebrating Hallowe'en is the same as celebrating death, and we should always choose life over death. I understand what she was trying to say. Yes, goblins and evil spirits are bad, but we never think of Hallowe'en that way. I am very sad about this. I do not want to go against God's will, but I also do not want to miss the mumming.

The good news is that Mama is doing better. She was in the kitchen making hoecakes when we got home from school. She gave Sapphire some water with molasses, and it quieted her down for a while.

I never did figure out why Sam says dressing up in kilts would scare colored folks.

October 31, 1931. Today is Hallowe'en. Jasper, Sardius, Beryl, and Daddy spent the whole morning on the back porch finishing up their jack-o'-lanterns, but I stayed inside so I could ask Mama about what Miss Weston had said about Hallowe'en being a celebration of death and an abomination unto the Lord.

My mama is so smart and sweet. She set me down close beside her and said that Miss Weston was partly right, but not one hundred percent right because she does not know the whole story. We should not honor demons or death, and we should not have anything to do with witchcraft. But God knows our hearts, and He knows that when we have mummings, we are not celebrating death deep down in our hearts. That is just the outside trappings of an old custom. What we are really celebrating is a family tradition that goes all the way back to old Scotland and Ireland, and we are only doing it in fun, so that does not count as courting the Devil. It is one of the ways our family has of remembering the old ways, the places that the older folks miss so much.

She told me that Great-Mam-ma loved the Lord with all her heart, but when she was a little girl in Ulster, everyone in their village dressed up on Hallowe'en, and all they did was have fun and just be together and take a day when they did not have to work. It was a way of reminding themselves that life does not always have to be so hard, that sometimes you can just have fun pretending to be bad. It is a way to mock the devil, not to honor him.

Miss Weston does not understand that. We come from a different place than she does. That is all right. We all are different, and we do things in different ways. Mama said that she thought it best if we just celebrate in fun without dishonoring the Lord in our hearts, and that we should not say anything to Miss Weston that might grieve her soul.

That made sense to me. My mama is very smart, and she always knows just what to say to me to make me feel right. Now I am going to get dressed up in my witch's costume and go have a good time at Pap-pa's and Miss Janey Jo's.

Cold, waning days, wind roving and brutal.

Darkness hovers upon the earth.
Joy and suffering collide.
The Spirit sits and watches,
The Great Dark lurks in the hidden places.

November

November 1, 1931. We had a very good time last night at Pap-pa's mumming. When he saw that I had on one of Mam-ma's old black dresses, he laughed and slapped his knee, saying that Mam-ma would enjoy seeing me put it to good use. Pap-pa, Sardius, Jasper, Uncle Woodrow and Daddy all dressed alike as scarecrows. Miss Janey Jo dressed up like a fancy lady. She wore an old-fashioned dress and a hat with about 10 goose feathers, and she carried a parasol. Beryl wore a sheet and said she was a ghost. Mama did not dress up, but I think she enjoyed the evening.

At church this morning, no one said anything to Miss Weston about the mumming, but she probably knew what we had done because she preached from Deuteronomy 18: 10-12, which goes like this: "There shall not be found among you any one that maketh his son or his daughter to pass through the fire, or that useth divination, or an observer of times, or an enchanter, or a witch, or a charmer, or a consulter with familiar spirits, or a wizard, or a necromancer. For all that do these things are an abomination unto the Lord."

Everyone was very quiet, not saying a word, not even "Amen" every once in a while. When at the end the hymns started up, every one sang loud, like they were happy with the sermon and pretending that they had not just spent the evening before acting like witches and goblins and being an abomination to the Lord.

Miss Weston did not come to dinner at Pap-pa's house today. I think it was because she is mad at us. Mama says she probably is not, but if she is, she will get over it. Missionaries cannot carry a grudge because that is a sin, and it is best if I do not bring it up. We have to keep to our own counsel.

Mrs. Carlton came over later in the day, carrying some goat milk in a bottle. She says babies do better on goat milk than they do on cow's milk and that maybe Sapphire will gain a little if she gets some more nourishment. Sapphire seems to like it fine. Mrs. Carlton took her on her lap and gave her a bottle of it. She sucked it right down, and she did not spit it back up again. Mama got very quiet, and when I went over to her to see if she was all right, she was smiling, I reckon that means she is happy that Mrs. Carlton brought that milk. I know I am.

November 1, 1931
Dearest Cecilia,

For the first time since I have been here I am at odds with the people of this community. On Friday, I discovered that not only do the children celebrate the heathen practice of parading around in ghoulish costumes in honor of Hallowe'en, they do it with the full accommodation and participation of their parents! I was so outraged that I gave them a stern lecture, which put everyone out of sorts, but I do not think it made any difference in their behavior. I know they disregarded everything I had to say and went right ahead and participated in who knows what kind of obscene rituals in observance of the devil's night.

Today, I let them know of my displeasure by preaching from Deuteronomy 18. You have never seen such guilty looks as on the faces of people in the congregation. But no one came forward to confess their participation in abominations, so I know my sermon did no good whatsoever. How am I to enlighten these people if they are so blind to their own sins and so unwilling to listen to the direct admonitions of Scripture? Sometimes I wonder if I am doing any good here at all.

With a heavy heart,
Emily

November 2, 1931
My School Journal, grade 7, Miss Weston's class
By Pearl Wallace

My friend Darlene's mother has a goat that has two babies, which are called kids. They are just darling, the way they leap around. There are two little girls, named Flossie and Barbara, and they are so tame we can hold them and tote them around like puppies. The grown-up goat is Matilda. Mrs. Carlton used to have a daddy goat, but she says that boy goats stink to high heaven, so she decided not to bring him with her from New Orleans. She said she would not be able to stand having him in the truck with her, even in the back!

Darlene's mother milks Matilda every morning and makes cheese from the milk, and she brings milk to my baby sister who is not gaining weight as she should. Goat milk is better for you than cow's milk, and Sapphire likes it very much. We are grateful that Mrs. Carlton brought it.

November 2, 1931. We pretty much have all the crops in, praise the Lord!

Daddy has gone off to tend to his still, so Darlene and her mama came over. Until he gets his supply back up, we can count on him being gone most days. I just wish I could find where he is hiding it. Jake Hatton and Pap-pa both are wanting more whiskey, and there is not a drop to be found out in the woodshed.

It was warm today for November, so we played outside all afternoon. We made up a scene from *The Secret Garden*, which is my favorite book, and we acted it out. Beryl played Mary, and although I wanted to play Dickon, I let Darlene because she seems out of sorts these days, and I wanted to cheer her up. I played

Colin, and it was more fun than I thought it would be because I got to throw a temper tantrum. I rolled around on the ground and screamed and carried on until we all got so tickled we forgot to finish the scene. We all started pretending to throw temper tantrums, rolling around, kicking and screaming, and laughing. Mama, Mrs. Carlton, and Uncle Woodrow came out to see what all the ruckus was about, and when they saw us laughing so hard, they all got tickled, too.

November 3, 1931. Good news! Jasper and Sardius collected the money from the fellow who bought Dandyman. Today Sardius laid out of school so they could catch a ride to town for it. Then they went to Greenbrier store and bought Jasper a new pair of brogans. Sardius got a pair of rubber boots that fit over his good shoes so he can go outside in the rain and the muck and not have to worry about keeping the cold and wet out, and they got all of us, including Daddy and Uncle Woodrow, new wool sweaters. Both Sapphire's and mine are pink, which I love very much. Beryl's is blue, Ruby's is green, and Mama's is a nice, soft red. Daddy's and Uncle Woodrow's are brown.

Jake Hatton bought a pint of whiskey today, and he paid me cash money. I hope I have enough saved up by Christmas time to buy everybody nice presents. I would like to buy something special for Mama. She deserves nice things because she never buys herself anything when we go through the Sears & Roebuck catalogue and pick out what we want. I also would like to get a pretty shirt and a tie for Jasper so he can go courting. He is struck on Mabel Hathaway. She is sweet, although she has a gimpy leg because she caught the polio when she was little, but not too bad. It makes her limp some.

I would like to buy a dress for Sapphire, a baby doll for Ruby, and a new coat for Beryl. All she has is my old coat, which started out being Daddy's, then Jasper's, and then Sardius', before I got it, so it is old as the hills and way too big for her. Also, that blamed old Ralph Lee tore the sleeve last winter. He grabbed it and slung it over a barbwire fence and ripped a great big hole in it. Mama tried to fix it, but you can tell it is patched. Beryl hates to wear it because she gets scundered if people think we are poor.

I also plan to buy Darlene a present, although I have not decided what yet, and I have not decided what I will get Sardius or Daddy, either. Daddy had better watch it, or I might not get him anything. He is behaving himself now, but it is a long time to Christmas yet.

November 3, 1931
Dear Jonathan,

You are a saint! Thank you for the very generous boxes of goods you sent to me. Many of the things are much needed here—especially the shoes and winter garments for the children. It has turned cold, and many of them do not have gloves, socks, or in some cases, even shoes.

Although the people here are very proud and will not accept any charity, Miss Halfacre, Mrs. Miller, and I are devising a way to soothe their excessive pride and convince them to take a few things to benefit them and their children.

Dear Jonathan, your kindness and generosity have exceeded my wildest hopes. I will write to the Ladies' Guild and to the Brothers of Christ's Words to thank them as well.

While you have already been most generous, since you ask, we could use more books for the children. I have started a library, and the few books I brought have flown off the shelves. If you could find books suitable for children of all ages, they will be very much used, I can promise you! Of course, we can always use more clothing, household items, food, blankets, and the general basic necessities of life. I also hope you are thinking of how we might fund that scholarship program.

I remain your devoted friend,
Emily

P.S. While some of the more fanciful hats will be amusing to the members of the community, it is not likely that they will find a home. The women here are not inclined to wear finery or anything they would call frivolous. While I am grateful for all you have provided, I encourage you to gather more sedate styles, if possible.

November 4, 1931. When I got home today, Darlene was sitting at the kitchen table with Mama! She was eating some pie and drinking coffee, and they were having the best time, talking in French. We all went outside to play, and guess who came over to spoil our fun? Ralph Lee Bittertree. He is the meanest boy I ever met, and he thinks he is high and mighty, too, and that gives him reason to treat everyone else bad. Today he had a squirt gun pistol, and he chased us around, shooting us with cold water. He was especially mean to Darlene, running up on her and trying to squirt it down the front of her dress. She tried to push him away, and he yanked at her sweater so hard he tore it. I kicked him in the leg, and then we ran inside and told on him, but he ran off before Mama could get outside to have a talk with him. He is a low-down varmint!

November 4, 1931
Dear Students and Parents,

As you know, The Reverend Miller suffered a severe heart attack on September 10 and has been very ill since then. His medical expenses are a burden to him and Mrs. Miller, and although all of you have been more than generous in your provisions for their daily needs, I know you all also will want to help them meet those expenses.

You are invited to attend a fund raising event for their benefit on Saturday, November 7, from 4 pm until 9 pm. Bring a vegetable dish to share. The Millers, Miss Halfacre and I will provide a barbequed side of pork. There will be games, contests, and plenty of prizes! Please come for an evening of fun and entertainment to help your pastor and friend. We appreciate all your help!

Sincerely,

Miss Emily Weston

November 5, 1931. Mrs. Carlton and Darlene were at the house when we got home from school today, helping Mama cook supper and tending to Sapphire. Darlene is the sweetest girl, and she is good at fishing and climbing trees, and she is smart, too. She also is not ascared of anything. I dared her to jump off the roof of the springhouse, and she did. Of course, then I had to do it, too, and so did Beryl, and we had a good time taking turns jumping until Beryl turned her ankle and had to quit. After that, we moseyed on in to the house. Uncle Woodrow had split up a big load of kindling, enough to last a good, long time, and he told us girls to stack it up on the porch while he came inside to help Mrs. Carlton make a pie.

We had a very good time. Uncle Woodrow was in fine spirits. He and Mama talked French to Mrs. Carlton and Darlene. He learned it at school, and then he learned to talk it when he was in France, during the Great War, the one that gave him the shell shock. They all got to jabbering away so that I could not understand a thing they said, so they started in teaching me, and Beryl, too.

It will be fun to learn to speak French. That way, Darlene and I could have a secret language where we could talk about things and no one around here would know what we are saying, except for Mama and Uncle Woodrow, of course, and maybe Daddy. He also studied French in school.

Mrs. Carlton was having the best time with Mama and us, cooking supper, laughing, and talking about what it is like down in New Orleans, when all of a sudden, she jumped up, saying, "I have to go. That's Billy Ray's car coming over the hill," and pointed out the window. She grabbed up Darlene by the hand and just flew out the back door.

It is a good thing Billy Ray's car is noisy. He has to drive on the road right above our house on his way to the bridge, so it takes him a while to get home after he comes by. The road follows the creek a ways before the bridge, then doubles back. Mrs. Carlton and Darlene can get home in plenty of time before he ever rolls up into the yard.

November 6, 1931. Today at school, we learned about Africa, which was very interesting because I think that is where Darlene's people came from. I thought Africa was just one big country, but it is a lot of countries. Almost everyone who lives in any country in Africa has black skin, which makes them Negroes. I wonder if there are any other white Negroes like Darlene over there? I wonder what it would be like to live in a country where most people look different than I do?

Darlene and I picked persimmons over by the old apple orchard and got enough to eat our fill and a bucket to bring home to make jelly. We went down to the creek and looked for crawdads. They call them crawfish down in Louisiana, and can you believe that they eat them? It was too cold to find any, even though Uncle Woodrow came by to help us look. He was in fine spirits, and he did not shake hardly any at all this afternoon. He seems to be about as happy as I have ever seen him.

Mrs. Carlton is so very sweet to Mama. She slipped over here again today when Daddy was not around to tend to Sapphire and give her some fresh goat milk. Mama and Mrs. Carlton are getting to be good friends, even though Daddy tries to turn Mama against Mrs. Carlton. He says any woman who used to be with a Negro is trash, and he does not want his children growing up with Negroes and trash, even if the Negro is whiter than he is. I do not think Mrs. Carlton is trash. She is the nicest lady you ever met, and she is as educated as Mama is. Her father was a schoolteacher in New Orleans, and she went for nurses' training before she met her first husband and dropped out. Darlene never met her daddy. He met with an unfortunate accident before she was born.

Mama and Sapphire are both doing better, thanks to Mrs. Carlton.

November 7, 1931. Sapphire's diapers and my shoes came today! The shoes fit, and they look nice enough, but they are not near as pretty as my Mary Janes. Mama was proud of me that I had enough money to buy them. I told her I had saved up my muscadine money and that Pap-pa had paid me for helping him feed his geese. She knew I was disappointed that they are ugly compared to my Easter shoes, but she says I will be glad to have them this winter when it is cold and wet. I wish I had enough money to buy a second pair to wear to church, but even if I did, it would be hard to explain the extravagance. Of course, Beryl was very happy to get my Easter shoes. She called them my birthday present to her. Even though they are too big, she put them on and dragged them around the house. Mama says we can stuff newspaper down in them so she can wear them come Easter. Her birthday is in two weeks.

The diapers are very nice, soft and white. I am glad I bought them because Mama is having to do a washing about every day to keep Sapphire clean and dry. It is hard to get things dry in this damp cold. I was thinking about giving them to Mama for Christmas, but I did not reckon she should have to wait that long, so I went ahead and gave them to her. She cried when she saw them. She pretended that she had gotten into some dust that made her eyes water, but I knew better. Poor Mama. Imagine crying over some diapers.

This evening, we are going over to the schoolhouse to help out Preacher Miller. His hospital bills are big, and he needs us to help him pay them. It is a pity the poor man is going broke on top of being so sick! I am taking some of my whiskey money to give, and Mama is taking her butter money. Sardius and Jasper will give some of their calf money, and Daddy sold one of his pups, so he thinks he has money to burn, besides giving some to Preacher Miller. The Wallaces will not be ashamed at not being able to do their part.

November 8, 1931. The big event Miss Weston put on to raise money for Preacher Miller turned out to be the best thing I have ever seen! I thought we would just be going to pay our respects, hear a sermon, and then slip some money in the basket, but there was a carnival, with games and all kinds of prizes that you would not believe! Everything cost a dime to play, which went to Preacher Miller's hospital bill.

First, Miss Weston had all us children line up, and one by one, we had to recite either the Lord's Prayer or a Bible verse, which we all could, and then we got to pick out anything we wanted from big baskets, and these prizes were just wonderful! They had been donated to Preacher Miller by Miss Weston's rich friends from up in Chicago, and you have never seen anything like them. I got a coat for Beryl that looks almost brand new, and that has saved me a lot of money. She thinks I got it for myself, but I will give it to her for her birthday coming up in two weeks. It is red, with big brass buttons, and is thick and warm, because it came from Chicago, where the winters are very cold.

Ruby recited John 3:16, and Miss Weston tried to give her a beautiful doll, but she picked out a pretty hat for Mama instead. When Mama saw it, her face went red, so I am not sure if she liked it or not. It was very fancy, with blue feathers that stuck way up high. Miss Weston told her to recite another verse, and she gave her the doll, anyway. Beryl got a pretty dress. It is pink, with ruffles!

Since she let Ruby go twice, I asked Miss Weston if I could play again so I could get a coat for Darlene, and she said yes. Right off the top of my head, I recited the whole Beatitudes, and Miss Weston was so impressed she picked out coats for both Darlene *and* her mother. I am excited about that, but I asked her to keep them for me because if Beryl sees me taking them home, she might feel bad that I would get coats for other people and not her. Or, she might figure out that the first one was for her. I have to be cagey about presents.

They had a contest for the big boys and grownups, too. Anybody who could split a wheelbarrow full of wood for the church stove in under 10 minutes got a prize. Everybody laughed when they heard the rules. It only takes about 5 minutes to split a wheelbarrow full of wood. Even I could do that. Jasper got himself a beautiful pair of fancy, black patent leather shoes. Sardius got a suit of clothes that need just a tiny bit of mending, and Daddy won a complete set of leather bound Encyclopedias that do not hardly look like they have ever been used. He says now we will know about everything there is to be known.

The ladies' prizes were out of this world! Miss Weston held a contest where she would give clues about a Bible story, and the first lady who shouted out the story she was hinting about got to pick out whatever they wanted. The nice thing about it was that there were so many prizes that everybody got at least one, and there were some left over. Mrs. Bittertree got a set of bangle bracelets, and you will not believe it, but Mama got the very best prize of all!!! A FUR COAT!!!

It is funny how it worked out. She did not mean to get the coat. She was pointing to a pocketbook, but Miss Weston did not hear her and thought she was pointing to the coat, which was under a big blanket right beside the pocketbook, and she dug it out and handed it over. Mama tried to tell her better, but by then Miss Weston had already started in on another set of clues. Mama sat down right on the floor and cried, and I did, too. My mama has a fur coat! She will be so nice and warm this winter. She says she will feel silly wearing it, but you should have seen her running her hands over it and holding it up to her face. She is downstairs right now picking out the initials that were embroidered in the lining, and she will put her own initials in it so that it will look like it has always been hers.

Everybody was jumping up and down and laughing and crying all at once. Just think! Our dimes went such a long way, and between us and the nice people from Chicago, we raised nearly $25 for Preacher Miller.

What a day! Miss Weston is THE BEST teacher ever!

Those people in Chicago must be very, very rich to be giving away such fine things, but Miss Weston says they are very snooty there. They stop liking their things after they have used them for a year or two, and they are always looking for ways to get rid of them. I cannot imagine that.

Cold, waning days, bitter nights.

There is singing and rejoicing on my frosty banks,
But it is not enough to rouse my silver children,
Lying solemn and still upon my bedrock.

Laughter rings from the bluffs above to the shallows below.
There will be sweet dreams
Underneath the bright stars and the still, cold Orb.
The earth spins faster, into the darkness.

November 8, 1931
My Dear Jonathan,

I only wish you could have been here last evening to see what your kindness and generosity, and the kindness of the Ladies' Guild and the Brothers of Christ's Words have accomplished. You have never seen such gladness as the good people of the Cheola community came together, bringing their hard-earned dimes and dollars to give to the Reverend Miller, and being granted such goods as they have never seen before. There were tears, laughter, and shouts.

Jonathan, you have been such a dear to coordinate all this, and I cannot begin to tell you how grateful I am, how grateful

Mr. and Mrs. Miller are, and even how grateful the people here are, even though they are not fully aware of the lengths to which you have gone to better their circumstances. Thank you a million times!

Your eternal friend,
Emily

November 9, 1931
My School Journal, grade 7, Miss Weston's class
By Pearl Wallace

This has been the best week I have ever had! Miss Weston had a day of games at the schoolhouse yesterday to raise money for the preacher, and she gave away wonderful prizes that were donated by her friends from Chicago. We all won the best prizes you can imagine!

I got coats for my sister and also for my best friend and her mother, who live across the creek from my house. They are from Louisiana where the winters are warm, and they do not have warm coats, so they will be very happy to get these. Miss Weston brought them to my pap-pa's house, and he and Miss Janey Jo will find a way to get them to Darlene and her mother without anybody knowing where they came from. It will be so exciting.

Both Darlene and her mother are very beautiful. Darlene has very white skin and very white hair, and she has beautiful blue eyes, but she has to wear dark glasses because light hurts her eyes. After school, I always run home as fast as I can make Beryl go in hopes that Darlene will be waiting for me so we can climb trees or go fishing in the river, or just play.

November 9, 1931. I just found out the worst possible thing about Darlene. She is a CATHOLIC!!! We were out climbing the big sycamore down by the creek, while Sardius and Jasper went to the river to catch some trout for supper. While we were up in the tree, we got to talking about where you go when you die, and Darlene said, "If you have taken your last rites and received absolution from a priest, you will go to heaven. If you do not, you will go to hell." I nearly fell out of that tree! I had no idea that Darlene was a papist. As nicely as I could I told her that everybody knows that Catholics are idolaters because they worship statues and the Virgin Mary, not God, and she said I was crazy and that I would surely go to hell if I did not go to confession, and then I told her you cannot be saved by talking to a priest. Beryl tried to back me up, but she got confused about the whole thing and ended up just hollering, "You're ignorant!" to Darlene, which made things worse, and I told her to shut up. We all got so mad at each other that we ran back to the house and told our mamas on each other.

Mrs. Carlton and my mama looked at each other, and then Mrs. Carlton just stood up and said, "Let's go on home, *cherie*. It's getting late and we need to get supper on the table."

Darlene started crying, "But Mama! Pearl will go to hell if she doesn't confess." That made me mad all over again, and I said, "No I won't! You will go to hell if you aren't saved by the Blood of Jesus." Mama did not say a word to help me out, but just put her arms around me and said, "We'll talk about it later, sweetheart." And then Mrs. Carlton and Darlene left. Beryl and I cried for a long time over their souls, and Mama did not say much to help us figure out a way to make them see sense. All she said was, "Honey, we'll pray for them. It will work out fine."

I bet the reason Darlene does not go to school is because she is a heathen papist. She has been brainwashed by the pope to believe that the Catholics are right. Mam-ma told me all about how those Catholics work. When her own mama and daddy were living in Ulster, Ireland, they had to live among the wicked Catholics, who used to do abominable things like drink blood and eat flesh at their midnight Masses. Great-Mam-ma's Daddy was an Orangeman who tried to make Ireland a Godly place, but those Catholics were too stubborn to let him help, and they persecuted them so much they finally ran them out of the country.

That is why they came here, to get away from the Catholics, and also because of the potato famine, which was caused by their ungodly Catholic practices. I am so miserable about it I could just die. How could it be that my very best friend is a Catholic?

November 10, 1931. I told Miss Weston about how Darlene is a heathen papist, and she listened, but she was not much help when I asked her how I could convince Darlene that she needs to get saved by the Blood of Jesus. Just like Mama, she said we should pray about it, but I do not think that will do it. Darlene is too far gone.

I was so woeful about it that Jasper offered to take me squirrel hunting and let me shoot his rifle. Pap-pa bought him one for Christmas last year, which is a very good thing because Daddy has only one. When Jasper and Sardius went hunting, they had to trade off using it.

Jasper let me carry the rifle and take every shot. I am not bragging when I say that I am a very good shot. I can hit a squirrel right between the eyes from 50 feet, and I can hit one pretty square at 100. Jasper says I am a real deadeye. I got three squirrels for supper, which me feel very much better. Mama was happy about it, also. We had collards, pan bread, and squirrel stew, which was very tasty.

After supper, Mama, Jasper, Beryl, and Sardius put on their new things for us to admire. Mama looked just beautiful in her fur coat and beautiful blue hat, and you should see how proud Sardius is of his new suit. I think he is even prouder of it than Beryl is of her new dress. Daddy had us call out what we wanted him to look up in his Encyclopedia, and he looked it up and read it to us. Then he pretended to read all kinds of crazy things, until we called him on it, like the Amazon River is full of crocodiles and housecats! We got so tickled our sides ached.

I did not put on the coat I got for Beryl because she would see how much it is too small for me and might guess it is for her. I just said I was too hot to go parading around in a coat inside.

Daddy says we got a sight more out of our money by giving it away than we ever would have if we had tried to buy these things. Mama says that is what happens when you do things in the name of the Lord. It is like fishes and loaves.

November 11, 1931. I thought about going to see Darlene today, but Mama needed me to look after Ruby and she did not want me taking her across the creek. Besides, I bet Darlene is still mad at me. I am not mad at her. I am just grieving for her lost soul, and I am praying that God will give me the words to make her see reason.

My favorite hen, Daisymay, has gone broody. It is late in the season, but I think she may be sad because she has nearly quit laying eggs and she wants what the other ladies have laid. Mama will not let her sit them, though, because we are not getting many eggs, it being so late, and besides, it will be very cold for the baby chickens if they hatch. I feel sorry for Daisymay. She is a good little hen. It is sad to see her trying so hard to find some eggs.

I hope Darlene comes to see me tomorrow. Maybe I can talk some sense into her.

November 11, 1931
Dearest Cecilia,

I so appreciate the encouraging letters that come from you, dear sister! You cannot imagine how I miss you and our long chats. Your counsel is more important to me than you can imagine.

I agree that I should try to encourage Pearl's friend and perhaps help her get some learning. I do not know how I will be able to persuade her to come to school, and I am not certain she will be accepted by the other children. If Mr. Wallace's attitude is representative of that of all the folk here, it would not be a good idea to introduce her into the classroom. This is especially true since I have learned that the child also is of the Catholic faith. You will not be shocked to know that the people here have a strong aversion to any interpretation of Scripture different from their own, being as how Father has similar attitudes. I am grateful that you, Mother, and I have learned to be more broadminded. That summer we spent with the O'Seanaseays broadened us in so many ways that we were not even aware of at the time. The training we got in Ireland is serving me well now as I try to introduce new ideas to the people here. They are kindhearted in general, but I must admit that they tend to be close-minded.

Please continue to pray for me—for all of us. It has become quite cold here, and some of the children still do not have enough warm clothing. If you get the chance, please try to gather some blankets and more woolen garments. I can take all sizes, from infants on up to large sizes for men. The older boys are as large as men. The stove at the schoolhouse malfunctioned today, which made conditions uncomfortable for some of the more poorly clothed. The boys got it started again in short order, but I hope it does not happen again.

I love you and miss you terribly!

Emily

P.S. I have been corresponding with Jonathan about the possibility of establishing a scholarship fund for some of the brightest of my students. If you see him, please encourage him, and also it would not hurt to garner enthusiasm for the project among our friends.

November 12, 1931. I found out today that Otis Merriweather is struck on me, which makes me mad because I do not want him plaguing me to death with his loud and loutish ways, not leaving me alone, getting me into trouble. He is in the sixth grade and is a year older than I am. I have never paid him much attention because he is always running around with the other boys and acting out. At dinnertime today, he pulled my hair as he ran by me. Five minutes later, he did it again. I slapped at him that time and told him to leave me alone, but when I did, he grinned at me. That is how I know he is struck on me.

I did not see Darlene today. I wish she would come over. Mama told me not to go see her. Billy Ray was home. Mama does not like Billy Ray any more than I do.

November 13, 1931
Dear Jonathan,

I do appreciate the letters you have sent of late, and I appreciate that you are continuing to find ways to provide for the needs of these good people here in the mountains of East Tennessee. We always can use warm clothing, and we always need shoes. Believe it or not, a couple of the children still are going without them, even though the ground is sometimes frozen in the mornings. They wrap their poor little feet in rags, then walk several miles to be here every morning. Education is that important to them. Even the children who do have shoes are often ill shod, wearing shoes that fit poorly or are full of holes.

Please continue to pray for me, and for all of us. I look forward to the Christmas holidays when we can get together for a nice visit.

Sincerely,
Emily

November 13, 1931. Sardius has noticed that Otis Merriweather is struck on me. We were eating our dinner when Otis came right up to me and told me I looked nice. I pretended not to notice while he looked at the ground and turned beet red, and Sardius was nice enough not to say anything, until we were walking home this afternoon. He started to tease me about it, but Beryl was listening in, so he changed the subject. Sardius is a good brother. So is Jasper. Neither one of them would scunder me about anything if they could help it. Beryl might, though, if she knew there was a boy who liked me.

Sapphire is getting fatter. Mama looks like she is filling out a little, also. That is good news! She is looking livelier. Daddy pinched her cheek tonight and she swatted at him, but she laughed when she did it.

November 14, 1931
My dear Cecilia,

I have been informed by the Reverend Miller that there are some people in a neighboring community not at all far from here who are extremely antipathetic toward people of the Catholic faith. He tells me that there used to be a robust Catholic church there, but a year ago, some men came one night, looted and desecrated the sanctuary, dragged the priest out of his bed, and beat him severely. He left the next week, the church was never used as a place of worship again, and the small Catholic congregation has been driven underground. I understand that they meet secretly in their own homes for worship. They go to Maryville about once a month to the only Catholic Church in the region to make confession. It is my understanding they are constantly in fear for their lives.

Cecilia, as you may imagine, I find myself alarmed at this news. When I see my neighbors and the parents of my students, I see only kindhearted, peaceful people. It is almost impossible to believe that they might harbor hatred toward other Christians simply because they worship in the way of Rome.

This disturbs me greatly. If Pearl's friend is vilified for being both colored and Catholic, I do not know how I can begin to counsel Pearl, and I certainly worry about what may befall her friend if the news is told abroad. It is too disconcerting to think about. Please pray for us all.

Love,
Emily

November 15, 1931, I still have not seen Darlene. It makes me sick to think that she is still mad at me. She is the only friend we have here in this holler. Mama tried to cheer me up yesterday by letting the hems out of my dresses that have gotten too short. She also fixed up my gingham. It did not have enough of a hem to let out, so she put some grosgrain ribbon at the bottom, and then added a pretty ruffle below it that she made out of a flour sack.

I wore it to church today. Mama stayed up late last night putting a wide collar on it just like one we had seen in the catalogue, and she surprised me with it this morning. I felt very fine in it, especially since it went so well with the sweater that Sardius and Jasper had bought me with their calf money.

Miss Weston said some things in her sermon that made me feel a little better about Darlene. She said that God's love is bigger than rules that people make up about what they think He wants us to do. Everyone who reads the Bible pays attention to different things, and because the Bible is so big, most of us do not pay attention to all of it. Sometimes we get caught up paying too much attention to some things that are not so important, and we do not pay enough attention to other things that are very important. The biggest, Number One Rule is to love God and Jesus with all your heart, and the Number Two Rule is to love your neighbor as much as you love yourself. I guess that means I cannot be mad at Darlene, even though she is wrong about which rules you are supposed to follow. I should love her even though she has got to repent of her sins to Jesus, not a priest.

November 15, 1931
Dear Cecilia,

I have had a heartening day. God revealed to me a sermon that I think has encouraged my little flock to be more inclusive of others, particularly in regards to interpretation of Scripture. I delivered it this morning to a surprisingly large number of congregants, and it seemed to be very well received. There were several "Amens" at important points.

As usual, I took Sunday dinner with the Aikens, and enjoyed my afternoon with them and with the Wallace family. After the meal, I managed to pull Mr. Woodrow aside for a long chat in which I asked him how to go about helping Pearl's friend and her mother. He warmed right to the subject, suggesting that I invite them to church first, in the hopes that they might be accepted by the community. I mentioned what Revered Miller had told me about the antipathy some people in the area have about Catholics, so he promised me would speak to them about downplaying their religious preferences and see if they might come with him next week. We had a very nice conversation. He seemed quite happy and relaxed. Because he seemed so eager to be helpful, I became emboldened enough to ask him to stop by the schoolhouse early tomorrow to take a look at the stove. It is getting so cold I would hate for it to go out again on a freezing day.

I feel quite lighthearted these days. My students are industrious and bright, I am invigorated by the crispy chill in the air. The Reverend Miller tells me my sermons are first rate. I cannot help but sing each morning on my way to school! God is good!

I love you.
Emily

Cold, waning days, sparkling, bitter nights

The Spirit sees rancor and is grieved.
The woman lures without capturing.
The stranger captures without luring.
The broken man's heart glistens with hope.
All will know sorrow.

I run, silent, dark, and cold.

November 16, 1931
My School Journal, grade 7, Miss Weston's class
By Pearl Wallace

I love summer, but wintertime is nice, also. Tennessee is a great state in which to live because we have all four seasons. In the winter, it snows enough so that we can go sledding. There is a big hill over by my pap-pa's place. In the spring, fishing is very good. In the summer, we like to go swimming. The river is nice for that, but it is very swift, so our mother does not let the little ones swim in it, and she is even nervous about me and my brothers going in. She prefers for us to go swimming in creeks. Our favorite place to swim used to be at the Y on Little River, up past Townsend, because it was so beautiful and peaceful, but loggers have ruined the place. Now, it is too muddy to swim, and there are no trees on which to rest your eyes. I wish that people would not cut down the trees because it turns the hills into a big, muddy mess.

I like the fall, also. It is very pretty when the leaves turn gold and red!

November 16, 1931
Dearest Cecilia,

The most extraordinary thing happened today! I am still shaking from it—whether it be from fear or astonishment, or simply my grieving over the pain of another, I do not know. This morning I went to school early, well before daylight, and found Mr. Woodrow there, having come to examine the stove, as he had promised yesterday. He had already cleaned it out and lit the fire, so he must have arrived quite early indeed. I opened a window because ash was lingering in the air, and a flying squirrel flew straight toward my face. As you can imagine, I shrieked quite loudly, and before I knew what had happened, Mr. Woodrow threw himself upon me, dashing me to the floor, and he rolled with me into the corner! There I lay, pinned underneath him as he shook so hard he fairly vibrated, whispering in a strange, strangled voice, "Be quiet. Don't move."

He pressed against me so tightly I could hardly breathe. My face was crushed against his neck so that I could not even cry out, even as he kept admonishing me to be quiet. I was so overwhelmed—he is so large and so masculine and was shaking almost in an animal way—that I could only lie there, trembling beneath him. At last, after several long moments, I managed to take a breath and squeak out a whisper, "Mr. Woodrow! You must release me!" whereupon, he suddenly seemed to come to his senses, realized what he had done, and he jumped up, pale, shaking, and stammering out an apology. Then he turned and fled.

I was so taken aback that it was some time before I could collect myself to even sit up. How terrifying it was that one moment he was lying on top of me, crushing me to himself, violently shaking, and the next, he had disappeared. I still do not have my wits about me. Every time I think of it, I get so distressed I can hardly think. I hope the students did not notice how disturbed I was over it. I had a hard time concentrating the whole day.

Cecilia, please pray for this dear man. It was a terrible thing to witness.

Your loving sister,
Emily

Cold, waning days, freezing nights.

The stars are as cold as the night,
But the great Orb begins to warm, to call to me.

I feel the stirrings of lust
Echoing in the warm bellies of my upright children.
They do not know what awaits them
As the Great Dark leers.

And the Spirit hovers above all,
Watching without murmuring.

November 16, 1931. Miss Weston seemed out of sorts at school today. She kept forgetting what she was talking about, and a couple of times she sat down all of a sudden, as if her legs had given out from under her. Sardius asked her if she was feeling well, and her face went as red as fire. I hope she is not getting sick.

Darlene's mother was here when we got home from school, but Darlene did not come with her. I am blue because I miss her. I have decided to tell her that I do not care if she is a Catholic because I love her so much.

Mrs. Carlton and Mama were sitting at the kitchen table, and Mama invited Beryl and me to sit down and have a cup of coffee with them. Beryl drinks mostly milk and sugar when we have it, but I drink real coffee with just a little milk, or cream when Mama does not make it all up in butter. Mama and Mrs. Carlton were getting along just fine, as if Mama did not know that Mrs. Carlton was bound for hell and damnation, and neither one of them said anything about what had happened until about 10 minutes later when Mama mentioned Sunday's sermon and how sometimes different people look at the Bible and see different things. Then Mrs. Carlton said, "Yes, as long as we follow the Number One and Number Two Rules, we should be fine."

Beryl had forgotten Sunday's lesson, and of course, she had to ask what the Number One and Two Rules were, and then Mama asked me if I would like to tell her, so I did. Mama smiled at me and said, "That's right, Pearl," and then she asked Mrs. Carlton if she loved God and Jesus with all her heart, and Mrs. Carlton said, "Oh, yes! I love Jesus very much because he suffered and died for my sins." Then Mama said, "Me, too," and I did not know what to think of all that, so I did not say anything.

Finally, curiosity got the better of me and I asked Mrs. Carlton when Darlene might come over to see us, and she said, "Maybe tomorrow," and that is all. I hope she does come. I miss her, and I also want another chance to tell her I love her even though she is wrong about religion. If she loves Jesus, it must be in the wrong way. Mam-ma told me for certain that the Catholics were full of abominations. She had seen it with her own eyes.

November 17, 1931
Dear Jonathan,

It is very kind of you to offer to personally come to escort me home for the Thanksgiving celebration, but I do not think the holiday is long enough to justify such a herculean effort. Of course, I would like to be at home to celebrate with my real family and with all my dear friends, but your offer is far more than I can accept. Even though I know your intentions are gentlemanly, you must realize that it would not be seemly for me to drive all the way from here alone with you.

Jonathan, as much as I enjoy your company, and as much as I regard our friendship, I must caution you again that there is no understanding between us. I do not know which direction the Lord will take me after this year, and I do not know what His intentions are for my eventual marital state. Forgive me for saying this, but I am beginning to think that you are anxious for me to return your affections merely because I have been reluctant. You never even mentioned the possibility of us getting married until I was already committed to my life here.

Of course, I am not foolish enough to believe that I will stay here forever, although there are times I would like to, when the days are so dazzling and the nights are so spangled with stars that one could believe they are close enough to be gathered in one's pocket like so many garden posies. This place is changing me, for the better, I believe, and if and when I do choose to come home, perhaps you will find me a better person for it.

I hope your holiday is warm and loving. Please give my best to your family,
Emily

November 18, 1931. Finally! Darlene and her mother were here today when we got home from school. And they were both wearing their new coats! They were so proud of them, and they were so surprised to get them. Mrs. Carlton said they just showed up on their back stoop yesterday, and they had no idea who had brought them, but they were mighty glad to get them. Mama winked at me, and I felt so proud and happy I nearly hugged Darlene. Beryl did, but I was still feeling a little bad about the fight we had, and it made me bashful.

Mama and I have talked about it, and she said I should not say anything at all about Darlene belonging to the Catholics, but to just pray and remember that different people make up different rules but that does not mean we are different in our hearts. I think that Darlene must be different from the Catholics of Ireland. I am sure she loves Jesus as much as I do, and God sees her heart. She cannot help it if she was brought up in the wrong religion.

We got some extra-good news today. Billy Ray is going to work over in Cocke County, on Big Creek, with the logging company. His cousin who is a foreman there got him a job, even though they have cut back the gangs to where there are not many crews left. They are not even cutting timber any more, but are taking apart the shantytowns and railroad. Some people are buying up all the land over that way to turn it into a big park that will let folks enjoy the mountains. I think that is a good thing. Those loggers have stripped all the trees off the hills over in Sevier and Cocke counties so that it is just a muddy mess. I do not know how they will put it back together again, but they say there is going to be a big push to plant it all back the way it was before the loggers came in.

I am glad that Billy Ray has a job now, moving all that logging equipment off the mountain, because, starting a week from Monday, he will be gone all during the week, and be home only on Saturday and Sunday. That means I will be free to sneak over to see Darlene after school. I cannot stand even looking at Billy Ray's hide. He looks at me funny when I am over at Darlene's house. Sometimes he is mean, and sometimes he grins at me as if he knows something on me. I suspect he is thinking about my daddy's drinking.

November 19, 1931. It was an exciting day. Mrs. Carlton bobbed my hair, and Mama's also. We were looking at the pretty ladies and their clothes in the Sears & Roebuck catalogue, and Mama said she was sick of her hair; it took so long to brush it out and pin it up every day. Mrs. Carlton said, "Why, Adeline, you would look pretty with your hair bobbed, and it is so easy to take care of. I can cut it for you." Mama looked surprised at first, and then she crossed her arms and said, "Well, all right, then," and went and got her sewing scissors that had just been sharpened last week.

Mrs. Carlton bound up her hair at the back of her neck, then she tied another ribbon around it just below that, and she cut it between the two ties. She says she will send Mama's hair off to someone she knows in New Orleans who will pay good money for it to make a wig out of it. The next thing we knew, Mama's long, long hair was lying on the table beside her, and Mama was looking like a movie star! She looked so beautiful that I said I wanted my hair bobbed, and Mrs. Carlton cut it the same way. She tied up my hair in string, too, and I hope she can sell it for a lot of money.

Mama and I now have very short hair that comes just to the bottom of our earlobes, and we have bangs! Mama put on some lipstick and some blacking on her eyelashes, and we all danced around and had a fine time pretending to be elegant and beautiful. Darlene looked a little sad. I know it was because her hair seemed so hopelessly kinky, but her mother took all the braids out, cut it short, and slicked it down with some petroleum jelly, and it looked just wonderful. I wish Beryl had cut hers, too, but she was too scared she would look funny.

Uncle Woodrow walked in on us while we were acting silly. He stopped in the doorway, looking from Mrs. Carlton to Mama to me to Darlene, while we all held our breath, waiting for him to speak. He broke into a big grin and said, "Excuse me, ladies. I thought this was Richard Wallace's house. I see I have stumbled onto a movie set by mistake!" I laughed so hard I had to sit down on the floor.

Daddy does not approve of Mama's and my new hairdo, though. He came in before supper while we were combing our hair and admiring ourselves, and he just stopped in the doorway, staring at us as if we were wild Indians. He turned straight around and went outside, but thank the Lord he did not go hitting the bottle. When he came back into the house, he was a little teary-eyed, and he was nice to us all evening.

It was good to see Uncle Woodrow. He had disappeared for a few days, and we always worry about him when he goes missing. He appeared to be in fine spirits. He drank coffee and ate some cornbread with molasses, and he did not shake any the whole time he was here. Ruby knocked some blocks over, and he jumped a little, but not much.

November 20, 1931. I am sorry to say Miss Weston does not like my new hairdo, either. When I walked into the schoolhouse, she took one look at me and turned white. She said, "Pearl, your hair is your glory. You were such a beautiful young lady, and now you look like you have turned into a boy."

That made me sad, but I do not want to have my long hair back. If Miss Weston does not like it, I am sorry, but having short hair makes me feel lighter, both on my head and in my heart. I also am looking forward to getting some money from that wig-maker. I want to buy a little dress for Sapphire, and maybe I can get another pair of patent leather Mary Janes.

Darlene and Mrs. Carlton came over today to bring over some fresh goat milk. Mrs. Carlton had gotten kicked by her cow again, and she told the story so funny! Darlene was limping a little, and when I asked her what was wrong, she said she was skipping rope and fell off the porch. Mrs. Carlton said that was not as funny as her getting kicked by a cow.

Today is Beryl's birthday, and Ruby's is next week. I cannot believe Beryl is nine years old already. Now we are only a year apart for the next few weeks. We had a little party after dinner tonight, but we will celebrate big on Sunday at Pap-pa's place. I will give Beryl her coat, and I am sure she will be thrilled to get it. She has been piling on sweaters so she does not have to wear that ragged old coat unless Mama makes her. I wish I had saved my Easter shoes to give her as a birthday present, too, because that would make it extra special for her. I have a sugar tit for Ruby made out of real maple sugar. I am glad she will not realize that Beryl's present is so much better than hers.

November 21, 1931. I have hit pay dirt. I was out in the barn today looking for Daisymay's nest, and I found a little hidey-hole made out of bales of straw over in the corner. Behind it were three dozen jars of whiskey! This is what Daddy has been doing when he stays out all day. He was making enough whiskey to keep him and his friends drunk all winter. I bet I can steal at least four or five, especially if I just get one every couple of weeks.

Now, I know it is going to be a fine Christmas. There is so much whiskey that I am thinking maybe I can make a deal with Jake Hatton where I give him wholesale prices so he can sell some of what he buys from me for a profit. He has mentioned that he could sell a lot of whiskey if I could just keep him supplied. I hate the thought of partnering up with somebody as low down as Jake Hatton. I know he will cheat me at every turn, but when you are engaged in criminal activity, you have got to keep your standards and your expectations low, and you have to keep your wits sharp about you.

Darlene did not come today, so I went to her house. Daddy would kill me if he knew because he still does not like me being friends with Darlene. He keeps his mouth shut when she and Mrs. Carlton come over here now, though, because he knows Mrs. Carlton has saved Sapphire's life with her goat's milk. We have not told Daddy that Darlene and her mama are Catholic. It is bad enough that Darlene is a Negro. He would bust something if he knew she was Catholic and she comes over here and sits in his kitchen drinking his coffee.

November 22, 1931. We all wore our new sweaters to church today, and Mama wore her fur coat. We looked as fine as anybody there, maybe even finer. Everyone stared at Mama and me, but we did not care. Miss Weston did not say anything about our hair. She pretended she did not notice it.

Miss Weston preached on heaven and how we will get Glorified Bodies that will not feel any cold or pain, and we will eat all we want, any time we want, and that we will never have any cause to be afraid. We will not just be sitting around on clouds playing harps all day long but will be doing our favorite things. I probably will be fishing or swimming in the river. I suppose there are fish in the River that flows by the Throne of God. It would be a waste of good water for there not to be.

Afterwards, we went to Pap-pa's house and we celebrated Ruby's and Beryl's birthdays. Beryl LOVED her coat! She cried and jumped up and down and hugged me until I thought I would be squeezed to death. Mama cried, also. She said she was very proud of me.

It was a very nice birthday party. I wish Uncle Woodrow had been here, but he did not go to church with us and so he could not come to the birthday party, which made me mad. He should have been more considerate of it being a big birthday celebration. Miss Weston came, but she did not seem to be happy the whole time she was there. She seemed nervous or something, looking around and jumping whenever anybody said something to her. I hope she is all right.

Daisymay has hatched out four sweet little chicks. Although Mama did not want her to sit eggs because it was so late in the season, somehow she managed to hide these away so that we could not find them, and now she is a proud and happy mama! They are staying in the barn since it is cold. Daddy's hounds are having to share their home with fluffy little chickens, but I do not think he minds. More chickens mean more eggs and meat.

November 23, 1931
My School Journal, grade 7, Miss Weston's class
By Pearl Wallace

My baby sister, who just turned one month old can smile. When I look at her, she looks right at me as if she knows me, and she grins like she is happy to see me. She is the most darling little baby ever!

I am very happy that Thanksgiving is this week. Mama is baking pumpkin and apple pies, and she also is gathering up Brussel sprouts that she will cook up with some brown sugar and ginger. Pap-pa will kill a goose, and who knows what Miss Janey Jo is going to put together! My mouth is watering just thinking about it.

I also am very excited that Miss Weston will be joining us for Thanksgiving dinner. She has family in Chicago, but it is too far for her to travel for just a long weekend, and so Miss Janey Jo was thoughtful to invite her. It will be very nice to have her with us. I know Miss Janey Jo will make us proud with her cooking and her fine table.

November 25, 1931. Otis Merriweather gave me a piece of gingerbread at dinnertime today. His mother packed an extra one for me. I thought that was very nice of her. She barely knows me, but she sent me some gingerbread just because Otis likes me. I think maybe he is nicer than I gave him credit for.

November 26, 1931. Today was Thanksgiving! We all went over for a feast with Pap-pa and Miss Janey Jo. It was a real treat for all of us that Miss Weston was there, too. We had a big goose that Pap-pa had killed early this morning. I am glad I did not see that because when I do I never can eat any, and it was very, very good!

I am not tenderhearted about most animals, especially about fish. I can kill them without thinking about it. I also can kill a squirrel, although I used to be squeamish about them, too. I got over that when a tribe of them wiped out just about our whole tomato crop last summer. They came at them the minute they started turning red, took out one bite from each of them, then threw them on the ground. We probably lost 100 tomatoes to them, so now I am not at all tenderhearted about them. Squirrels are good eating, too, and I figure we have to eat. If I let my heart get in the way of my stomach, then I will starve to death. Jasper says they are just furry rats, but I do not like to hear that because I do not like to think about eating rats.

Although I can kill a squirrel any time, and a rabbit if I do not think too much about it, and certainly possums and raccoons, I hate to see a bird die, except for roosters. Of all the roosters we have had, there have been only about five or six good ones. The rest are just awful, fighting each other, jumping on the hens, grabbing and pulling on their combs, and mashing them down to the ground. They flog the little children, too. I think most of them do not deserve to live. Other birds, though, I do not like to think about killing. I think of them in the air, flying free, and imagine their spirits soaring up there. When they die and their spirits leave their bodies, it is very sad. One minute, it is a living creature, running around, flying, enjoying life and the sunshine and all of its friends, and the next, it is limp and its eyes have gone empty. So I do not watch when Pap-pa kills a goose. I do not like to think about how we just robbed something of its life so we can enjoy eating it.

I am thankful today, for my life, and for all the people in it, even Daddy, who was sober and was as nice as he could be. He swung me up on his shoulders, although I am too big to do that, but I liked it because I felt safe, knowing Daddy was steady and he would not fall over and drop me. He has big, strong shoulders, and I like it when he runs with me on them, bouncing me up and down. I also am thankful for my sweet Mama and my brothers and sisters and for my Pap-pa and Miss Janey Jo and their big table that will hold all of us, even Uncle Woodrow, and all that food. And Miss Weston, too. It was nice to see her not so prim and proper.

She sat back and laughed a lot today, and when Pap-pa offered her a wee dram of sherry, she stopped for a second, then flickered her eyes over toward Uncle Woodrow, blushed, and said, "Well, Mr. Aiken. I normally do not imbibe, but since it is a special occasion, I will not refuse your hospitality," and then she took a little glassful! After that, she was very scundered when it looked as if no one except Pap-pa and Miss Janey Jo was going to drink any. She did not say anything, but her face went white when everyone at the table turned Pap-pa down, and then she looked at her lap and got very quiet. I did not know what to do, but then Mama spoke up and said, "I do believe I will have just a sip, although Richard is avoiding all alcohol at present." Then Uncle Woodrow, who never drinks at all, ever, said, "Yes, I would like a little glass, too." I could tell Miss Weston was very grateful to both Mama and Uncle Woodrow. So was I! They all drank a toast to Pap-pa's health and then to Miss Weston, the special guest of honor. It was very nice.

November 26, 1931
Dearest Mother and Father,

Happy Thanksgiving! I am sorry to miss spending it with you, but rest assured, I did not spend it alone, and I had a very good time becoming more acquainted with the good people here in the Cheola community.

The Reverend Miller is continuing to improve, but slowly. He and Mrs. Miller had dinner with Mrs. Miller's sister and her family while I went to the Aikens' home for the holiday. Although the Millers need me to be with them most of the time, today I got a little break and was able to socialize more in the community.

I hope all of you had a grand day and that Thomas and Jonas did not eat too much turkey! I miss you all and love you very much.

Your daughter,
Emily

November 26, 1931
Dear Cecilia,

Happy Thanksgiving! I had a wonderful day today at the Aiken's home, eating one of the finest meals I think I have ever had. It was a beautiful, clear, crisp day, and I feel full of the joy of living.

I did have one awkward moment, although it passed quickly and did not leave any lingering discomfort. Mr. Aiken offered me a glass of sherry after dinner. I am so used to Father and Mother drinking sherry after dinner that I completely forgot about it being illegal! I do wish Congress had made an exception for fine wine drunk at meals when they passed the Prohibition amendment. I can understand why they needed to outlaw hard spirits, but I am sure wine has never hurt anyone. Our Lord certainly had nothing against it.

I digress. Right after I had accepted a tiny glass of sherry, I suddenly remembered that spirits of all kind are illegal and that Mr. Wallace has a weakness with drink. He declined a sip, as did Mrs. Wallace and Woodrow, and I was so embarrassed at my lapse of judgment, I nearly died. But suddenly both Mrs. Wallace and Mr. Woodrow changed their minds, which made me feel infinitely better. It would have been better if we did not have the specter of Mr. Wallace's failings hanging over our heads, but even with that, we had a nice, cozy afternoon together.

I am happy to report that Mr. Woodrow did not seem to be suffering from any ill effects after his frightful episode of last week. He seemed to be in fine spirits, although he was a little distant with me. That is understandable, considering how embarrassed he must have been. I wish I could tell him I hold no hard feelings for him over it, that in fact, it made me more sympathetic to his situation, but knowing his pride, I refrained from even mentioning the episode. I look forward to the day we can discuss his illness in comfort together. Together, perhaps we can devise a way for me to help him overcome it.

I hope your day was fine and comfortable among our blessed family. I miss you all! Give my love to Thomas and Jonas.

Much love,

Emily

Cold, short days, bitter nights.

Rage tears along my banks,
Hurling and tearing, flinging fear and pain.
The in-between child cries are muffled with tears,
The woman suffers in proud silence.
Dark more dense than winter hovers,
Grinning and gaining, stinking of hate.

November 27, 1931. We did not have school today on account of the Thanksgiving holiday. Darlene came over, but she did not want to play much. She said her stomach hurt and she just wanted to sit inside and play with Ruby, so we stayed in the kitchen most of the day, eating leftovers from yesterday and talking about what we are going to be when we grow up. I want to be a missionary like Miss Weston. Beryl wants to be a wife and a mother, and Darlene says she wants to be an actress. I was surprised to hear that, because Darlene is bashful sometimes. You would not expect her to get out in front of people!

Jasper and Sardius also surprised me. Jasper said he wants to be an airplane pilot like Mr. Charles Lindbergh, and he wants to build his own plane and fly all over the world. I always thought Jasper would be a farmer. He is so good at it, and he already has a good start on it. He knows about everything there is to know about farming. Sardius had to think about it long and hard. At first, he said he wanted to be a teacher, but then he changed his mind and said he wanted to be a preacher! I cannot imagine Sardius being a preacher any more than I can imagine Darlene being an actress. Both of them are just too bashful.

We did not see Mrs. Carlton all day. Mama asked after her, but Darlene said that Billy Ray was keeping her home today. That sounded a little strange to me, the way she said he was "keeping" her home, as if he were holding her against her will. Mama looked funny when she said it, too, but no one said anything.

November 28, 1931. Darlene and her mama came over early, right after Billy Ray took off for Johnny Joe's barn and Daddy left out to "take care of some business," as he called it. Of course, I know what kind of "business" he was talking about. At least he is only making whiskey, not drinking it, which suits me fine. Uncle Woodrow came over to chop some wood, although to tell the truth, we have a good supply of wood already laid by. I guess he thinks it is going to be a hard winter.

All of us young-uns went outside to play human croquet. It was boys against girls. We were having the best time when Doodlebug, our mean old rooster jumped up and flogged Darlene on the back of the leg, just in that soft spot behind the knee. Darlene had not done a thing to him. He just decided he did not like her and lit into her like he meant business. I could see that he drew blood, so I lifted up Darlene's dress a little to look at it better, and I saw some big, red, crusty welts that looked as if she had been hit hard enough with a strop to bring the blood. I could not help myself. I just said, "Oh, Darlene!"

Darlene jerked her dress down very quickly and ran inside to her mama. No one but me saw the strop marks, and when I followed Darlene inside, Mrs. Carlton was saying, "We'll take care of this at home," and she and Darlene left without hardly saying goodbye. Uncle Woodrow looked worried, and he went outside right after that, and that's the last we saw of him. I wonder if he knew Darlene was hit hard enough with a leather strop to bring the blood, and it made him techy. I told Mama later, and she just shook her head and told me to pray about it, which made *me* techy. She ought to say or do something to keep Darlene from being beat that bad.

I did not say anything to the others besides Mama about Darlene's strop marks because I did not know what to say. Daddy is a sorry drunk who yells, cusses, and throws thing, and he has whipped all of us a few times, when we deserved it, but he has never really hurt any of us. Usually he just lays a few switches across our legs with a hickory that still has most of its leaves on it. We holler and carry on like he is killing us, and then afterwards, we go out and snigger about how he did not even make a mark on us. Mama has never so much as raised her voice to us. I reckon Darlene is right when she says that Billy Ray Carlton is worse than my daddy.

The only good thing that has come out of this day is that we will have Doodlebug for supper. Jasper wrung his neck right after he flogged Darlene. I am glad, because we all hated Doodlebug. He gets it into his head to run at you when you are not looking, and more than once, he has scratched or pecked all of us. I am surprised he lasted this long.

November 29, 1931. Daddy was in a good mood again this morning, and he went to church with us to listen to Miss Weston preach and to Beryl and me sing. Ruby almost got up with us, but she got bashful at the last minute and would not get up there. We sang *The Old Rugged Cross*, and Mama cried. Even Miss Weston looked a little teary-eyed, and I saw Daddy blowing his nose, but I am not sure if it was just because he has a cold coming on. He and Mama held hands on the way home, and he carried little Sapphire most of the way.

We had a fine time at Pap-pa's house at dinner. Daddy was a little on the quiet side, but Uncle Woodrow and Pap-pa were funnier than ever, telling stories about all the trouble they got into as young'uns. Miss Weston's face went red, she laughed so hard. Mama laughed a lot, too.

When we got home, we saw that the gate was open and three of the dogs had gotten out. Daddy started to get mad, but Jasper reminded him that he was the last one out, and he remembered Daddy closing the gate and latching it. We got the dogs rounded up easily enough, but it is a mystery how the gate got open.

This afternoon, I made a big order from the Sears & Roebuck catalogue so I can start getting ready for Christmas. I ordered some yarn so I could make Sardius a hat and Mama a pair of mittens. I just did not have enough money to buy her a dress, and besides, she needs new mittens with the cold weather, and her old ones are full of holes. The yarn for Sardius' hat is bright yellow. When he wears it, he will think the sun is shining down on him even on the darkest, dreariest days. A skein cost 45c. Mama's yarn is a soft, pretty red that looks warm. It was expensive at 98c, but it is pure angora wool, and so it is extra fine and soft. I also ordered some paper dolls with five sets of clothes for Beryl that she can cut out and pin onto the cardboard dolls. They are beautiful! They cost 45c.

I spent most of my money on a beautiful little dress for Sapphire. It is pink, with little pink roses embroidered all over it, and it has ruffles at the cuffs and hem. I must say, I am very proud of it and think it was worth every penny! I cannot wait to see her in it. It is a little big for now, but by Easter, it will be perfect. It cost $2.42.

I still have to get presents for Jasper, Daddy, Pap-pa, Miss Weston, Darlene, Mrs. Carlton, and Miss Janey Jo, so I had better get busy and sell some whiskey soon. Daddy's stash inside the hay bales is getting bigger and bigger, thank goodness!

November 29, 1931
Darling Cecilia,

It has been another wonderful Sunday. I have become quite comfortable preaching, and my little flock appears to be comfortable with me as well. What a fortuitous circumstance that I have come here! I am growing more confident, more secure, and happier with each passing week.

Today, I sat at the Aikens' table again, and we had such a jolly, comfortable time together. I am beginning to feel a part of the family; we are all so familiar with each other. Woodrow was in fine form, telling the funniest stories and making me laugh so hard I had a hard time remembering that we are not kin. I nearly punched him in the shoulder—a most unladylike thing to do! But if I had, I do not think he would have thought less of me. He is so kind and generous of spirit, and I do believe I can say or do anything around him and he would make me feel perfectly accepted and cared for.

Cecilia, I do wish you could meet him! He is quite beautiful, lean and lithe, with broad shoulders and those stunning, marvelously expressive eyes. It makes me wish I could be an artist so I could capture the beauty of his physique in oils. He reminds me of the sculpture of David in Florence—the very epitome of masculine grace and loveliness.

It is late, so I must be off to the luxury of my bed and my pillow. I hope your dreams are as sweet as my own are these days.

Love,
Emily

Cold, waning days, bitter nights

Joy cavorts with grief,
Riding high in my currents,
Swirling in my eddies,
Dancing amid the rocks.
I hear the laughter of some,
Even as others cry out in pain, rage, and fear.

My children do not know
What they do not know.

November 30, 1931
My School Journal, grade 7, Miss Weston's class
By Pearl Wallace

After I have finished my studies at the Moody Bible Institute, I will go to Africa on the mission field, where I will teach the people about Jesus and how to dress properly. I also will teach them how to read and write and to cipher. I hear that in Africa the people are wild, and sometimes they eat missionaries, so I will have to be careful not to let them catch me. However, if I pray about it, God will protect me so that I do not end up on somebody's dinner plate.

Prayer is a great thing. When we pray, God protects us and guides us, and He talks to us through prayer. We will ask Him for something, and He will think about it, and if He thinks it is good for us, then He will grant us the desires of our heart. Psalm 37:4 says, "Delight thyself also in the Lord; and He shall give thee the desires of thine heart."

November 30, 1931. This was a wonderful day. Daddy came home late this afternoon as happy as a cow in clover because he got a job! The railroad is hiring bulls to make sure hobos do not ride the trains without paying, and since he belongs to the union, he was one of the first in line. Union members back each other up. They will go on strike if the railroad hires a scab over a union man. His first day of work will be next week.

His job will be to ride the train and throw hobos off when they try to sneak a ride for free. Daddy said since he is a big man, he will be able to heft anybody and throw him off. Beryl asked him if he would hurt them when he threw them off, but he laughed and said he was just raffing about. He would not really do any throwing. That was just a saying that means he will ask them if they have a ticket, and if they do not, he will tell them they are not allowed to ride. We were glad to hear that. I feel sorry for those hobos. They only steal a ride because they are out of work and they are looking for food and a job. If they get thrown off a moving train, they could break a leg, and then they could not even walk to the next town. That is just not right.

Other than the fact that he has to be mean to the hobos, I was very glad to hear about Daddy's job in almost every way. If he has a job, he likely will not drink so much. The bad part about it, though, is that if he is not making any whiskey, I am going to lose my business, and I need that money. Christmas is coming up, and Easter is not much further after that.

November 30, 1931
Dear Jonathan,

I am sorry I have not written to you in a while, and regret that I have been so neglectful, particularly since you have faithfully written to me at least once a week since I arrived here. Your letters cheer me, particularly the ones in which you tell me about how all our old friends are doing.

Jonathan, although I do care for you very much, I must remind you that there is no understanding between us. I got a letter this week from Marilyn Baker, who seemed to imply that you and I are practically engaged. You know that is not the case, so please make sure that no one gets the impression that I will be retuning in the Spring to marry you. I still do not know God's plan for my life, and until I do, I cannot be making any plans beyond this school year.

I will tell you that I am not certain that I will be returning to teach again next year, although I also am not certain that I will NOT. I admit that teaching under the conditions that I face is difficult, but at the same time, there are students for whom I feel responsible. They are very bright and eager to learn. It would be a waste and a pity to leave them here to fend for an education without my help. If only I could find a way to help these few students continue their education in a proper school, I would feel better about leaving the area at the end of the term.

I hope all is well with you. Please continue to pray for me and for my dear students.

Emily

November 31, 1931. I might like Otis Merriweather. Today he slipped a piece of peppermint candy onto my desk when Miss Weston's back was turned. I snatched it up before she turned around and put it in my pocket and ate it when I got home this afternoon. I feel a little bad that I did not share it with Beryl, but it was hard candy and I would not be able to break it in two without smashing it into powder. I reckon I could suck on it for a little while and then give it to her, but then I would have to endure it while she sucked it all the rest of the way down, and I do love peppermint.

We got to play with Darlene all afternoon today. With Billy Ray gone during the week, Beryl and I go over to her house about any time we want to. Back behind the house, between the porch and the outhouse, is a big spruce tree, and we climbed up it and jumped over to the roof where we could get a good view of the river and the mountains beyond. It is very pretty there, except for that patch over by Hickory Ridge where the loggers clear-cut the whole mountain. That part is ugly, but if you look in the other direction, all you can see is sparkling river, then green and blue trees and winter skeletons all over.

Darlene says she comes up here all the time to look at the sparkly river, and sometimes when she wants to get away from Billy Ray. We stayed there for a while, but Darlene was not in a talking mood, so when it got too cold to just sit and look, we came on down and Beryl and I came home.

December

December 1, 1931. Sardius and I got into a fight at school today. In our history lesson, we learned about slavery, which is very bad. Negroes did not come to America like everyone else. Indians did not come to America, either. They were born here. The rest of us came for religious liberty and because there was not enough food in the old country. Negroes are different. They were captured and brought here as slaves, and they were treated badly. I did not know that until Miss Weston explained it today. I thought that the slaves came over on their own because they were looking for work, just like everybody else.

At lunchtime, we all got to talking about the slaves, and I said it was wicked to capture people from their homes where they were happy and make them work and do things they do not want to do as if they are animals. Sam Hutchinson, whom I never have liked ever since he called me a smarty-pants back in the fourth grade, said that Negroes are animals and working as slaves was the best that could happen to them. He said if somebody owned them, they took care of them, fed them, and gave them a place to sleep out of the cold. It was better for them because all they knew was to run wild and eat each other. That made me mad, because I know that Darlene knows better than to run wild and eat people. She would not like being a slave, either, so I told Sam he was ignorant, and he called me a name I do not want to write down here. Sardius hauled off and gave him a good clout on the chin.

Sam knocked him down and jumped on him, and I lost my head and jumped on Sam. I got in a few good licks before Miss Weston showed up and dragged me away. Otis Merriweather pulled Sam and Sardius apart.

We all had to stand in the corner for the rest of the afternoon and listen to the others snigger at us behind out backs. It was mortifying, but not as mortifying as knowing Miss Weston caught me fighting. She said she was very disappointed in me, which makes me feel just terrible. I wish she would let me explain, but she said there was no good reason for fighting, especially for girls, and she did not want to hear my excuses. I feel sick. And hungry. Mama made us skip supper tonight because of it. I did not get to play with Darlene today, either.

December 1, 1931,
Dearest Cecilia,

It was a disappointing day today. I do not feel encouraged about being able to invite Pearl's friend to attend school, or even church services. Today, I taught the children about the disgraceful practice of slavery, and some of the children were quite vocal in their approval of it. One even went so far as to call Negroes "animals." I am proud to say that my Wallace children came to the defense of people of color! Little Pearl actually initiated a fight over it, which drew in her brother and several others. It was quite a sight. I secretly felt so proud of her that I found it difficult to punish them! But discipline is paramount, so I did my duty and gave them all the same punishment for fighting. I did not feel it was appropriate to punish a child for expressing an opinion, no matter how wrong or cruel it was.

I have heard from Marilyn. Did you know she thinks Jonathan and I are practically engaged? I suspect Jonathan has been talking out of school. I certainly hope she did not get the idea from Mother! Please try to keep everyone in line for me.

All my love,
Emily

Cold, waning days, bitter, sparkling nights.

Lovers warm my banks with sweetness.
I murmur songs in my most gentle voice.
Ice rimes my banks, but no one feels the chill.

On the other side, close to the horizon
Dwells the Darkness.
The Spirit broods and waits.

December 2, 1931. Thank goodness Mama is through punishing Sardius and me. She is very tenderhearted, so she cannot stay mad at any of us for long. Miss Weston did not act any different this morning, so I suppose she has forgiven us, too. Mama says I ought to apologize to her for fighting, but I do not feel so inclined. If they would just listen to us and let us explain WHY we were fighting, they would probably give us a certificate of honor and not be mad at us. Maybe I will make a certificate of honor and give it to Sardius for Christmas so he will know I think what he did was brave and sweet.

Daddy was home all day today. His job does not begin until next week, so I was hoping he would use the time to build up his whiskey supply, but I guess he thinks he has enough for now. There is a new batch out in the woodshed, four jugs and twenty-six quart jars, on top of what he has in the barn. I figure I can get at least 10 pints out of it easy without him noticing. I skimmed off one whole pint today, which I sold to Jake Hatton. Pap-pa has been asking me if I can get him some, too.

Darlene and her mother came over to bring some goat milk, and because they are saving Sapphire's life, Daddy does not have much choice but to be welcoming. He even smiled at Mrs.

Carlton, and he patted Darlene on the shoulder just a little. Uncle Woodrow was here, and he was so nice to Darlene that Daddy had to be nice, too, to keep from being shown up. Uncle Woodrow is a real gentleman, and I know that makes Daddy think more about how he treats people.

They did not stay long. Uncle Woodrow said he needed some help over at his place. He has a chicken that he thinks might be egg-bound. Mrs. Carlton knows how to unclog them, so they all went to tend to that chicken. Mrs. Carlton loves chickens and all kinds of animals. When she found out that Uncle Woodrow keeps rabbits, she said she wanted to see them, too. Daddy would not let Beryl and me go with them. He said he needed us to help him out in the barn, and then, after they left he plumb forgot that he had something for us to do.

Uncle Woodrow is going to move in with us for the winter. He and Daddy made him up a little room in the barn loft with a straw-tick mattress covered in a pretty quilt, and they even put a rag rug on the floor. It looks homey and cozy. Daddy will be gone from Monday until Saturday morning, and Uncle Woodrow will be here to help with whatever needs doing. I am happy to have him here. He is good at playing games, and he makes Ruby laugh. Most days we cannot even tell he is suffering from shell shock, he is so jolly.

December 3, 1931. It is starting to get very cold. I do not mind the cold so much as the dark. Daddy, Sardius, and Jasper make sure the stove does not go out overnight, and since we sleep in the loft right over the kitchen, it is nice and warm up there when we are getting dressed in the mornings. In general, Beryl is hard to get going in the mornings. I like to make it to the top of the ridge in time to catch the sunrise and spend a little time just dawdling for a while because it is so pretty, but if I am having to baby Beryl along, I usually do not get there in time to see the sun make its little "Pop!" It does not pop too often since it usually comes in behind clouds, which are pretty, too, but it has been clear this week, and I get to see that little line of gold coming across the mountain, outlining the hills so pretty. The sun seems stronger in the winter, more glary, but I think that is pretty, even when it runs straight in my eyes and makes me blind. If I get to just the right spot when the sun comes up, all I can see is bright gold, and I think that is what heaven must be like, except in heaven, we will have special eyes so that you can see through the gold and it does not hurt them. It is like the day is jumping out at you, full of surprises, all bright and happy, and it does not give a tinker's hoot whether you care about it or not, or whether it blinds you or not. It is coming no matter what anybody thinks or wants.

December 4, 1931. Sardius laid out of school today to help Pap-pa and Jasper kill a hog. I am glad they did it while Beryl and I were in school so we did not have to be there to see it. I love pork, and hogs are big, mean critters that you do not feel sorry for when they get killed, but it is a messy, ugly business that I do not like to see. Pap-pa is kind not to make us girls come help. He pays Jasper and Sardius for helping him butcher it and render it down, and he also gives them a ham, some bacon and lard, and some hogshead cheese. I love head cheese. It is the best thing you ever tasted fried up and put on a flat hoecake.

Daddy went over to help with the hog killing, but Jasper said he was not very much help. Daddy is tenderhearted toward animals, and he tends to look the other way whenever blood is spilled. Of course, Uncle Woodrow takes off for the woods when he even thinks there might be a killing going on. I am pretty sure that Pap-pa thinks Mama married into a family full of lady-men who do not have the gumption to do what-all needs to be done on a farm. He does not say anything, but I see how he looks at Daddy and Uncle Woodrow sometimes when they go pale and look the other way. I am glad I have a little stronger gut, but I wish it were stronger still. I want Pap-pa to be proud of me, even if he cannot be proud of Daddy.

We had a good time with Darlene and her mama today, as we always do, and Uncle Woodrow slipped back home to spend some time with us. It feels good, having Darlene and her mama in our house, helping Mama cook and clean. Uncle Woodrow is sweet, too. We are all family. We love each other so much!

I sold Jake Hatton another full pint of whiskey this evening. I made him pay me before I gave it to him. I have learned how to handle him, although I do not think I will ever get that 50c that he owes me. The last time I reminded him about it, he acted as if he did not even remember drinking my whiskey. He said he is not sure it was to him that I sold that whiskey. As if there could be anybody else! I know the difference between Jake Hatton and my pap-pa.

December 5, 1931
Dearest Cecilia,

It is cold, perhaps as cold as what you are experiencing, although it is not as dark. The daylight lingers a little longer here. I do not mind admitting to you that I am lonely. The Reverend and Mrs. Miller try to be good company, but the long evenings are tedious and somewhat sad because it is clear that the Reverend is not going to recover his health any time soon. I long for music in the parlor and the laughter of our friends. The people here are kind, but I am always aware that I am an outsider.

I read a lot to while away the time, and I find I am sleeping more than usual, and dreaming strange and beautiful dreams. One dream has been reoccurring for some weeks now—I dream that I am wrapped in the blue and white rag rug that lies in the Miller's parlor. It engulfs me entirely, so that I can hardly breathe, but rather than feeling suffocated or trapped, I feel free and blissfully euphoric. The rug lifts off the floor, like a magic carpet, sweeping me up high over the mountains, where I drift, watching the beautiful landscapes below me, the bright stars above me.

When I wake, I am smiling, and feeling as if a beautiful future lies before me! Even writing about it makes me long to curl up in bed and go to sleep, so I will end this letter and turn off the light.

Good night, sweet Cecilia!

Emily

December 5, 1931. Many things happened today. I got up before daylight with Jasper and Sardius because we wanted to go fishing. This is Daddy's last Saturday before he leaves to be a bull for the Railroad, and we are going to surprise him with a big feast for supper. It is cold, so I put on a pair of long johns and some old trousers. I did not dream that I would see Miss Weston today!

We started down to the river, and we could see Mrs. Carlton through the kitchen window. We pecked on it instead of going to the door because Billy Ray is at home, and I did not want to see him. When she let us in, she had a big, bloody sore on her head just above her ear. I asked her about it, but she just said she was glad we were here, and she thought it was a good idea if Darlene went fishing with us.

Once we got out the door, I asked Darlene about the sore on her mama's head, and Darlene made a face like she was about to cry, and she pulled at her hair. After a minute, she said, "That Billy Ray is the meanest S.O.B. that ever walked. I'm going to kill him one day."

She would not tell me much more, but I got the gist of it. Billy Ray had bashed Mrs. Carlton's head against the stove and split it open. He *is* a mean S.O.B., and I do not care who hears me say it. I tried to take her mind off it, and we had a pretty good time fishing, even though we all were mad at Billy Ray. At least we caught a good mess of trout by the time the sun was full up, and we gave Darlene six big ones to take home for their dinner. That might sweeten up Billy Ray some.

Jasper and Sardius went on home, but Darlene begged me to stay awhile, so I did. We sat up on the roof in the cold and watched the river until I got to shivering and decided to come on home.

When I got there, Beryl met me in the yard, breathless, telling me that Miss Weston was visiting at the house. She had been hiding out, waiting on me so I would not be scundered to death, walking into the house and right into Miss Weston. I was very grateful to her to go to the trouble, because here I was, wearing trousers, with short hair, no doubt looking just like a BOY! Miss Weston would be very disappointed in me, for sure. We did the only thing we could think to do. We climbed in the bedroom window, into Mama and Daddy's room, and I rooted around in the closet until I found a skirt that did not look too bad. It hung off me, but we found some pins in her sewing chest and Beryl helped me to pin it up some. I was ascared to death and shaking by the time we climbed back out of the window and came around to the front door.

Mama looked at me funny when I came in, but she did not say anything. Mama, Daddy, Jasper, Sardius, and Miss Weston were all sitting in the living room drinking coffee, and Miss Weston held Sapphire on her lap. Ruby looked as if she was not paying any attention, but when I came in, she said, "Pearl's wearing the wrong clothes!" I just about died before Miss Weston smiled at me. She did not say a word about me wearing a skirt pinned together and nearly dragging on the ground.

"Hello, Pearl," she said, as nice as could be. "I dropped by for a visit with your folks and to see your new baby sister," and that was all there was to it. I sat down, and we had the nicest visit about school and how well Sardius and I are doing. Daddy was the very picture of politeness, and he sat still right there in the living room the whole time.

December 5, 1931
Dear Jonathan,

Thank you for your kind efforts on behalf of my students! I have talked to the Wallace family, and they were quite agreeable that their sons might continue their education in Chicago rather than stay here in East Tennessee to work on the family farm, provided they are able to earn scholarships for their room, board, and tuition. I have not yet told them that you are looking for sponsors for them. It will be delicate, getting them to agree to accept anything they might consider "charity."

Their eldest daughter, Pearl, also is very bright—she may be the brightest of the lot, and although she is only going on 11 years old, she will most certainly be ready for high school at the end of next year. I think it would be best if we could find a family to host her for at least the first year or two. A boarding school might overwhelm her at such a tender age. Once I can convince the family to allow their sons to accept assistance, I will begin to work on them for Pearl's sake. I do not think it would be amiss to tell the family who hosts her that she is available for light housework in return for her room and board. It will sit better with the family if they know Pearl will be earning her keep.

I never thought that having a well-connected friend such as you could be so beneficial to my life as a missionary. I cannot tell you how much I appreciate you going to the trouble to seek out the help of so many important people. Thank you, Jonathan! I pray daily for your health and happiness.

Your friend,

Emily Weston

December 6, 1931. Miss Weston preached from the Book of Esther today. It was about how we all have a Destiny. We may not know what that Destiny will be, but at some point in our lives, we will be called upon to do something important. We might not even know we are fulfilling our Destiny when we do it. We may just be living our ordinary lives, but sometimes we might do something as simple and easy as encourage someone, and that may end up being a great thing. I like the idea of having a Destiny. I am going to try hard to find mine. This also is a good thing to write in my Journal that I turn in tomorrow.

Today is Daddy's last day before he goes off to be a bull for the railroad tomorrow. We had a nice time at Pap-pa's house for dinner. Pap-pa got out his fiddle and played for us, and Miss Janey Jo made us all get up and dance a reel, even Mama. Although she is still very skinny, she has gotten a lot stronger since she was out all night looking for Sapphire, and she danced for a long time before she got too breathless to stay up with the rest of us.

It is a pity that Uncle Woodrow would not dance. I could tell Miss Weston wanted him to dance with her. She kept tapping her foot and looking over in his direction, but he did not look as if he saw her. After a while, he jumped up and went outside. I bet Uncle Woodrow would make a nice husband. I wonder if Miss Weston might be willing to marry him if he asked her?

December 7, 1931
Dear Cecilia,

I am in a terrible quandary—again! The doctor has ordered that the Reverend Miller leave the cold climate for the duration of the winter. He says his heart is so fragile that he is afraid he will get pneumonia breathing the frigid air, and he does not want him to be tempted to bestir himself to help Mrs. Miller bring in wood or to shovel a path to the woodshed. This puts me in a terrible position, for if I stay here, I will be quite alone for the next 4 months! Mrs. Miller's sister has offered to come stay a few days a week with me, but she has a family and that would be placing too much of an obligation on her shoulders.

I do not feel unsafe being here alone. The Millers do not lock their doors, even when they go away overnight, and the people in the community are absolutely harmless. What worries me is that Father and Mother might find out that I am here alone. I have no doubt they will insist I come home immediately, and even petition the board to see that I lose my post here. I have considered asking The Reverend to refrain from letting anyone know—not the board nor anyone in the community, and certainly not Father. Do you think this is dishonest? I know I have already been less than honest with him by implying that someone else is preaching on Sundays. I am quite frantic. If I have to leave here in the middle of the school year, I will be devastated.

Please counsel me, dear sister!

Emily

December 7, 1931
My School Journal, grade 7, Miss Weston's class
By Pearl Wallace

God has given every one of us a destiny. Esther had a very important destiny to save her people from death and destruction, and she fulfilled her destiny very well by being courageous and smart. I hope I have an important destiny and that I will also be courageous and smart when the time comes to fulfill it.

For now, my destiny is to help take care of my baby sisters, and to be nice to my friends and my family. I know it is my destiny to live here and to be a part of my family because I am so happy doing it. I love living on the Little Tennessee River. It is the most beautiful river in the world, and it flows right by my house, just like the River of Life flows by the Throne of God.

December 7, 1931. Daddy left before daylight this morning to go to town with Mr. Sutton, the mailman. He did not wake us up to see him off, which made Beryl sad, but not me. I was having a good dream this morning about it being summertime and I was eating watermelon, and I felt so warm and good I would have hated to get out of bed just to watch him leave and then feel sad about it all the rest of the morning. Just getting up and having him gone makes it feel like any other day. We will see him on Saturday, anyway.

Now that Daddy will be gone during the week, Darlene and her mother are going to come over every day after school so Darlene can look at my school books. I have most of what we need because Daddy bought books for Jasper when he was in the seventh grade, back when Daddy had enough money to buy such things. Mama and Mrs. Carlton also are teaching us to speak French, and we have already learned a lot!

When we got home from school this afternoon, they were already at the house. Even though Mrs. Carlton's head still has that big old sore, we all were in such fine spirits that she did not even care. Uncle Woodrow brought in a whole load of wood for us, and he got the stove to roaring. It got so hot in the kitchen that we moved into the front room for a while, then we young'uns went out to the barn to play with the baby chicks.

Uncle Woodrow told Mama not to bestir herself to make supper, that we could just have cold cornbread and buttermilk, and Mrs. Carlton said she had some apple pie at her place she could go get. Uncle Woodrow left out also to go put on a clean shirt, but the funny thing is, when he came back, he had on the same shirt! He had plumb forgotten to change it. He slapped at his forehead and carried on about how forgetful he has become that he made us laugh until our sides ached. Thinking back, though, it troubles me a little that he could be so forgetful. I wonder if the shell shock is doing that to him?

We had so much fun that we forgot we were supposed to start our lessons together. We put a quilt on the floor in the living room in front of the fireplace and pretended to have a picnic for dinner, then we played Charades.

December 8, 1931. We are doing fine without Daddy. Uncle Woodrow is staying here until we get used to having him gone. Last night he slept in the barn loft, but tonight he disappeared again, which he is wont to do sometimes. I worry about him being out in the cold night, and this night was wet, as well, but Mama said he knew how to take care of himself and not to worry.

Darlene came over and stayed for supper, and then we played Shadow Buff until Ruby got so sleepy she fell asleep on the couch. Mama said Darlene should just stay here for the night because the rain was so cold. Jasper offered to run over and tell Mrs. Carlton, but it turns out that Mama had already mentioned that Darlene might stay so that Mrs. Carlton would not be worried.

I have decided I am not going to worry about getting caught for selling whiskey. Al Capone killed people and did a lot of other bad things, and the law was out to get him for all his meanness. I figure that if they catch me, I will pretend I did not know running whiskey was against the law, and I do not mind pointing the finger at Jake Hatton as my customer, although I would never tattle on Pap-pa. I will make out as if Jake Hatton made me think it was all right and I do not know any better, being just a little girl.

December 9, 1931. I think Mama misses Daddy, although I do not know why. Sometimes I find her just sitting and looking out the window, like she is expecting him to come up the front steps, and she ups and says something nice about him when we are talking about something completely different. It is a mystery to me why she likes him so much. He is not much help to her even when he is here. She is better off with just Sardius, Jasper and Uncle Woodrow, who are always helpful and kind to her. You never know when Daddy is going to be helpful and kind and when he is going to come home drunk and mean. I do not like the feeling we all get when Daddy slips out to the woodshed. We do not know if he is going to have just a sip and come back feeling happy, or if he is going to come back to the house cussing and carrying on. Sometimes I wish he would just stay away all the time so we would not have to put up with the strain of not knowing how he will be.

The little girls have gone to bed, and the rest of us are just sitting around the stove, talking. Mama is sewing, as she always does of an evening, while I write this. Jasper and Sardius are teaching Darlen how to make a cat's cradle. I do not know where Uncle Woodrow is off to.

I love summertime, but winters can be nice, too, because there is not that much to do except stay by the warm stove, play games, and talk.

December 10, 1931. I love being out in the barn these days. Little chicks are the most fun things to play with! Darlene, Beryl, Ruby, and I played out there all afternoon before supper. Uncle Woodrow, Jasper and Sardius were up in the loft raking up some loose hay, and then Jasper and Sardius came down and chased us girls all over the barn. Uncle Woodrow sat up in the loft, his long legs dangling over, looking down on us and laughing fit to be tied.

Mama and Mrs. Carlton cooked up a big supper with biscuits, fried ham, and green beans, and when Mrs. Carlton came out to the barn to call us in, we were ready for it! She looked about as pretty as I have ever seen her. She had on a yellow and red flowery dress with a wide belt that made her waist look small. Her long hair hung down her back in beautiful waves. The front of it was pinned up on top of her head, so that it covered up the sore, and she looked just like an angel. She reached out to ruffle up Ruby's hair, and said, "Ruby, you look like you could use some of my special butternut cake. You all go on in and have your supper, and I am going to run over to my house and get it. I just have to put the icing on it, and I will have it back over here in time for dessert."

Well, supper was delicious, and it was a good thing Mrs. Carlton was late coming back with that cake. We were so stuffed, we barely were able to make room for it. It is too bad Uncle Woodrow did not join us for supper. He sure missed a good one!

Cold, waning days, frozen nights.
Desire fills the air, softening the bitter nights.

My children drown in passion.
Some are fulfilled;
Some drink deep of possibility.

The upright father is filled with pride,
The mother with hope.
The children slumber in their innocence,
But the in-between one aches with loss.

I murmur softly to them all
As the Spirit mourns for those who embrace their rage.

December 11, 1931. At school today, we learned about entrepreneurship. Henry Ford and John D. Rockefeller are entrepreneurs. Miss Weston says that it is entrepreneurs who will pull this country out of the Depression, but Daddy says that the Rockefellers and the Fords are the cause of it, that they built their own riches on the backs of the working man.

I think I agree with Miss Weston. I like to think that I can make my own destiny by being an entrepreneur. Now that I study on it, I think I already am one. I see a need for goods in the community, and I find and sell the needed goods. It is too bad that what I sell is against the law, but then, if it were not, I would not have a business. Daddy says that making whiskey should not be against the law, that the law of nature entitles every man to have the right to use his crops as he sees fit. On the other hand, men like Rockefeller might be acting within the laws of men, but they break what he calls "moral laws." I think that is the same as breaking the laws of God, but I am not sure what all those are.

It is true that God does not like drunkenness, and to put a fine point on it, my selling whiskey would be wrong if I made people drunk, but I have never seen Pap-pa or Jake Hatton drunk. They just sip, which I do not think is wrong in God's eyes. In Proverbs, it says, "Give wine unto those that be of heavy hearts." Everybody has a heavy heart these days. I think this Prohibition law is just wrong. It is making me rich, though, so I will not complain about it.

If I could figure out how to make whiskey myself, I could get rich in a hurry. I would not have to worry so much about when Daddy is going to bring in a new jug, and once word got out, I would have all the customers I could get. All the moonshiners around here weld their stills together with lead, and anybody with any brains at all knows that will poison you. Daddy's still is copper, and he welded it together with pure silver so that his whiskey is the best in the county. He will not sell it, though, because he says he does not want to go to prison, but I know for good and well he is just too lazy to make more than he and his old cronies can drink. That is all right. If he got in on this, he would run me out of business.

The yarn and paper dolls I ordered from Sears & Roebuck came today. Mama was curious that I got a package, but she did not ask. She knows that Christmas is coming up. The paper dolls look so pretty, it was all I could do not to open them and play with them. I know Beryl will love them! I started working on Sardius' hat, but I did not get very far before I had to pull all the stitches out and start over again. I think I may have to get Mama or Miss Janey Jo to help me.

December 12, 1931. Daddy got home good and early this morning, and we were right glad to see him. He told us all about being a railroad bull, how there are a lot of roughnecks who jump on after the train is rolling along. They run beside it for a while, then they grab onto a railcar door and jump up into the car like it is the easiest thing in the world. The bulls look out for them to jump on, but there are so many of them, it is hard to catch them all. He kept us all in stitches telling us about the crazy people who ride the trains.

I worked some more on Sardius' hat, but I think it may be hopeless. I surely will have to get Miss Janey Jo to help. She is an excellent knitter. So is Mama, but I want everything to be a surprise, so I will keep it from her if I can.

I slipped over to Darlene's house this afternoon after I saw Billy Ray's automobile running by up on the road, leaving. Darlene and I went up and sat on the roof for a little while, but then Billy Ray came back, so we scampered back over to the tree and down before he could see us. I lit out for home, before I was tempted to tell him what I thought of him for beating Darlene and her mother.

December 13, 1931. Sapphire is sick. She never was very strong, but now she has a snotty nose and she cries all the time, and she coughs. Mama is feeling poorly, too. She was up all night long with the baby, and Daddy ended up going out to the woodshed, then he came back in and started cussing at Mama and Sapphire, too. This morning Mama was a nervous mess, and I could tell she was torn up because she said she was too tired to go to church. I feel so sorry for my mama I could just cry myself. Sometimes I get so mad at Daddy I wish he was dead. We would be much better off without him. But then, I get to thinking about how he tries so hard to be good to us most of the time, and I feel bad about even thinking that.

If Mama had some money, she could take Sapphire to a doctor. Mama generally does not truck much with doctors, especially the one who tends to people in this holler. He is old and hard of hearing, and he does not seem to know much about anything. Mama calls him an incompetent quack. He was tending Mam-ma on the day she died, and he also was tending to Little Harrison when he died. If she got a doctor for Sapphire, she would need to take her into Maryville to find one who knows his business.

I am going to bed now. I am tired because I was up most of last night listening to Daddy carrying on and Sapphire crying.

December 14, 1931
My School Journal, grade 7, Miss Weston's class
By Pearl Wallace

I am working on Christmas presents because Christmas is right around the corner! I sneak and work on the shirt I am making for my brother Jasper whenever I can, and I work on a tie for my father when Jasper is in the room.

I am making Daddy's tie with scraps from a pair of Pap-pa's old suit pants. When Pap-pa was courting his wife, Miss Janey Jo, he used to get dressed up in his finest suit to go see her. It was a long way to go by road, so he would cut across the pasture. One night he was making his way back home, and a big bull got loose and chased him all over the field. He had to jump over the barbwire fence, got tangled up, and tore his trousers to shreds. I am grateful to that bull! These trousers were made of very good wool, and it will make a fine tie for Daddy.

December 15, 1931. It was so cold this morning, and we were all so tired out from being kept awake by Sapphire's crying that Mama asked Uncle Woodrow to take us to school in the wagon. It felt like a holiday, riding over the icy road. Uncle Woodrow is a great deal of fun. We had a grand time jogging along the old road behind Charley.

We were the first ones to get to the schoolhouse. Miss Weston was very happy to see us. She gave us hot coffee and some biscuits. We had such a grand time! Miss Weston laughed at everything Uncle Woodrow said, and the more she laughed, the funnier he got. By the time the first students got there, we all were just in stiches. I could tell Miss Weston was sad to see our little party come to an end. She walked out to the wagon with Jasper and Uncle Woodrow to say goodbye to them, even though it was past eight o'clock and the students were all at their desks waiting for school to start. It took her a good long while to come back to the classroom, and the boys started acting out something awful while she was gone. Otis Merriweather usually joins in when the boys act out, but today he came over and sat beside me, and when Sam Hutchinson started making fun of us, he turned around and shook his fist at him and told him to get away. Sam backed down right quick because Otis is bigger than he is, and he knows how to use his fists. It is nice to know Sam will leave me alone when Otis is around.

I am mad at Walt Bittertree. Darlene came over to play with me after school today. I ran inside to get us a slice of cornbread, and while I was there, old Walt came in, all in a lather, telling Mama "that little n girl is outside sitting on the porch, looking like she owns the place!" That made Mama and me both mad as blazes, and I almost said something, but Mama put her hand on my head and said, as cool as a cucumber, "Yes, Mr. Bittertree. Darlene is our guest this afternoon. We think highly of her and her mother, and we would appreciate it if anyone who does not share our feelings would not speak disparagingly."

Old Walt looked like Mama had slapped his face. He just stood there for a minute, turning red, then he muttered something about getting on home and high tailed it out of there. I followed him right out to make sure he did not say anything mean to Darlene as he went by. The nerve of him! Walking right into our house and insulting our friend!

December 15, 1931
Darling Cecilia,

It has been the most wonderful day! My students are all working hard. As it turns out, I love living on my own and having the large Miller house all to myself, and this morning, I had a veritable party for breakfast at the schoolhouse. Woodrow and Jasper Wallace brought Pearl, Sardius, and Beryl to school in the wagon because of the bitter cold, and they got here so early, we had a chance to visit. The time just flew by; we were having such an agreeable conversation! Mr. Woodrow is not only very funny, he is extremely intelligent, caring, and thoughtful, as well as being a perfect gentleman. I am glad we have had the chance to become friends. Of course, friendship is all that we claim. I do not worry about him thinking there is more to our relationship than that.

Jonathan is working very hard on behalf of the Wallace children to get them sponsors to attend school when they have completed their studies here. I have been in contact with Wheaton Academy, and they assure me that scholarships are available to extraordinary students who pass rigorous academic standards. They are sending me the appropriate paperwork now so I can begin the testing.

Cecilia, Jonathan seems quite settled in his opinion that he and I are going to get married sometime after the school term is over, but truthfully, I am not nearly as enamored of him as I once was. Being here has broadened me considerably, and I am no longer so awestruck, now that I have had a chance to see a bit of the wider world. I am even considering staying and making my home here. I could easily buy a place here and support myself modestly from Grandfather's legacy, for I have discovered that I prefer the simple life in these hills to the more hectic social atmosphere of Chicago. I am thinking I no longer desire the sumptuous life that Jonathan wants to offer me. What would you think if I decided to settle here permanently?

Of course, I would miss you, Jonas and Thomas, and Mother and Father enormously, but we could visit regularly. Perhaps Mother and Father would consider having a summer home here. The area is so appealing that George Vanderbilt has built an enormous estate near Asheville. I have not yet seen it, but I hear it is an architectural marvel. We would not have to be apart for very long. Besides, our family is all beginning to scatter. Jonas will be married this time next year, Thomas will be traveling with the army, and no doubt, you will be marrying soon, as well. We are all finding our paths in life.

These are just thoughts, Cecilia. I have no definite plans, just dreams, and I must say, I do dream sometimes of building a life here.

Hugs and kisses to you, my sweet sister!

Emily

December 16, 1931. I do not miss Daddy while he is at work. It is nice to come home to some peace and quiet when I get back home from school. Darlene and her mother were at the house this afternoon, and so was Miss Janey Jo. Mrs. Carlton was sitting in the rocking chair singing to Sapphire while Mama took a nap, and Miss Janey Jo was in the kitchen cooking up a mess of black-eyed peas and making onion poultices for Sapphire's little chest. Darlene, Beryl, and I had the best time all afternoon, listening to Darlene's mother sing and playing hopscotch out on the front porch. Uncle Woodrow came by, and he sat beside Mrs. Carlton and joined in with the singing. They all stayed for dinner. By the time they left, Sapphire was doing better. Mama may not have to take her to the doctor after all.

Since we are studying for exams at school, Miss Weston said we did not need to turn in our Journals next week. That is a relief. It is hard to make up stories to tell when there is so much real life going on around me. We are all very tired from studying and listening to Sapphire cry and cough half the night. Tomorrow is my last exam, so I am going to bed early.

December 16, 1931

Dearest Mother and Father,

I am very much looking forward to coming home for the Christmas holidays! I intend to leave first thing Saturday morning and take a leisurely two days to make the drive. My old schoolmate, Jenny Sunlee, who lives in Indianapolis, has invited me to spend the night with her and her family, which will be perfect. I anticipate I will have a whole afternoon and evening to visit with her and catch up on the events of her life. I am absolutely certain that I do not need Thomas and Jonas to come get me. It would be a waste of their time and of gas. I am, after all, 22 years old, quite an adult, and capable of traveling on my own.

The Reverend and Mrs. Miller also are looking forward to being away over the Christmas holidays. He has recovered well enough to make the journey all the way to Miami, Florida, where he has a cousin who has been badgering them to visit. They say they will be glad to get away from the house for a while, especially since they have grown so attached to me that they will feel quite bereft while I am gone. They are such dears to be so fond. I feel as if they have become as close as a favored aunt and uncle. I miss you, and look forward to seeing you very soon.

All my love,

Emily

December 17, 1931. Today is my birthday! Mama made me a big cake, which used up all the eggs she has been saving for several days. The hens are not laying much because there is not enough daylight to keep them going, so I feel special that she has held back enough eggs just to make me a fancy cake. Daddy was not here to help celebrate, but Pap-pa and Janey Jo came over, and we had a fine time. Pap-pa gave me a hair clip. He glued onto it a beautiful rose that he carved out of pine and dyed red. It looks wonderful on my new hairdo. Jasper gave me a big stick of peppermint, Sardius gave me an embroidered handkerchief, Beryl made me a beautiful card, and Ruby gave me a pretty mussel shell she found. Miss Janey Jo made me a new blouse made out of lawn that is very fine and makes me feel grown up. I will save it for Sundays.

Mama made me the best present. She gave me *two* beautiful new dresses! She made them out of Mam-ma's old dresses by taking them apart, then re-cutting them to fit me. One is brown, with white trim. The best part of that one is the white flower

Mama made out of a lace handkerchief (also Mam-ma's) and sewed at the throat. It looks very grown-up and fine. The other one is blue, with a yellow and white collar and cuffs.

Sapphire did not cough once today, I am happy to say. That is her birthday present to me, and I think it is the best one, even better than the dresses.

It has been a very good day.

December 18, 1931. Today was the last day of school before Christmas, and it was special. Miss Weston brought cookies and hot cocoa for all of us! We sang Christmas songs, and there were no lessons at all, except for a Bible lesson. We went outside and cut some pine boughs, then brought them back inside and laid them all around in the windowsills and on the desks. They made the room smell very good! We took turns reading the Christmas Story from Luke, and then we play-acted the scene where Mary and Joseph tried to get rooms at the inn, but were turned away. We had a very good time with the baby doll Miss Weston brought to be baby Jesus.

Otis Merriweather sat down beside me, and no one said a word to us about him being struck on me, so I felt all right talking to him. I told him about how awful Ralph Lee Bittertree was, and he told me about his aunt who is married to a low-down man who beats her, and when his uncles and cousins in his clan over by Madisonville found out, they pummeled the tar out of him. "He'll never lay another hand on my aunt," he said.

Otis' uncle is the Sheriff over in Madison County, so I wondered why they did not sic him on the man. He said it does not do any good to arrest him because the judge will not do anything except tell him to behave better, and it would just make the feller mad and meaner. I think that is a disgrace. The Bible says a man should love his wife like Jesus loves the church, and a man who disregards the words of the Lord is breaking the most important laws, in my opinion. Shame on that judge for not throwing that scoundrel in jail!

I wish the law would protect women against their no-good husbands. It would be nice if Mrs. Carlton could have Billy Ray thrown in jail, but I expect Otis is right that if she tried, it would just make him meaner. A woman just needs to depend on her family to make sure her husband treats her nice. Mama has her daddy only 4 miles away, and even though Daddy has never laid a hand on her, he knows that if he did, she would sic Pap-pa on him. It is nice to know that Otis' clan also takes care of his aunt. I would expect Sardius and Jasper to do the same for me and my sisters, and maybe Daddy, too, although I am not sure I could depend on Uncle Woodrow. He does not have it in him to be rough.

I wish Mrs. Carlton had brothers or a daddy to help her. Maybe I will talk to Sardius and Jasper about it, and my Pap-pa, too. Maybe I can talk them into coming to her rescue. I hope they would come to Darlene's rescue, too, and teach both Billy Ray and Ralph Lee Bittertree a lesson they will not forget.

December 19, 1931. I am happy to say that it is the middle of the day, Daddy is home, and he has not had anything to drink. He has two full jugs out in the woodshed and over a dozen jars, and I found another four jars under the house. This is very good because I have a new customer, and think I may be getting another one soon. Walt Bittertree found out I had a business going from Pap-pa, who accidentally let it slip to him when Mr. Bittertree found him sipping the other day. Although I am mad at him for calling Darlene that nasty name and acting like she has no business at our house, I have to set my feelings aside when it comes to business. He bought a half pint from me.

Also, Jake Hatton says he knows of a fellow over in Big Gully who will take all I can get to him. I wonder if Daddy will notice if I siphon off some and replace it with water? I better not try. It would be a shame to lose my only source of revenue just because I got greedy.

This afternoon, Pap-pa took me over to Greenbrier store where I finished most of my Christmas shopping. I got a beautiful pure linen handkerchief embroidered with tiny roses for Miss Weston. It cost 25c. I also got some peppermint candy for Darlene and Ruby. I waited until Pap-pa's back was turned, and then I was able to sneak and buy him some pipe tobacco. It is Virginia's Finest, the most expensive brand, but I figure I got most of my money from him, so it is good to give it back. I am not getting a Christmas present for Jake Hatton. He is a pretty good customer, but he is not kin, and I do not count him as a friend.

December 20, 1931. Today was the last day of church before Miss Weston goes home to Chicago for Christmas. It was a beautiful service. Some of the men had come early and had built up a big fire in the stove, and the piney smell from our school decorations was strong in the air. Mixed with the smell of wood smoke, it all seemed delicious. Miss Weston preached on pretty much the same thing she had told us about on Friday. We sang Christmas carols, and then Miss Weston passed around hot chocolate to everyone and handed out peppermint sticks to all the children. It was the best Sunday service to which I have ever been!

She came to Pap-pa's house for dinner again, which makes me very happy. Daddy always acts like such a gentleman around her when he is sober, so I do not have to worry about him scundering us all. Uncle Woodrow is always a gentleman, and so is Pap-pa. I think Miss Weston enjoys being around us all. Of course, Mama and Miss Janey Jo are very sweet to her, and Uncle Woodrow can keep her laughing about the whole time. She tries to behave ladylike when he gets to teasing her, then her face turns red, and she starts to giggle, then she just busts out laughing. It is good to see her having such a good time with us.

I gave Miss Weston her handkerchief, which made her cry, and then she laughed and said, "Pearl, your handkerchief is coming in handy right now!" as she dabbed at her eyes with it. She is the sweetest lady and the best teacher I ever had.

Daddy did not have a drop to drink all day. Hallelujah!

December 21, 1931. I am glad Darlene and I are free to go back and forth between our houses any time we want to except on Saturday and Sunday when Daddy and Billy Ray are home. Mrs. Carlton and Darlene stay over at our place almost all the time during the week. Mama and Mrs. Carlton cook up a storm, and you never smelled such good smells as what comes out of our kitchen on those days! Uncle Woodrow and the boys say that Billy Ray and Daddy are missing the best parts of the week. It gets dark so early now, we eat supper by lantern light, then sit around in front of the fireplace, play games, and feel as if we are on top of the world.

Sapphire is two months old today. She is doing very well, and Mama seems as fit as ever. I think Mrs. Carlton is good for both of them. Darlene and I are learning French up a storm. Darlene has a head start on me, being Cajun and speaking it since she was a baby, but I am catching up fast. Mama says I have a knack for it. *Je suis heureux à ce sujet.* That is French for "I am happy about that."

December 22, 1931. *Nous préparons pour* Christmas! Jasper, Sardius, and Uncle Woodrow cut down a pretty little cedar and dragged it into the front room, where it takes up a whole corner. It makes the house smell sweet. Mama had a few chestnuts to put in the coals, which she said were likely the last we would get because the blight has pretty much taken out all the chestnut trees around here. We had a good time roasting them and cutting out paper snowflakes for the tree. It was a cozy, happy time. Of course, Mrs. Carlton and Darlene were here to help trim the tree. They brought over a pecan pie that was the best thing I have ever tasted.

I have Christmas presents for everyone, thanks to my business income. Jake Hatton has bought a whole quart of whiskey, for which he paid me cash without arguing about it! Pap-pa buys a half-pint about every month. I do not think Walt Bittertree will be buying very much. I always thought he was a teetotaler, so I was surprised that he wanted any at all. I do not count Jake Hatton's friend as a customer yet because you should never count your chickens before they hatch. I do not worry that I have spent all my money, though, because I know there is always someone out there who is thirsty.

I have all my Christmas presents ready. For Mama, I have wool mittens that I knitted myself. I made Daddy a bow tie to wear to church. For Jasper, I have a new shirt I made, with Miss Janey Jo's help. It is blue. Sardius will have a certificate that says "Bravest Brother Award." He will know that is for taking up for me when Sam Hutchinson called me a name. I also have finished his wool hat, finally! It turned out exactly as I hoped it would. I have paper dolls for Beryl and peppermint candy for Ruby. For Sapphire, I have the beautiful, beautiful pink dress!

I got some peppermint candy for Darlene, but I don't have anything for Mrs. Carlton except for a card that I have made. I drew a picture of the river view from the top of her roof and colored it with colored pencils. I think it looks very pretty.

For Pap-pa, I have pipe tobacco, and I also will give him a pint of Daddy's whiskey, but I will slip and do it when nobody is looking. Miss Janey Jo will get three white goose feathers I found and dyed pink with beet juice. They are very pretty, and they will make a fancy touch for her hat.

Uncle Woodrow: I made him a patchwork pillowcase out of bright red, yellow, blue, and white scraps from Miss Janey Jo's scrap bag. It will look good on his bed.

I already gave Miss Weston a handkerchief.

I am ready for Christmas!

December 23, 1931. Today is the day of the winter solstice, the darkest day of the year. From now on the days get longer and brighter. Tomorrow is Christmas Eve! I can hardly wait!

We have not had snow yet, but it is cold enough to snow. I am hopeful because it is easier for Santa Claus to take off in his sleigh if there is a good snow on the ground, and that makes it more likely that he will make it all the way back to this holler. This year I am hoping he will bring me some rubber boots to wear over my shoes so that my feet do not get wet on sloppy days, but I reckon I would be happy if he would just find a way to keep my daddy from getting drunk, for Billy Ray to stop beating Darlene and her mother, and for my mama and Sapphire to be strong. I know all that is a lot to ask, but we are allowed to dream at Christmastime.

> *Cold days, icy nights.*
> *The Earth stands immobile and frozen,*
> *But I surge beyond my banks,*
> *Reaching for the Orb who beckons with her silvery cry.*
> *We will dance for days in the splendor.*
> *Joy seeps from the warm houses,*
> *The Spirit smiles to see love flourishing in the stillness.*

December 24, 1931. It is Christmas Eve! It is also the full moon, the one the Cherokee call the Full Cold Moon. This will be the third full moon in a row that Daddy has not gone foxhunting. It is like a miracle.

I went over to Darlene's house to give her and her mother my presents, but they were not home, so I left them on the porch. I hope Billy Ray does not steal them.

December 25, 1931. *Joyeux Noël!* This has been a wonderful, wonderful day. Daddy came home late last night after we were all already asleep. He brought very many packages with him that Santa had given him to give to us. Daddy says Santa sometimes has a hard time making it all the way back into our holler, and so he brought our presents to Maryville early and gave them to Daddy to give to us.

They were all just wonderful. I did not get my boots, but I got a packet of writing paper and a whole set of colored pencils, new stockings, and some warm gloves. And peppermint candy! And an orange! Everyone loved the presents I gave them, too. Mama wore her mittens all day. She almost did not take them off for dinner. Miss Janey Jo got her best hat and stuck all three goose feathers in it, and then she wore it the rest of the day.

For dinner, we had a huge feast of ham with gravy, biscuits, corn, green beans that Miss Janey Jo had canned over the summer, sweet potatoes, white potatoes, and turnips. For dessert, we had fruitcake with raisins. I think this was the best Christmas we ever had.

Daddy did not drink one drop of whiskey today. Daddy and Uncle Woodrow played for us while we all danced, including Mama. We all took turns dancing with Sapphire, who was wearing the dress I got her. It was too big, but Mama tied a ribbon around it and cinched it in so it looked fine. It will fit her perfectly for Easter.

December 26, 1931. Daddy was sober all day again today, which makes me think that maybe Santa Claus got my message, but I have my doubts because I know things are worse for Darlene and her mother. Darlene came over by herself with goat milk for Sapphire, and some delicious bread that we ate for dinner, but Mrs. Carlton did not come. Darlene does not ever lie to me, but tonight she told a big one. She said that her mother did not come because she would rather stay with her husband when he has been gone all week. We all know that Billy Ray does not give Mrs. Carlton the choice. He will not let her step foot out of the house when he is home.

Darlene did not ask, but she had her nightgown with her, which meant that she was hoping we would invite her to spend the night, which Mama did, even though Daddy gave her the evil eye. Then, when Mama offered to let Darlene take a bath, she turned her down, saying she had already had a bath. That was a lie, also. She is a little stinky. I am afraid she might have some bruises and cuts she does not want us to see. I can tell Mama is thinking the same thing.

We all got quiet, wondering what that mean old Billy Ray is doing to them. It is best to keep quiet in the face of other people's troubles so they do not think you are pitying them, but I would give anything to make Darlene feel safe and happy.

December 28, 1931. Daddy left early this morning as usual, and Billy Ray did, too, so Mrs. Carlton and Darlene came over for about all day. We played games again, and Mrs. Carlton and Darlene stayed through supper. By then it was time to go milk, so Uncle Woodrow was very nice to walk Mrs. Carlton across the creek. Darlene stayed here to help us do our own chores, and then we waited for Uncle Woodrow to come back so we could keep on with our games, but I reckon he went on to bed up in the loft because he never came back. I wish he would not just disappear like that. At least he does not disappear for long, as he used to. These days he disappears only for a few hours at a time. I suppose we should count our blessings. Darlene is going to stay the night again tonight. That is a blessing!

Cold days, bitter nights
Lovers lie together snug among feathers,
While children play nearby in warmth.
All is safe when the cruel one is away,
But Darkness lies waiting amid the naked greenleaves.

The Earth sleeps, but even in her sleep,
She turns her face toward the bright brother.
I run silent, holding my silver children close.

December 29, 1931. Today was very fun. Beryl, Darlene, and I slept late because we had been up most of the night swapping stories. When we woke up, it seemed very bright outside, and we could hear Jasper, Sardius, and Uncle Woodrow out there laughing and hollering. When we looked out the window, there was snow all over the ground! Of course, we rushed right out to play in it, even before we ate any breakfast. Darlene, who had never seen snow before, could not believe her eyes. She kept picking up globs of it and licking it off her fingers.

We built snow forts and had a big snowball fight. Darlene does not have any mittens, so Jasper was sweet to take his off and give them to her to wear. Then he could not help much with the snowman we made, so he just stood aside, telling us what to do while he kept his hands in his pockets. We put the hat I knitted for Sardius on him, and then Jasper ran in and got Daddy's kilt, which we got to keep on him for just a little bit because Mama came rushing out the minute she saw it and made us take it right off. She said Daddy would kill us if he knew we were treating his kilt so badly. That made Uncle Woodrow laugh because he thinks Daddy is silly the way he carries on about the Wallace clan and what he calls his "heritage." Uncle Woodrow does not even wear a bit of tartan pinned to his shirt when he goes to the Highland Games.

Afterward, we made snow-ice cream, which was delicious!

December 31, 1931. This is New Year's Eve. We are all going over to Pa-pa's house to spend the night. Even Darlene is going with us. I hope we can stay awake until Midnight to ring in 1932! The fun in the snow is still going on.

January

January 1, <u>1932</u>!!! Happy New Year! 1932 is here at last! It snowed again last night, so we got to go sledding down Pap-pa's big hill. Everyone but Darlene, Beryl, Ruby, and I went home to tend to the chores, so it was just us girls with Miss Janey Jo all day long. She dug out Mam-ma's big work boots for me to wear so I would not get my new shoes wet. They were way too big for me, but I put on four pairs of socks, and although I was very clumsy walking around in them, I was fine once I got on the sled. She also found a pair of mittens for Darlene, which she said Darlene could keep. Miss Janey Jo is very kind. I am glad Pap-pa married her, even if he did not wait a decent interval after Mam-ma died.

When it was about time to go home, Miss Janey Jo asked us to stay for supper and to sleep over again. We were ascared that our mamas would be worried about us, but Pap-pa said he would just ride over there and let them know we would be home tomorrow. When he came back, he had Sardius with him. We had a grand supper, then Pap-pa played his fiddle and Miss Janey Jo brought out some material she had put aside, and we made a little rag doll for Sapphire while Sardius and Pap-pa whittled out some legs for it. I barely can keep my head up to write this. We stayed up past Midnight last night, and now it is ten o'clock, and I am very, very sleepy.

They say what you do on New Year's Day sets the tone and that you will do the same thing every day for the whole rest of the year. If that is the case, then I will do nothing but play all year long.

January 2, 1932. Darlene and I slept late this morning. Sardius had already walked home before we got up, and Pap-pa drove us home in the buggy so we would not get our shoes muddy. The snow is melting, making the path just one big pig sty. Darlene went straight home, and I did not see her the rest of the day.

As soon as she left, Daddy took a bag of sugar out of the cupboard and disappeared. Uncle Woodrow said he was going to check on the raft Sardius and Jasper were building over in his old shed. I asked him if I could go with him, but Mama reminded me that I needed to help Ruby with her reading. Mama has been too busy to help her much, and she is afraid she will forget the words she already knows if we do not keep working with her.

Ruby loves *Baby Chatterbox*, especially the part where baby keeps saying, "Baby, baby, baby loves kitty, kitty, kitty, and kitty, kitty, kitty loves baby, baby, baby." She reads it over and over and then laughs her head off, and reads it again! It plagues me to death. I have been trying to get her interested in *The Wind in the Willows*, which is one of my favorites, but she keeps wanting to go back to *Baby Chatterbox*. After we had read it about ten times, she finally let me read *The Wind in the Willows* to her. She remembered some of the words and picked them out without my help. I am very proud of her.

January 3, 1932. Darlene spent the night with us again last night. She showed up right after supper with a bruise on her cheek, so I knew she had had a rough time with Billy Ray. I know that is why her mother lets her come and stay at our house so much, to keep her away from him.

Although we went to bed early, we did not go to sleep. After Beryl and Ruby fell asleep, we were still talking, and Darlene told me the worst thing! She asked me if I knew where babies came from. I told her I surely did, being as how I have seen firsthand how worn out Mama gets every time she has to go out looking in the cabbage patches for a new little one. Then Darlene said that was wrong, and that babies come from something just awful that fathers do to mothers. I do not know where she heard that outlandish tale. I tried to tell her she was wrong, but she got very quiet and would not answer me. After a while I figured she was asleep, but then I heard her crying. She would not say what the matter was, but she let me put my arms around her and pet her for a little while, until she got quiet again.

I feel so sorry for Darlene, I could just cry myself. I would like to talk to Mama about what she told me, but I'm ascared she will think something is wrong in the head with Darlene and she might not let me play with her any more. I do not know where she heard that awful tale about what men do. I know my own Daddy is a sorry drunk, but he would never do that to my sweet Mama. She would leave him and go back to her daddy if he tried.

January 4, 1932. Today was the first day of school in 1932. We did not have many lessons today. Miss Weston was tired after her long trip. She drove all the way from Chicago by herself. She is very brave!

Darlene came over right before supper because Billy Ray is not working over at Big Creek this week on account of the weather over there is too bad, and he is in a black mood. She had her nightdress in a sack, tied up so that it looked like a big, soft ball. We were out in the front yard, tossing it back and forth, when Ralph Lee Bittertree came into the yard.

I cannot stand Ralph Lee Bittertree's hide. He is the meanest boy, and about as ugly as they come, with a long, scrawny neck and a big Adam's apple that bobs up and down when he talks. He has yellow teeth and greasy hair, and he always has a scrawny stubble on his chin. I just hate the sight of him.

Anyway, we were tossing the sack back and forth, and all of a sudden, he ran up and grabbed it out of Darlene's hand, and he shook it out and flapped her nightdress around, holding it up to himself, mincing around like a silly woman. Darlene tried to snatch it from him, and he hauled off and backhanded her, threw the nightdress down in the mud and stomped on it! I got so mad I punched him in the stomach, but he hit me back, hard, and then he said, "You little n— lover! You just wait till the fellers over by Madisonville get their hands on you and your n—friend. They'll burn down both your houses!" and then he stalked off. Before he got out of the yard, he turned and spit at us.

I was so mad I ran into the house to tell Mama, but Jasper caught me on the front porch before I got inside. He said, "Don't go telling on him to Mama, Pearl. It will just rile her." Then put his arm around me and Darlene until we both felt a little better. Darlene was whimpering, but as soon as he started petting her, she snuggled up against him and quit sniffling.

I wish I could kill Ralph Lee Bittertree dead, and I wish I could kill Billy Ray dead, too. That job Billy Ray is doing can be dangerous, and it would be fitting if he got knocked in the head taking apart one of those big machines. Darlene and Mrs. Carlton would be as free as birds!

After supper, we all sat around the fire and swapped stories. Uncle Woodrow seemed a little blue, so we tried to cheer him up by singing rounds. It didn't work very well. He just got more and more sad, and then he finally got up and went out to the barn to go to sleep.

It is past my bedtime. Darlene and Beryl are already asleep, so I think I will go to bed, too.

January 6, 1931
My darling sister,

I am back in East Tennessee, safe and sound, and none the worse for my journey. I quite like driving across the country! The time alone is perfect for meditation.

It was so good to see you again, but now that our visit is over, I find I am missing you more than ever. How I wish you could come stay in this beautiful old house with me! It feels quite empty with the Millers gone, but I have surprised myself in that I do not feel at all lonely. Rather, aside from missing you, I find myself feeling gloriously emancipated. I come and go as I please, although there are not very many places I have to go. Perhaps I will take advantage of the fine weather we are having and go for a drive up in the mountains to enjoy the spectacular winter wonderland.

I did enjoy seeing Jonathan again, but to be honest, Cecilia, he does not seem quite the dashing man I always have imagined him. I care for him, yes, but after getting to know the people here—their independence, their hardiness—Jonathan seems rather sedate and stodgy. He has his routines, his work, his friends. It is all so predictable. I am not certain I would be happy living the kind of life I have imagined living with any man from our set.

Enough of this! As I told you, I spent the whole trip back here, which I am beginning to consider "home," in meditation, and have made some surprising discoveries about myself.

Much love,
Emily

January 6, 1932. I am over the moon! The wig company has sent me $43 and Mama $56!!! They said my hair was a beautiful color, and very much in demand, although it was so fine it could be made into only one wig. Mama's hair is thick and over two feet long, and could be made into several. It is light brown, which is not as highly regarded as the color mine is. Now we are rich! Mama says this will be our special secret and we should not tell anyone about it, except Mrs. Carlton. She especially does not want Daddy to know about it because she wants to spend it the way she wants to, and not how he wants to. Her plan is to tithe ten percent, plus a little extra to go to missionaries in Africa or India, to help the children who are starving over there. The rest she will save for Sardius to go to high school next year. She might have to spend a little bit on the roof, also. Daddy does not like it when she gives money away, especially when she sends it to missionaries. He says we cannot afford to give money to savages over in Africa when we are all starving to death here. Mama sees it differently, though. She says if we give faithfully to the Lord out of the bounty we have received, He will always provide for our needs. That makes tithing the best investment there is.

Mama gave me $5 of my money to do as I wished. I decided to tithe on the whole $43 right now so I do not have to keep up with how much I owe the Lord. Ten percent of $43.00 is $4.30, which leaves me only 70c to spend, but it is better to make sure the Lord has His whole portion without having it hanging over my head. However, with Jake Hatton coming over so often, and getting me new customers, my money stash is growing quickly. Mama is right. I have tithed faithfully, and the bounty keeps coming!

The rest of my hair money she put into an envelope and hid under the floorboards under the rag rug in the front room. She said it should be saved for when I graduate from the eighth grade. I can use it to pay for room and board in Maryville if Daddy is not able to put me in his boarding house when I am in high school. Of course I want to save it. It is nice to know I do not have to worry about how much money Daddy will be making in a year and a half. I will be able to go to high school even if he has lost his job again.

January 7, 1931
Dear Jonathan,

I am back safe and sound, and as promised, here is the letter I said I would write to you as soon as I got the chance. The drive down was just lovely, and it gave me time to think about the conversations we had over the holidays.

I must admit, coming home for Christmas was not quite what I expected. The swirl of parties and all the excitement was more than I have become accustomed to, and I found it a bit overwhelming. You must forgive me if I seemed distant and preoccupied. I did not mean to—it's just that I found myself feeling out of place. Dedicating myself to the Lord's work has changed me in ways I did not imagine, and I find it difficult to step easily back into the gay life I once found so comfortable and fun.

As for our more private conversations, I admit that I am not fully resolved as to what the Lord is leading me to do. I know you think I will be best utilized in His work as your wife and helpmeet, but you have not seen the work that I do here, how important it is, and how much of a difference I am making in the lives of these people I have come to care for so deeply. Please forgive me for not being able to give you an answer at this time. I have much to take care of here before I can begin to consider moving back to Chicago. Getting some of the brighter children out of this unbearably hard life, finding a way to get them educated and on the road to reaching their full potential, is my first priority. I know you understand this, and I am so very grateful that you have gone to such lengths to help me.

I remain always your devoted friend,

Emily

January 7, 1932. Darlene did not come over today, and I had to tend to Ruby so I did not get to go over to her house. I hope she is well, but I am worried about her. It is probably too cold for her to walk over here. She has the new coat I won at Miss Weston's contest, but being from a warm place, her blood is thin and she can't stand the cold wind. I am glad Miss Janey Jo gave her those mittens, and now I wish she had a warm cap. Miss Janey Jo also gave me Mam-ma's work boots, so I am wearing them when I walk to and from school. It wears me out to walk in them, but it saves my new shoes from the mud and the wet. I change into my new ones when I get close to school so no one sees that I am wearing a dead woman's old shoes.

There is not much going on around here. Uncle Woodrow has disappeared again, Jasper is busy whittling out an airplane, and Sardius is studying. Beryl wants to play with her paper dolls, but Ruby will get into them and tear them up if we let her see them, so I have nothing to do but play with Ruby, and it is too cold to stay outside. I wish Darlene would come over.

January 8, 1932. I went over to see Darlene before supper just to say hello. Her mother met me at the door, but she did not invite me in. She just stood behind the door, cracked it opened a little bit and said that Darlene could not come out because they both were sick.

Mrs. Carlton was acting so funny I wanted to know if Darlene was really sick or if maybe Billy Ray had hurt her again. I climbed up on the roof and sat there a while, but I never heard anything, so I came on back down and came home. I sure do hope that it clears up over at Big Creek so Billy Ray can get back to work over there. Maybe he will go back and a big snow will come and he will freeze to death. He could thaw out in hell. That would serve him right!

Miss Weston came by soon after that with a pretty little sweater for Sapphire. She had already given her a blanket that day she came when I had to crawl in the back window and put on Mama's skirt, but today she said she loves buying baby clothes. Since Sapphire is the only little baby she knows, she could not help herself.

Miss Weston also brought two dresses for Darlene! She said they were left over from the carnival, and she did not know what to do with them, and was hoping that Darlene could put them to good use, to keep them from going to waste. I was so happy about that I wanted to run get Darlene to come right over, but by then it was time for supper, and I remembered that she was feeling bad. I hope we can give them to her tomorrow.

Uncle Woodrow came in while Miss Weston was here, and she started acting funny. She kept glancing over to him and laughing at just about everything he said, and when Mama invited Miss Weston to stay for supper, she said she had to get on back home, and then looked at Uncle Woodrow and asked if it was safe to go out to her car in the dark by herself. He jumped right up to walk out with her. I think maybe she is struck on him. I wonder if he is struck on her, also. It would be wonderful if my Uncle Woodrow and Miss Weston got married! I wonder what I can do to make them like each other better.

January 9, 1932. When Daddy got home this morning, he seemed very tired and sick. He and Mama went into the bedroom, and I could hear them talking. It made me sad. I wish I did not feel sorry for Daddy, but he did seem pitiful. I wonder if he does not like having to tell those hobos they have to get off the train? I surely would not like to have to do it.

This is a mean old Depression that is making everyone suffer, but Daddy says as soon as we kick the Republicans out of the White House, things will get back on track. Daddy thinks it will be between Mr. Smith and Mr. Roosevelt, and he is pulling for Mr. Roosevelt because he is the best man for the job. It is impossible that Mr. Hoover will be reelected because he has done everything in his power to ruin the country, along with all the other Republicans who have been in government ever since ugly old Abe Lincoln, who denied us our state's rights.

I am happy that Mama will be able to vote for Mr. Roosevelt, too. Miss Weston says that women were not able to vote until 1920, which I think is the most disgraceful thing ever. Imagine, one half of the population the United States not being able to vote for who is going to run the country!

I think that women make better decisions than men do. They are not as hotheaded, and they do not get into shouting matches. It was women who got whiskey outlawed, also. Some of them got tired of seeing their husbands coming home drunk, spending all the money on liquor that was supposed to be used for food, that they just said they were not putting up with it any more. I am not sure how they did it, but they got the Constitution changed so that not a drop of whiskey is allowed to be in the whole of the country.

I wish Mama could just put her foot down like the women in the Temperance Movement did and not let Daddy make any whiskey, although if she did, I would not have a job today. It is funny to think about it. Not letting Daddy make whiskey would run me out of business, but not letting anybody in the country have whiskey makes me rich! If it had not been for the Women's Temperance Movement, I would not have a job.

January 10, 1932. Beryl, Jasper, and I sang *Shall We Gather at the River* today at church. Miss Weston had not asked us to prepare anything, but just before the service started, she asked us if we could do it since we missed singing it back when Sapphire was born. Mama mentioned that the boys were good singers, too, so Miss Weston asked them to join us. Jasper did, but Sardius would not. He is too bashful to sing in public. We did a good job, I think.

Frozen days and nights.
Ice rims my banks,
I murmur quiet lullabies to my silver children.
They lie cold and languid in the deep shadows.
The Great Darkness suckles danger in the forest,
Even as the flaming Orb speeds his entry into the days.

January 10, 1932
Dear Cecilia,

It has been cold and dreary here. My classes are going well, but it seems that no one is as happy as they normally are. Today, I went to dinner as usual at the Aiken home, but a gloomy pall hung over the table. I am afraid Woodrow is sinking into a black mood. He did not even speak to me today, other than to greet me perfunctorily, and he barely looked at me during the entire afternoon. It was depressing to see him so low.

His black mood affected everyone else, as well. The conversation at the table is usually lively, but today hardly anyone spoke at all. I tried to initiate some banter, but it was lost in the general glum atmosphere. Now I feel strangely restless and lonely. Hopefully, tomorrow will be much brighter!

I miss you, dear sister.

Emily

January 11, 1932
My School Journal, grade 7, Miss Weston's class
By Pearl Wallace

My Uncle Woodrow is a very fine man. He served in the Great War in France, where he learned to speak the language very well. He already knew French because he learned it as a child. He went to a very good boarding school where they taught him all the classics, including French and German. He also knows some Latin.

Uncle Woodrow also is good at fixing things. He helps out around our house a lot. He helps in the fields, plowing, planting, and harvesting. He also helped to fix our roof when it sprang a leak during a big storm recently. Uncle Woodrow is kind to animals and to everyone he meets.

I think it is time for him to get married. He would make a very good husband for a woman who is educated and who enjoys reading, especially if she knows the Bible well and likes conversations about it.

January 12, 1932. It was warmer today. Darlene and I went down to the creek after I got home from school. We were looking for crawdads, and all of a sudden, I could see Jake Hatton standing on the other side, hiding behind a tree, motioning to me. Of course, Darlene saw him, so I broke down and told her about my side business. I know I can trust her. We both have secrets that we can trust the other to keep.

Poor old Jake was twitchier than ever today, muttering and cussing, and that made Darlene get tickled. She kept a straight face while we were talking to him, but when we headed to the woodshed to get his whiskey, she got to snickering, and then she busted out laughing. I tried to shush her, but she laughed so hard she got me tickled, too, and the next thing we knew, we were about beside ourselves, laughing and running up to the woodshed.

She helped me to siphon off a half-pint, and then she decided she wanted to try some whiskey. I warned her about how nasty it is, but she just turned the jug up and took a big swig! You should have seen the face she made! I got tickled and laughed so hard that it turned over her funny box again, and we were just killing ourselves trying not to make any noise, but we did! Jasper stuck his head into the woodshed to see what the ruckus was about.

He caught us red-handed with our hands on the jugs, and of course, he thought we were drinking! He gave us a stern talking to, but we convinced him that Darlene just wanted to try a taste and that she hated it, and I hate it also. I think he believed us. I hope so. I made him promise not to tell Mama, and he swore he would not, if I promised him never to drink again. He made us leave the woodshed before he finally left us alone. We pretended that we were headed back to the creek, and then, after he left, we snuck back to finish pouring off a half-pint for Jake Hatton. We were able to slip back over the creek without anybody else seeing us. It was a close call, but it was funny at the same time.

It was all we could do to keep our faces straight while we were giving Jake his whiskey. Darlene kept turning her back, and I could see her shoulders shaking. It is a good thing Jake was so happy to get it that he did not even notice her. I told Darlene I could use another customer, if she needs me to supply her some whiskey, and she said I was crazy to even think it!

After we gave him his half-pint and I got my 25c, we went walking across the creek, over to the big beech grove. That is such a pretty place, even in the wintertime because the leaves stay on the trees and they are such a nice, buttery color that they make the cold winter sunshine glow as soft as summertime. The Cherokee believed that a beech grove was sacred, and so are oak groves and the groves of other trees that keep their leaves all winter long.

I got to telling Darlene a story about a haint who used to live in beech groves, and I had just gotten to the real scary part when we heard a rustling in a rhododendron hell right beside us. I about jumped out of my skin, thinking it was a bear, while Darlene thought it was the wood spirit coming to eat somebody. She grabbed onto me, about dragging me down to the creek! It turned out to be just her mother, thrashing her way through the rhododendron, her hair all messed up from getting it tangled up in the branches. She sort of looked like a haint for a minute! Darlene and I shrieked, and then, when we saw who it was, we nearly died laughing. How her mother got caught up in a rhododendron hell mystifies me! Once you get into those things, it is near impossible to get back out again. It would be like a wood spirit had got ahold of you. Mrs. Carlton jumped when she saw us, too, and she hollered out real loud, "Darlene! Pearl! How come you to be here?" Then we all had a good laugh over it.

January 13, 1932. Beryl caught a chill and so did not go to school today. Sardius and I left early because it takes me so much longer to walk in Mam-ma's old boots, so we got to the ridge in time to watch the sun come up. Although it was freezing, we stopped and sat on a log to watch it blaze up as if the world were on fire. It was one of the prettiest mornings I have seen in a while, and just about freezing to death was worth it to see that sunrise.

Today, Miss Weston asked Sardius to stay behind after school. After everyone else left, Otis Merriweather hung about at the door fussing with his coat and gloves. I could tell he was waiting on me. He always likes to tell me goodbye at the end of the day.

Miss Weston wanted Sardius to stay for about an hour, but he did not want me to walk home alone in the cold. Then, guess what? Otis Merriweather jumped up and offered to walk me home! It was a good thing no one else was still in the room to see that. I would have been scundered to death! Miss Weston put her hands on Otis' shoulders and told him to take good care of me and to be a gentleman, and Otis turned about a hundred shades of red, but he promised solemnly, which made me feel like a grand lady.

I am glad I got to walk with Otis. I have been thinking about how his uncles and cousins took care of his aunt when her husband beat her, and I wonder if there is a way we could stop Billy Ray from being so mean to Mrs. Carlton and Darlene. I cannot imagine my daddy and my Uncle Woodrow going over to teach Billy Ray a lesson, so I asked Otis if his family ever go take care of women outside their clan. He said, yes, they keep an eye out in all the communities around here for anything that needs to be taken care of, and you do not have to be in the clan, or even Scottish, for them to come to your aid.

We talked a long time, and I ended up telling him about how Billy Ray Carlton beat Darlene bloody with a strop and hit her in the face, and how he knocked Mrs. Carlton's head against the kitchen stove, and he said he would talk to his uncle about getting his clan over there to knock some sense into Billy Ray. I felt much better after talking to him. Otis is about the nicest boy I know outside of my brothers, although he is a little rough sometimes. I hope his uncle and cousins can make sure Billy Ray leaves Darlene and her mother alone from here on out.

I went over to Darlene's house to tell her about it, but no one was home.

January 14, 1932. Guess what happened yesterday? Arkansas just swore in the first woman to the U.S. Senate! Mrs. Hattie Caraway is actually from Tennessee, having been born and raised right here in our own Great State, so I know she will do an excellent job.

Miss Weston says that women do not belong in politics because they are exposed to too much ugliness, and on that she and Daddy agree. However, Miss Janey Jo, Mama, and I have different opinions. I hope Miss Hattie Caraway can do something to end this Depression we are in, and I am glad she is against ending Prohibition. If people can buy whiskey legally, then my business will be over, and I will be too plumb broke to buy new shoes for Easter. Miss Weston also is in favor of keeping prohibition, but for a different reason than I am! Ha ha! It is a good thing she will never see this version of my Journal.

Jasper caught Ralph Lee Bittertree peeping through Mama's bedroom window this evening. He was just coming in from milking and found him with his face mashed right up to the glass and his hands cupped around his eyes. Jasper threw a rock at him, and he lit out through the woods. He did not see anything because Mama was in the kitchen at the time. She tacked up a quilt across her windows to keep that nosey Ralph Lee from peeping in again, and we will be sure to keep an eye out for him. I surely hope his daddy has not told him anything about my side business. He might have been peeping in to catch me at it. I would not be surprised if he sics the law on me.

This is all I have time to write. Darlene is coming over to spend the night again tonight, and I have to take Jake Hatton a pint of whiskey before she gets here. He has a friend who wants it. As much as I love Darlene, I think it is better if I do not take her along. I do not need her making fun of Jake Hatton. She gets to mocking him, and you should see her hippy-hopping, cussing and twitching, just exactly like he does. Now, neither one of us can keep a straight face when we see him.

January 15, 1932. A funny thing happened today. I was on my way to Darlene's house and saw a big buck standing right out in the clearing by the creek, then he went moseying off into the woods, and I followed him. I sort of wish I had had a rifle with me, because I know I could have got him, and he would have made some fine eating, but I did not, so I had to content myself with just looking and following. He went over to beech grove, which is so pretty with the light coming though the leaves and turning the whole place into a glowing fairyland.

When I was coming through there, I saw Uncle Woodrow and Mrs. Carlton sitting on a log under the giant tree, and they were having the biggest time, laughing. Uncle Woodrow then stood up, took his hat off, took her hand, and bowed low, and she laughed again. I felt funny coming up on them like that, and I did not want them to think I was spying on them, so I eased back and went on over to Darlene's. I keep going over in my mind about why they were sitting there laughing, and it makes me feel odd and a little scared. I bet that if Billy Ray Carlton could see that he would be fit to be tied.

I mentioned it to Darlene, but she just shrugged and said sometimes her mama likes to go for a walk in the woods alone, and maybe she just happened to come across Uncle Woodrow. I reckon that is what happened.

January 16, 1932. Daddy is home for today and tomorrow. He is not drinking as far as I can tell, but he seems dull, not at all like he usually is when he is sober. I hope he is not sick.

I did not see Darlene today. I wanted to go over to see her, but Mama up and decided that we young'uns should go spend the day with Pap-pa, and she shooed us out the door right after breakfast. She even let us take Ruby along. Jasper carried her on his shoulders most of the way.

I am glad we went, even though it seemed strange not to spend time with Daddy or with Darlene. We had a good time with Miss Janey Jo and with Pap-pa. Pap-pa and Jasper each whittled out a cross for Beryl and me to wear around our necks. Pap-pa's was a little better, but not much. I let Beryl have that one to keep Jasper from feeling bad about not being as good a whittler as Pap-pa is. Sardius did not play with us much. He mostly sat by the fire and read his book. He is getting very serious about school these days.

Miss Janey Jo cooked up a great big dinner, then packed up the leavings for us to bring home, and then Pap-pa brought us back in his wagon. Daddy was looking more chipper when we got home, and we had a fun evening together.

January 17, 1932. Daddy did not go to church with us today. Instead, he stayed home and got drunk. You would think he would behave himself right after he begins his important new job. I am disgusted with him, and I hope he suffers from a terrible hangover all day at work tomorrow. I hope his boss does not notice, though. I would hate for him to get his walking papers so soon after he started his new job.

I am happy that he did not seem to notice that I have stolen a gallon of his whiskey.

Miss Weston preached on the Breastplate of Righteousness today. I am sure it was very good, but I was distracted because I kept thinking about Daddy and how disgusted I am with him. Mama looked glum all through the service, also. We went to Pap-pa's for dinner, and Miss Weston came, also, and so did Uncle Woodrow, but it was not the same without Daddy. Everybody seemed quiet and sad.

January 17, 1932
Dearest Cecilia,

These long winter days are becoming quite dreary, and for the first time since I have been here, I find myself missing the bright society of our old friends. It would be such a pleasure to attend a party or a ball, to feel the crisp cold on a snowy day and enjoy hot chocolate with a group of rowdy young people! The cold here is damp, so that it gets into your bones and makes you chilled from the inside out.

The church service this morning was adequate, but I was less than inspired, and it showed. Afterwards, I had my usual Sunday dinner with the Aiken family, but everyone seemed quite glum. I tried to draw Mr. Woodrow out, even asking him to go for a walk with me, but he was uncommunicative and cut the walk short, saying he was cold and wanted to get back to the fire. I feel singularly distressed. He is a mysterious, lonely man! Breaking his barriers is more difficult than I thought it would be, but I will not give up trying. He is deserving of a happy life, and I believe that someday, I will be able to draw him out of his sorrow. Please pray for me, dear Cecilia! The house is cold and empty, and I am lonely and sad. I love and miss you.

Emily

January 18, 1932
My School Journal, grade 7, Miss Weston's class
By Pearl Wallace

At school we learned about the rotation and revolution of the earth around the sun. My teacher, Miss Weston, says that if we could see the earth from heaven as God sees it, it would look like a small, blue marble swimming in a black pond, filled with sparkling diamonds, which are all the stars. All the stars are suns, and to the planets revolving around them, they are bright, like our sun. Our sun is just one tiny speck of light when it is seen from far, far away.

It makes me happy to think that God is watching us from out in space, holding our little blue marble in the palm of His hand, breathing His life into it. Even though to Him we are tiny specks, even smaller than chiggers, He still loves us because we are His own children, and He knows about all our sorrows.

January 19, 1932. Jake Hatton was waiting down by the springhouse when I got home from school today. Of course,

I blessed him out for coming so close to the house and risking people seeing him. He did not even apologize, but started twitching and hopping around, excited as all get-out. One of his friends needed some whiskey since the federals found his still and all six gallons of whiskey he had just made last week and busted it all up. They did not catch him, but now his important customers are in need, and he says if I will sell him just one gallon, he will pay me extra.

I asked him how much extra, and he said half again, but I felt a stubborn spell coming on, and I just crossed my arms and said, "double." Jake about had a fit, but I would not budge. I figure anybody as desperate as he seemed would give in if I stood strong enough. Finally, he gave in, but when I told him he would have to pay me cash up front, he hemmed and hawed, cussed and twitched, then finally agreed to pay me half now and half at delivery, which will be tomorrow. He gave me $2.00, although he tried to cheat me by saying that there are only six pints in a gallon, but I told him I knew my arithmetic better than that, and I scratched out the numbers in the dirt with a stick. There are two pints to a quart, four quarts to a gallon. That means there are eight pints in a gallon, and at 50c per pint, that makes $4. I told him he had to pay me $2.00 now and $2.00 on delivery. He stood over my ciphering for a long time, muttering and jerking, then he tried to cheat me again by paying me mostly in nickels, dimes, and pennies so he could shortchange me. I am on to him, though, and I counted out every red cent right in front of him so that he had to pay me the whole $2.

Now, I feel like I have fought a great battle and won it, but I also am ascared. A gallon is a lot of whiskey to steal, and if Daddy is sharp when he comes home this Saturday, I may have to pay with my hide.

January 20, 1932
Dear Cecilia,

I have just heard the most terrible news about a situation over in Alcoa. One of the colored men living there caught a white man in a compromising position with his wife, and violence ensued. The white man was killed, and now the community is up in arms over it. The colored man is being held in jail, but there is talk of a lynching. I heard this from Ruth Halfacre, the other teacher here at the school, and we are trying to keep it concealed from the children, because we know this would frighten them.

Cecilia, I have to admit that I am terrified! I have heard about lynchings going on in the Deep South, but I never dreamed they could occur here in the mountains of Tennessee. People actually are suggesting that they might storm the jail, drag the poor man out, and hang him! I understand police have been sent over from Knoxville to help maintain order, and I am sure they will do their best, but the very possibility of such violence makes me quake.

Please pray for the situation here, Cecilia. I think of the poor child who is friend to Pearl. I think her name is Darlene. It is awful to think that she might be dragged into this somehow. Alcoa is some 20 miles away, but anger can flame up anywhere, once it has been ignited. Please pray for me, as well.

Love,
Emily

January 20, 1932. Today was just awful, and I feel terrible for poor Beryl. Since I am the oldest girl, I get new underwear whenever I outgrow mine, and Beryl has to make do with my old drawers and things. Today she had on a pair of my old step-ins, and halfway through the morning, when she was playing outside at recess, the elastic gave way and they fell down! Thank goodness they did not make it all the way to the ground. She caught them halfway with her knees as they dropped, but then she had to waddle to the outhouse with her knees mashed together to keep them up. I could see them drooping down below her dress, and her face was red as fire, so I ran over and walked behind her so no one could see what was going on. We made it to the outhouse all right, but the poor thing cried for the longest time. These step-ins are about as raggedy as they can be, and we both would die if anyone could see how poor they look. Mama would, too. Thank goodness we managed to hide them from everyone. She took them off and stuffed them in her pocket. I bet it was uncomfortable having to go through the rest of the day without any drawers on.

I wish it had happened to me and not to Beryl. I would have been scundered about it, but she was mortified. She ended up crying again all the way home, and she would not let me tell Sardius what had happened. He is so worried about her he is about beside himself. I think Mama may have let him in on it later, though, just to stop his hovering. Mama was very sweet about it. She says she will make Beryl all new drawers and throw these old ones away. They are ready for the ragbag, anyway, and she is sorry she made Beryl wear my old hand-me-downs in the first place.

I got my other $2.00 today! Instead of stealing four quart jars from Daddy's stash behind the hay bales, I took just three and poured just a little from each of the other jars into a new jar. I am praying I do not get caught. Oh Lord, if you ever wanted to protect me, please do it now!

January 21, 1932. Guess what I did today? I ordered Beryl 7 new pairs of step-ins from the Sears & Roebuck! Darlene helped me pick them out. There are 7 different colors, one for each day of the week: pink, blue, turquoise, white, yellow, green, and tan. Darlene had the smart idea of having them sent to Pap-pa's house so no one will see that I am getting a package.

It is good to have Darlene to trust with my secrets. She says she will help me if I ever decide to start making whiskey on my own. I wish she knew how to make it. That is the only thing that is holding us back.

I am feeling bad about keeping secrets from Mama, but she would not approve of my breaking the law. She very much believes in living an upright, respectable life. It is hard to hide the fact that I have money from her. I already am pushing my luck buying all those Christmas presents. If Mama figures out I have money to burn, she will also figure out where it likely came from. I will be sure to tell Pap-pa to save that package for me when it comes. Now I need to figure out how to get them to Beryl with no one suspecting that I bought them.

I also ordered Daddy a handsome, all-cotton handkerchief and a pair of bobbing floats for Jasper. Their birthdays are coming up. I should have ordered Sapphire something. It is her 3-month birthday.

January 23, 1932. When Daddy got home today, he had a black eye and his hand was bandaged up. He did not say anything other than the hobos are a rougher bunch than he had counted on. Mama looks worried, but Daddy laughed about it. He said he had had quite a time of it, but those hobos will not be back on his train. Then he announced that tonight is the full moon of the Wolf, and that he was going hunting. This is the first time he has even acted like he wanted to go hunting ever since Sapphire came to us, and even though Mama was not happy about it, she just said, "Well, be sure to dress warm." Daddy left out right after supper.

He is out there now, along with Harvey Madison, Walt Bittertree, John Jay Breem, and a couple others of his cronies who go hunting with him. I can hear the hounds baying back and forth all over the hills, and I can hear the rifles going off. I can only imagine how drunk Daddy is getting. I wish I could just leave and run over to Pap-pa's for the rest of the night.

Darlene did not come over today. I wish she was here now. I would like somebody to talk to, and Mama has already gone to bed. Beryl has, also. Jasper and Sardius are having their own conversation. I am very lonesome.

January 24, 1932. Today was a very big day. During the invitational, which was *Jesus Gave it All*, Sardius got up and walked down the aisle. He has dedicated his life to Jesus! Miss Weston was grinning so hard I thought her face would split in half. Mama cried, saying she had always hoped he would make a preacher. Jasper and Uncle Woodrow shook his hand and told him they were proud of him. Miss Weston looks as proud as if he were her son. I am proud of him, also. Sardius will make a good preacher, or a missionary, depending on what his calling will be. He always has been the kindest boy, and he loves to study the Bible.

What a wonderful, exciting day, except for the fact that Daddy did not have any part of it because he was too drunk to stand by the time he got home last night. I hope he is ashamed of himself, missing such an important part of his son's life. After church, we all, including Miss Weston, went to Pap-pa's for dinner and shared the good news. Miss Janey Jo looked tickled and hugged Sardius. Pap-pa did not look as pleased, but he shook his hand and said he was happy for him. Sardius is glowing like a new penny. Miss Weston is, too.

When we got home, Daddy was still drunk, but he was pitiful rather than mean. When we told him the news, he cried, then went to bed and passed out. I heard him in there weeping later on. He does not hardly ever cry when he is drunk, just those times when there has been a tragedy, like when my baby brother died two years ago right after he was born. I hope he does not think Sardius' dedicating his life to Jesus is a tragedy.

January 24, 1932
Dear Mother and Father,

I have some wonderful news! I have written to you before about my favorite family here in the Cheola community—the Wallace family. Well, you will be very pleased to know that God is working here in a very big way. Today, their second to eldest son came forward during the alter call, to declare his calling to preach the Gospel! He says he made the decision because of my inspiration. He has shown himself to be a wise, dedicated student who loves the Lord with all his heart. Until recently, he did not realize he could have opportunities to expand his learning, but with my encouragement, he recognizes his own potential and wants to take advantage of it to help others come to know God.

You see, my efforts here are not wasted. Now that Sardius has made the leap to follow God, I know others will come forward. I am grateful that I have had some influence in this wonderful event! I hope you are, too.

Much love,
Emily

Cold, gray waxing days, frozen nights.

I have been dancing with the Great Orb for days
Lost in the splendor of her light,
In the frenzy of her lust,
In the ecstasy of mine.
Her light shines through the darkness;
Cold heat, mingling with the stars.

My upright children are a confusion
Of joy and pain, of relief and weight.
But the Spirit smiles on all
As the Darkness sits sullen.

January 25
My School Journal, grade 7, Miss Weston's class
By Pearl Wallace

My brother Sardius has dedicated his life to Jesus! I am very proud of him. He says he will be a preacher or a missionary, depending on what God calls him to do. I hope he is a missionary because I want to be one also, and we can go to Africa or India and serve God together. It will be very much fun to lead people into the Path of Righteousness and to see them be saved and baptized. I cannot wait until we can do that.

My mother and father are very proud of Sardius, also, and so are my Pap-pa and my step-grandmother. We had a nice time yesterday, celebrating God's blessings and helping Sardius plan for his future.

January 26, 1932. Today, Miss Weston got a big surprise. She was teaching the eighth-graders their History lesson, and we seventh graders were working on pictures we were drawing of the Universe. I was trying to figure out just where Heaven might be, when all of a sudden, the door flew open and the best-looking man I ever saw in my life stood in the doorway. He was tall, with soft, black hair, white skin and pink cheeks, wearing the most beautiful coat made of fine wool, a dashing gray fedora, and a long, white wool scarf. He looked just like a movie star, with big, white teeth and flashing eyes!

Miss Weston was writing on the blackboard when he came in, and she turned around, dropped her chalk, and went as white as a ghost. Then she turned red, got a mad look on her face and marched right up to him, grabbed his arm, and walked him out the door without saying anything to us. We all tried not to look, but of course none of us could resist, and we rushed to the window to peep out at them. It was hard to keep quiet the whole time they were outside. I know Miss Weston was freezing because she did not have on her coat, but they must have been out there at least ten minutes. When she finally came back in, she was nearly blue from the cold, but she did not say a word. She just went back up to the blackboard, picked up her chalk, and finished writing the word, "diaspora," which she had only gotten halfway through when she had been interrupted.

After school, she asked Sardius, Beryl, and me to stay for a minute, and when Otis Merriweather fooled around in the back of the room pretending to be looking for something after everyone else left, she said to him, "Otis, you might as well leave now. You will not have a chance to speak to Pearl this afternoon," and he turned bright red and scurried out the door.

Then Miss Weston turned red herself, cleared her throat, and finally stammered out, "I have a visitor who came unannounced, and it will be difficult to find accommodations. I hate to ask this of you, but do you suppose your grandfather might be able to host him for the night? I assure you he will be leaving first thing in the morning."

We were dumbfounded. Miss Weston lives in Preacher Miller's house, one of the prettiest in this section of the country, and it is plenty big, especially now that the Millers have gone to Florida for the winter. I wanted to ask her why her guest did not stay at her house. In these parts, you do not turn away company who has come from far away to visit, but Sardius jumped right in and said, "Of course, Miss Weston, I am sure our grandfather will be happy to offer accommodations for the night."

I nearly guffawed at the way he said it. Beryl did giggle, but I gave her a little shove and she quit.

Then, the most amazing, wonderful thing happened. Miss Weston took us outside and put us in her very own automobile! The man who had come to the schoolhouse was sitting in his automobile, a very fancy, shiny one, and he looked about near frozen to death. When we came out, he jumped out, and Miss Weston just said, "Follow me," to him, and she got into her automobile and drove us to Pap-pa's house.

Miss Janey Jo met us at the door, and she was as nice as could be and brought coffee and hot chocolate so we could warm up, and we all sat in the front room until Pap-pa came in. Then Miss Weston said, "Mr. Aiken, I am in a very difficult position, and I must beg your indulgence. My acquaintance, Mr. Dean, has arrived unexpectedly, and we are having trouble finding accommodations for him. May I throw myself upon your mercy and beg a bed for him for the night?"

Of course Pap-pa said yes right away, and he asked Miss Weston to stay for supper, but she said, no, she had to get us home, and she shooed us out the door and into her automobile without even looking at Mr. Dean again. Then she drove us straight home without saying another word to us.

What a strange adventure! I think Mr. Dean did not get the reception he was expecting to get when he barged into that schoolroom. I bet she was mad at him for coming because she is struck on Uncle Woodrow and she did not want Uncle Woodrow to know she had another suitor.

January 26, 1932
Dear Cecilia,

I have been through a most embarrassing incident. This afternoon, Jonathan showed up at the schoolhouse unannounced! He did not warn me he was coming—apparently he left in the middle of the night and drove straight here, and then just appeared at the door, expecting me, no doubt, to be pleased. I nearly died! My students saw everything, and I am certain word will get around that I have had a man come calling for me, made especially bad because I am now living alone in the Miller house.

Of course, I could not let him even darken the door of the Miller home, so I made him sit out in the freezing cold while I finished the day's lessons. Then I put the Wallace children in my car and instructed Jonathan to follow me to the Aiken home, where I begged a room for him for the night. The Aikens were very gracious, taking him in with open arms and a great deal more sympathy than I had for him. I did not even tell him goodbye. I just took the children home and came back here for the night. I hope that is that last I see of Jonathan Dean. The nerve of that man!

I hope the Aikens did not let him know that the Millers are not at home for the winter. If word gets back to Father, I shall be in a world of trouble. Surely, they would not tell him. They are very discreet. It is midnight, and I am still so upset I cannot get to sleep. I hope he has realized that I will not allow my position to be compromised by his unwanted advances and that he leaves tomorrow without attempting to see me again.

Your distressed, but loving sister,

Emily

January 27, 1931

Jonathan:

I do not know what you had hoped to accomplish by arriving at my place of work uninvited and unannounced. Did you not realize that your appearance would compromise my position here in the community? As an unmarried woman, I must live absolutely above reproach, and to have a man from out of town come and expect to stay overnight is anathema to my reputation. How dare you take such a cavalier attitude with my good name? It would have been bad enough if you had come only to my home, but you allowed all my students to see you, which means that word is already all over this community that I have been entertaining a strange man. I can only hope that the Aikens will do what they can to mitigate the damage you have done to me.

What on earth made you think you would be welcomed by showing up like that? Do you have no consideration for my feelings, for my reputation? I am violently upset at your behavior, and I expect a letter of apology both to me and to the Atkins family who were so generous to put you up for the night.

Emily Weston

January 29, 1932. I missed 2 days of school because I had a cold, and I sure was glad to be going back today! Mama dosed me with so much garlic that I cannot stand myself. She made me swallow

3 buds this morning before we left. I hate to admit it, but that must have worked, because I could feel my cold leaving me as we walked across the ridge this morning. I felt perfectly fine all day.

Darlene and I had a fun time this afternoon. We made popcorn during our French lesson, then read by the fire until it was time to start supper. Mrs. Carlton has the prettiest singing voice. She sang to us while Uncle Woodrow played Daddy's banjo, and it was such a good time. Billy Ray can just stay away. Everyone is so much happier when he is gone.

January 30, 1932. Daddy started drinking as soon as he got home today. It is 4 o'clock and he is still at it. Mama is in the bedroom crying. Sapphire has been squalling all day, too. I have done nothing but tend to Ruby and try to put some food on the table, and Beryl has been too mopey to be much help. Jasper and Sardius have been out chopping wood and mending the fence where one of the dogs chewed a hole in it. Uncle Woodrow is nowhere to be found. I have not seen Darlene. It is a miserable, cold day.

January 31, 1932. We all went to church today, except for Daddy, who is nursing a hangover. Everyone is gloomy except for Sardius, who was happy to be going to church. Usually church cheers me up, too, but today Mama seemed so blue that it was hard to get my spirit in a good mood.

I gave Pap-pa some whiskey today and asked him to buy Mama a sack of cornmeal instead of paying me. Her birthday is coming up next month, and I think it is better to give her something she can really use instead of getting her something just for pretty. I would like to get her something pretty, but I know she will appreciate good cornmeal more. She is like that. She cares more about her family than she does herself. We have about run out on account of Daddy stealing a good bit of our corn crop to make whiskey last summer.

February

February 1, 1932
My School Journal, grade 7, Miss Weston's class
By Pearl Wallace

My sister, my best friend Darlene, and I are taking French lessons. Both my mother and Darlene's mother speak French very well. Darlene's mother knows it because she is from Louisiana, where they speak French every day. My mother knows it because her mother believed that all young ladies ought to know a second and third language. Mama also learned German, but she does not hardly ever use it because no one likes to hear it since the Great War, in which we fought the Germans. They gave my Uncle Woodrow a case of shell shock back in 1918.

After Darlene, Beryl, and I learn French, we will go to France where we can speak it every day. I also might become a missionary in France. I think a lot of the French are Catholic, so they need someone to set them straight about the Gospel.

February 2, 1932. It is Groundhog Day, and guess what? He did not see his shadow! It rained all day, and although it was miserable to walk to school in the cold and wet, and to be stuck inside all day, we were happy because we will see an early spring. I, for one, am ready for spring. I have about had enough of the cold.

We are running low on whiskey because Daddy has been hitting it hard the last few weeks, and Harvey Madison and Luke Roundtree have been helping him. There probably is not more than about 6 quarts left out in the barn. Jake Hatton left me a note today, but I had to turn him down on account of I am afraid to take any more. I hope Daddy is feeling fit enough to make some more soon.

February 3, 1932. It is all over for old Al Capone! They sentenced him to go up the river for 20 years yesterday. That is something I do not like to think about. I sure hope they do not catch me. I would not like to spend nearly twice as much time in prison than I have already lived.

Cold, dark days and nights.

I am slow and languid. Replete.
I fall between my banks, indolently watching.

Sickness rears a head. I smell it, but I do not care.
A clean passion flares to mask it.

My children can tend to their own,
Although they are blind in their paths.
I cannot fathom enough to give voice.

February 4, 1932. Darlene told me that somebody stole some of her mama's step-ins off the line today. I do not think Beryl would do something like that, but she might if she were desperate enough. Mama has made her one new pair, and she pins the old ones together so they do not fall down, so Beryl should not worry about them. I will be glad when her new ones from Sears & Roebuck show up.

Now I think on it, I do not think Beryl would steal Mrs. Carlton's step-ins no matter how desperate she might be. For one, she has never stolen anything that I can think of, and second, they would be way too big for her.

February 5, 1932. February is my least favorite month. It is dark, dreary, wet, and cold, and there is nothing to do. Jasper loves it because he has time to get back to his studies. In the wintertime, he spends every minute he can reading. Mama is pushing him to finish up the tenth grade before plowing season begins. He has to finish several more books and take some tests, but I know he will do it. He loves to read and to learn, almost as much as Sardius does. In a way, he may love it more, because he has to give up so much to make it happen. He works very hard during the days, then he stays up late at night studying. It makes me feel bad that the rest of us get to be lazy, with school being our main job, while Jasper has to keep up work around here, and squeeze in learning late at night.

Even though it is cold and dark, in some ways, it is happier around here with Daddy gone. Maybe it is because Billy Ray is also gone, and we have the run of the place to ourselves without his meanness hanging over us. Even Mama seemed happier today. You never saw such a fine time as we all had over supper tonight. Mrs. Carlton baked a cake, although she had to get eggs from Uncle Woodrow as well as us, but it was worth the effort to find them. Mama made black-eyed peas with potatoes, and Jasper had caught four trout.

Je suis tellement pleine que je pouvais exploser! (That's French for " I am so full I could explode ! ")

February 6, 1932. Daddy is home for his birthday today! Pap-pa and Miss Janey Jo came over for supper to help us celebrate, and Pap-pa brought Daddy's handkerchief, Jasper's fishing floats, Mama's cornmeal, and Beryl's step-ins. He called me outside to give them to me, and we hid everything except the handkerchief up in the barn loft. Mama and Jasper will get theirs on their birthdays next week, and I am saving the step-ins for when I can figure out how to get them to Beryl without anybody knowing it was me.

Daddy was sober, but he did not look very happy. He looks tired, and he is jumpy. It seems as if he and Uncle Woodrow have changed places. Uncle Woodrow is jolly, while Daddy looks like he is spooked about something. He was happy to get my handkerchief, though, and once the celebration got started, he seemed much better.

All was going fine until Billy Ray came over with Darlene and Mrs. Carlton. As soon as Billy Ray walked in the door, everyone got quiet. We all know what Billy Ray does to Darlene and Mrs. Carlton, and we all were burned up that he would have the nerve to show his face to us. He was loud and friendly, as if we all were his best friends. No one said anything, but everyone there wanted to kill him. I could tell that Jasper cannot stand to be in the same room as him. Almost as soon as he got here, Jasper jumped up, saying he was going to start hauling water for our baths, and he and Sardius went out with their buckets. I wanted to go, too, but was curious about how Billy Ray would act around Daddy and Uncle Woodrow. He generally acts like they are all big buddies, but there is no reason to. Daddy has not asked him to go hunting with him ever since he moved back. Uncle Woodrow does not hardly speak a word to him anymore.

Daddy and Uncle Woodrow tried to be nice for a little while, but when Billy Ray slapped Mrs. Carlton on her bottom, Uncle Woodrow got a mad look on his face, jumped up and walked out of the room without saying anything. It makes him mad to see anybody hurt anybody else. Billy Ray sat real quiet for a minute, then he got pouty, and he yanked Mrs. Carlton's arm, saying it was time to go home.

It was a bad end to Daddy's birthday party, but at least we got a lot of water for our baths, on account of Sardius and Jasper doing so much hauling. Mama is bathing the little ones now, and

Beryl and I get to go next. I am looking forward to a nice, hot one. It is cold outside! I hope Billy Ray did not take our slight against him out on Mrs. Carlton and Darlene.

February 7, 1932. Mama managed to get Daddy up and dressed and off to church with us. Miss Weston preached from the book of James. James was Jesus' brother. All his brothers and sisters thought Jesus was crazy, until He was raised up from the dead, and in the early years, they spent a lot of time trying to keep Him out of trouble with the priests. After He was risen, James became his biggest follower, and he did not care who knew it!

That makes me wonder if Jesus were my brother, would I believe that He was the Son of God? I worry that I might not. It makes me feel bad that I would think He was crazy and talk about Him behind his back. As good as Sardius is, I would not believe him if he told me he was Jesus. It is just too hard to imagine what that might be like. I wonder why their mother did not tell them?

If Jesus were my brother, I wonder what he would say about my bootlegging business. Would he make me stop, even if it meant that we all might starve? He did a little bootlegging himself, sort of, when He turned the water into wine, although He did not make any money from it. If His mama were cold and hungry, He could make a miracle and give her anything she needed. Since I am not God, I have to work miracles in my own way, and somehow, I do not think He really minds.

Beryl got a bad headache this afternoon, so I decided it was time to give her the step-ins. I hid them in the chest of drawers where she keeps her things. Tomorrow when she goes to get dressed, she will find them, and will she ever be surprised!

February 7, 1932
Dear Cecilia,

If, a year ago, you had told me that I would turn a cold shoulder to Jonathan Dean while he begged me to look upon him favorably, I would have laughed at you! How much I have grown and learned in the past few months. It seems that I have been here for much longer than that. I have matured and increased in wisdom in so many ways that I cannot count. Jonathan seems like a feckless, spoilt child to me now.

I think about how much I tried to get him to notice me, how I slavered at his every word, how I longed for him to look at me, and when he did, I nearly melted with childish infatuation. Now I know that is just what it was—infatuation. I am learning that love is much deeper, much more selfless. I know now that love means looking at someone and understanding his pain, and being willing to do anything to help relieve that pain. It means to be able to sit back and wait, and hope, and be resolved to let things take their own measure of time.

I have been reading about the lives of the saints, and I am beginning to understand that real love is patient, kind, compassionate, giving. Not given to selfish impulses. Jonathan is none of those. He has become whiny and needy. He angered me so much, by coming here without my permission, that I have not written to him at all except to chastise him mightily. He, however, has written me three letters since then! It is such a relief to know that my sentiments have matured so much during my time in these beautiful, hard, rugged, quiet mountains. Jonathan wants what he cannot have. When I considered him a shining idol, he wanted little to do with me, but now that I am standing upright on my own two feet and no longer find him so charming, he is throwing himself at me. Men! How childish and foolish they can be.

I am off to bed now. I had a lovely day, which started with me preaching a very good sermon, and then going to my usual sumptuous dinner with the Aiken and Wallace families. It has been such a successful day, and I am quite overcome with the joy of it!

Love,
Emily

February 8, 1932
My School Journal, grade 7, Miss Weston's class
By Pearl Wallace

Darlene and Mrs. Carlton come over to my house almost every day. They come to bring goat milk for my baby sister and for our French lessons. I always rush home after school because I know they will be here when we get home. It is something to which I look forward every day. When we walked in today, there was a big fire roaring in the fireplace, with popcorn going, and plenty of hot coffee and milk. It is such a nice, cozy feeling, coming in from the cold drizzle and getting to eat popcorn and listen to Uncle Woodrow tell stories. Winters are not all bad.

February 8, 1932. Beryl found her step-ins, and before I could stop her to tell her not to blab about it, she went running to Mama. I guess I should not have just hid them for her to find like that. I pretended I did not know where they came from. Mama thinks Daddy did it, and I did not tell her better. Now I just have to get to him on Saturday when he gets home before Mama does. I will tell him I bought them out of my muscadine money.

Beryl is, of course, very happy. She wore the blue ones today, and she says she will wear the pink ones tomorrow. She almost went prancing out in front of everybody to show them off!

February 9, 1932. We had right much fun at school today. Miss Weston knows we are all feeling restless with the weather being so dreary and we cannot go outside because of the mud and slush. She let us skip our lessons and instead play games all afternoon. She brought out some jacks, jackstraws, marbles, and a cup and ball set. While we were playing, Sardius was stuck in a corner, working on an essay that Miss Weston wanted him to write. I do not think it was fair he had to miss the games to do schoolwork, but I did not say anything. Miss Weston must have her reasons, and Sardius did not seem to mind. Beryl wore her pink drawers today to school. When she put them on, she said she was tickled pink, so they match!

February 10, 1932. We have an assignment to write about one of Longfellow's poems, either "Evangeline" or "Hiawatha," but I cannot decide which one. I like "Hiawatha" because it is about Indians, and I like thinking about the Indians who used to live here, up on the bluff above the river. However, the Indians who lived around here were Cherokee, while Longfellow wrote about Hiawatha, who was Iroquois, but they also were peaceful.

I think I will pick "Evangeline." I like the way "Hiawatha" ends with Hiawatha getting saved by the blood of Jesus, but otherwise I do not have any connection to the Iroquois after all. I like "Evangeline" because Darlene is a Cajun, just like Evangeline was. I think she will be excited to hear the story of Evangeline so I am going to go over there tomorrow after school and tell her about it.

February 11, 1932. As it turns out, Darlene knows all about Evangeline. Her mama told her about the story last year so she could know a little about her history. That is a sad story, as sad as the Cherokee having to walk The Trail of Tears all the way from Tennessee to Oklahoma.

Here is how the story goes:

The English won Acadia (that is up in Canada) from the French in one of their wars, and they did the meanest thing. They shoved them onto different boats without paying any attention to keeping friends and families together, and burned their homes. Many got shipped off, back to Europe or to different ports along the Eastern Coast. They never saw their husbands, wives, children, or sweethearts again.

Evangeline spent her whole life looking for her betrothed, Gabriel, and she ended up down in Louisiana, where Darlene used to live. Many other Acadians went there, too, and eventually they came to be called "Cajuns" because they forgot how to say

"Acadians" right. Evangeline finally found Gabriel, but he was very sick, and he died in her arms. It is a very sad story.

Evangeline and Gabriel loved each other, and they never stopped, and that is sweet, but I do not think I would be as faithful as Evangeline was. If I lost my betrothed and had no idea how to find him again, I would have to figure out a way to get on with my life. To tell the truth, if a likely man happened by who had a lot of money and was nice to me, I might be tempted to marry him. If I knew I could make it on my own, though, I might not marry at all. If you ask me, men are not always what you expect or hope they will be, and they can go bad on you. Look at my daddy. He went bad on Mama right before her eyes. Overnight he went from being a nice, handsome, hardworking husband and father to a shiftless drunk who says mean things and starves us all.

I never knew my Uncle Woodrow before he lost his nerves, but they say he was a very strong, handsome man, too, before the Great War. Now I would not have him, nice as he is. I would have to take care of him instead of him taking care of me the way it is supposed to be. Gabriel could have been that way, too. You just never know about men, so I reckon it is best just to stay away from them altogether if you can. That is what Miss Weston has done. She does not have a husband, and she is doing just fine. I suspect her daddy is rich, though. She has a fancy automobile, and you should see her pretty dresses! She did not get all that teaching down at Cheola School, or preaching, either.

As I was saying, Darlene knows about Evangeline, and we had a nice discussion, an argument really, because I thought Evangeline was crazy to waste her life pining after Gabriel, and she thought it was the right thing to do. I do not know. Gabriel was very nice, and it turns out he was the faithful sort, too.

February 12, 1932. Sunday is St. Valentine's Day. Someone slipped a piece of paper that was cut out into the shape of a heart into my coat pocket when I was not looking. I found it when I was walking home. It said, "Be Mine, Valentine!" It did not have a name on it, but I know who gave it to me. Of course, I kept it hid from Beryl and Sardius. Some things need to be kept private. When I got home, I put it in my cherrywood box along with all my money.

February 13, 1932. Daddy got home early this morning and took off again before any of us even got out of bed, so I did not have the chance to tell him to take the credit for Beryl's step-ins. I do not think Mama had the chance to mention them to him, either. I reckon he noticed how low his whiskey is getting, so he is probably going to spend today and tomorrow laying in a new supply. I am glad he is gone because Darlene got to spend the whole day here, and tonight she is going to stay the night. Billy Ray is home, and by the way Darlene is acting, he is having one of his mean spells. I wish he would just die. Poor Mrs. Carlton is over there with him all by herself.

February 14, 1932. Today is St. Valentine's Day! Daddy gave Mama a box of chocolates and a yellow ribbon, and he gave us young'uns our own box of candy, which we ate right down.

Good news! Darlene went to dinner at Pap-pa's house with us today. Mama said that she could come even though she did not go to church with us because people might not be nice to her considering that she is not exactly Caucasian and that she is a Catholic.

February 14, 1932
Dear Jonathan,

I received your beautiful card and gifts yesterday, which I found touching, if a trifle excessive. The box of candy is so large I will be sharing it with my students this week. I am willing to wager that none of them have ever tasted fine Belgium chocolate, and so it should be quite a treat for them! You were very kind to send it.

I am sorry I have not replied to any of your letters for the last month. I have been very busy with my students. You know that Sardius Wallace has been called to preach, and so I have been working with him to prepare him for Wheaton Academy this summer. Of course, I am eternally grateful to you for your part in arranging for him to be able to apply for a scholarship there, and his brother, Jasper, as well.

Since you have so kindly offered, I will happily take you up on your offer to send another shipment of goods for the benefit of the community. It is nice to know that you are so enthusiastic about helping me do the Lord's work here among these good people.

Sincerely,

Emily

Cold, waxing days, frigid nights.

The earth slips through the darkness,
Turning slowly toward the light.
My silver children still sleep, languid and soft.
My upright children rejoice in love.

I smile, as does the Spirit.
The scent of greening warms the air.

February 15, 1932
My School Journal, grade 7, Miss Weston's class
By Pearl Wallace

My best friend is a Catholic, which means that she does not believe that you have to be washed in the Blood of Jesus to be saved. She thinks you just have to go to a priest and confess your sins. I wish she would go to church with us on Sunday and walk down the aisle during the invitational and really get saved.

The sermon was very good. Miss Weston preached about how Gideon was so afraid to mind God that he made God pass some tests to prove He was really talking to him. God should have gotten mad at him for doubting Him so much, but He did not. He just patiently passed all the tests Gideon gave Him with his wet fleece and his dry fleece, until finally, Gideon believed Him and went off to fight the Midianites. Miss Weston says our faith should be stronger than Gideon's, but it is good to know that God will be patient with us if it is not. I am glad about that. Sometimes my faith is not always as strong as it should be. Maybe if my faith were stronger, Darlene would be saved. I am wishing for it with all my might.

February 17, 1932. Today was Mama's birthday. She is 35 years old. We will celebrate her birthday, along with Jasper's, on Sunday. Mama is the sweetest soul on this earth. She hates to make us work hard, and she especially hates for us to miss school. Mama very much wants her girls to become ladies so we do not have to make our way in the world by hard labor. I do not mind hard work, and I wish Mama would let me help her more.

Jasper's birthday is tomorrow. Mama said that he was her birthday present 16 years ago, and she knew she was going to get him, but she did not have the chance to go out looking for him on this day because she was too busy celebrating her own birthday. That worried me because if Mama knew he was out there waiting for her in the cold and snow, why did she not go out and find him as soon as she could? I asked her about it, but she said she was just raffing about that. Of course, she would have laid out of her own birthday party if Jasper were ready. In fact, she went out the very minute she knew he was there, and she did not make him lie out in the cold any time at all.

February 18, 1932. Today is Jasper's birthday. He is 16 years old. Even though we will not celebrate his birthday until Sunday, when Daddy can be here, Uncle Woodrow decided we should have a party anyway. Mama baked him a cake, and Darlene and

Mrs. Carlton came, which made up for Daddy being gone. Mrs. Carlton and Darlene gave him a beautiful quilted jacket that they had made out of flour sacks and an old blanket that they had used to line it and make it warm. It is very colorful. I think Jasper likes it, although it is a little loud.

February 19, 1932. Sardius stayed at his desk at dinnertime today and ate while he was taking a special test Miss Weston wanted him to take. I did not want to sit with the sixth graders because Sam Hutchinson was sitting with them, so I went off by myself over by the stove where it was warm, and then Otis Merriweather came over and sat down beside me. We talked about Sardius being called to dedicate his life to Jesus. Now that he has, I probably cannot count on him to take up for Mrs. Carlton and Darlene. He would likely consider it sinful to hurt Billy Ray Carlton. Jasper would do it, but I hate for him to have to go it alone, since I cannot trust Daddy to do it right, and Uncle Woodrow would as soon die as do violence to any living soul. I reckon I am going to have to rely on Otis and his family. He had said they consider it a community service to take care of women who have low-down husbands, so I asked him about it again.

I was confused about Otis claiming to be a Scot. When we go to the Highland Games every summer, we meet people from a lot of different clans, and I never have met any Merriweathers. I had always heard that the Merriweathers were English, so I was wondering how they had a clan. Otis explained that his clan that helped his aunt was not the Merriweathers, but the Cluecluckers, which, he believes, are on his mother's side. I have never heard of them before, but I reckon there are a lot of Scottish families I have never met. I told him all about the Highland Games at Maryville, and he said he would try to get the Cluecluckers to go next summer if he could.

As far as he knows, the Cluecluckers do not have a tartan. Daddy says that you can tell people have family pride and dignity if they display their tartan. He says only trash just plain forgot their lineage when they left the Old World and came to the New one. I suppose that is what happened to the Cluecluckers, but I did not tell Otis that. Being that his daddy is a Merriweather, his pride has been watered down with English blood, which does not have any heritage to be proud of. The English are just a bunch of rogues. I did not say that to him, though, since it would not be polite to point it out.

Now that I think on it, I realize that Miss Weston is English, too, so I reckon not *all* the English are rogues. I have decided not to hold it against her. She cannot help it if her ancestors were born on the wrong side of the border, just like Darlene cannot help it that she was born into the Catholics.

February 21, 1932. Today at dinnertime, Miss Janey Jo put on an even better spread than usual for Mama's and Jasper's birthdays, with a goose and about every kind of vegetable that grows in Pap-pa's garden. She also made a pound cake for dessert, and she wrote, "Happy birthday Adeline and Jasper" in sugar icing that she dyed pink with beet juice. Mama cried, and I think it made her feel a lot better about Miss Janey Jo marrying her daddy, because after that she patted Miss Janey Jo's hand and smiled at her. I just about ate my weight in roasted goose, so by the time we got to the cake, I could not hardly eat a whole piece!

Everybody gave Mama and Jasper presents, which were all very nice, but Miss Weston gave them the nicest ones of all, and to tell the truth, they made our presents seem a little poor. She gave Mama a beautiful lace collar and Jasper a leather bound journal that he can write his thoughts in. Miss Weston said she feels so much a part of the family, she just had to do what she could, which made me feel very good.

I gave Mama her cornmeal and Jasper two bobbing floats, which he liked very much. They cost 6c.

Tonight is the full snow moon. Jasper and Uncle Woodrow will begin plowing, enough to get in some cold season vegetables, but not enough for it to be too hard on them. We do not begin the main plowing season with this moon, thank goodness, because we will get several more hard freezes before it is time to do the spring planting. Still, the little bit that needs to be done is no picnic. It is miserable trying to plow the hard ground when the snow and wind are coming at you. We just try to get in some onions and garlic early on, while the moon is still waning, and then we move on to collards, cabbages, and Brussels sprouts.

Thank goodness Daddy did not go fox hunting tonight. He has to go to work tomorrow.

February 21, 1932
Dear Cecilia,

We had a lovely celebration yesterday—it was for the birthdays of both Mrs. Adeline Wallace and Jasper Wallace, the eldest boy, who just turned 16. He has become an exceptional young man! Like his father and uncle, he is beautiful to look at, strong, lively, and of the finest of intellects. I cannot tell you how impressed I am by this family. Anyone would be proud to be associated with them.

As usual, the conversation was lively, ranging through a variety of topics, from the humorous to the sublime. I do wish you could have been here to see it all! Our little society in Chicago would pale in comparison. All anyone talks about at home are other people, society events, and the weather. Here people talk philosophy and poetry. Although they spend their time toiling in the soil, they do not talk much about crops or the weather. Their minds are on much loftier subjects.

Mr. Woodrow has challenged me to think about politics, and about the rights of women and coloreds. I must say, I was taken aback at how broad-minded he is. He would give Father a good run for his money; he had such a grasp of the problems they face and how it translates into problems of our entire society. I could talk to him for hours and never be bored.

It is late, so I must be off to bed. I hope your dreams are sweet.
Emily

Waxing, snowy days, bitter nights.
I taste hope, sweet and green.
But it is too soon for Spring;
Is it mine? My ardor for the Great Orb?
Not only mine, but the yearning of the stranger
Who cannot see beyond the bend,
Beyond the cascades, where the boulders lie in wait.

February 23, 1932. Jasper plowed most of the day, but it started to snow just as we got home from school, so Mama made him come in early. Uncle Woodrow came in, too, and we had a fine time just sitting in front of the fire telling stories and eating supper in the living room. Mrs. Carlton and Darlene brought a cheese pie and a quart of buttermilk, which we managed to make disappear in about a minute! Then we played Shadow Bluff the rest of the evening. Winters can be hard, but they are cozy, too, when you have a good fire going and all your loved ones are around.

February 27, 1932. We laid out of school for the last 2 days to help with the planting. Just as soon as Daddy got home today, he changed into his overalls and went out to help. Mama let us wait until after breakfast and it warmed up a little bit before we had to go out. We got all the carrots, beetroot, and turnips in, with plenty of time to spare. Now we wait until March until we start the next round of crops.

It feels good to be done with that. I am going to take a bath and go to bed directly.

February 28, 1932
Dear Jonathan,

Thank you for your kind letter and your promise that you are finding more funding for my students. If they are relieved of the burdens of having to provide any of their own expenses, it will go well for us all. I can see them both being quite accelerated in their academic pursuits and ready for college in no time at all!

In answer to your question, I am not sure about my plans for the summer. I do intend to come home for at least a short while, to spend some time with my family, and perhaps to visit some schools in order to ascertain the best academic opportunities for some of my other gifted students. You are welcome to help me search out the options, and I always am grateful for any financial help you can secure. Being a missionary means that I must rely on the goodness of those who have wealth and wish to use it for the Lord's work. I have found that it is not advantageous to be shy about asking for support!

Things are going well here. I have fit into the community as smoothly as a hand in glove, and I have come to love it dearly.

Your eternally grateful friend,

Emily

February 29, 1932
My School Journal, grade 7, Miss Weston's class
By Pearl Wallace

February 29 happens only once every four years, when there is an extra day in February. It is the one day that women are allowed to ask men to marry them. I wish Miss Weston would ask someone from around here to marry her! I would like it very much if she lived near us forever, and maybe even became a part of my family.

Thank goodness I am not old enough to be getting married, since I do not know of a single boy around here that I would like to ask to be my husband. There is a boy at my school who is nice, but he is not enough of a gentleman for my liking. If I decide to marry someone, I am going to make sure it is someone who is tall and handsome like my Daddy and Uncle Woodrow, and is also nice, sober, educated, and fun.

March

March 1, 1932. We ate the last of the potatoes today, because Daddy got into them again. Last year he stole about eight bushels, and we ran out at about the same time last year. By my reckoning, we should have at least 10 bushels still down in the cellar. When Jasper came up from the cellar this evening and said they were all gone except the eight little shriveled up ones he had in his hands, Mama went white and she pressed her lips together very hard for a minute before she said, "Oh, well, we can eat these tonight, and we still have plenty of other things to last us the winter." Jasper pointed out that we could not eat these because we have to use them for seed, but Mama said we can borrow some from Pap-pa when planting time comes.

I really hate it that we have run out of potatoes, but Mama is right. We will not starve. We still have plenty of green beans, as well as two sacks of cornmeal, so we can feast on cornbread and muscadine jelly, and we have enough apples to last us awhile. Also, there are plenty of fish in the river. And we can hunt. I am glad we live in the country. We can always live off the land!

I hope Daddy has made plenty of whiskey out of these potatoes. Pap-pa, Walt Bittertree, Jake Hatton, and Jake's friend are all wanting some, and there is hardly a drop to be found.

Waxing days, bitter winds, frozen nights.

The great orb turns her face from me, and lets me rest.
I seek the comfort of my silver children;
My creeping children still slumber in their burrows,
But soon, soon, they will wake and know hunger.
My upright children fear the starving,
And the Darkness that lurks like a copperhead.

March 2, 1932. Today was very windy. Spring is coming, and I say it cannot come too soon! Sardius, Beryl and I ran all the way home after school so we could go fishing before supper. We stopped at Darlene's house on the way so she could go with us. We caught nine big ones, so we all will feast! Darlene's mother was mighty happy to get those trout. She said she had been hankering for some for the longest time.

Sapphire sat up all by herself for a second today!

March 3, 1932. I am ascared I am growing too fast. My shoes that I bought just last October are getting tight, and I do not know if they will serve until Easter. I want another pretty pair of patent leather ones. I have plenty of money to buy them. I just have to figure out a way to make Mama think I got the money from Pappa by working for him.

There was some very bad news in the papers today. Mr. Charles Lindbergh, who was the first person to fly across the Atlantic all by himself, had a little baby who was kidnapped night before last. The kidnappers are demanding $50,000 to give him back. I feel very sorry for Mr. and Mrs. Lindbergh. I was only five years old when Lindy made his famous flight, but I remember it.

I am too sad to write any more today.

Waxing, cool days, cold nights
Green shoots nibble at my shore,
My silver children, my creeping children

Wake and shimmer, stir in the thickets,
In the shallows,
Seek out one another, and begin their seductions.

The cruel man lashes out
In fear and pain and anger.
The woman stands her ground,
The in-between child learns to hide.

March 5, 1932. I got up early and went out to the barn to see if Daddy had resupplied his stash behind the hay bales. They are very well hid, so that you have to either crawl over a high stack of them, or worm your way through a little pathway through them. I am little enough to be able to slip in through the cracks. I got back in there all right, but Daddy has not added to the store, so I will not be able to take any more from there. The woodshed is getting low, also, and so is the springhouse. Jake and his friends are just going to have to do without. I cannot risk taking any more without Daddy figuring it out.

While I was in there, I heard somebody come in. I kept quiet, because I do not want anybody to catch me hiding back there with Daddy's whiskey, but I was able to peek out between the bales to see who it was. Uncle Woodrow and Mrs. Carlton were standing just in front of the door, just a little apart, facing each other. I could not see Uncle Woodrow's face because his back was turned to me, but Mrs. Carlton's face was a mess. She had a black eye and a big, long bruise all along the side of her cheek. Her lip was busted and swole up.

Uncle Woodrow's shoulders were shaking. "I can't stand this, Celeste," he said. "You have to get away."

"And where would I go?" she answered. "I can't leave Darlene. At least she's safe for now, but I can't just leave her. I don't have a penny to my name. He'd come after us."

Uncle Woodrow just sank down onto one of the hay bales, his head in his hands. "I'll come with you," he said. "We'll manage."

Mrs. Carlton shook her head. "I have to get back. He'll be waking up soon, and I have to get breakfast on the table. He'll be nice enough for a while now. He got it out of his system, and we'll be safe, especially if Darlene stays away." Then she went out the door, leaving Uncle Woodrow sitting on the hay bale, sobbing his heart out. He is so tenderhearted. It just about breaks his heart to see anyone suffer, especially someone as nice as Mrs. Carlton.

I could not leave until he did, and so I just sat there a good long time until Uncle Woodrow finally eased himself up and went out. I waited for a few minutes, then slipped on back home. Darlene was there, having breakfast with everybody. Uncle Woodrow was not around. I expect we will not be seeing him for a while. Mama asked me where I had been, but I did not have much of an answer. I just said I had been out to the outhouse.

I bet I will not see Mrs. Carlton for a while. No doubt, she will be keeping her face hid from everybody for the next couple of weeks. Daddy is nowhere around, either. The boys have gone to the river. Darlene is as low as a snake's belly. It is mighty quiet around here.

March 6, 1932. I am happy because Darlene came with us to Pappa's house for dinner! I am hoping that now that she is spending some time with Miss Weston, she will get saved and baptized. She has already been baptized once, but that was when she was a baby, so it does not count.

Miss Weston came to Pap-pa's house with us for dinner. While were eating, Miss Janey Jo surprised us all. She said, "Darlene, I have always wanted to have a little girl come and live with me. I know your mama needs you during the week, but on the weekends, she has Billy Ray to keep her company. How would you like to come stay with us on Saturdays and Sundays?"

Darlene's mouth fell open, and so did mine. It would be just wonderful if Darlene could get away from Billy Ray when he was home. Miss Weston spoke up, saying, "What a wonderful idea! I could come over here sometimes on Saturdays and maybe we could do a little reading together."

Mama got excited, too, saying that Miss Janey Jo would be so happy if Darlene would come and spend some time with her. Before we knew it, it was decided right then and there that Darlene would come every weekend. Darlene is very excited and happy, and I am, too. Planting season is coming up, and I will not be able to spend time with her, but I know she will have fun with Miss Janey Jo and Miss Weston.

March 7, 1932. We have started the spring planting. It has warmed up, melting the snow so that we have been able to plant for the past 2 days. We had to miss school, but one thing that really brightened my day was that I ordered my Easter shoes. I told Mama I was going to use my hair money, but she said she was going to pay for them, now that Daddy is working. She also bought Beryl, Ruby, and me some socks. Beryl and Ruby can get by with my old shoes for Easter this year, but Mama says that if Daddy keeps his job, she will buy everyone new shoes for Easter next year. Won't we be a sight—all of us in our shiny new shoes!

I hope spring does come early, as the groundhog promised it would because we are running low on everything. We will be lucky to make it until the first crops come in. When Easter comes, I will wear my new patent leather Mary Janes, and I will have a new dress, too. It will be very nice to celebrate the risen Christ with all new clothes and shoes.

Mrs. Carlton and Darlene also are doing some planting, so Uncle Woodrow went over to help them.

March 13, 1932. Daddy got busy as soon as he got home yesterday, and we got the rest of the early planting done. I am very relieved it is over! Today is Sunday. Hurrah! A day of rest! My back is killing me.

I was very surprised to see that Otis Merriweather came to Miss Weston's church today. His family goes over to that trashy Holy Roller church over in Big Gully where the people do not respect the Lord or His holy temple. They holler and carry on as if the Lord cannot hear them unless they are screaming their lungs out. The preacher is ignorant, too. He does not even have an eighth grade education, and cannot hardly even read, so he just thumps on the Bible and makes things up that are not true while pretending to read it.

Otis slipped in sometime during the singing to sit in the back row, so I did not see him until the end of the service, then he crept outside before I got out, but I could tell he was waiting for me when we walked past the big cedar tree in the front yard. I told everybody to go on, that I had left my hair clip inside and that I would catch up to them. Beryl offered to go back with me, and it took me a long time to talk her out of it. Finally, Sardius said, "Come on, Beryl, I will race you down to that fence over yonder," and she could not pass that up. Sardius always lets her win, so she loves to race him. Sardius knew Otis was waiting for me. He is the sweetest, kindest brother of all.

After they all went on, I slipped back to the cedar, and sure enough, Otis was there. He stepped right out and tipped his cap as gentlemanly as could be, and he asked me if he could walk me home. I did not object, so we turned and started walking toward home as slowly as I could walk. I did not want Daddy looking back and seeing me walking with Otis Merriweather! He does not like the Merriweathers because they do not have good breeding. I have not told him that Otis' mother has Scottish blood. He may not believe me because nobody has ever heard of the Cluecluckers.

Otis and I talked all the way back to the house. I reminded him that he was supposed to talk to his uncles about talking or beating some sense into Billy Ray. I told him about how Billy Ray beat Mrs. Carlton's face bloody and begged him to do something, but he said he would not see his uncle until Easter because they live all the way over toward Ten Mile and he does not hardly ever get over that way. The family will be getting together for Easter, though, and he said he would do everything he could to get them over to take care of Billy Ray.

We went to dinner at Pap-pa's and Miss Janey Jo's as usual, and it was good to see Darlene there. Dinner was very good, especially since Darlene, Miss Weston, Uncle Woodrow, and Daddy were there. We had fried chicken, with mashed potatoes, gravy, biscuits, green beans, coleslaw, and chess pie for dessert! The only thing that put a damper on things was knowing Mrs. Carlton was stuck over in our holler with Billy Ray. I could tell Darlene was grieving about it, but she put on a happy face for us all.

I am pretty sure that Miss Weston is struck on Uncle Woodrow. She sat beside him today and talked to him and nobody else the whole time. Uncle Woodrow is nice to her, but since he is bashful, he does not make on over her like she makes on over him. I bet he is tickled about it inside, though.

Warm, waxing day, shorter nights.

The wind howls over the tender grass
That edges to my water,
Braving frost and Spring swells.
I howl, too, full and rushing, tumbling,
Running, free and wild,
Impatient to couple with the sea.
The laughing child seeks peace for her friend,
But she will deliver only sorrow.

March 13, 1932
Darling Cecilia,

What a wonderful weekend I have had! Pearl's friend, Darlene, is now staying every weekend with my friend, Janey Jo Aiken. While that is a good thing, the circumstances of why she is there are not. Her stepfather is so abusive that everyone is worried about her safety. He already has beaten her bloody several times. You can see bruises all over her face, arms, and legs. The poor child has been a punching bag for a despicable, violent man.

Yesterday, I went over to help entertain her and to see what I could do to help with her learning. She is surprisingly academically advanced for her age, and for the fact that she has had little formal schooling.

She actually is a charming little girl, and rather interesting looking. She has features that set her apart as being from African descent, but she is afflicted with albinism, a condition I do not think entirely regrettable. Her skin is milky white, and her hair is the palest shade of blonde, although it is kinky. Her eyes are a beautiful blue, large and luminous. I think that she may grow into her thick facial features at some point and become quite striking.

We had a lovely day sewing, cooking, reading, and walking about the farm, feeding and observing the animals. She has a lively curiosity, a sweet nature, and an abundant sense of humor. I like her very much! It is such a pity that she probably will never be accepted within white society. I have been wracking my brain to try to figure out a way to get her into a decent school up North, but it will most likely be difficult. Perhaps I can find a respectable school for Coloreds. I hope the fact that her skin is not black does not mean that Negroes will ostracize her. What a predicament!

Today was a good day, as well. I had a nice conversation over dinner with Woodrow about ways to help Darlene. We talked about the plight of people of color and what we as a society owed to such benighted souls. While Woodrow was initially receptive, in the middle of the conversation, he suddenly became unengaged. It was clear something is troubling him. I hope it is not the memories of his unfortunate experiences during the Great War.

I miss you and love you, sweet Cecilia. I am happy to hear that you have captured the attentions of Harry Hamilton. What a catch he would be!

Good night. Please remember to pray for us all.

Emily

March 14, 1932
My School Journal, grade 7, Miss Weston's class
By Pearl Wallace

Our neighbor Billy Ray Carlton has a nice little flat-bottom boat. Mrs. Carlton and Darlene can handle it just fine. They pole up and down the river as if they have done it their whole lives, which, in fact, they have. They used to live on what they call a bayou, which is like a very slow, swampy river. Our river is very swift, but Mrs. Carlton and Darlene are not troubled by it. They put their backs into it, and Darlene holds the boat in the current while Mrs. Carlton picks up her pole and pushes upstream. They say the Little T. is not as dangerous as a bayou because the bayou is full of alligators and also snakes that live in the trees and drop on your head when you paddle underneath. We have snakes here, but I have never seen one in a tree, except for little black snakes and green snakes, and they do not count.

Last week, we took the boat all the way over to Gracie May's Island. Someone has been camping there and has made a sturdy lean-to. We crawled in there and pretended it was our house. We had a good time fishing until it was time to go home for supper.

March 15, 1932. Darlene and her mother spent most of the day with Mama and the little girls today. With Billy Ray being gone during the week and on his best behavior on the weekends ever since he beat Mrs. Carlton so bad, things are getting happy again. By the time we had gotten home from school, they were all very jolly, sitting around, chattering in French, eating biscuits with persimmon jelly. Mrs. Carlton still looked pretty rough, but she was smiling and laughing as if she did not feel a thing. Uncle Woodrow was telling a big tale about an old fellow who called his rifle his "Hell by 90," and claimed to have shot an eagle that was so high up in the sky that it took him 24 hours to fall to the ground. Mrs. Carlton topped that one with a story about a fellow down in the swamps who caught alligators by their tails and slung them around until they were so dizzy they could not walk. Then he lined them up in the mud and walked across the swamp on their backs. Jasper had to top that with a story about a fellow he had heard about who would not shoot at a squirrel until he had at least three in a row lined up in his sights so he could get all three with one shot. By the time they were done, we were all just slapping our knees, laughing fit to be tied.

March 16, 1932. My new shoes and socks came today! They are just beautiful, so shiny, with thin straps across the tops that stand out against my white socks. I am not supposed to wear them until Easter, but I did put them on and prance around a little bit before supper. Darlene tried them on, but they were too small for her, so she could not wear them very long without them hurting her feet. I wish Darlene could have new shoes for Easter, too. She is wearing the ugliest old clodhoppers you ever saw. They are too big for her, and she clomps around in them looking like a poor little orphan.

March 18, 1931. I forgot to write in my Journal yesterday, there was so much excitement. Ralph Lee is in big trouble. He went on a rampage the other day, stealing tobacco and a pistol from Greenbrier store, and then late that night, he went to Mable Hathaway's house and climbed into her bedroom window. She woke up as he was trying to get into the bed with her, and she screamed her head off. Her daddy busted in and just about killed him before he trussed him up and threw him in the woodshed. He had to lie there all night until Mr. Hathaway went in to get the Sheriff to arrest him the next morning.

　　Now Ralph Lee is sitting in jail, and his mama has been over here crying fit to be tied. Mr. Bittertree says he will not go bail him out, that he will just sit there until he has served his time and has figured out how to behave himself. He says Mrs. Bittertree has made a baby out of him for the last time.

I feel sorry for Mrs. Bittertree. She has only the one son, so it is natural that she would dote on him. If she had a houseful of young'uns, she might be a little more prudent about raising them, but an only child is a treasure that she feels must be coddled. I also feel the least bit sorry for Ralph Lee, if I look for it. Mostly, though, I am glad he got what was coming to him. I hear he will be in jail for a long time for stealing that pistol.

I also felt very sorry for Mable Hathaway. I told Jasper that I cannot imagine how fearful it would be to wake up to Ralph Lee's nasty old breath on my face, and that I could see why he would want to kill him, being as how Mable was his sweetheart. Jasper smiled at me then and told me that Mable was not his sweetheart. She has been struck on Tom Savington over by Sweetwater for months now. Jasper said he never had a chance with her. Now I feel sorriest of all for Jasper.

March 19, 1932. The most amazing thing happened today! Daddy was home early, and I could tell he was planning on leaving to go work at his still, but before he got out the door, Miss Weston came by. It was a good thing I was still up in the loft getting dressed, because I had just put britches on, but I had the chance to change into a dress before I went down. Mama, Daddy, Jasper, and Sardius were all sitting in the front room, talking to her.

She floored every one of us, except for Sardius, who seemed to be in on it. Miss Weston wants him to go to Chicago this summer to begin high school at a fancy boarding school! He will have a scholarship, which means that all his room, board, and schooling will be free.

That about dumbfounded us all, except Sardius, who looked about as excited as if he had just seen Santa Claus in the flesh. It was plain that he really wants to go. Miss Weston said Sardius is so bright she believes he should have every opportunity to get a good education. After high school, he probably can get a scholarship to go to college as well!

There was a general ruckus, where Mama cried, then laughed, then cried some more, then she hugged up Sapphire very tight and hugged Sardius, and said this was the answer to prayer. Daddy looked worried, but what could he say in the face of Mama's and Sardius' happiness? He started to say something about Sardius being needed here to help run the farm, but Mama jumped all over him. "Richard Wallace, we will be fine. There is no better investment than an education for your children, and there are better things to do than work your life away toiling on a farm. With you working, we can always buy what we need to eat."

He finally nodded his head. When Mama has won an argument, he knows better than to take it up again. Mama is sweet, but no one had better stand between one of her children and something good.

Then things got crazier still. Miss Weston cleared her throat and said, "And I believe that Jasper has a great deal of potential, as well. I understand that he has been keeping up with his studies even though he has not been able to go to school. If you will allow us, I would like for him to take some tests. If he does well, I feel confident that we can make the same offer to him."

You could have heard a pin drop. Then Jasper jumped up, shouting, Mama started crying again. Daddy looked like somebody had walloped him with a stick of firewood, but nobody noticed him. Sardius, Jasper, and Mama were all hugging each other and me, and Miss Weston was laughing, and Daddy could not get a word in edgewise. We all know that Jasper will pass those tests. He has already completed the schoolwork up through the 10th grade. Jasper is smart.

I was so excited, I wanted to run tell Darlene, but then I remembered that she would be at Pap-pa's house today, and since I was about to bust with the good news, I just grabbed up Beryl and squeezed her until she squeaked.

We all worked hard today, planting and getting food cooked for everyone, but nobody minded one bit. It was like we were floating on air the whole day.

March 20, 1932. Daddy got drunk today. He was gone by the time we got up this morning, and Mama never even mentioned his name. She just said we all had to get dressed and go to church and be faithful to the Lord for all his blessings, and we left, wondering what we would come home to.

We went to Pap-pa's for dinner, except for Daddy, of course, and everybody was happy about Sardius' scholarship and Jasper's maybe scholarship, but the day did not feel right. We were all worried about what Daddy was up to and what kind of mood he would be in. Even Miss Weston seemed a little nervous. Uncle Woodrow did not hardly say a word.

Daddy got home about the time we were getting ready for bed. I do not want to write down what he said or did. It just makes me sick to think about it.

March 21, 1932
My School Journal, grade 7, Miss Weston's class
By Pearl Wallace

I am very proud of both of my brothers! Sardius has won a very important scholarship to study at Wheaton Academy in Chicago, Illinois, and my other brother Jasper will probably also win the same kind of scholarship. All he has to do is pass some tests, which I am sure he will do. He is very smart, and he has kept up his studies at home even though he has not been able to attend school for the past year.

Both of my brothers are going to go far in life. Sardius will become a preacher or a missionary and Jasper will build and fly airplanes. Perhaps he will break Charles Lindbergh's record when he flies solo around the world. I hope to become a missionary with Sardius and perhaps Jasper will fly us to the far away parts of the world where there are no roads so we can share the Gospel to people in the darkest places.

March 21, 1932. Mama had to drag Daddy out of bed this morning to go in to work with Mr. Sutton. I have never seen him this bad. I cannot tell you how glad we all are that he is gone.

Today is a big day in the life of a farmer. Tonight is the full moon, the Worm Moon, by the Cherokee reckoning. That means that it is the time when the ground is warming up and the worms are coming out, and it is time to start in on farming for serious. It is going to be a hard two weeks, especially for the men and boys. They have to turn the soil here, at Uncle Woodrow's and Pap-pa's place, and they probably will help out Mrs. Carlton, too. Billy Ray does not work a lick when he is home. He is as trifling as he is mean, so Mrs. Carlton and Darlene will starve if she is not able to make at least a small garden.

We have passed the Spring equinox. That means from now it will be warming up, and the days will be longer than the nights, but no one feels like celebrating that. Poor Uncle Woodrow, Jasper, and Sardius got started early this morning, plowing over at Pap-pa's place while Beryl and I traipsed off to school. It is bad to have to walk to school in the cold and the wind, but we get there sooner or later. Jasper, Sardius, and Uncle Woodrow have to be out in it all day. It is cold today, and that makes it worse. When we got home, they were still out there.

By the time they finally came in, they were filthy, chilled, and bone tired. Their faces were as red as fire from windburn, and their hands and lips were chapped. Mrs. Carlton made up some honey and beeswax to rub over their hands and faces. Darlene and Mrs. Carlton helped us cook dinner and carry water for the baths. As tired as he was, Uncle Woodrow helped, but Sardius and Jasper were so plumb wore out that Mama told them to just sit until supper.

After they all had had a good soak, Mama sent them on to bed while we finished the dishes and cleaned up their muddy mess. It is hard to be a man. Women have to work hard, too, but at least most of them do not have to plow if there is a man around.

March 24, 1932. Beryl and I have laid out of school to help at home. The boys and Uncle Woodrow have dirtied their clothes so much that Mama cannot stand for them to put them back on, even though they will just get them filthy again plowing every day. She has been scrubbing clothes and doing spring cleaning. Beryl and I stayed home to help carry water, take care of Sapphire and Ruby, and to cook the meals.

Warming, waxing days

I have been in a frenzied embrace,
The Great Orb still holds me.

I am full and strong, singing like a winter wind,
Surging with white spray and power.

The Spirit grieves with a memory,
Death grins for now,
But will weep at the reckoning.

March 25, 1932. It is Good Friday, the day they hung Jesus on the cross to die. I am glad that real Christians do not think of Jesus hanging on the cross, but instead think of Him as risen and sitting at the right hand of God the Father. The poor Catholics never think of Him in any other way but always hanging on that cross, always suffering. Mrs. Carlton wears a cross that has Jesus hanging on it. You can see the nails in His hands and feet. It is too sad to think about it.

March 26, 1932. When Daddy got home early this morning, he did not even sit down. He told Jasper and Sardius not to get up for another hour and went out to the field and started plowing. I am very glad he let the boys get some extra sleep. They need it.

Even though Daddy is a wonderful man when he is at himself and not drinking, we are all mad at him. The last time we saw him, he was cussing out Mama and all the rest of us, and telling her to pack up her rags and just get out of his life. Even though he is nice now, it still stings when I think of how he was last Sunday. I cannot get over his meanness. None of us can, except for Ruby. She forgets.

I do have to admit, though, that Daddy put in a good day's work, which took a burden off everyone else.

Tomorrow is Easter Sunday. I am glad we get to take the day off.

Cool, waxing days, shorter nights.

Holiness walks upon the land, upon my waters,
It stills the running rapids and
Holds my silver children,
As well as my creeping ones.

My upright children sleep in solemn peace,
Secure that Life will triumph.

March 27, 1932. It is Easter Sunday! The Lord is risen! Today we gave thanks for the Risen Christ and for the season of planting and for the warm weather that is coming. I wore my new shoes and the new dress that Mama made for me for my birthday. It has tucks all down the front. It is blue and yellow, and I feel beautiful in it.

Daddy did not go to church with us today, but stayed home and plowed with Uncle Woodrow and Pap-pa because we have only nine more days in the killing time to finish the first plowing and for all of the second plowing. Thank goodness the second plowing goes easier. He let the boys come on to church with us, though. It was a good Easter Sunday, but Mama does not like it when Daddy does not come to church with us. Miss Weston asked about him and about Uncle Woodrow, and I think Mama was scundered that they did not honor the most holy day of the year, but instead went out and plowed all day. I am glad they did, though. The plowing has to get done, and it is not their fault that Easter is early this year.

Warming, waxing days, cool, clear nights

My upright children rejoice in the Spirit
They wear their fine things,
Proud, humble, thankful.
The Spirit laughs aloud,
Watching Death slink into the grave.

March 27, 1932
Dear Mother and Father,

A glorious Easter to you! Our Lord is risen! Praise Him from whom all blessings flow, and blessings to you, too.

I wish you could be here to share this holy day with me, and to see the beauties of spring in this enchanting place. It was such a pleasure to worship with my church family here. If you could see how much they all love their Lord Jesus, how they listen to the sermons, and how they praise with their songs, you would know why I love them all so much. And if you could see the glories of these mountains, so blue, green, and white with blossoms, you would know why I love being here so much!.

I hope your day has felt as holy and as glorious as mine has. Peace be unto you, dear family. I love you dearly.

Emily

March 27, 1932
Dear Jonathan,

Yesterday, I received the beautiful little chocolate Easter egg you sent. What a lovely thought for such a special occasion as this most holy of celebrations. You can be assured that I will enjoy it enormously. You are so very kind to me, and I am blessed to call you friend.

Your comrade in Christ,
Emily

March 27, 1932
Dear Cecilia,

Blessings to you on this glorious day! I miss you, but I wish you were here rather than I were there. You cannot imagine how beautiful this spring is becoming, with the whole earth greening right before my eyes, flowers popping out minute by minute, the sun glowing like a golden ball. The air is so sweet, and so pure you almost feel as if you are breathing the Holy Breath of God. I am in love with this place and all the people here!

The day would have been perfect, except that not all of the men were able to come to church services this morning because they are pressed to get in the spring plowing. As you may imagine, I was saddened to see so few of them in the congregation this morning, but their places were taken up by a number of women and children who do not normally attend my church services. It was gratifying to see many of my own precious students in their seats today. Praise God from whom all blessings flow!

Good night, my sweetest of sisters.
Emily

March 28, 1932
My School Journal, grade 7, Miss Weston's class
By Pearl Wallace

It is plowing season. We plant by the signs, so we have a two-week time period between the full moon and the dark moon to get the plowing done. That is the killing time. This is also the time to plant the below ground vegetables like potatoes, carrots, and radishes. We plant the above ground vegetables during the waxing moon. In Ecclesiastes, it says, "To every thing there is a season, and a time to every purpose under the heaven: A time to be born, and a time to die; a time to plant, and a time to pluck up that which is planted; A time to kill, and a time to heal; a time to break down, and a time to build up."

My father, uncle, and brother Jasper do the heavy work of plowing, although my father has to stay in Maryville Monday through Friday, where he works for the railroad. He has a very important job on the trains making sure only the proper people ride them. It is hard for him to have to work all during the week and then come home to plow on the weekends. Sometimes he has to miss church on Sundays because of it, but he says that is one of the sacrifices that farmers have to make.

March 29, 1932. It is Easter break so we do not have to back to school again until tomorrow. Miss Weston thinks about her students and takes into consideration that people have to take time off school to do the plowing and planting. She spreads out our breaks over the spring planting time so people do not have to miss too many of their lessons. If she had taken the whole week, she could have gone home to her family in Chicago, but she knows we will have to take more time off later on when planting begins. She also did not want us to miss church on Easter Sunday. It would not be the same to have to go to the Holy Roller church over in Big Gully.

Sardius, Jasper, and Uncle Woodrow hit the fields early this morning. Daddy has gone back to work. Mama and I helped in the fields some, but after dinner, she sent me out to catch some trout so that I did not have to work all afternoon.

I stopped off at Darlene's house to see if she could join me, but before I got across the creek, I saw a truck and a car parked up on the dirt road above our house. At first, I though it must be somebody lost, and I almost hailed them, but I could see through the trees that seven men had gotten out, and they had set about to pulling sheets out of the back of the automobile. I thought that was strange, so I kept quiet.

I could not figure out what they were up to! All of them set to putting on those sheets over their clothes, like white robes, and they had pointy hoods that covered their faces, with eye-holes cut out. One of them took a big wood cross out of the truck and hoisted it over his shoulder, but then he laid it down, fiddled with his mask and hood, then yanked it off and tied a handkerchief around his face.

One of the other men said, "Hank, you're out of regulation." Hank just snorted, saying he couldn't see a thing through those G.D. eyeholes, and he picked up the cross again. Then they all began cutting through the woods. It was the oddest thing I had ever seen, grown men dressing up like ghosts for a mumming.

I almost laughed out loud, but all of a sudden, I got a funny feeling creeping up the back of my spine as if something was telling me that these men were up to some meanness. I stayed quiet, slipping back up into the woods and hiding so I could see what they were up to. They came through the trees, walking as if they had some place important to go, and before they got to the creek, they turned and went over toward Darlene's house. I followed them until I got close enough to hear them talking.

They knocked at the door, but it looked like no one was home. I figured Darlene and Mrs. Carlton were out on the river already, and Billy Ray would be over at Big Creek. They knocked a few more times, then just stood on the front porch, looking like they did not know what to do.

One of them spat on the porch and said, "They ain't home." That told me right away that they were ignorant trash and that I had better not let them see me, but then, another one mentioned Billy Ray's name and I realized who they were. They were Otis Merriweather's uncle and cousins come to take care of Billy Ray. That made me feel better, but still, something did not seem right, so I stayed hid and waited to see what they would do. They just walked around the yard, peeking in the windows, until finally, they figured out that no one was home, and they turned and left, walking back through the woods, their heads hanging like they were disappointed. I waited until I heard the automobiles start up, and then I went on to the river to try to get those fish for supper.

I wish I had told Darlene and Mrs. Carlton that they might be coming. I did not count on them being dressed up as if for a mumming. I just figured they would come and knock on the door like anybody and politely ask to see Billy Ray. I realized then that Darlene and her mother might be ascared to see seven men dressed up like ghosts standing out on their front porch.

I would have told Mama about it, but when I got home, Ruby was throwing a tantrum right on the kitchen floor, and Sapphire was screaming, too. Beryl was trying to comfort Ruby, but she was not doing much good at it. The boys and Uncle Woodrow were coming in, hungry for their supper. By the time we got it all sorted out and everyone was happy again, it was time for bed and I did not want to go running to Mama when she was so tired.

Warming, waxing days, cool dark nights

The taste of evil hovers in the air.
It poisons the greening.
It seeps into my lifeblood.
Miasma filters through my bedrock.

The Spirit grieves while Darkness sways,
Dancing the dance of Death

March 30, 1932. We were back at school today. I told Otis about his folks turning up at Billy Ray's house yesterday and asked him why they got all dressed up as if they were going to a mumming. He said he reckoned they had to hide who they were because they did not want to start any feuding. That made sense to me. If Billy Ray knew who was giving him what-for, he might get up all his family or friends and go pay Otis' family back. I know all about feuding families. The Hatfields and the McCoys up in West Virginia fought for over 11 years, and before it was all said and done, nearly a dozen folks were murdered. The Wilsons and the Joneses from over on Indian War Path got into a feud over the Jones' dog killing some of the Wilson's chickens, and it lasted nearly a year. Sammy Wilson is still in jail for cutting off Andrew Jones' ear. I reckon if I was going to go meddling in another family's business, I might think it a good idea to dress like a ghost, too.

I wish there was time to talk all this over with Mama and Uncle Woodrow, and even Sardius and Jasper, but they are all so busy with the plowing, and so tired at the end of the day, I do not want to burden them. Beryl is too little to talk about such things, so I reckon I will just keep my mouth shut for now.

March 31, 1932. Maybe it was not such a good idea for those Cluecluckers to be coming out to work on Billy Ray. They might ascare Mrs. Carlton and Darlene, and it might not be worth it even if they did have to give Billy Ray a good talking to. It might even make it worse, and now I feel bad that I have turned them loose. I think I will tell Otis tomorrow to call them off. You never know what things you set in motion when you start getting other people involved in your business. In this case, it was not even my business. It was Darlene's and Mrs. Carlton's.

I did not have a chance to go over to Darlene's house to tell them about the Clueclukers coming to see Billy Ray. I had to help in the fields after school.

April

April 1, 1932. Otis Merriweather is out of school the rest of this week helping with the plowing at his place, so I was not able to tell him to tell his cousins to leave Mrs. Carlton alone. Then the Cluecluckers came back today, and it turned out just terrible!

I was on my way over to Darlene's house to warn her and her mother about them. I had just about made it to the creek when I heard their automobiles coming up through the woods up on the hill. I took off running so as to get to the house to warn Darlene and her mother not to be ascared. I went around to the back to keep those Cluecluckers from seeing me, and it is a good thing I did. They came through the woods fast, coming into sight even before I made it to the back door, marching right into the front yard, that big old cross laid across the shoulder of that man I reckoned was Hank. I did not want them to see me, so I shimmied up the big spruce behind the house and up onto the roof, then tiptoed up to the peak of the roof to peep over. They were in the front yard, talking about Billy Ray. I got a little ascared listening to them, their white robes dragging the ground and those pointy hoods making them look like big ghosts. I did not move, lying flat up on the roof, peeping over, listening in to what they were saying.

When they walked up on the front porch to bang on the door and holler for Billy Ray to come out, I could not see them anymore, so I slipped down to the porch roof and hid in the ivy growing up there. I was just able to lean over and see what was going on. Mrs. Carlton came to the door, cracking it open just a little, but she did not let them in.

"We have come to talk to your husband, ma'am," one of them said. "We have heard he has not been acting as a man should, mistreating you and your daughter, and we want to set him straight."

Mrs. Carlton eased out on to the porch. She was shaking, and I have never seen anybody as ascared-looking in my life. "He isn't here," she said, quiet-like.

"Ma'am, I know he is your husband, but you do not need to be protecting him. We are here to help you. You have nothing to fear from us, or from Billy Ray, once we have had a chance to speak to him."

Mrs. Carlton shook her head and wrapped her arms around herself as if she were freezing, although it was as mild a day as I have seen. "He isn't here," she said again, and this time, she sank back onto the door.

The men began to argue with her a little bit, cajoling in soft voices, and although they sounded as nice as could be, those white robes and their hidden faces made them seem evil as the devil. The man who held the cross never said a word. He just stood aside, holding that cross out in front of him like a shield.

After a while, the head man asked if they could come in and check for themselves, and then Mrs. Carlton suddenly stood up straight, put her hand on her hip, and said, loudly, "Gentlemen, I appreciate your concern, but this is my house, and I am a woman of my word. My husband has not been home all day, and I will not allow any strange men inside when he is not here. I am sure you can appreciate that." She crossed her arms again, and you could tell she meant business. The fellows murmured among themselves, and then finally, they bowed at her and told her to tell Billy Ray that they would be back, and they stepped off the porch. Mrs. Carlton went inside and shut the door.

They did not leave right away. They stood in the front yard for a few minutes, and I could hear everything they said, being hid up in the wisteria and ivy up on the roof. The tallest man among them whistled.

"What a looker!" he said. "I wouldn't mind coming back some dark night and getting me a piece of that."

The others laughed. "Sam, you'd better watch it. We're here to protect her, so don't be getting any ideas."

The one holding the cross said, "Did you see that little n-- in there?" The others looked at him. "In the window. Looking out at us."

"Naw," laughed another. "I saw a little girl. She was as white as a lily."

The man with the cross shook his head again. "No, kinky hair, and a Negro face. I seen her with the light shining on her. She may be white, but I know good and well what she is."

The others argued with him awhile, and finally the one they called Sam said, "Well, I know her mama ain't one! And if she is, I may just change my appetites."

They argued for a while longer before they finally decided to knock on the door again to try to get a look at Darlene. I do not know what came over me, but I got so ascared for what they might do if they saw her that I slipped back over the roof, climbed down the spruce, and ran around to the front of the house.

I just ran right up to them, grinned at them like a crazy person, and said, "Hey, fellows! Are you the Cluecluckers? It is too bad Billy Ray is not at home, but to tell you the truth, he has been a whole lot better to his wife and child since I told him you were coming. You need not bother yourselves with coming back. I think he will behave from now on. My daddy and brothers are looking out for him."

They all turned and stared at me, and then they started backing off. Within a minute or two, they were headed back to their automobiles. I could hear them starting up, and they roared off down the dirt road. I went up and knocked on the door, but no one answered, and I got to feeling bad that those men had shown up on account of me, so I went on home.

We had some fried chicken that Miss Janey Jo brought over for supper, but I could not eat much of it, I was so worried. I wanted to tell the others about it, but they were all about dead on their feet. Mama asked Beryl and me to wash the dishes without her, and she went on to bed with Sapphire without hardly eating a bite herself.

I am thinking just now that it is April Fool's day, and I am feeling like the worst kind of fool there ever was. I wish I had not said anything to Otis about Bill Ray. There may be more trouble than I had reckoned on.

April 2, 1932. It was a terrible, terrible day. When Daddy got home this morning, he was a pure mess. His face was all bruised up and his nose was swole up to about the size of 3. His knuckles were skinned up, too, and he was limping. He said he had an altercation with a big old hobo that did not like to be told to get off the train. Then he went to bed with a poultice. At the time, I was glad he did not go out to the woodshed first, but now I am wishing he had drunk himself senseless. I had no idea what kind of trouble I was in.

As soon as Daddy was in bed, Uncle Woodrow came in and asked Mama to come outside for a little while. The rest of us young'uns went out to the field, and as we went out, I could see that Mama, Mrs. Carlton, and Uncle Woodrow were all standing in a huddle. After a while, Mama came out to get me. By the tone of her voice and the look on her face, I knew I was in big trouble

Uncle Woodrow and Mrs. Carlton were sitting at the kitchen table. Mrs. Carlton looked just awful, and I knew it had something to do with those Cluecluckers. As it turns out, it was way worse than I had reckoned on. Mrs. Carlton had heard everything I had said to them, so she knew I had something to do with those men coming to take care of Billy Ray. I told her about how Otis Merriweather's uncle and cousins looked out for women who had bad husbands and how he said he would send them here because of the way Billy Ray had been beating Mrs. Carlton and Darlene.

They all three got very quiet, then they looked at each other. "We might as well tell her," said Mama. Mrs. Carlton nodded her head, and then Uncle Woodrow took a shaky breath and he told me the most awful thing. Those men say they are looking out for the good of the community and that they go around taking care of people who cannot take care of themselves, but they use that as an excuse in order to pester and even kill people they do not like. They especially do not like Negroes, Catholics, or Jews. The fact that they had seen Darlene and recognized her as one means that they probably will be back, and they might try to do something terrible to her.

About that time, we heard Billy Ray's car coming by, so Mrs. Carlton jumped up and ran out the door. Mama did not say anything to me, and neither did Uncle Woodrow. He went back out to the fields, and Mama went into the bedroom to talk to Daddy.

The day went from bad to worse. Daddy got up for dinner, and even though neither he nor Mama said anything while everybody ate, I knew I was going to get it. Daddy looked mad at first, and Mama looked ascared and sad. She kept looking at me, and her eyes would well up, and then she would look away. She did not look at Daddy at all. As soon as dinner was over, they sent everybody else out to plant, and then they called me into the living room, and I knew they were going to bless me out good, and maybe even whip me for siccing those Cluecluckers onto Billy Ray. My stomach was in knots, not just because I was in trouble, but also because I knew I had done something bad to Mrs. Carlton and Darlene.

Daddy sat down on the couch and made me sit right next to him. Mama sat across from us, not saying a word. Daddy's mad face just crumpled for a minute. He looked so sad and mad and beat up all at the same time, but then he drew a big breath and said, "Pearl, honey, do you know about Pandora's Box?"

I shook my head, "No, sir."

"Well, it is about a girl who found a very pretty box, and she opened it. What she did not know was that it contained all the demons and the devils in the world, and when she opened it, they all flew out and went around wreaking havoc. Do you know what that means?"

I did not know exactly, but I did not want to say so. I told him I figured he meant that my siccing the Cluecluckers on Billy Ray opened up a world of trouble for Mrs. Carlton and Darlene.

"That's right, sweetheart. Those men are bad. I want you to stay away from them, and if they ever come back while you are over there, I want you to come straight home. Is that plain?"

"What about Darlene and Mrs. Carlton?" I asked.

"You can come get me if I am home, or you can go get Woodrow or your Pap-pa, but you keep Jasper and Sardius out of it, you hear?"

I could not figure out why he did not want Jasper or Sardius to help Darlene and Mrs. Carlton. "But, Daddy," I said, "they can help. They've got your rifle. It's too far to go get Pap-pa. And you know Uncle Woodrow is not tough enough to run them off."

Daddy stood up, his face turned red, and he shouted, "Just wind your neck in! You've got no business sticking your nose into Billy Ray's business!" Then he told me to stay away from Mrs. Carlton and Darlene from here on out, and never to go over to their house again, and he stalked out the door. Mama cried a little, looked at me as if she wanted to say something, and then burst into tears and went back into her bedroom.

Daddy did not get home again until suppertime, drunk as a skunk. Mama did not hardly do anything all day, but just stayed in the house, trying to do a little sewing. She did not say a word to me about Darlene the whole time. Later on, she said she felt a sick headache coming on, and she went to bed, leaving Beryl, Ruby, and me to take care of Sapphire, then supper, and then everyone's baths. It is a good thing there was plenty of goat's milk in the springhouse, so we were able to keep the baby fed.

At first, I just felt bad, and then I got to thinking about how Daddy said he did not want me helping Mrs. Carlton or Darlene even when those bad men came, and he made it plain that he was not going to help out any, either, and that made me madder. Mrs. Carlton and Darlene do not have anybody in the word to take care of them, and Daddy ought to know better than to just let bad people run over a helpless woman and child. He owes it to Darlene, and to me, to protect what needs to be protecting. By the time we got the dishes done, I was about to boil over.

Mama came out of the bedroom about then. Her eyes were red and swole up, and she looked so pitiful that I got over my mad spell right quick, especially when she put her arms around me and said, "Pearl, I am so sorry. We will do what we can to help Darlene and Mrs. Carlton. Daddy didn't mean it when he said to keep away from them. He is just ascared for you."

I stomped my foot. "Well, if he was so ascared, why did he leave out and go get drunk? He can't do me a bit of good lying drunk around here. I reckon I just have to take care of myself. Thank goodness I have Jasper and Sardius to lean on!" Then I felt terrible about saying it. Poor Mama's face just crumpled up and she went back into the bedroom. I feel sick.

Warm, calm, waxing days.

The taste of hate and fear sits like a vapor over the land
And in my waters clear to the bedrock.
I wait for the evil that blackens the hearts of men
To blacken the sun as it blackens the Great Orb,
Who turns away her face in disgust.

April 3, 1932. It was a bad day in so many ways. I did not hardly sleep a wink all last night, worrying about what those Cluecluckers might do, and I am sick that Daddy has told me to keep my nose out of it.

I also am sad because Mama and Daddy did not go to church with us today. Mama had a sick headache and Daddy's hangover was too bad. It burns me up that poor Sardius will probably miss school again tomorrow to make up for his sorry ways. I also was still a little mad at both of them for telling me to stay away from Darlene, so I got Ruby and Beryl up, and then we went off to church by ourselves. I left Sapphire at home, but I made sure Mama was up and taking care of her before we left. I could not stand it if something happened to her. Just thinking about that little Lindberg baby makes me want to cry. Poor Jasper and Sardius had to stay home and plow.

I stayed after church so I could talk to Miss Weston. All this has been weighing on me something terrible. I was hoping Miss Weston might be able to shed some light on things, and maybe she can help me find a way to take care of Mrs. Carlton and Darlene.

I asked Miss Weston straight-out why some people do not like Negroes. She hemmed and hawed a little bit, then she sat down beside me, held my hand, and said, "Some people do not understand that God made everyone to be a little different than everyone else, and when they see differences in people, they think there is something wrong with them." I told her that is what Mama said, but it did not make sense to me. A lot of people are different and they get by with it. No one hates me because I have straight, white hair and no one hates Walt Bittertree because he walks with a limp, and no one hates Uncle Woodrow because he shakes sometimes. Why would they hate Darlene?

She said that some people think certain types of people who are of a different race are not as good as others. Negroes have it especially rough because some people look for ways to make themselves feel better when they realize how bad white folks treated them. They enslaved them, beat them, and put them in chains. If you believe someone is as good as you are and is the same as you on the inside, you cannot in your heart justify treating that person badly—beating him, or putting shackles on him for no reason other than you want to make him work for you.

It makes people feel better if they can say Negroes are not really people, not really children of God.

I remembered what Sam Hutchinson said about Negros being animals, and it all made sense to me, but it made me very sad for Darlene. She would feel terrible if she knew Sam said that about her. I keep thinking that those Cluecluckers are going to try to do something awful to her, and it is my fault. I told Miss Weston about how the Cluecluckers came to the house asking for Darlene, and then I begged her to do something to stop them. After she heard me out, she said she would go to the Sheriff and tell him that the clan was harassing women and children. But when I told her that Otis Merriweather's cousin *is* the Sheriff and that he is likely in on it, she went pale and put her hand to her face. We just sat there a long time, feeling sad, until she finally said we should pray and that she would think of something. This is getting worse and worse!

The only good thing that happened is that Daddy was plowing when we got home. Even though he had told me to stay away, I went over to Darlene's house anyway, but no one was home.

April 3, 1932
Dear Cecilia,

Trouble upon trouble has come to my quiet little paradise. Today, I just found out that the Klu Klux Klan has been to Darlene's house, and that they are bent on doing violence to her. Have you heard of them? They are an organization that harasses and even kills people of color, and, I have heard, Jews and Catholics as well. I found out about them when I was at school from one of my professors who was working to expose their crimes. They are well known throughout the South for murder and violence.

I suspect that it was the Ku Klux Klan that burned down the church in Memphis that I told you about last August. I feel lost and helpless, unable to do anything. I wanted to report them to the law enforcement, but as it turns out, the sheriff in these parts is related to the men involved, and it may be that he is a part of the organization as well! To make matters more agonizing for me, the group is family to one of my students. How could this be? How could these darling children, so earnest and so innocent, be a part of a den of such evil? How could the gentle, kind people of this community harbor so much hatred in their hearts? I do not know where to turn, what to do, how to stop it, or even what to think.

Oh, Cecilia! Please pray like you have never prayed in your life. I, myself, have been on my knees all afternoon and evening, and all I feel is a deep, empty pain throughout my whole being. Where is God in all this?

With a heavy heart,

Emily

April 4, 1932. Poor Charles Lindberg paid over $50,000 in ransom money to get his baby boy back, but Daddy says he probably will never see him again. I cannot imagine how much money $50,000 is. If someone kidnapped our little Sapphire and demanded $50,000, or even $5,000, there is no way we could even begin to pay it. I do not even think we could come up with $500. We would have to sell our farm to do it, but we would. Sapphire is priceless to us.

I had another talk with Miss Weston at dinnertime today. I still don't understand why people think Darlene is a Negro when she is pure white, and since I cannot get a good answer from Mama, I was hoping Miss Weston would know.

She was very nice about it, and we had a good talk. She said people look at one or two things about a person and make up their minds, even if it does not make sense. She said that kinky hair, a wide nose and big lips are what make people know that Darlene is a Negro, and they completely ignore the fact that her skin and hair are white. That just confused me more. Sarah Boyd has kinky hair, and lots of people have fat lips and big noses, and nobody holds it against them. Miss Weston looked sad and said that Darlene has just the right combination of things going against her, and once ignorant and ungodly people make up their minds about something, they cannot get it out of their heads, and they think they are justified to be mean.

That just burns me up. Darlene cannot help how she looks, and nobody has the right to be nasty to her because of it. It burns me up that Daddy told me to stay away from Darlene's house, and I just dare Mama to say anything! I got so mad that I promised myself that nobody could stop me from doing whatever I can to take care of Darlene, and I went over there right after school to tell her that. No one was home again. I peeked in all the windows, but I could not see anything but an empty house. It would have been nice to go up on the roof and look at the river and think for a little while, but I went on back home because I knew Mama and the boys would be worn out from plowing all day, and I started feeling bad about not helping out. I have not been much help to anybody of late.

My soul is heavily burdened. I do not know to whom I can talk about this. I have brought a load of grief upon my friends and my family. I wish I could do something to end this terrible mess!

April 5, 1932. Sardius went back to school with us today. Tonight is the dark moon, so he is taking a little break before we have to start in planting peas and broadbeans tomorrow. It was very, very nice to be able to have him walking with us, and I took the chance to tell him about what all had been happening with the Cluecluckers coming. I did not hardly get started before he shushed me and pointed to Beryl. I did not get a chance to talk to him again until we got away together at dinnertime, and then I told him everything.

Sardius was very sweet. He told me that it was not my fault that those bad men had come to bother Mrs. Carlton and Darlene. He soothed me and petted me on the back until I calmed down, and then he said we should report this to somebody. But when I told him about Otis Merriweather's uncle being the Sheriff, he did not know what to do either. He got quiet for a long time, and then he said, real quiet, "Let's pray about it."

I wished that I had talked to Sardius earlier. I have been praying every day for Jesus to tell me what to do, but Sardius would have more weight with the Lord. I am a terrible sinner whose word would not be worth much, but Sardius has given his life to Jesus, and he is a much better child of God than I am. I just nodded my head as Sardius put his arm around me, and we prayed for all we were worth. I just about hugged him. Sardius is the smartest and best boy I know.

It felt good to unburden myself before the Lord. I promised Him I will quit selling whiskey if He would just find a way out of this mess and to save Darlene from worldly harm.

This was the prettiest day we have had so far this year. A whole grove of serviceberry trees are blooming along the fenceline over by Jimmy Holland's pasture. We stopped to pick some for Mama and Mrs. Carlton. Mama loved hers, but Mrs. Carlton and Darlene were not home. I left them on the front porch. I hope they cheer them up.

April 6, 1932. I have not seen Darlene for five days, and the more I think about her, the sicker I get. I wish I could go see her, but we are spending every minute out in the fields until dark, and she has not come over here once.

April 7, 1932. All of us were back at school today, including Otis Merriweather. I collared him at dinnertime and told him he had better tell his uncles and his cousins to leave Darlene and her mother alone. He looked at me as if I had slapped him. He had no idea that his cousins could be mean to Mrs. Carlton or anybody. I said they sure and well were mean, and I did not want to see them sticking their noses around where they did not belong any more. Otis about cried and tried to get me to tell him why I wanted them to leave Billy Ray alone, but I was not about to tell him that

Darlene is a Negro or a Catholic. He might be on his cousins' side. I had already gotten Darlene into enough trouble.

When we got home from school, Mama let on that she was worried about Darlene and Mrs. Carlton. This was the first time she has mentioned them since Daddy had told me to stay away from them. She had not seen either of them, although they were still bringing Sapphire her goat milk. Somebody puts it on the steps early of the mornings, then disappears for the day. Mama said she had gone over there several times, but they were never home. I am as low as a snake's belly, but I am glad Otis is going to call off his family.

April 8, 1932. When we got home from school today, guess who met me as I was coming down the path? Darlene! But it was a different Darlene than I have ever seen before. Her hair was nearly as straight as mine! It fell in the prettiest curves from the part on the side of her head down to her chin, and she had on pretty pink lipstick. When she took off her spectacles, she did not look like anyone from around here, but like a foreign princess or a movie star! We rushed into the house together to show Mama.

Mama stopped in her tracks when she saw her. At first, she lit up with a smile, then she ducked her head, looking sad. Mrs. Carlton came in behind us, looking nervous. "What do you think, Adaline? Will it work?" she said.

Mama looked at Mrs. Carlton with a kind of sad expression that made me worry. "Oh, Celeste. She is beautiful, but…" Then she stopped, glanced at Darlene, and said, "Darlene, honey, you are just beautiful! I love your new hairdo," and I felt better.

Beryl was crazy over Darlene's slick hair and her pink lipstick. We all wrapped our arms around each other and danced around until we all fell down laughing. What a wonderful day this has been. Now even if those men get a good look at Darlene, they will not be able to say she is a Negro.

Mrs. Carlton and Darlene were mighty relieved when I told them I had talked to Otis and told him to tell his cousins to not come back. Things are going to be better from here on out.

Oh, and Jasper and Uncle Woodrow got most of the peas planted today. They have a little more to do, but they say they can ease off some. They are going to take tomorrow off before they start in on the beans.

It is funny how things go from good to bad and back to good again in no time at all.

April 9, 1932. One good thing about those Cluecluckers coming is that they scared off Billy Ray. Mrs. Carlton told him about how they came asking for him, and he lit out right after that and has not been back since. Billy Ray is the biggest coward in the world. I cannot imagine anybody more low-down than a man who will leave his wife and child alone when he thinks some bad men will be poking around. If he had any backbone at all, he would be waiting for them with a loaded shotgun.

Now that the Cluecluckers have been called off and Billy Ray has taken off for parts unknown, we had us a big time today. Daddy has to work overtime at the railroad to take the place of some of the men who are out sick, so he will not be home this week. That is fine with me. We can use the extra money, and he was not here to put a damper on our fun. Darlene did not need to go over to Pap-pa's, so we decided to go fishing. The river is swole up very high. When it is high and swift, Mama does not like us to go down there by ourselves in case we fall in, so we talked Jasper and Sardius into going with us. It did not take much talking. We all had a grand time, and we caught ten trout betwixt us!

Warming, waxing days.

The taste of green seeps deep and soft.
The greenleaves bud and swell,
My body is full of freshness,
My silver children wake to my roaring song.

The upright ones rejoice in fullness,
But they do not see the Darkness looming.
I sing of Spring but wait for calamity

April 10, 1932. It is Sunday, which is usually my favorite day, especially since Darlene and Mrs. Carlton joined us for dinner, but today Uncle Woodrow seemed a little tetchy. At dinner, we were all making on over Darlene's beautiful, wavy hair, and Miss Weston mentioned that Darlene looks almost white, and all of a sudden, Uncle Woodrow held his hand up to let us know to be quiet. Then he turned to Darlene and said,

"Sweetheart, don't you let anyone tell you that you aren't perfect the way you are. It's okay to disguise yourself now, when you may be in danger, but one day, you will know that you need to be proud of who you are and what you are, and you won't need to hide from anybody. It isn't you that needs changing. It is the ignorant and bigoted people who don't know any better. And don't you ever forget it."

Everybody got very quiet, and then Miss Weston blushed. Mama spoke up and said, "Of course, Woodrow. Darlene is perfect the way she is. But for now, I think it is a good idea she keep herself disguised as long as there is tension around here. Don't you agree?"

Uncle Woodrow just nodded then went back to eating, but he was quiet and a little tetchy with everybody but Darlene and me the rest of the day.

April 10, 1932
Dear Cecilia,

It was an uncomfortable day. I think the crisis with Darlene may be over, but things are still a little tense among my newfound family. Pearl informs me that the Klan has been called off, and Darlene has managed to change her hair enough that she might be able to pass for white. If they should come back, perhaps they will not molest her or her mother. Still, I am wary. Pearl does not know what these people are capable of. I told you about the men who tried to lynch the colored man over in Alcoa. They did not succeed, but things were breathtakingly tense for some time, and now the poor man has been sentenced to death. What a tragedy! He was caught up in his anger and jealousy, and it was entirely the white man's fault. The jury did not see it that way, however, and now he will be taken away from his family and his loved ones. The misery just will not end!

We were discussing this at dinner today, and I mentioned how pleased I was that Darlene might be able to pass for white with her straightened hair, and suddenly Woodrow gave me a hard look. Then he turned to Darlene and told her she needs to always remember that she is just as good as everybody else. I could not agree more, but as long as there is trouble between the races here and as long as ignorant people harbor evil in their hearts against people of color, I think it is necessary that Darlene try to blend in as much as possible.

Woodrow spent the entire remainder of the meal talking to Darlene and Pearl. I know he is concerned for the child and wants her to be at ease, but I was a little surprised that he conversed with them almost exclusively, when he usually is attentive to my thoughts and words. I ended up talking to Mrs. Carlton and Mrs. Wallace the whole time. Mrs. Carlton is surprisingly beautiful, and very gracious. She is unusual, but I can see why some might find her attractive.

I simply am too drained to write any more. Give my love to everyone, and please do not stop praying!

Emily

April 11, 1932
My School Journal, grade 7, Miss Weston's class
By Pearl Wallace

Sunday is my favorite day of the week. I love to go to church to hear from the Word of God, and I also love to go to my grandfather's house for Sunday dinner afterwards. We always have a nice crowd. Miss Weston, my teacher, comes for Sunday dinner, and so does my Uncle Woodrow. My father was not able to come yesterday because he had to work overtime at the Railroad, but we managed to have a good time without him, even though we missed him very much.

The reason we had such an extra-special good time this Sunday is because my best friend, Darlene, and her mother came to dinner with us. Darlene has come before, but this is the first time her mother has been able to. She usually stays home and cooks Sunday dinner for her husband, but since he was gone yesterday, she was able to join in with us! It was a very good time.

April 11, 1932. I was happy over the weekend, but today has been another awful day, even worse than any I have had before. The Cluecluckers came back. We did not go to school today because of the planting, and I ran over to Darlene's house at dinnertime. We had gone up on the roof to eat, and we were just sitting there, enjoying the sunshine, when we saw them coming through the woods, all dressed up in their white ghost costumes. The same man who had carried the cross before wore a filthy handkerchief over his face instead of the hood the others wore. It gave me chills to see him, and I could feel Darlene grow stiff with afright. We both threw ourselves down flat on the roof and eased over the top so that we were on the back side of the house, and we just laid there, still and quiet as we could be while those Cluecluckers walked up to the front porch and knocked on the door.

It took Mrs. Carlton a long time to come to the door. They kept knocking and knocking, and I could imagine them going around, peeking in the windows, and I was scared to death they would come to the back and look up to see us. I thought Darlene should not have anything to worry about now that her hair was as straight as a white girl's, but she just froze up when she saw them and shook her head when I whispered that she did not need to be ascared of them now.

We stayed quiet while they kept banging on the door. Finally, Mrs. Carlton opened it. I could not hear a thing anyone was saying, so I whispered to Darlene that I was going to go listen in. Although she grabbed my hand, shaking her head, "no," I was dying to know how Mrs. Carlton would handle it. I pulled myself away to slide over the peak of the roof and down to the roof of the porch, where I hid in among the wisteria and ivy. I could hear them plain as day.

Mrs. Carlton was saying, "I told you. My husband is not here. He has gone hunting with several of his friends, and I expect them back sometime, but I assure you, he is not at home at present. In case you are interested, he has been very well behaved ever since I told him you had come. I thank you for that, but your work is done, so you might as well go on your way. There is no need for you to come again."

I inched my head over the roof and peeked through the wisteria. The man with the handkerchief across his face had put down his cross and had his face mashed up against the window with his hands cupped around his eyes, looking in just as brash as a trashy old peeping-tom. He backed up and looked at Mrs. Carlton in a mean way.

"Is your daughter at home, ma'am?" he asked.

Mrs. Carlton froze, and from where I was, I could see how ascared she suddenly was. She stood there for a minute, then she asked him why he had his face covered. He did not answer her, but asked again if Darlene was at home, and he picked up his cross and lowered it down toward her head in a mean way.

Finally, she said, "She is not here, either, and I ask you gentlemen to leave at once. You have no business with me or my daughter. The Wallaces live just across the creek from here, and I believe everyone is at home, including both Mr. Wallace and his brother, as well as his sons. If you do not leave at once, I will call out to them."

I knew she was bluffing. Daddy was not home, although Uncle Woodrow and the boys were about somewhere, but they could not hear her from there no matter how loud she hollered. I figured the only thing to do was to skitter back across the roof and down the back and go get them before things got out of hand. I had a bad feeling about this, and all of a sudden, I was not so sure about how much Darlene looked like a white girl. If they looked at her up close, they might be able to figure out she is still a Negro, no matter how much her looks had changed.

I did not know what to do. Uncle Woodrow would not be worth much. If he even saw these men dressed up in their dirty sheets, he would no doubt fall into a shaking fit, and Sardius is too skinny to really scare these fellows. Only Jasper has some heft to him, and there is not much he could do against seven men set on meanness. I laid there for a minute more while I thought about it. Jasper could shoot them, or I could bring him and Mama and everyone and act like we were just ladies coming over for a visit while Uncle Woodrow drove the wagon over to get Pap-pa. But it would take a long time for them to get back here, and there was no telling what might happen in the meantime.

No matter how I looked at it, it looked bad. But then, while I was lying there, trying to decide what to do, one of the other men said in a little nicer tone. "We would like to meet the little girl who lives here with you, ma'am. I reckon she is your daughter? Do you know where she is?"

Mrs. Carlton lifted her head and told them straight to their faces that Darlene was off spending the night with her schoolteacher, Miss Emily Weston, and she would not be back today. The men looked at each other, then the tall one, the one they had called "Sam" stepped right up to Mrs. Carlton and raked his hand across her chest, picking up the cross she wears on her necklace.

I know that is a Catholic cross because it has Jesus hanging on it, and I knew it was trouble by the way the man was looking at it and then looking at Mrs. Carlton with a sort of hungry look on his face.

"Are you Catholic, Ma'am?' he asked. Mrs. Carlton took a step back, but he hung onto that cross, stepping up to her and getting close to her face, then he yanked at the necklace. It broke and came off in his hand.

After that, I could not believe my eyes what happened. He kind of sneered at her, and then he reached his hand inside her dress, and grabbed her titty, hard! I just about fell off the roof! I would have hollered at him then, but I was so shocked that all I could do was just draw in a breath and hold it. A woman's titties are private to her and to her baby, and no one is ever allowed to touch them, not even her children, and especially not a grown man! My mama has told me that if anybody ever tried, I was to kick him in his private parts and scream bloody murder. That man had reached right in and grabbed one of Mrs. Carltons', and I could not make it seem right in my mind that anyone could do such a thing. Mrs. Carlton's face went red. She let out a little shriek, then she hauled off and slapped him. At the same time, one of the other men jumped in and grabbed the fellow.

"Sam, you lay off," he said. "We are not here to insult the lady." Then the others stepped up, grabbing Sam to pull him away. Sam kind of glared at them, then glanced at Mrs. Carlton who stood in the doorway, her hand to her neck, shaking so hard she could barely stand.

"I am truly sorry, Ma'am," said the one who had stopped Sam. "Our fellow has no right to insult you. There is no need for you to fear us. We will not be back." No one else said anything. They just turned and stepped across the yard and into the woods. The man who had apologized to Mrs. Carlton turned and waved at her as they made their way into the woods. I nearly died because when he looked back, I had half stood up on the roof, and I was ascared he had seen me, but he turned again and went on into the woods.

We watched them go, waiting, still as mice, for a good 5 minutes before I scurried back over the roof to Darlene. She was lying flat on the roof, shaking and sobbing quietly into her hands. After a while, Mrs. Carlton came out, walking around the house, calling to us softly, and when we peeked over the edge of the roof, she put her hand to her mouth and started to cry.

I have never felt so bad in my life.

April 14, 1932. I do not know where Darlene is. She and her mother have been gone since yesterday. I wish Daddy would come home. Mama is a nervous wreck. We have switched to planting Brussels sprouts and squash. We are working such long hours I do not have time to write.

April 15, 1932. It was a hard day of planting. Darlene and Mrs. Carlton are still not at home. Goat milk shows up on our back step every morning, but neither Mama nor I have seen hide nor hair of them.

April 16, 1932. Daddy did not come home again today. He sent word with Mr. Sutton that the Railroad is having trouble with the hobos and they need every man to keep them in line. As much as we are glad when Daddy gets to work overtime, we are starting to miss him, and I can tell Mama is worried. It is not good that the hobos are getting out of hand and hurting people. I hope Daddy stays safe. It was bad enough when he got beat up last month. They might could hurt him bad.

I also wish he would get home and get busy with his still soon. We are about plumb out of whiskey. It will be nice when things get back to normal.

We have finished up with most of the planting so that Uncle Woodrow and Jasper can handle it from here on. I am sick to death of working and worrying over Darlene. The only good news is that we get to go back to school on Monday.

April 18, 1932. It is Monday, and I just realized I have not written in my journal to turn in to Miss Weston. We all are laying out of school because we just did not have it in us to go after what all happened. I will try to write it just as it happened, as near as I can tell it, anyway, because it is all so jumbled up in my mind that I am having a hard time sorting through what really went on.

Darlene stayed home this weekend because Billy Ray turned up on Friday and he decided she could not go over to Pap-pa's house. I did not see her all day on Saturday, and now I wish we had sneaked her out of the house anyway.

Sunday started out really good because it was Miss Janey Jo's birthday, and Mama decided we were going to spend the whole afternoon celebrating with Pap-pa and her and not do a lick of work. She said we all needed a true day of rest, and the best way to make that happen was not to even get near the fields all day. Then, before the day was over, it turned out to be horrible, more horrible than any I have ever had.

Miss Weston was at dinner with us, and we had a very fine time playing games afterward, then we ended up staying until late in the evening. We spent the afternoon looking at Pap-pa's new calf and riding his old saddle horse, and then Pap-pa up and decided that we needed to do some target practice. Uncle Woodrow and Miss Weston went back into the house because neither one of them can stand being around guns. I was hoping that they might start courting when I saw them walking back together, but now I know better. Miss Weston is for sure struck on Uncle Woodrow. She smiled at him all evening, laughed at nearly everything he said, and once she reached over and poked at his shoulder, but he is not struck on her, I am sad to say. I know for a fact that he is struck on someone else, namely Mrs. Carlton.

I am getting ahead of myself. We practiced shooting at tin cans until it got too dark to see anymore. By the time we made it back, Janey Jo, Mama, and Miss Weston had already made supper, so we stayed until Ruby fell asleep on the floor and Beryl was yawning her head off. Mama finally said we had to get back because of it being a school day tomorrow, and Miss Weston offered to drive us home. It was a very tight squeeze, but we all got in. Mama and Uncle Woodrow sat in the front and held the little ones. I sat in the back with Jasper and Sardius. Beryl sat on Jasper's lap. We giggled all the way home because we were all packed in so tight we hardly had room to breathe. That ride back was the last good thing I remember.

After that, it felt like the whole world caved in. One minute, we were riding along in Miss Weston's fine car, laughing like we did not have a care in the world, and the next minute we were rolling into the yard, and Darlene was stumbling up from the back, screaming like a panther. Her dress was torn and bloody, too, and I could see she had bruises and bloody marks all up and down her arms and legs. We all jumped out of the car to tend to her, but she was so riled up we could not hardly understand a word she was saying at first. She just gasped and screamed, pulling on my arm, hollering something about Billy Ray trying to kill them. Mama rushed into the house with Sapphire and Ruby, but the rest of us took off running over to Darlene's house.

We could hear the screams before we got to the creek. By the time we made it to the house, all I could hear was shrieks— shrieks from Darlene right beside me and shrieks from Beryl, who by this time, had caught the hysterics. And then there was Darlene's mother, sitting in the middle of the floor, her bloody hands held out in front of her and shaking as if she had the palsy. Blood streamed out of a gash along her collarbone. Beside her lay a big black skillet smeared with blood. Billy Ray was sprawled over in the corner, his head lying in a puddle of blood. Beryl let out one more shriek, and then lit out for home.

All of a sudden, it seemed as if everything went into slow motion. Uncle Woodrow shoved me aside and threw himself at Mrs. Carlton, getting down on his knees in all that blood, gathered her up in his arms, and then sort of collapsed into her, sobbing and shaking, rocking her like a baby, covering her bloody head with kisses while she screamed and hollered. The rest of us stood rock-still, except Miss Weston, who grabbed onto the doorframe and slid to the floor, hanging onto that doorframe as if her knees had turned to water. She stared at Uncle Woodrow for a long time while he kissed Mrs. Carlton, and then she began to sob.

Then everything just went crazy. While we were all looking at Uncle Woodrow and Mrs. Carlton, Billy Ray came to. He pulled himself up to his knees, and then he staggered to his feet and lunged toward them. He had a knife clenched in his fist. Jasper saw it, too. Before Billy Ray had time to take a second step, Jasper tackled him. The knife skittered across the floor, finally stopping in a slow spin right beside Uncle Woodrow.

Billy Ray jumped up and took a swing at Jasper, but he ducked just in time. Sardius head-butted him in the stomach, but not hard enough to do any good. Billy Ray shoved him off, and just as he stood up straight again, something whizzed by me, and the next thing I knew, Billy Ray was standing still, looking at the knife sticking out of the middle of his chest. Uncle Woodrow still had one arm around Mrs. Carlton, who half lay in his lap, sobbing and quivering. The other arm was held out straight, as if it had been frozen when the knife left his hand. That arm was as still as stone, while the rest of him wailed and shook like he had the palsy. Then the arm that held the knife began to shake, too, until he fell face first onto the floor, weeping and shuddering, making noises like a trapped animal.

It is funny what I remember and what I do not. I do not remember Billy Ray falling, nor what Jasper, Sardius, or Darlene did after that. All I remember is poor Miss Weston looking at Uncle Woodrow and Mrs. Carlton with their arms around each other as if her heart was broken. She sat on the floor, staring for what seemed like a long, long time, where nobody spoke, until she finally shook herself and said. "We need to get these children out of here, and Mrs. Carlton needs attention," and she held out her hand to Jasper to pull herself up.

Everybody but me started moving, but I could not remember how to pick up my feet. It felt like they had just grown to the floor. Sardius put his arm around Uncle Woodrow, coaxing him to get up, while Jasper gathered Mrs. Carlton in his arms and carried her out the door. Uncle Woodrow was not worth a hill of beans. He just kept stumbling and sliding back down to the floor, crying fit to be tied. Finally, Miss Weston went over to him, helped Sardius hoist him up, and pulled his arm over her shoulder.

"Come on, Woodrow," she said. "This is no time to fall to pieces. We have to get Mrs. Carlton some help."

I was so ascared I forgot to follow them out. The next thing I knew, I was standing alone on a bloody floor with a dead man at my feet, and I could not make it make any sense. In all the times that I had imagined Billy Ray dead, I had not seen anything like this. In my mind, I could see him as cold and still, and I could imagine saying, "Good riddance to bad rubbish," but seeing him like this was far past what my mind had told me it could be like.

Somehow, Billy Ray dead was more real than he ever could have been when he was alive. He was hard and still, his muscles outlined underneath his soft, splotchy skin. The skin of his face and neck seemed tender, like a baby's. His hands were rough, hairy, and bony, but at the same time, they seemed helpless, pitiful. All the meanness had left him, as if it had run out with his blood. I could not stitch it together in my mind that all that blood had been inside of him just a few minutes before, and he had been alive. Now his spirit had fled, and I did not want to know where it had gone.

As I looked at him, I thought that the right thing to do would be to take the knife out of his chest, but the thought of touching him turned my stomach. I made myself reach for it, but then it came to me that even if I took it out, he would still be dead. There was nothing I could do to help him at all. My knees went to jelly. I staggered out as fast as I could, but my legs just quit working. I fell off the porch and lay in the grass, gulping in great breaths of air, hoping that Jesus would forgive us for what we had done, but not being exactly sure what it was that we had done. It just seemed that evil had pushed its way inside us, and I was sorry we had not done anything to stop it. I wished I had never hated Billy Ray.

I laid out there in the grass beside the porch for some time, crying, praying, afraid for what would happen next. I tried to get up, but I was so sick and dizzy, I could not get my legs up under me. Just when I was beginning to think I would have to lie out there all night, I saw Jasper coming back for me. He walked up to where I lay, sat down beside me, and then he put his big, strong arm around my waist and hefted me up. He did not try to hurry me along, but he had to hold onto me because my legs were twitching so bad, I could not take a single solid step by myself.

We were nearly to the creek when all of a sudden, Jasper stopped, holding his breath as he looked around. "Shush," he said, hustling me over to a pokeberry bush. After another second, he ran back to the house, pulled the door shut, then sprinted back to my hiding place in the pokeberry.

I could not understand why he was acting like that. "Listen, and be quiet," he whispered, and after a few seconds, I could hear hushed noises coming through the woods. Three white figures came out of the darkness of the woods—men wearing sheets. One was very tall, and I knew him to be Sam. Another did not have the sheet over his head, but wore a bandana tied around his face. That was Hank, the one who had the meanest spirit toward Darlene. I could tell because of the bandana and the way he walked, sort of hunched over. He carried the same cross I had seen before. They came on as quiet as cats, creeping and stopping to listen, until they stood in front of Billy Ray's dark house, not five feet away from us. I was trembling so hard I could hear the leaves of the pokeberry bush rustling around me. Jasper kept his arm tight around my waist, hunkering down over me as if he could protect me. He kept his hand over my mouth for a minute, until I felt like he was smothering me and I pushed it away. I knew better than to make a sound.

"Be quiet," Sam said. "We want to be out of here before they wake up." He took the cork off a jug and doused kerosene all over the cross while another one of them dug a hole with a spade. I could smell it, strong and sharp, like the breath of the devil. When the cross was good and soaked, they dropped it into the hole, scotched it up with rocks, then tossed a match. It went up in blue flames. As the fire whooshed up, swallowing up the cross, the men lit out toward the woods.

It was an awful sight, that cross on fire, the flames spewing up into the black sky, the smell of kerosene strong in the cool night air, and I all I could think of was Jesus hanging on that cross and burning, while evil men stood nearby, casting lots and jeering. I wanted to scream, but no sounds came out of my throat except for some gasping sobs, and then Jasper's hand was over my mouth again and he was dragging me out of the pokeberry bush and across the creek, through the woods, and on up to our little house, all lit up with light and voices.

I do not know what happened after that for a while. I just sort of blanked out, and then Mama's hand was on my forehead and she was holding a cup of whiskey to my mouth. I choked some of it down, and although it tasted awful, it gave me a warm feeling in my stomach, and after a minute, I felt back to myself a little. Darlene sat beside me, holding my hand and crying, while Mrs. Carlton half-sat, half lay on a chair at the kitchen table. Her eyes were closed. She moaned a little bit, then fell quiet. Uncle Woodrow sat beside her, holding her hand, shaking bad enough to rattle the whole house

"Are you feeling better now, Pearl?" Mama asked. I nodded, not sure if I could speak. She looked at me real close, stroked back my hair, and smiled at me, her eyes sweet and gentle. "Good. I need to finish stitching Mrs. Carlton up before the laudanum wears off," and she put my hand in Jasper's, walked over to where Mrs. Carlton lay, and picked up a needle that had been lying on her collarbone. As calm as could be, she took to stitching. Mrs. Carlton moaned and cried out, but Mama did not seem to notice. She just kept on sewing while Mrs. Carlton cried and Uncle Woodrow sat beside her and shook.

The whiskey was making me feel better, enough so that I was able to look around. Miss Weston sat on the couch, holding both Sapphire and Ruby in her lap. Darlene and Beryl huddled on either side of her. Jasper hovered over me until I waved him away. He was making me feel smothery. Sardius was nowhere to be seen.

Miss Weston spoke up, "Jasper, can you build us a fire? Darlene is cold. And is there any more of that whiskey left?" Jasper handed the cup to her, and I could not hardly believe my eyes when she took that cup and took a big swallow before giving a sip to Darlene. She set Ruby down, put Sapphire in Beryl's arms, and crossed over to Uncle Woodrow.

"Drink a little of this, Woodrow. I find that it can help in times like this," she said as she cupped her hand around the back of his head and tilted the cup up to his lips. He drank it, and I wondered if maybe I was having a dream, where nothing was normal. Nobody was behaving anything like I expected them to. Mama calm as ice while she sewed up a moaning woman, Miss Weston serving whiskey to everybody as if it were a tea party. Uncle Woodrow scared to death, but sitting right there in the living room, not running out the door.

Jasper built a fire, even though it was as warm as an April night can be, for Darlene was shivering enough to rattle her bones, although I think the whiskey had quieted her down a bit. A little while later, Sardius came in with Pap-pa and Miss Janey Jo. As soon as they got here, Jasper pulled them out to the porch, where they stayed out talking for a few minutes, then Miss Janey Jo came back in to sit with the rest of us, and we waited, not knowing what was going to happen, fearful to sit, and yet afraid to go out. It was as quiet as the grave, except for Mrs. Carlton's moanings and Uncle Woodrow's occasional gasp for breath. Miss Weston settled in the corner with Sapphire, staring at the fire for a long, long time. Miss Janey-Joe cuddled up to Darlene and Beryl, with Ruby on her lap. Mama laid another blanket on the little girls and took me in her arms, holding me and stroking my forehead, which quieted my heart. Uncle Woodrow held Mrs. Carlton's hand. No one said a word while we waited for Jasper, Sardius, and Pap-pa to return.

They came in through the back door much later. Pap-pa stood in the open doorway, looking big and calm, then he leaned against the doorjamb as he flickered his eyes over at Miss Weston. "Ladies, we need to pray," He said. "It may be that the Lord has shown us a way out of the bind that we find ourselves in tonight." Everyone gathered around, and Pap-pa knelt in front of the fire and prayed a short, simple prayer: "Lord, we can't help but think this is Your will. Tell us if it isn't." Then he got up as everybody started whispering in urgent, soft voices. I could not hear what they said, but I did not care. I was so tired that I closed my eyes for just a minute, and when I opened them again, they had all stopped talking. Miss Janey Jo was sorting through the woodpile.

"No, Janey Jo. There is no need for you to go," Pap-pa said. Janey Jo laughed. "Don't you think for one minute that we will let you boys go and have all the fun," she said as she pulled out three sticks of fatwood. She handed one to Miss Weston and one to Mama.

I fell asleep again after that, and the next thing I knew, I was lying in my bed with Darlene and Beryl beside me, and daylight was coming in through a fine mist of rain, along with the barest whiff of charred wood. Mama was shaking Darlene and me awake.

It is still April 18, and I have much more to tell about what happened, although it seems like a week has gone since Uncle Woodrow killed Billy Ray. We are not at school because Mama said we needed our sleep, and besides, the Sheriff would likely want to talk to us.

Mama waited for us to rub the sleep out of our eyes before she sent Beryl downstairs. "Miss Janey Jo and Pap-pa are here," she told her. "And after breakfast, they are going to take you home with them so Miss Janey Jo can help you start that new dress she has been promising you."

Beryl jumped right up and scuttled downstairs. Darlene and I started to get up, too, but Mama stopped us. She sat down on the side of the bed, laid her hands on our arms, and spoke to us in that sweet voice of hers.

She told us that the Sheriff had come by last night, and they had filled him in on what had happened. He had wanted to wake us, but she told him we were all so tired from all the excitement of Janey Jo's birthday that we would not be able to make any sense. I am very glad she did not let him wake us. I was not sure what I should tell him. I did not want him to know that Uncle Woodrow had flat-out killed Billy Ray dead. He would surely get the electric chair for that.

"The Sheriff will be coming back," she told us. When he does, he will want to talk to you both, and you will need to tell him the important things that he needs to hear. Pearl, I want you to tell him what has been happening to Darlene and her mother for the past few weeks. About those men who have been bothering them. Now, you need to go over it in your mind. Can you tell me exactly what you have seen?"

I started to tell her about how Otis's clan had come to the house to make Billy Ray treat Darlene and her mother better, but she stopped me.

"There is no need to let on why you think those men came. You do not need to be dragging Otis Merriweather into this. It will be hard on him and his mother if they get involved. Let's just stick to what you saw at Darlene's house, not what you and Otis talked about or what you thought, all right?"

I thought that was wise. Otis could get into a lot of trouble if it came out that he knew anything about this, and he could not help it if things turned out different than he expected. I thought about it, then said, "Some men came asking about Billy Ray."

"That's right," Mama nodded. "And how were they dressed?"

"At first they wore regular clothes, but then they changed into sheets with eye holes cut in them. One of them couldn't see through his eye holes, so he wore a bandana."

She laid her hand on my arm again. "The Sheriff does not need to know that you saw them in regular clothes or indicate in any way that you might be able to recognize them if you saw them again. If you do, you might be putting Otis and his family in trouble.

Mama was right. There was no need to tell that I saw their automobiles or that one wore a bandana because he could not see through his eye-holes or that one of the others had called him "Hank." I ran the scene through my mind, careful with my words. "They wore sheets. One of them carried a big wood cross."

Mama asked me how many times they had come. I reckoned there were four times, because that is all I saw them, but they could have come more. Darlene kept quiet. I could tell she was too ascared to say anything.

"So you saw them come to Mrs. Carlton's house four times? Where were you when you saw all this? What did they do each time?"

"The first time they came, I was on my way to Darlene's house. I saw them coming through the woods, but they didn't see me. I hid behind a tree and watched them."

I told her how they had knocked on the door, then went around the house peeking in the windows and how they just left when they figured no one was home.

"That's good, Pearl. And how about the next time?"

I told about how they came the second time and how I was ascared of them so I had climbed up on the roof so I could see what all went on without them seeing me. I described how Mrs. Carlton had come to the door, looking ascared and how they tried to get her to let them in but she would not, saying her husband was not home and she would not let them in as long as he was away. Then they stood on the porch and said some nasty things about her and Darlene. I talked about how they had knocked on the door again and I got so ascared for Darlene and about what they might do to her that I shimmied down off the roof and told them there was no need to come back, that Billy Ray was not at home much these days.

Mama frowned. "Maybe you should not say you talked to them or that they saw you. I am sure the Sheriff is a good man, but he might not be thinking about your safety. He might mention to the wrong people that there was a witness, and that could put you in danger. These are evil men, Pearl. They might hurt you if they think you know too much. Can you just say they went away on their own?"

I realized that since Otis' uncle was the Sheriff over in Madison county, maybe he was in on some of this. It about made my hair stand on end, and right then and there, I realized that more was at stake than any of us could ever imagine. Uncle Woodrow might be blamed for everything. He could get the electric chair, and the rest of us might be staring in the face of the devil himself. I stopped, thinking it through before I told her about how they had come back to ask to see Darlene and how one of them tore Mrs. Carlton's necklace off her neck and then grabbed at her titty, and how the other one pulled him away and apologized, and how Darlene had been so scared and how Mrs. Carlton had cried.

Mama looked at Darlene. "Darlene, sweetheart," she said. "Is that right? Do you remember it the same way so that you could tell the Sheriff just how it happened the way Pearl has said?" Darlene nodded. "Do you have anything else to add to what Pearl has told me?" Darlene began to cry as she shook her head.

"I was real scared," she said.

Mama petted her on the head. "I'm sure you were, honey. I would be, too. Now, Pearl, tell me about the last time you saw these men."

I started telling about how I had been lying in the yard because I was too weak and trembly to move after Uncle Woodrow had killed Billy Ray, but I caught myself before I got any of it out. I took a breath and started again, speaking slowly, making it up as I went.

"I went to Darlene's house."

Mama smiled and nodded. "Yes, you and Jasper went over there because we had run out of firewood. Darlene and her mother were here all evening, and Mrs. Carlton told you to run over to her house and get some so we could make some popcorn. Isn't that right?"

"But Mama, we have firewood in the woodshed. What if the Sheriff checks?"

Mama smiled. "No, sweetheart. We burned all we had left for supper. There might have been a little bit the last time you checked, but I used almost all of it doing the washing."

I knew for good and well that was a flat-out lie, but Mama's face was as smooth and untroubled as an angel's. It was easy to change my thinking and believe we had gone to get some wood from Billy Ray's woodpile. "Yes," I said. "But as we were walking back, we saw them coming through the woods. There were just three of them this time, and they were carrying that big cross and a jug of kerosene," then I just told the rest of the story as it happened, until I realized that the law would wonder why we let the house burn up with Billy Ray in it. "Shouldn't we have gone over there and done something?"

Mama just smiled, "Why, honey, we were afraid of those men! We are just women and children. Your father is in Maryville, Uncle Woodrow and Sardius were at his place, and Jasper had to ride over and get them and Pap-pa to help us. By the time everyone got here, the place was in flames and there was nothing we could do. Besides, we had no idea Billy Ray was in the house. When Mrs. Carlton and Darlene came over for supper, he had been out all day, and they did not expect him back. He often stays out all night, being as how he has a drinking problem. It appears that he came home sometime during the evening and passed out in the house."

I am no fool. I knew what she was up to. None of us wants Uncle Woodrow to get the electric chair, and we had to get our story straight, but I was flabbergasted at how Mama could sit right beside me, as sweet as can be and lie her head off. I have never known her to tell a lie, not ever, even when it would make things easier if she did. But here she was, straight-faced, looking me right in the eye as she made up one story after another. She ignored my surprised look and went right on. "By the time they all got here it was too late. The house was in flames. Of course, you girls had all gone to bed by then, and you did not see any of the really bad part."

"But what about that cut on Mrs. Carlton's collarbone? How are we going to explain that?

"No one will see anything under her dress. She is tired and weak, though, because she is so scared and upset over her husband being burned to death, and the whole ordeal has taken its toll on her. The Sheriff probably will not bother her too much and will rely on what you, Darlene, and Jasper have to say." She stood up. "Now, let's go on down to breakfast. Miss Janey Jo and Pap-pa are here. We want to be sure we remember everything right when the Sheriff gets here."

We went on downstairs. Miss Janey Jo hugged me, and so did Uncle Woodrow. "You are a very brave and a very smart girl," Miss Janey Jo said, "and we are proud of you." Uncle Woodrow just petted me on the head with a quivering hand and fought back tears. Mrs. Carlton tried to smile at us even though her face was trembly.

There was a big breakfast spread on the table: salted ham with eggs, biscuits and gravy, and plenty of butter and jelly. We all sat down, and Pap-pa prayed. He said, "Lord, we thank you for giving us deliverance. We know you have pulled us from the gates of fire, from the evil intent of men. You have blessed us beyond measure. Help us to deserve what you have done for us this day."

Uncle Woodrow did not eat much. He shook so hard when he lifted his coffee cup to his mouth, he spilled some all over his shirt. Mama just smiled at him. "Woodrow has difficulty with fire or any kind of violence. Just knowing that the Carltons have been threatened has brought on some very bad memories from the war."

Beryl spoke up, "Poor Uncle Woodrow. When he saw Mrs. Carlton screaming and bleeding, and Billy Ray lying on the floor, he just. . ." Mama cut her off. "

"Beryl, you did not go to Darlene's house last night. You were in bed asleep during the whole ordeal."

Beryl said, "But Mama!" and Mama leaned over and said,

"You were so tired that I took you up to bed myself. If you think you saw anything, it must have just been a bad dream. You may have awakened when the fire got going and it is all jumbled up in your head. "

It was a good thing Beryl had run off before she had had a chance to see the really bad part. I spoke up, "Yes, I woke up, too, and I could see the fire through the trees. Beryl was crying in her sleep, saying something about Mrs. Carlton being hurt. I knew she was having a dream. She does that a lot."

Beryl did not catch on. "But Mama!" she said. "I know what I saw," but Miss Janey Jo cut her off.

"Beryl, I am looking forward to getting started on that dress. Hurry up and finish your breakfast so we can get on over there," Beryl likes nothing better than sewing up new clothes for herself, and she suddenly forgot all about the night before.

We were just finishing up when Jasper sat up straight, made a little gasping sound, and said, "I just realized…" His eyes went wild as he groped for words. Janey Jo pushed back from the table.

"Let's go get you dressed so we can leave now," she said to Beryl. We'll take the wagon, and Pap-pa can walk back when he is ready." As she hustled Beryl up the ladder to the loft, Jasper whispered, "We left the k-n-i-f-e in him." I felt my heart just about jump out of my chest. The last time I had seen that knife, it was sticking out of Billy Ray's chest, and I was talking myself out of taking it out of him.

Everyone froze. We had all plumb forgotten about the knife! Pap-pa jumped up and tore out the back door, followed by Jasper and Sardius. Uncle Woodrow put his head down on his arm and cried. Mrs. Carlton looked as if she were about to cry, too. How could we have forgotten something as important as the knife? I could feel the blood leave my face. Darlene broke out in big sobs.

We waited for a long time, and when Pap-pa and the boys did not come back, Mama finally told me to run over there and see what was keeping them. Darlene wanted to come with me, but her mother stopped her. "You don't need to be over there, *cherie*. Last night was bad enough, and it may upset you to see the house burned down. You just stay with me." So I went over there by myself.

The Sheriff's car was parked out in the yard, and four of his men poked through what was left of Billy Ray's house. It had burned clear down, although part of the floor still was strong enough to hold them, and two of the walls still partly stood, but most of the walls had collapsed in on it, and the roof, too. The burnt remains of that cross lay over on the front porch. The fire was completely out, thanks to the rain that had been falling since early this morning, but smoke still curled out of some of the piles here and there. Billy Ray's body lay over by the well, covered up with a sack. His feet stuck out, and I could see that he was lying on his back, but it was obvious there was no knife in his chest. I wondered if there was any hope that he had burned up so much the knife had fallen out.

Pap-pa and one of the Sheriff's men lifted a big, charred beam and threw it aside, then poked around through the rubble. Nobody paid any attention to me, but I was afeared to go join the search. I did not know what I would do if I happened to stumble across the knife. "What are you all looking for?" I called out.

Pap-pa glanced up. "Nothing, honey. You can go on back home. We are just checking the scene to see what we can see." He added, casual like, "It looks like Billy Ray died of smoke inhalation. He probably died without ever waking up. It's a pity he let himself get so drunk. People who drink like that usually come to a bad end."

That lightened my heart. Nobody had found the knife yet, but still, I was beside myself with worry, and I could not stay still, so

I sort of wandered around in the yard. The big spruce at the back of the house still stood, but it was mostly a charred hulk. I knew it would not live, and somehow that made me sadder than seeing the smoldering remains of Darlene's house.

The whole place stank of brimstone. It made me think about Billy Ray burning in hell. I sure had hated him, and he deserved whatever punishment God was choosing to dish out to him, but it made me feel sweaty and hot to actually connect in my mind Billy Ray suffering in the eternal fire.

I feel sick and dizzy just thinking about it. A lot more happened, but I cannot think straight enough to write it down.

Warm, waxing days; rain freshens the earth.

Death has come to claim his own.
Evil and Good have vanished together in smoke.
I hear the sobs of the stranger, locked out of tenderness,
I taste the fear of the woman, singing in harmony with hope,
The terror that rages and flames,
The dread that weighs like icy steel.
Green has crumbled into dust.

April 18, 1932.
My dear sister,

I am utterly, utterly undone. All this school year, I have believed that I am ministering to the people of this place, that I have been accepted and loved, and that I have a home here among the people of these beautiful mountains. But I have been deluded and deceived. I have deluded and deceived myself. I am not loved, am not accepted. I have done no good here. All I can think of is that I must get away. I have to get back home to safety and the arms of those who truly love me.

I cannot tell you what has happened, at least not yet. I do not trust myself to recount it correctly, and I do not want you to know the worst of it. Let me step back and find a moment to breathe before I divulge the source of my pain and sorrow. I tell you this much only to ask you to please pray for my deliverance from this heartbreak, from the terrible pain I feel. I am sick to my soul.

Emily

April 19, I think. I believe it is Tuesday. Mama let us sleep late this morning. I did not wake up until it was full daylight. Darlene was still asleep, so I dragged myself down the ladder to the kitchen, where Jasper, Sardius, and Ruby were just finishing up breakfast. Mrs. Carlton and Uncle Woodrow were not there. Beryl is still over at Pap-pa's house.

Mama told me that the Sheriff would be wanting to talk to me this afternoon, and we went over what all I would be telling him, then we went up to the loft and woke up Darlene and went over the story again. Mama did not hardly have to say a word while Darlene and I talked. She just nodded and smiled. We had it all straight.

I went to the outhouse right after breakfast. It was such a beautiful morning, it almost made me forget what had happened, except for the lingering smell of wet char in the air. It was hard to make it straight in my mind that such awful things had gone on, and I felt so heavy with grief, I did not want to go back to the house, where there were so many bad thoughts and fears. I wandered up the creek, as far as I could get from Billy Ray's house, from the smell of the burned wood. I climbed up the hill up past the beech grove to look out at the sun shining on the river so pretty, just like it always has. Behind me was a jumble of badness, but in front of me, it did not seem that a single, solitary thing had changed. It was almost easy to believe it was just another spring day, full of birdsong and sunshine.

All of a sudden, out of nowhere, a fog rolled in and it began to rain, one of those fine, drizzly mists that make you feel like you are in a cloud. Something caught my eye as I gazed out toward the river, but when I looked again, I did not see a thing. A minute later, I glanced up again and saw Jake Hatton hiding behind a tree, sticking his head out just enough to peek around it. When he saw me looking at him, he grinned as he motioned for me to come over. I shook my head. We were scraping the bottom of Daddy's whiskey stash, and I did not dare try to take any more. Also, I was afraid that the Sheriff might come by and see me talking to him. It would not be good if he found out my business with Jake Hatton.

He motioned again. I shook my head again, and finally, he jerked his arm hard, telling me I had better follow him, and then he disappeared into the rhododendron hell to get out of the rain, which by now had turned into a steady drizzle.

I realized I had better mind him. If I did not, he might tattle on me to the Sheriff, and that was the last thing I needed. I followed him a little ways in, along a crooked path, and before I got too far, I saw him crouched down amid a tangle of swollen pink buds, grinning at me. He patted the ground beside him, and I sat down. His hat was pulled down over his face, his collar turned up against the wet.

I said, "Jake, I told you, I don't have a drop of whiskey to sell you right now. It's almost gone, and Daddy will kill me if he knows I've been selling it to you. And if he does, you'll never get another drop from me!" I hoped that would keep him quiet.

He grinned at me, winking and twitching. "You got secrets, little A-hole? Huh? Huh? A-hole. A-hole?" I stomped my foot. He was making me mad.

"You quit cussing at me, Jake Hatton, or I will never sell you another drop!"

He hung his head. "Sorry, G.D. it. It won't stop, G.D. it. A-hole. A-hole."

"Shut up!" I hollered, but as I looked at him close up, I could see a world of sadness in his face. The whole right side twitched as if he was in pain, while his eyes looked like wells full of hurt. Water had gathered in the corners.

"So sorry, G.D. it," he kept muttering, while a tear slipped down his cheek, and then he started to sob, and he tried to reach in his pocket, but by then he was twitching around so much that he seemed to forget what he was reaching for and got all involved with his twitching. It was then I realized that he truly could not help it. Jake Hatton had not been to war, so he was not suffering from shell shock, but he sure was suffering from something. I stopped to wait for him to get over it.

Finally, he quit twitching long enough to reach into his pocket, and Lo and Behold! He pulled out a bloody knife that looked like the very one that I had last seen in Billy Ray's chest. "You want this, little A-hole," he said, then he chucked it down at my feet. I sat looking at it a long time.

"What is this?" I asked him, careful not to give away my feelings.

"I saw the G.D. clan. I saw them, G.D it. I saw them, and I saw all of it. I figured you didn't want the G.D. law to find it."

I picked it up, and when I looked at him again, he was grinning that crooked grin of his, his eye winking so hard that the whole side of his face jerked, and then he reached out, and ever so lightly, he petted my head with a twitchy finger. "I got me some whiskey," he said. "Not as good as yourn, but I'm G.D. okay for now. You be careful, now. You don't want them after you," and then he turned and crawled out of the rhododendron, into the rain and the mist between the trees.

By the time I got back to the house, Pap-pa was there. He looked worried and wet, and he smelled like soot, so I knew he had been back over to Billy Ray's house looking for the knife. I called him out to the back porch. You should have seen the look of relief that came over his face when I pulled that knife out of my pocket! His eyes, bloodshot with soot and lack of sleep welled up. He did not say a word, he just reached out and folded his arms around me, pulling me to him. I could smell the soot and the sweat on him, and my heart began to sing like a bird. With Pap-pa on my side, I know nothing bad will ever happen.

Later on, after dinner, the Sheriff came by. We all were on the back porch eating some hoecakes and strawberry preserves that Mama had brought out to us.

He was a fat, greasy-looking man, and the minute I laid eyes on him, I felt a meanness about him. Jasper got up and stood behind me while Pap-pa eased up to me and Darlene with a meaningful look in his eye.

"Pearl," he said, "the Sheriff wants to talk to you two about what's been going on here the past few weeks. I told them that some men had been bothering Darlene and her mother, and they want to clear a few things up." He and the boys settled down on the porch steps while the Sheriff came and stood right over Darlene and me. He was big, and he stood way too close. I got the feeling that he did not like me or Darlene and he wanted to scare us.

I was determined not to be ascared, but I could tell Darlene was frightened because she was shaking so bad she was practically rattling the chair. I got up, stepping between him and Darlene. My knees were shaking, too, but I was bound and determined that Sheriff was not going to see it, and I for sure was not going to let him loom up over Darlene and scare her even more.

"I'll tell it," I said, looking him in the eye as brazen as I could be. "Darlene was so ascared by those men she can't hardly even think about it without falling to pieces." And then I started in at the beginning, telling the story I had pieced together and practiced in my head. I did not say too much, leaving out everything but exactly what I saw and heard once those men showed up in their white sheet getups. I could tell Pap-pa was proud of me. He was looking at the ground while I talked, but there was a little smile around the corners of his mouth. I could not see Mama. She was behind Darlene and me, quiet as a cat, but when I got to the part about how the man had grabbed Mrs. Carlton by the titty, I felt her lay her hand on my shoulder.

The Sheriff asked a few questions, but mainly he just looked at me, nodding, looking grim and a little bit worried. I could see him thinking, and I wondered if he knew Otis' uncle, the Sheriff over in Madisonville, who was family to the Cluecluckers.

Finally, the Sheriff just nodded, thanked me for my cooperation, and asked Darlene if she had anything to add to what I had told. She looked at him very ascared-like, and shook her head, but added, "They scared me real bad, sir. They were mean, and they hurt my mama and made her cry."

I expected him to maybe feel sorry for her, but I could tell that he did not. In his eyes, there was a look that said he did not like her, that she did not matter, that she had no rights to be making complaints against anyone who would hurt her, and he was mad that he was forced to believe that the Clueclukers had done wrong. We let him know we were willing to swear on a stack of Bibles that they had tried to hurt an innocent woman and child and burned down their home, and when it all shook out, he knew he would have to at least make a show of trying to put things to rights.

In the beginning, I thought that if we told him everything that had happened, he would have to do the right thing, but as I looked at him, I realized that those Cluecluckers just might get away with everything. The Sheriff was on their side, and it burned me up so much that I did not feel at all bad that we had fudged the story just that little bit. If we had given him the least suspicion about Uncle Woodrow, it is likely they would have found a way to pin it all on him—everything, including the fire—and those mean S.O.Bs would be free to keep on doing exactly what they had done to Darlene and her mother.

It still burns me up every time I think about it.

April 20, 1932
My dearest Cecilia,

My soul is heavily burdened. I still am unable to write about what has happened here. I will let it suffice to say that there has been violence and I have been a witness to it. It also has awakened in me a strong realization that I am not the kind, helpful person that I thought I was when I first came here. There is evil in my heart. I had thought I was coming here to help the people of this community to grow in the light of God's love and to shed my own light of learning to the children. I did not realize that I was arrogant and condescending, that I was coming from a place of privilege, and that I would be hurting the very people I thought I had come to help.

Father has done us a disservice. Our whole community in Chicago has done us a disservice. They have made us believe we are superior to people who struggle simply to survive. Our wealth and our education have made us think we are of a special, chosen group, and if we deign to stoop low enough to help those less fortunate, then we should be elevated even higher than we already are. What a foolish, arrogant notion! In reality, we all are such sinners, believing we are better than any other of God's creatures.

At present, I am heartbroken and so discouraged I do not know what to do, except beg forgiveness, pack my things, and come home to the arms and hearth of my loving family. I realize now that I have been callous and unfeeling toward Jonathan, using him and his good nature to further my own selfish goals. I have to beg his forgiveness for the way I have treated him.

Oh, Cecilia! Please pray for me that God will show me a way to atone for my excessive pride!

With a broken heart,

Emily

April 21, 1932. We went back to school today. Miss Weston is as nice as always, but she seems very tired and very sad. She has dark smudges under her eyes, and she moves as if she is swimming in molasses. At dinnertime, I wanted to talk to her a little bit, just to let her know how much I appreciate what she has done for us, but when I saw her up close, her eyes were so red, I could not bring myself to mention it. I wonder if we will ever be able to talk about what has happened. I know she must feel terrible about the part she played in saving my Uncle Woodrow from the electric chair, but I hope she knows how much we all love her for it. I am glad we did not tell the Sheriff that she was there that night. I cannot imagine her being able to lie for us.

It is the full moon tonight. It is time to plant sweet potatoes. Jasper got up and went out to get an early start this morning. I wonder how he had the energy to go plant after all we had been through. Sometimes I think it is not worth it to try to scratch a living out of dirt. I hope he passes those tests with flying colors. This farm will break him down into an old man before his time. I have not seen Uncle Woodrow for days. We figure he will be back soon, and if he is not, I will be mad at him. I think Mrs. Carlton needs him more than she needs Darlene right now.

Darlene and Mrs. Carlton are staying over at Pap-pa's house for the time being.

April 22, 1932. Just when I thought things could not get worse, they did. Sardius, Beryl, and I were in school this morning, when Jasper came running in to tell us to come home. Daddy had been in a bad fight with those hobos, and it looked like he might not live. We got home as fast as we could.

Pap-pa, Janey Jo, Uncle Woodrow, Mrs. Carlton, and Darlene, were all sitting in the living room. Mrs. Carlton held Sapphire in her arms, and Ruby was sitting on Pap-pa's lap. They jumped up when we came in, and Janey Jo held out her arms to us. We all started crying. From the looks on everyone's faces, I knew it was bad.

It was a little while before they let us into the bedroom to see Daddy. Mama was kneeling beside the bed, lost in prayer. She had her head on his hand, stroking his arm as she prayed. Daddy lay still as death, white beneath the bruises. His arm was in a sling with a splint, and one of his legs laid out on top of the bed covers. It was splinted and bound, too. A big bandage was wrapped around the top of his head.

Mama moved to the chair when we came in. She just looked at us as if she could not bear the sadness, then looked at Daddy again and stroked his hand.

"Come and kiss your daddy, children," she said, and we stood in line to lean over him and kiss him between the bruises and bandages. Then we stood around, not knowing what to say or think. I did not know it would hurt this bad to see Daddy this bad off, knowing he might die.

April 22, 1932
Dear Cecilia,

Things are getting more painful here every day. This week, Mr. Richard Wallace was attacked by a gang of men who have been riding the train illegally. Mr. Wallace's job is to keep them off the railroad property, and apparently, they have become extremely resentful to the point that they have attacked railroad personnel.

Mr. Wallace is near death, I am told. I have not been by to see him or the family yet. I do not feel it is my place to intrude during their time of hardship. I will wait a few days to see how things develop before I go. If the poor man dies, I do not know how the family will survive. The boys have scholarships to attend Wheaton Academy beginning with the summer term, but if they leave, the farm will not be tended, and I do not know how Mrs. Wallace will fare by herself. She has very young children, and she is not strong enough to run a farm by herself.

Cecilia, life here is so very, very hard! I do not think I have it in me to withstand the terrors or the hardships anyone who lives here must face on a daily basis. Please continue to pray for me. I feel so lost and incompetent! I see now how foolish I was to think I could ever improve the lives of these people.

Love and tears,
Emily

April 23, 1932. Mrs. Carlton and Darlene spent the day here today. Mama did not let us girls go out to the fields today. She said Beryl and I should just play with Darlene and try to be happy, but we could not be happy. The boys and Uncle Woodrow worked in the fields all day by themselves. Mrs. Carlton cooked supper so Mama could sit with Daddy.

I have not been this sad since the baby boy that Mama brought home three years ago died.

April 24, 1932
Dear Cecilia,

I think I have preached my last sermon. The Reverend and Mrs. Miller have returned, and his health is much improved. He let me know that he is ready to get back into the pulpit. I am glad about that. I feel so disheartened I was not up to doing a good job today. I just gave a lackluster sermon about how God wants us to be kind to one another.

I am quite sure I will be coming home at the end of the term. Life here is just too hard to bear. I look forward to getting back into my old life, seeing my old friends, and most of all, dear Cecilia, to spending time with you! And I am wracking my brain to try to find a way to help the children I have come to love so much.

I love you,
Emily

April 25, 1932
My School Journal, grade 7, Miss Weston's class
By Pearl Wallace

My father was attacked by a gang of ruffians who beat him up badly, broke his arm and his leg, and bashed his head in. We do not know if he is going to live. The doctor says that he has some swelling in his brain and that if he lives, he may not ever be able to talk or even move again. My mother sits by the bed day and night. She wipes his face with a washrag and she prays over him all the time. I have not seen her cry yet, but her eyes are red and swollen, so I know she is crying when we do not see her. We are all so sad, we do not know what to do.

All our neighbors are very nice. They have come to bring food. Mrs. Carlton, my best friend's mother, comes every day to take care of my baby sister Sapphire, and my step-grandmother takes care of Ruby. Mrs. Bittertree came by with a cake today. Mr. Bittertree offered to help with planting potatoes. My grandfather and my Uncle Woodrow also are helping as much as they can.

I am praying for my father to live and to be well. I know he is saved, so if he dies, I am not in fear for his soul. But I do not want him to die.

April 27, 1932. Mama sent Beryl and me to school, but Sardius stayed home to help get the sweet potatoes in. When I got home today, I went in to see Daddy. I stared at him a long time before I reached out to touch his cheek, and he woke up. At first, he looked at me like he did not know me. Then his eyes lit up and he tried to reach out to me, although his hand would not move. He gave out a long cry, like he was trying to tell me something important, but I could not make any sense of it.

Mama came in with some soup so I could feed him. Jasper helped to drag him up on the pillows a little bit, and then I spooned some soup into his mouth, but most if it dribbled out and down his chin. My heart is breaking because my Daddy might die. I hope he knows I love him, even though I have been mad at him for most of my life.

April 27, 1932
Dear Jonathan,

I was happy to get your letter today. I know I have been remiss in writing you, but it has been a very hard time for us all here. I have told you about the Wallace family. The father, Richard, has been injured very badly and may not live. Their neighbor's home has been burned to the ground, and the owner, Billy Ray Carlton, died in the fire. We have a mother and child homeless and fatherless, and another family on the brink of being fatherless. I feel worthless and helpless to do anything.

Jonathan, I realize now that I have no place here. I do not belong here. In my arrogance, I inserted myself into this place, into the lives of these self-sufficient and good people, thinking I could civilize and instruct them. I was so wrong! They were gracious to accept me, but they have always stood apart from me—they have no need or desire for anything I can do for them.

I am ashamed to think how my pride has come between you and me. You have been nothing but kind to me, and I have repaid you with my foolish snobbery. Please forgive me for treating you so badly. I hope you do not hold my deplorable behavior against me.

Sincerely,
Emily

Warm, waxing days, greening earth

Hope lies in shards.
Love struggles through pain.
My upright ones suffer with broken hearts and broken bodies.
I wait, tasting the grief and the yearning.

April 28, 1932. I feel bad going to school when Sardius cannot because of the planting. Jasper has not been studying for his exams, either, and Mama goes out to the fields to work in between taking care of Daddy and Sapphire. Mrs. Carlton is a big help, but she is trying to plant her own garden.

April 29, 1932. Miss Weston is worried about Sardius missing so much school. She brought Beryl and me home in her automobile so she could go over his lessons with him. When we got home, everyone was still out in the field. Uncle Woodrow had gone to help Pap-pa, so it was just Sardius, Jasper, and Mama. Mama had tied Sapphire up to the apple tree so she could not get into anything while Ruby tended to her. Mama is particular about her babies and she always makes sure they are tied up good and proper to keep them from scooching away.

Ruby had gotten into a mud puddle, and of course, had completely forgotten about taking care of Sapphire. Her dress was just covered with mud. Thank goodness she was barefooted, or she would have soaked her shoes. When we got to them, Sapphire had a big fistful of dirt she was putting in her mouth. We were too late to stop her, so I had to try to rake it out as best as I could. She eats dirt every chance she gets, and it is a constant trial to Mama. I was mad at Ruby for not tending to her, but Ruby looked so sweet, looking up at me through all the mud on her face, her big, blue eyes just shining, that I could not bless her out.

Mama and Jasper came over when they saw us. They were so tired, they could hardly stand, and they were ragged and dirty, too. Mama's hair stuck to her head from all the sweat, and Jasper looked as if he needed to be propped up. I felt just terrible, knowing that I had not been here to help them. I might not be worth much in the fields, but I could at least have tended to Ruby and Sapphire, and I could take care of Daddy, also.

Beside them, Miss Weston looked like she had stepped out of the catalogue. She had on a pure white blouse, a soft gray skirt, and a wide belt that cinched her waist in so pretty. She had on her lavender hat with the netting that came down over her face, and her shoes were shining and clean. I wanted to tell her not to step out into the field so as not to get them dirty, but before I could, she swooped over to pick up Sapphire, and got dirt all over her blouse and skirt.

Mama about died. She reached for Sapphire, but Miss Weston pulled the baby away, saying, "Mrs. Wallace, please let me help. I have done nothing all day but be in the classroom with your precious children while you have been laboring in the fields. Why don't you let me take these babies into the house and get them cleaned up for you?"

Tears came into Mama's eyes. She was both scundered and grateful. Then tears came into Miss Weston's eyes, and she suddenly turned to Beryl and me and said, "Come, girls. Let us go start some supper for your family. They have been working hard today, and we need to give them a little rest." Then she marched to the house, followed by Mama. Mama would have told her she did not need help, but by the time she got to the house, she could barely drag her feet across the threshold. She sank into a chair in the kitchen, and said, "I am beholden to you, Miss Weston."

Miss Weston gave Mama some water, then called Jasper in. About that time Uncle Woodrow and Sardius came home, and they both looked as worn out as Mama and Jasper did, although they were a little cleaner by the time we saw them because they had stopped at the well and washed some.

Miss Weston was so nice. She tied an apron around her waist, fried up some fatback, made biscuits, and cooked some wild burdock that Uncle Woodrow and Sardius had picked on their way to the house. The evening might have been nice, except that we all knew Daddy was lying in the room right next to us, maybe not long for this world.

May

May 1, 1932. Mama sent us young'uns to church today, but she had to stay home because she is afraid to leave Daddy for very long. Preacher Miller is better now, and back in town, so he has taken over preaching again. He gave a pretty good sermon, but it was not half as good as Miss Weston's. She always makes the Bible make sense, and makes it come to life. Preacher Miller talks about things I do not always understand.

We did not go to Pap-pa's house for dinner, but they came over here with food so we would not have to cook. Mrs. Carlton and Darlene came with them. It is hard for them to get over here every day, but they do manage it most days. Mrs. Carlton has taken her goats over to Pap-pa's and she and Miss Janey Jo bring milk over to Sapphire nearly every day. They cook enough dinner to last us through supper and breakfast so Mama does not have to do anything but take care of Daddy and help out in the field when he sleeps.

Uncle Woodrow is still very shaky, but he acts a little better. It seems that he is trying very hard to be strong. At dinner, when we were saying the blessing, he held Mrs. Carlton's and Darlene's hands, and he takes pains to take care of Daddy when he can. He also is working very hard in the fields.

Daddy is doing a little better. He can move his hands and legs, and he can swallow food if somebody feeds him, but he cannot move his arms. One is too broken up and the other just will not move. The whole side of his body is all twisted up. He cannot speak, either, but sometimes when he sees us, he will cry out the most awful sounds and try to move toward us. Mama says we can cuddle up with him for a little while, but when we do, he cries and makes those sounds again, and water runs out of his eyes. It is hard to look at him when he is this way.

May 2, 1932
My School Journal, grade 7, Miss Weston's class
By Pearl Wallace

My father has an automobile, although with the Depression on, it is hard to find parts to keep it running. We all used to pile into the back (it is a truck with an open bed), and Daddy would careen up those mountain roads just as fast as it would go. There is a place over by Big Gully that has a little hill, then a dip, and when he goes over that fast, we all fly up in the air, and we have to hang on tight to keep from falling out! It is a great deal of fun to go over the Big Gully hill fast, and we always beg him to go as fast as he can so we can go aflying. When we come down again, it feels as if our stomachs have stayed up for a second or two. It is a wonderful feeling.

Daddy is stove up right now, so I guess we will not be going over the hill at Big Gully for a while yet. I wish we could. Back when we were doing it, I never thought that there would come a time when Daddy could not drive. I wish I had paid more attention to how fun it was then.

May 3, 1932. Mama made all of us go to school. She says we are done planting sweet potatoes but that we will start planting corn with the new moon this week, and she wants us all to get our lessons to bring home so we can work on them in between planting. She wants to put in an extra large crop of corn this year. This did not make sense to us at first because it is pretty clear that

Daddy will not be stealing any to make whiskey, so we probably can get by with planting less. When Jasper questioned her about it, though, she said she plans to make cornbread and sell it down at the highway. I have never heard of anybody wanting to buy cornbread, but Mama knows more about that than we do.

May 4, 1932. Miss Weston is working us hard. She does not even let us take a recess, and she makes us work while we eat our dinner. She says I do not have to turn in my Journals for the rest of the year, which is a big relief. I cannot think up good things to write, that sound like my life is normal, anyway.

Mama makes us work on our lessons from the time we get home from school until now, and it is nearly 10 o'clock.

May 5, 1932. It is the new moon, so we planted corn all day. After supper, Mama made all of us study, even Jasper. I am so tired I cannot hardly move. Mama looks wrung out, but she smiles at us when she looks at us.

Old Al Capone went to prison yesterday. I feel the smallest bit sorry for him. I know how easy it is to get lured into a life of crime. Since Daddy is too sick to drink his whiskey, I am selling all I can. I sold Jake Hatton a whole quart yesterday, and I reckon I will sell it until it is all gone. With Daddy not working, we sure will need the money. I am glad I still have my hair money underneath the floorboards in the living room.

May 6, 1932. Something good happened today, but at the same time, it is not good. Hank Delany was arrested for setting fire to Billy Ray's house, and there may be other arrests. Mama, Uncle Woodrow, and Mrs. Carlton are very worried about that. If this goes to trial, I will be called to testify since I am the main witness. Jasper will be called as well, and so will Darlene. If a jury gets a good look at Darlene, things may not go well.

Daddy cries every time one of us goes into his room. Beryl sang to him today, and he let out such a wail that it scared her and she quit. Then he cried even louder so she had to start up again.

I do not know what we are going to do. I do not think that Daddy is ever going to get better. If he cannot work, we will go back to trying to scratch out a living from this farm. That means Jasper and Sardius will not be able to go to that fancy boarding school in Chicago.

May 7, 1932
My dearest sister,

I have spent the last week reflecting on my sins and my ambitions, and I have come to realize that I should have accepted Jonathan's offer of marriage last fall when he made it. At that time, I was so infatuated with this place and with the idea that I was going to improve the lives of my students and their parents that I rejected him out of hand. Now I am reflecting on what a good man he is and always has been, and I so wish I could take back my cruelty to him. He has suffered through my manipulations, my scorn, my inability to see his goodness. I am not even sure I have properly thanked him for sending all those supplies and money to help me. What kind of woman treats such a loving man that way?

Do not tell him I have made these confessions to you, and do not tell Mother and Father, either. I have to deal with the heartache brought on by my own arrogance all by myself. Thank you for at least letting me share my shame with you. You are a good sister, and I love you.

Emily

May 7, 1932. Miss Weston showed up early this morning, just as we were going out to the cornfield. Mama called us back in and set us down at the kitchen table. Miss Weston looked very pretty and fresh next to Mama, who is so worn out you can almost see through her. Her hair is flat and dingy, and even though she smiles a lot, there is no sunshine in it. It is as if she is just stretching her lips out away from her teeth while her eyes look like the eyes of a trapped animal. We all see it, but no one says anything.

Miss Weston folded her hands on top of the table and said, "Jasper, your mother tells me you could pass the final exams for the tenth grade. I want you to come to school with the others next week and take those exams. I expect you to be going to Chicago with your brother next month and begin your studies."

We all were flabbergasted. There is no way Mama can do without Sardius and Jasper with Daddy laid up so bad. Both boys shook their heads.

"No, Ma'am," said Jasper. "Sardius can go, but Mama needs me here to tend to the crops this summer. I am going to run the farm from here on out."

"Me, too," said Sardius. "I want to be a farmer. I have made up my mind."

Mama laid her hand on Jasper's shoulder. "No, honey. Both of you are going to go to Chicago with Miss Weston. I am confident you will do very well on your exams. You do not need to be worrying about me or your Daddy or this farm. We will make do."

"But Mama!" they both said at once.

She held up her hand. "I am not arguing about this. It is settled, and that is that." And then she poured Miss Weston a cup of coffee and started talking about the weather, as if she did not know that we had sacks and sacks of corn waiting to be planted, Daddy was lying helpless in the bedroom, and she had a family to feed and no way to feed them. I could not help but to speak up.

"Mama, your hair money won't go that far, and…"

She cut me off. "Pearl, you will not contradict me. Now, Uncle Woodrow and your pap-pa are already out in the field, and they are expecting you to help them. Go," and she shooed us out the door. I think Mama has taken leave of her senses.

May 8, 1932. We planted all day today, so we missed church, but we left off for dinner. Miss Janey Jo, Mrs. Carlton, Pap-pa, and Darlene came over with food. It would have been a nice time, but we are still all so sad about Daddy and so tired from working that we did not have it in us to do more than eat before we went back out to plant more corn. We have 6 acres planted already. I do not understand Mama. Not only do we have to plant all day on a Sunday, but she makes us keep up with our lessons. We all are about to drop in our tracks.

May 8, 1032
My dear Jonathan,

How I wish you could be here with me today, to see the glories of this beautiful spring day! I would take you walking along the river so you could see the otters frolicking amid the spray, the bluebirds feeding their young in the hollow trees, and the white clouds foaming above our heads, flirting with the sun. It would be magnificient to talk to you, to show you all the secret, delightful places I have discovered during my time here, and if I may be so bold to say, talk about my feelings for you. It has taken me a long time to understand how much you mean to me, and now I hope to make up for it. I had to be dashed upon the shoals to clear my head and realize how perfect you are. I should thank my mother for having seen it so much sooner than I did.

I will be home in less than three weeks! I can hardly wait! I do hope you will receive me with kindness.

With fondest regards,
Emily

May 9, 1932. Miss Weston is giving us the rest of our Spring break this week. We are taking the whole week off, even though we really have only 3 days left on it, but she says we will go a little later in the year to make up for it.

We started out planting early, but then somebody from the court came by to talk to me. Mama kept him in the house for a long time before she sent Ruby out to fetch me. I reckoned she wanted to make sure he was on the right side before she let him ask me any questions. As soon as I came in, she sent Uncle Woodrow over to Pap-pa's house to fetch Darlene and Mrs. Carlton. He took the wagon and was back again in under an hour with them. Mrs. Carlton had a cooked goose with her, which we were mighty glad to see.

By the time they got here, I had already told the fellow my side of the story. He asked Darlene the same questions as he asked me, and she backed me up right down the line. Mrs. Carlton put in her two cents. We all agreed as to exactly what happened. Then Mama called Jasper in, who told what he saw, and that was about all there was to it.

After the man left, I got to thinking. Hank Delany might could get the electric chair for killing Billy Ray Carlton. That set me back on my heels. Hank is a mean S.O.B., but we all know good and well he had nothing to do with Billy Ray's death. The more I thought about it, the more it made me realize that it would be a terrible sin to let an innocent man die for something he did not do. I was just poking a hole in the ground to put in a piece of corn when it hit me about what we might be guilty of, and all of a sudden, it felt like the whole earth started to shake. My knees gave way, and I just started to sob, and I could not stop myself. I laid down in the dirt and cried and cried. Mama came running to me and gathered me up in her arms, but I still could not stop. Finally, Uncle Woodrow came, picked me up, carried me back to the house, and laid me on the couch.

After Mama brought me water and held me for the longest time, I was finally able to get ahold of myself enough to explain that I was ascared we might cause an innocent man to go to the electric chair! It scared me to death to think about it. Jesus would never in all eternity let us get by with that, and even if He did, I do not think I could let myself get by with it. I do not want Uncle Woodrow to go to the electric chair, either, and I just do not know what we could do about it.

Mama shushed me. "Pearl, honey," she said. "You do not need to worry about that. Hank Delany is the first cousin of the judge in Madison County, and it is likely that the judge himself is a member of the clan. Nobody is going to the electric chair. We just have to make sure everybody believes that Billy Ray died in a house fire, and to do that we have to make them believe that the clan set that fire. They will be looking for any way out of this that they can, and if they get the least suspicion that your Uncle Woodrow was there that night or that Mrs. Carlton might have had something against her husband, then they're going to find a way to point the finger at them. You just have to trust me. They will find a way to get Hank Delany off. They probably will call it an accident, or someone will give him an alibi. They won't let one of their own be found guilty. If by some crazy chance they do, we will find a way to make them doubt what happened. Believe me, honey. I won't let anything happen." Then she wrapped her arms around me and laid me down on the couch. She brought me more water and a wet washrag to put on my forehead, and then next thing I knew it was suppertime and everybody was filing in to eat. Darlene sat on the couch with me and held my hand until I felt like getting up.

May 10, 1932. I do not know what is wrong with me. I feel like the world is a heavy place to be. It is all I can do to get out of bed of a morning. Mama does not let me go out to the field with the others, but just coddles me and puts a book in my hand and tells me to read. Darlene came by, but I did not want to play with her, either. I just want to stay in bed and sleep.

May 10, 1932
Dear Jonathan,

You are such a treasure! After all I have done and said to you, I find it hard to believe that you still want me. I feel very comforted by that, but I must tell you, dear Jonathan, that I have changed a great deal since I have come here. I am not the same society-loving girl who left last August. Now, I have come to realize that the world is a broken place, that people are broken, that good people will suffer, no matter how good our intentions are. Still, I feel I must do all I can to help alleviate that suffering.

I will not say that I do not want to marry you. I just cannot look that far in advance. At this time, the only thing I can think of is how I can get my special, gifted children away from the poverty and despair that faces them in this place. I have you to thank that Jasper and Sardius will be attending Wheaton this summer, but I still have to find a place for Pearl, their sister. She is precious, Jonathan! So smart, so wise beyond her years, so kind hearted and innocent, and facing such hardships as you cannot imagine. She will be ready for high school in a year, and she is far too young to be going to a boarding school, even if her brothers are there. She is very close to her mother and sisters, and I believe it would be cruel to put her in an institutional environment at her tender age. She has never been out of the mountains of East Tennessee. The culture shock alone would be enough to undo her!

I beg you to counsel me. I realize now how much I love you, and I truly want to marry you, but I cannot ask you to wait until I have got Pearl sorted out and on her way, nor can I ask you to include her in your life, to raise a child not your own. But my mind is made up. I cannot marry until I have brought Pearl into a loving and comfortable home. Tell me what to do. Is it possible we could find a home suitable for Pearl, good people who will take her in and give her a sense of family? If we could, she could attend school with her brothers and still feel safe. Please tell me what to do! And please forgive me for my willfulness.

With fondest regard,
Emily

May 11, 1932. I wish Daddy would get better.

May 12, 1932. Darlene came to see me today, but I did not want to play with her. I feel bad because I am too weak to go help with the planting. Mostly I sat by Daddy's bed and watched him sleep. When he woke up, I listened to him cry. Oh, Lord Jesus! Make him better! I am sorry for ever wishing him dead. Please do not let them send Hank Delany or Uncle Woodrow to the electric chair. Please help Mama.

May 13, 1932. Poor baby Charles Lindberg was found dead yesterday. I am so sad I cannot stop leaking tears. Who would do that to a baby? They paid the ransom and everything, and still he was killed. It makes me want to sit down and give up on the human race. Beryl is begging me to go to the creek with her, but I just cannot get my legs under me.

May 14, 1932. Miss Weston came to see me today. She brought me some peppermint candy, and she went over some of my lessons with me. Exams begin in a week. I cannot remember anything. I keep thinking about Billy Ray lying in the fire with a knife in his chest, and then I think about Jasper's hands. They are so rough and chapped that he has to hold his pencil funny. Mama's hands are rough and chapped, too. Just when I find a way to think about something nice, I remember poor Charlie Lindbergh lying in his grave, and sometimes Daddy cries out, and it all comes back to me.

May 15, 1932. Mama got us all up this morning and made us go to church. Mrs. Carlton and Darlene sat with Daddy so Mama could go. Everyone came over for dinner at our house, even Miss Weston. She looks sad every time she looks at Uncle Woodrow, and I feel so sorry for her I want to cry again. Uncle Woodrow and Mrs. Carlton try not to look at each other when Miss Weston is around, but sometimes they cannot help it. It seems that the looks that pass between them sometimes are the only good things that happen.

Miss Weston says I do not have to turn in my Journal entry for tomorrow. I am glad about that. I cannot think of anything to write. All that comes into my head is how much everybody is hurting.

May 16, 1932. Even though we are supposed to be back at school today, we had not finished with the planting, so we stayed home one more day. I had planned to get out there early to start to make up for my laziness over the last week, but before I could get out the back door, Mama came, put her arms around me, and said, "I'm glad you have gotten your feet back under you. Let's celebrate that by going for a walk." That sounded good to me. It's not often I get Mama all to myself.

We went down to the river. It was a beautiful morning. The river seemed extra swift, and the smell of honeysuckle was so strong it made my mouth water. Here it is the middle of May, the prettiest month there is, and I had not hardly noticed it. Mama joshed with me a little bit about missing out on so much prettiness. By the time we made it back to the house, I was feeling a whole lot better about everything.

Mama did not want me to, but I went out in the fields to help plant corn the rest of the day. We got it all done, and then we celebrated. Pap-pa, Janey Jo, Mrs. Carlton, and Darlene came over. We took food into Daddy's room, and he looked at us without crying, and he even ate a little. He is able to move his arm a little bit. I think I saw him smile once with his eyes.

May 17, 1932. You will never believe what happened today. Mr. Dean came back! We were just getting out of school, and as we went out the front door, there he sat in his fancy automobile, waiting. We all ran over to him, and Sadie Maclean hollered at Miss Weston, "Your man is here!"

Miss Weston came out, and you should have seen her face! She just lit up all over, and then she laughed, turned red, and ran over to the car. Mr. Dean got out, and he held out his arms. I think he was hoping for a hug, but he did not get one. Miss Weston just took his hand and held it for a minute before she dropped it. Then she said, loud enough for everyone to hear, "Mr. Dean. How nice to see you, although I did not expect you. Have you come to visit the Aikens?" Mr. Dean laughed then, and picked up her hands and held them.

"Yes," he said. "I was just there, and Mrs. Aikens has invited you and the Millers for dinner. Come on, I will take you home to get them so we can all go over there together." Then he opened the door for Miss Weston, got in himself, and they drove off. Everybody cheered. It was just like a scene from a movie!

May 18, 1932
Darling Cecilia,

What a week it has been. Jonathan has paid me another surprise visit! This time was much better—he arranged to stay with the Aikens before coming to the schoolhouse to see me, and he graciously waited in his car until the end of the day, when I came out after school was dismissed.

As you can imagine, I was very surprised, especially since I gave him such a lecture the last time he drove down unannounced and uninvited, but this time it seemed much different, much more comfortable. I think he wanted to make a statement, that he is not afraid of me, and that he genuinely wants to marry me. To prove that, he drove all the way here as soon as he had gotten a letter from me telling him that I want little Pearl to come live with me in a year, in order to personally offer to open "our" home to her!

Cecilia, do you understand what I am saying? He wants to marry me enough that he is willing to take Pearl in and let her share our lives! What a generous spirit! What a loving thing to do! All of my prejudices against him have simply dissolved, and all I can think of is that I have been foolish and callous to put him off for so long.

There is more. I told him about Darlene, and although he has not yet met her, I explained her situation, and he generously offered to let her come, too! I hope he means it, and I hope he will not change his mind when he sees her, but I am oh, so hopeful. If Pearl has Darlene with her in Chicago, she will be so much more comfortable, and if Darlene has an opportunity to get an education, her horizons will be so much broader than any of us might imagine. Jonathan acts as if it will not be a problem to bring a mixed child into his home, especially when the home is going to be as large as he says it will be. He even suggested that I teach both girls at home for at least a couple of years

So, sweet Cecilia, I think what I am trying to tell you is that I am engaged to be married! Be happy for me. I am blissful! I am so in love with Jonathan at this moment, I find it almost impossible to wait. I cannot believe I actually spurned him for this whole year. He is a saint!

Love and kisses,
Emily

May 18, 1932. Our first day of exams was not that bad. I think I did better than I thought I would. The boys feel good about theirs, also. Beryl is the only one who is complaining about them being hard. I told Daddy all about them. He smiled at me with his eyes and made grunting noises like he was laughing.

Uncle Woodrow is not sleeping here anymore. I think he is sleeping over at Pap-pa's place because every morning he brings Sapphire her goat milk.

May 19, 1932
Dearest Mother and Father,

I have some news that I hope will make you happy. Jonathan and I have set a wedding date for August!

The school term will be over next week, and I plan to pack up and leave by May 28. I will stop overnight to see Jenny Sunlee, and then will be home on the 29th or 30th.

I am very much looking forward to being home. It has been a wonderful year of serving the Lord, but now I am ready to resume my life with my family back in Chicago.

Much love,

Emily

May 20, 1932. We had our last exams today. Beryl cried because she thinks she failed hers. Both Jasper and Sardius act like they are happy. I know I did well.

The full moon is tonight. The Cherokee call it the full flower moon. I know Daddy will be looking at it and wishing he were out foxhunting. His hounds are already baying. They know they are supposed to be hunting tonight. Poor Daddy.

Something good happened today. Amelia Earhart left all by herself from Newfoundland, up in Canada in her little plane to become the first woman to make the same flight as poor Charles Lindbergh did five years ago. She will go to Paris, France. It took Lindy 33½ hours, and even though I feel sorry for him about his little baby being murdered, I hope she beats his record, just to show that women can do anything a man can do, and do it better! I hope this is not mean. Lindy is a good person, but so is Amelia Earhart, and she deserves fame, also. I am praying for her safety.

May 21, 1932. This morning, Mama told Jasper and Sardius to not even think about going out to the fields, but to spend the whole day hunting or fishing, whichever they chose. Pap-pa and Miss Janey Jo came over right after breakfast. Uncle Woodrow stayed at Pap-pa's place with Darlene and Mrs. Carlton. I wanted to ask Mama if I could go with Jasper and Sardius, but before I got the chance, she said to me, "Pearl, why don't you and I go for a walk?

I have missed talking to you." Beryl looked like she wanted to come, too, but she never leaves the house if she can help it during May and June. Being outside makes her sneeze so much it gives her a headache. Mama and I slipped out before Ruby even knew we were going.

I just love having Mama all to myself, and I hoped we could take a good, long walk because I wanted so much to talk to her about what to expect if Hank Delany has to stand trial and how she was so sure he would not get the electric chair.

She just said, "Don't worry, Pearl. Hank is already a free man. There won't be a trial, unless Celeste makes trouble about it, and of course she won't. People would just as soon pretend nothing ever happened." She stopped to smooth my hair down. "You look beautiful with your hair short," she said before she looked out toward the river and added. "I think some good will come of this. Even though nobody is going to be punished for what they did, a lot of people around here don't like what happened, and I doubt that those men will come back to bother Darlene or her mother again. Maybe people will think twice before they go butting into other folks' business from now on."

We walked alongside the river for a while, then Mama sat down on a rock. She patted the place beside her. "Sit down, sweetheart. I want to talk to you about something."

I sat. I got a funny feeling going up my back. Mama had turned very serious.

"Pearl," she said, "you know your brothers are going to go to Chicago in two weeks. It is very important to me, to them, and to all of us that they go. They have to get out of here, get an education, and make something of themselves. If they stay here, they will miss out on what the world has to offer. They will miss out on having a good life. Do you understand that?"

I did understand it, even though I was worried about how we would be able to make it without them to help on the farm, but I did not say anything. I hated to let Mama down by letting her know I could not even begin to make up for what Jasper or

Sardius do, let alone both of them. Beryl cannot do a lick of work, especially in the spring.

Mama did not stop to let me say anything. "I have some news that may disappoint you. Miss Weston will not be back next fall. She wanted to tell you herself, but I thought I would give you some time to get used to the idea. She is getting married to Mr. Dean. I believe you met him when he came to visit her at the schoolhouse."

"But Mama, I don't want her to go!"

"I know, sweetheart. But I have some very good news. She wants you to go to Chicago, too. She and Mr. Dean have invited you to live with them. She will teach you at home until you are ready for high school. Even though I could teach you, I think it would be best if you went to stay with Miss Weston and had a chance to get a really good education."

I felt panicky. "I can't leave you, Mama!"

"Of course you can, my darling. I have Beryl, Ruby, and Sapphire to keep me company. And Daddy, and Uncle Woodrow, and Celeste. And you know what? Miss Weston also says she wants to bring Darlene to Chicago. She is a very bright girl, and she would be a lot better off up there than down here. You should know there is nothing here for her."

"Mama, Darlene can't leave her mama any more than I can leave you." I was crying by then.

Mama laughed. "Darlene would be much happier in Chicago, and so will you. Did you know that Mrs. Carlton and Uncle Woodrow probably will be getting married?"

I nodded my head, not knowing what to say. I could not imagine either me or Darlene going to Chicago. I looked around me. "Do they have mountains there?" I asked.

"No, it is very flat. But they do have a river. And a big lake. It is very beautiful."

I got to thinking about it. "Could I come home for Christmas and maybe for summer? And Easter? Or could you come see me?"

Mama drew a breath, and I noticed her blinking hard before she looked away. "I don't know, my darling. My place is here, at least until Daddy gets better. And it costs a lot of money to travel. But you will be there with Miss Weston, Jasper, and Sardius. And, we hope, Darlene. That is almost like being home, isn't it?"

I thought about it some more. Mama had gotten up with her back to me. She gazed out at the river for a few minutes before she turned to me with a big smile on her face.

"You don't have to think about it too much for now, but I just want you to know that this is my plan for you. As bright as Jasper and Sardius are, you are my very smartest baby, and I know you will go far."

In a way, it was tempting to think of going to live with Miss Weston and Mr. Dean in Chicago. I could imagine myself being there with Jasper, Sardius, and Darlene, but I knew it would be impossible. Mama could never make it without help.

"Mama," I said, as nicely as I could. "You don't have any money. I mean, you can have my hair money, but I don't think Daddy is going to be able to go back to work. Without Jasper or Sardius to help you, you can't run the farm by yourself. And who will help you take care of Daddy and the little girls? You need me too much to let me go.

Mama laughed. "So you think you will help me make enough to get by? How many customers do you have?"

I did not think I had understood her right. I just looked at her.

"Pearl, I know why Jake Hatton comes around the house. I know that Walt Bittertree and your Pap-pa get a little thirst now and then, and I also know your Daddy makes the best whiskey in the county. I would think that by now you would have at least a dozen customers."

I was flabbergasted into admitting. "I don't. I just have that one feller that Jake Hatton gets some for sometimes." I was stammering. "How did you know?"

"I know more that you think I do. I am ashamed to say that I let you get by with it because we needed the money so badly. It was worth it to see you be able to get yourself new shoes for Easter. And I have to say, Pearl, that I am proud of how you spent your money on your family. You have a good heart."

I cried then. I hated the thought of Mama being ashamed because of something I had done. She didn't let me cry long. "Honey," she said, "you may be breaking the law by trading whiskey, but sometimes the law is wrong. Especially when people are starving and the only way out is to sell something that people want and need. If the law is against it, then it is the law that is wrong, not you. I did not say anything because I knew Sardius would have trouble with it, and so would Jasper. Both of them see things in black and white, and they would be disappointed in their mother if they knew I let you get away with this. It's going to be our secret, all right?"

I could not do anything but nod my head. She laughed, then tousled my hair, and she said, "Do you want to see how we are going to manage while you and Japer and Sardius are in Chicago making something of yourselves? Come here."

She stood, turning up toward the bluffs above the river. I followed her all the way up to the old Indian cave, and then we picked our way past the entrance. Not far into it, Mama reached behind a big rock to pull out a lantern, which she lit, then walked on into the cave while I followed.

We walked several hundred feet, sometimes through passages that were so low we had to stoop down to make our way through. Finally, we came to a big room with a smooth floor. In the middle stood a gleaming copper still. Along one side of the room stood dozens of barrels and dozens of jars of whiskey. Right alongside the still ran a little creek. The ceiling was very high, and I could see little shafts of sunlight slanting down onto the floor and lighting the place up. The smell of caramel, whiskey, and smoke hung in the air.

"This is your Daddy's still." He does not know I know about it, and my guess is that he will never be back up here. He makes good, clean whiskey. He has a good recipe, and the water that flows through here is the best there is. His still is solid copper, welded with silver, so what he makes is about the best there is for moonshine. But Pearl, he does not make fine whiskey. Your pap-pa and I, well, we know how to make fine whiskey. He taught me how to make it when I was just a little older than you are."

She pointed to the barrels and told me how they were oak and that the insides were charred. "Pap-pa just moved these up here this week. He has been saving them in his barn for years, but he never let your Daddy know about them because he knew he would drink it all up in no time."

She told me how new whiskey tastes rough and nasty, but if you put it in charred barrels and let it stay there for a long time, it becomes smooth and almost sweet.

"You don't have to worry about me, Pearl, or about how I will be able to buy food or even clothes for your baby sisters. Your pap-pa and I are going into business. He makes the finest barrels, and I can make a good mash and run a still. We can get by with selling new whiskey for now to people who want something cheap, but the real money will come in a few years when Prohibition is over and we can sell what has been sitting in these barrels for years. There will be nothing better than Wallace Tennessee Whiskey when the time comes. Now, come here, and I'll show you."

She pulled the cork out of one of the barrels. "You know what new whiskey tastes and smells like," she said as she dipped a tiny dipper down into the barrel through the hole. "Now look at this." She pulled up the dipper and showed me a beautiful amber liquid that smelled sweet, woody, and comfortable. She gave me a sip. It went down hot, and I nearly gagged, but I could tell what she meant. Despite the burn, it was rich and smooth. "This has been double distilled. Your pap-pa made it and put it in the barrel ten years ago. You'll never taste a better whiskey."

My mouth fell open. "But why would pap-pa buy bad whiskey from me when he had this?"

Mama waved her hand toward other barrels. "He was just storing it up in these to give it time to get good." Then she laughed. "Pearl, I hope you never develop the kind of taste for whiskey that your Daddy did, but I do hope you come to appreciate how good this is."

Then she asked me how long it would take me to get at least a dozen customers.

I have been thinking about it all day. It looks like maybe I will be going to Chicago after all.

May 22, 1932. Three things happened today. First of all, Miss Weston got to preach one last time. It was the best sermon I have ever heard on how God will sometimes lead us into scary places, but He always will be with us to guide us. After she preached, she did not have an invitational at all, but announced that Jasper and Sardius have both won scholarships to study in Chicago. She also announced that she would be leaving us to get married in August to Mr. Dean.

We all cried, but no one cried more than Beryl. She sobbed all the way home from church and then all through dinner. Miss Weston tried to cheer her up by saying that she could come and visit her in her new home, but Beryl would not be comforted. "You don't understand," she said. "You are teaching me how to be a better person, and you aren't done yet!" I know what she meant.

The second thing that happened was that Daddy smiled with his mouth. It was a crooked smile. He still cannot speak but only makes grunting or moaning noises, but I know he knows me and can understand everything I say.

The third thing that happened is that we found out Amelia Earhart landed safely in Ireland yesterday. She had to crash-land, so she did not make it all the way to Paris, but she sure beat Lindy's record. Only 15 hours! Half of Lindy's time!

May 22, 1932
Dearest Cecilia,

I am all packed up. I am taking fewer things away than I brought with me, since I am leaving all my lesson material and books for the children here. They need it far more than I do!

In looking back over this school year, I am both hopeful and sad. It has been a hard year, much harder than I dreamed it could be, but I hope I have learned from it. I so look forward to being both mother and teacher to Pearl and Darlene, and I look forward to being a good wife to Jonathan. I love him even more now than I did before I came here. His steadfastness, generosity, and willingness to overlook my arrogance have made me realize how dear he is to me.

Overall, I like to think that my time here has been mostly successful in spite of my misinformed and misdirected intentions. I have loved these children, and I think I have been a good influence over them, if only in that I have taught them that God loves them. I have made some headway improving their lives, but I know I was foolish to think I had been accepted into the community and was "civilizing them!" Now I realize that my world and this one are so far apart that I can never even understand their needs. I feel ashamed when I think about what my hopes were.

I love you and miss you terribly,
Emily

May 23, 1932
My School Journal, grade 7, Miss Weston's class
By Pearl Wallace

This is the last Journal entry I will write. I know it is not required, but I want to turn in this last one as a gift to Miss Weston so that she can have it as a keepsake to remember one of her seventh grade students for the 1931-1932 school year.

I have learned very much from my teacher this year. I thought teachers were supposed to teach you things in books, but Miss Weston has taught me many more things than one can learn from books. She has taught me that knowing that God loves me does not mean that He will make my life easy. It means that He cares enough about me to be with me even when times are bad. Even when I do not get what I want, He gives me the strength and courage to get through it. He lets me see that maybe what I think I want is not the best for me and that maybe I should go ahead and let things happen and see the good that comes out of it.

Miss Weston has also taught me about what it means to love others, to respect them, and to let them do what they need to do even if it means that you cannot have what you want. She knows how to be happy for other people's happiness. If we can find joy in the happiness of others, we will always know joy.

Last of all, Miss Weston has taught me that God's Word is very big, so big that we cannot possibly know it all, and that we need to be as big as we can in order to try to live by ALL His rules. Even when we cannot live by or even understand all His rules, we can know we are pleasing to Him if we do our best to live out the number one and the number two rules that He has set out in His Word:

Love God and Jesus with all your heart, and love your neighbor as yourself.

Pearl Adeline Wallace

Warm, waxing days, spangled nights.
Blossoms perfume the air, green blankets the hills.
The great Orb slips into a waning Gibbous,
Letting me go--softly, gently.
I sigh with pleasure
As do my upright children, lying tender in the grass,
Watching Evil slip into the Shadows
To wait anew.

The Earth has turned.
I travel madly, joyously, without a care,
Watching all my children leap and stumble
Toward the glimmer.

Acknowledgements

I have a number of people to thank just for the fact that I lived long enough to finish this book. In January 2017, I was diagnosed with glioblastoma multiforme, grade 4, a deadly form of brain cancer that took my aunt and my cousin a few years ago. Sadly, the prognosis was not hopeful. If I survived the surgery, which was not guaranteed, there was the aftermath of possible paralysis and a long, painful regimen of chemotherapy and radiation. By the grace of God, I had a brilliant surgeon, Dr. Suvajynar Jauikumar who, with his able team, was able to remove the tumor.

Thanks to my husband, Michael, who refused to believe the "inevitable" and a group of friends who spilled many tears on my behalf and begged God for my life, things worked out differently than expected. The surgery had no apparent side effects. As my husband predicted, I spent 1 day in ICU, 2 more in the hospital, and I managed to walk into church the following Sunday to thank the hundreds of fellow believers who had prayed for me.

I also owe a thanks to my daughter-in-law, Julie, who badgered me into transferring to the Duke Cancer center, and for also badgering Dr. Henry Friedman, the oncologist heading the brain cancer program, into accepting me as a patient. Also on my list is my radiation oncologist, Dr. Grace Kim, and my ongoing oncologist, Dr. Dina Randazzo and her team, who continue to monitor my progress and dispense medicines and wisdom.

My publisher, Light Messages, refused to give up on me as well. Wally and Betty Turnbull, the founders of Light Messages and firm believers in the power of prayer, immediately set about to put in a word or two for me with the big man upstairs. They, along with my friends Anne and Matt Holway, Delores Crotts, Phil Hollingsworth, and countless others who refused to let me die, pleaded for my life and/or encouraged me to look into alternate therapies. Thanks to God's grace, I lived long enough to finish this book, nearly finish another, and begin two more. It looks like I will beat expectations by a long shot. Hallelujah!

Also on this list of people to thank are those who read early drafts of the manuscript, gave feedback and encouragement, fed me, visited me, drove me to and from appointments, and in general, gave me cause to live: my daughter, Mary Elizabeth, and her husband, Nick, who painstakingly researched the kind of diet I needed, scoured local markets for the right foods, and cooked; my son George, who helped my husband hold down the fort while I crawled into a hole to recover; and my grandchildren, Corinne, Ellie, Wells, and Eve, whose happy little faces gave me hope, faith, and determination; Carole Talant and Anita Lang who encouraged me to look into alternate therapies; my writing partners, Winklings Summer Kinard and Elizabeth Hein, who poked, edited, encouraged, and improved my writing; my proofreader, Meghan Bowker; Genia Holder-Cozart, who gave me gracious feedback regarding my treatment of racial issues; and my editor, Elizabeth Turnbull, for her tireless, sensitive editing, and for forcing me to confront the specter of white privilege in East Tennessee as it existed in 1931.

There are many more, far too many to list here, but I remember and thank them all, for driving me to appointments, for cooking, for sending cards and notes of encouragement, and for the many, many prayers offered up on my behalf.

About the Author

Deborah Hining is proud to be a bone fide hillbilly, having grown up in a very isolated village in the hills of East Tennessee. She earned her B.A. in Communication and M.A. in Theater from the University of Tennessee and her PhD in Theater from Louisiana State University.

From an early age, Deborah wanted to be a poet, and her greatest ambition was to see one of her poems published in a book. Now, after a long and checkered life with many detours, she has realized her ambition, having published two award-winning novels. *A Sinner in Paradise* won the bronze medal from *Foreword Reviews* Book of the Year in Romance, and the sequel, *A Saint in Graceland*, also received the bronze medal for *Foreword Reviews* Book of the Year in Religion. Both allowed her to indulge her love of poetry.

Deborah now is back to her roots, living on a farm in Chapel Hill, North Carolina, with her husband, children, and grandchildren.

More fiction from Deborah Hining

A Sinner in Paradise
Deborah Hining

Winner of the *Foreword Reviews* **IndieFab Book of the Year Bronze Medal** in Romance and the **IBPA Benjamin Franklin Award Silver Medal**. Readers will quickly fall for Geneva in this exquisitely written, uproarious affair with love in all its forms, set in the stunning landscape of the West Virginia mountains.

A Saint in Graceland
Deborah Hining

Winner of the *Foreword Reviews* **INDIES Book of the Year Bronze Medal** in Religious Fiction. Grieving her mother's death and yearning to see more of the world beyond her mountain home, Sally Beth sets out on a journey that leads her across the American Southwest and ultimately to a remote mission station in Tanzania, where she finds a new kind of freedom in the African plains and the people who dwell there. But when war comes to the mission gates, its horrors shatter her world. She must find a way to rebuild her life and choose whether or not to serve the people she's grown to love—a choice that will shake the simple faith of her childhood and ignite her passion for a wounded man.